ANTIQUES TO DIE FOR

ANTIQUES TO DIE FOR

Josie Prescott Antiques # 3

JANE K. CLELAND

2008

THORNDIKE
CHIVERS

This Large Print edition is published by Thorndike Press, Waterville, Maine, USA and by BBC Audiobooks Ltd, Bath, England.

Thorndike Press, a part of Gale, Cengage Learning.

Copyright © 2008 by Jane K. Cleland.

The moral right of the author has been asserted.

A Josie Prescott Antiques Mystery.

Excerpt from "Once by the Pacific" from *The Poetry of Robert Frost* edited by Edward Connery Lathem. Copyright © 1928, 1969 by Henry Holt and Company, copyright © 1956 by Robert Frost. Reprinted by permission of Henry Holt and Company, LLC.

LIBRARY OF CONGRESS CATALOGING-IN-PUBLICATION DATA

Cleland, Jane K.
 Antiques to die for / by Jane K. Cleland.
  p. cm. — (A Josie Prescott antiques mystery) (Thorndike Press large print mystery)
  ISBN-13: 978-1-4104-0788-7 (hardcover : alk. paper)
  ISBN-10: 1-4104-0788-8 (hardcover : alk. paper)
  1. Prescott, Josie (Fictitious character) — Fiction. 2. Appraisers — Fiction. 3. Antiques — Fiction. 4. Murder — Investigation — Fiction. 5. New Hampshire — Fiction. 6. Large type books. I. Title.
 PS3603.L4555A58 2008b
 813'.6—dc22   2008014362

BRITISH LIBRARY CATALOGUING-IN-PUBLICATION DATA AVAILABLE

Published in 2008 in the U.S. by arrangement with St. Martin's Press, LLC.

Published in 2009 in the U.K. by arrangement with the Author.

U.K. Hardcover: 978 1 408 41261 9 (Chivers Large Print)
U.K. Softcover: 978 1 408 41262 6 (Camden Large Print)

Printed in the United States of America
1 2 3 4 5 6 7 12 11 10 09 08

THIS IS FOR DENISE MARCIL,
MY LITERARY AGENT AND MY
FRIEND

AND, OF COURSE, FOR JOE

AUTHOR'S NOTE

This is a work of fiction. All of the characters and events are imaginary. While there is a seacoast region in New Hampshire, there is no town called Rocky Point, and many other geographic liberties have been taken.

CHAPTER ONE

"Josie? Josie!" Gretchen, my assistant, shouted from the front office, her voice echoing across the cavernous warehouse. "Josie? Where are you? Rosalie and Paige are here."

"I'm in the Barkley corner. Send them over!"

Her high heels click-clacked on the concrete floor, then stopped. I could picture her pointing to the far back corner where the furniture we'd just purchased from Isaac Barkley's estate was situated.

I was squatting to examine the inside of a tallboy drawer, checking for extra holes that might indicate the pulls had been changed. Isaac Barkley had some spectacular objects, but I'd identified two reproduction pieces as well.

"Josie?" Rosalie's sweet voice rang out a minute later.

"Here! Behind the tallboy."

"You are not!" she said, a bubble of laughter in her voice. "I'm looking at the tallboy as I speak."

I poked my head out and saw her. Her back was to me as she faced a highboy.

She wore a dark blue down parka over jeans. She was slender and pretty, the kind of pretty that derives as much from a vivacious personality as from facial features. Her kid sister, Paige, looked just like her, except that Paige's hair was a lighter shade of blond, almost platinum. Rosalie and I were about the same age, early thirties, and Paige was twelve.

"That's not a tallboy. That's a highboy!" I said, standing, brushing the grit from my palms onto my jeans as I walked toward her.

Rosalie turned to face me and rolled her eyes. "Oh, please. Tallboy, highboy. They're men and they're big. What's the difference?"

Paige grinned.

I laughed and shook my head. "Highboys are older, dating from the midseventeenth century. They're chests-on-stands. Tallboys weren't introduced 'til the turn of the eighteenth century and are chests-on-drawers."

Rosalie nudged Paige playfully. "Learn something new every day, right, Paige?"

"It's interesting," Paige said.

10

"See," I said to Rosalie, nodding in Paige's direction. "A smart girl." To Paige, I asked, "How's your vacation going?"

"Great! We went skating this morning."

"Paige went skating," Rosalie quipped, making a funny face. "I went falling!"

Paige giggled. "She's really bad."

"Watch it, cutie!" Rosalie said, trying not to laugh. "Paige is the athlete, that's for sure, not me." She waved it away. "Never mind all that! Josie, we're here to kidnap you! I'm dropping Paige off at her ballet lesson, and you and I are going to lunch."

"Cool," I said, enjoying their banter. "What's the occasion?"

"No occasion, just a random crime."

"Excellent. I'm all grubby from crawling around the furniture. Go and chat with Gretchen while I clean up, okay?"

"We're always glad to chat with Gretchen."

Ten minutes later, as I entered the front office, Gretchen said, "I know, I know. You're right. I guess it just wasn't meant to be. But I think it's really too bad."

"What wasn't meant to be?" I asked.

"Marcus Wetherby is divorcing Angelina for the second time," Gretchen explained.

"Who are they?"

"Don't you know anything, Josie?" Rosalie teased, laughing. "Marcus is the hero on the soap opera *Follow Your Heart.* He's a pilot with a girl in every port. Angelina, his first and his third wife, just caught him with Melina in Madrid."

"Not only did I not know that, but I didn't know that *you* watched soap operas."

"I don't. I'd never heard of it either until Gretchen filled me in just now!"

I laughed. There was no gossip too mundane to interest Gretchen, who was always glad for a chitchat about the latest happenings.

Sasha, my chief appraiser, sat at her corner desk, engrossed in a catalogue describing important nineteenth-century Eskimo artifacts. Fred, my other appraiser, wasn't around.

"Did Fred leave for the McIver job already?" I asked Gretchen.

"Yes. He said that since he was going to be in Exeter for that appraisal, he thought he'd stop at the university library."

"Oh, yeah?" I asked. "Why?"

"Let me find the note." She rustled through a pile of papers. "Here it is — he's checking that print you found against a book by Dame Juliana Berners called *A Treatyse of Fysshynge wyth an Angle,*" she read, stumbling over the fifteenth-century spelling.

"Right," I said. "That's good."

Tucked into a box of art prints I'd purchased as a lot was a slightly foxed woodcut that looked as if it might be a rare angling print, and I'd assigned Fred, an expert art historian and my newest appraiser, the job of authenticating it. He was at the university library to compare our print to their original. My fingers were crossed, but I wasn't optimistic that he'd be able to prove that we had a page from one of only a few extant copies of Dame Juliana Berners's 1496 book, one of the rarest publications on earth.

"We're off to lunch. Do you need anything from me before we go?"

"Nope," she said cheerfully. "I'm all set. Have a good time!"

I shrugged into my heavy wool coat. Gretchen's wind chimes jangled as I pushed open the front door. It was a bright, sunny day and whip cold, typical for January in Portsmouth, New Hampshire.

"What a doll Gretchen is!" Rosalie said as we crunched across patches of snow to our cars.

"Complete and utter. I have no idea what I'd do without her. Where am I being kidnapped to?"

"Murray's, if that's okay. It's close to Paige's ballet school."

"Perfect."

At lunch, we sat and talked with the ease and comfort of kindred spirits. I'd known Rosalie for more than a year, which qualified her as one of my oldest friends in Portsmouth. We'd met at an installation I was overseeing at Heyer's Modular Furniture.

Rosalie was a Ph.D. candidate ghostwriting a biography for Gerry Fine, the newly appointed CEO of Heyer's. I was installing a boatload of antiques for him, and we'd run into one another at his office — literally.

Absorbed in reading her notes, she'd been backing out, ready to leave. I'd just hung a bracket that was, according to my level, properly mounted, but according to my eye, wasn't. I was backing up to get a wider-lens view of it. Bottom to bottom, we collided.

"Oh, my God!" I exclaimed, startled.

"That's a heck of a way to meet someone," Rosalie said, laughing a little.

"Well, we obviously have a lot in common — we both walk backwards."

"And we both concentrate so hard we don't even notice our surroundings."

"I'm sorry," I said.

"Don't apologize. It makes us sisters under the skin." She extended a hand. "I'm Rosalie Chaffee."

Her radiant smile and laughing eyes drew an answering smile from me. We shook, completed our introductions, and chatted in a friendly way.

On the face of it, Rosalie and I didn't have a lot in common. Rosalie seemed to genuinely admire Gerry, the top executive of Heyer's, whereas I thought he was a pompous ass. She was in New Hampshire temporarily while finishing her education. I was a businesswoman who'd started a new life in Portsmouth and was eager to put down roots. She was raising her sister on her own after their parents had died in a car crash four years earlier. I lived alone, and had no family. She was boy crazy. I was in a solid, monogamous relationship.

But we had many common interests. We shared a love of murder mysteries, cooking, guavatinis, and good-natured debates about politics, love, men, business, and books. Rosalie was smart and open-minded and loads of fun to be around. We never ran out of things to talk about or tired of each other's company.

The next morning I arrived at Heyer's

Modular Furniture early, eager to hang a small Joseph Henry Sharp oil called *Crows in Montana* and get back to my office.

Before my staff began the laborious process of sorting, cleaning, and polishing every inch of every item, I personally examined everything. My warehouse guys would do the hands-on primping and my appraisers would do the authentication and write up the catalogue copy, but it was my responsibility as the owner of Prescott's Antiques, Auctions, and Appraisals to determine whether the contents merited a stand-alone auction or whether we'd generate more buzz and realize greater profits if we combined these objects with others. After years of trying to develop a decision-making model, I'd given up. As far as I could tell, successful merchandising was half art and half timing.

Inside, I hurried to Gerry Fine's office. The two-room suite overlooked a man-made pond at the rear of the building. Gerry's private office was accessed through a smaller room, an anteroom, where his assistant, Tricia Dobson, sat behind a big mahogany desk facing the corridor. Tucked off to the side of the anteroom was a windowless storage room that had been converted into a little office for Rosalie.

Tricia, Gerry's older, pleasant-faced as-

ant, looked up from her typing and ..iled as I walked in. "Hi, Josie."

"Hey, Tricia. You look awfully happy for this early on a Thursday morning."

"We're two weeks away from Florida."

"Oh, that's right. Where are you going?"

"Boynton Beach."

"Nice."

Holding a plastic container filled with various-sized picture hooks, nails and screws, wire, and a screwdriver in one hand, I lifted the painting, gauging whether I could carry it, along with all the parapher-nalia to install it properly, to the CFO's of-fice where it was to hang, or whether it would be more prudent to wheel it on a hand truck. It was only three by six inches, and light, but I didn't want to risk dropping it.

"Josie, do I hear your voice? Are you there? Tricia!" Gerry boomed from his in-ner office, startling me. The plastic contain fell and the clasp sprung open, spill hardware on the carpet.

"One sec!" I called, squatting to everything up.

Tricia calmly started toward his dictation pad in hand.

"Hurry!" Gerry called.

I left the scattered nails and scr

they'd fallen on the far side of Tri
slid the painting between the v
cia's credenza, and stepped to the
that connected her anteroom to Ger.
fice.

"Yes?" I asked from the threshold.

"It's Rosalie . . . I mean . . . they just called and told me," Gerry stammered, looking from Tricia to me and back again.

I'd never seen Gerry flustered. On the contrary, typically, he was smooth, confident, and in control. Now, though, his anxiety was palpable and contagious. I glanced at Tricia. She was staring at him, then turned to look at me.

"Who called to tell you what?" I asked, my worry meter whirring onto high.

"The police. She's dead."

"What?" I asked, gaping.

He jerked his thumb toward the phone. "That was the Rocky Point police. They want me to come down and identify the body."

"You," I asked, confused. "Why you?"

"They said they found her Heyer's key ard and called HR. Since she worked for e privately, not for the company, HR lled me."

looked at Tricia for answers or support. e was gripping the notebook so hard her

knuckles were white. Still, she didn't speak.

"Rosalie's dead?" I repeated stupidly.

Gerry's tone shifted from hapless confusion to sarcastic irritation. "That's what they said."

My heart began to race. How could Rosalie, my friend, be dead? "How did she die?"

"I don't know. All they said was that she washed up on the beach."

"Oh, my God! That's horrible!" I crossed my arms, covering my chest, an instinctive, protective gesture.

"Drowned? Rosalie drowned?" Tricia whispered. "She was so young."

Paige, I thought. *Where's Paige?*

"Yeah. So, Edie has the limo and I didn't bring her car. Tricia needs to stay here and hold down the fort. Will you take me?" Gerry asked me.

Gerry had negotiated a car and driver as part of his compensation package, and if he had no outside appointments scheduled, his wife, Edie, got to shop in style. Sometimes, when she'd commandeered his company car, he tooled around in her BMW, but evidently, today wasn't one of those days.

I was hot and cold at the same time. Chills ran up my arms and down my spine, yet my palms were clammy and I was having trouble breathing. "Sure," I agreed. "Now?"

"Yeah," he said, standing up, grabbing the suit jacket he'd draped over his leather chair. "Let's go."

Gerry was tall, with almost blond curly hair that he wore too long, and a deep suntan, thanks to the Portsmouth Suntan Salon. In the year plus since I'd begun helping him and his wife decorate his office suite with antiques they'd purchased from my company, he'd left during working hours several times to go to the tanning salon, whispering his plans to me with a wink, as if he and I were buddies or co-conspirators. At first I thought he was flirting with me, but then I realized that he was just vain and bragging.

The sun was blinding, reflecting off the bright white snow that dotted the landscape. The ground was winter brown, and the ocean was blue-black, glittering with sun-sparked diamonds.

As I drove up Ocean Avenue, I pressed the preprogrammed button on my cell phone, slipped in my earpiece, and heard the Chaffees' home number ring and ring, until finally a machine picked up. My throat caught listening to Rosalie's bubbly message. I glanced at Gerry. He stared out of the window toward the ocean.

After the beep, I said, "Hi, Paige. It's Josie.

Josie Prescott. If I can do anything, anything at all, call me." I added my number and hung up.

"Paige is Rosalie's sister," I explained to Gerry. "She's only twelve."

He nodded, but didn't reply. In fact, he was quiet the whole way and I was relieved. It gave me time to think, to try and assimilate the shocking information — Rosalie was dead. Yesterday, at lunch, Rosalie was full of weekend plans and lively conversation. How could she be dead?

While I waited for Gerry to finish his grisly duty, I slipped a George Benson CD into the player and watched the ocean. Small swells rolled in toward shore. Listening to George Benson's rendition of "On Broadway," a song that just tore me up it was so beautiful and mournful all at once, I wished I could forget all the memories connected to Rosalie.

Twenty minutes later, Gerry returned to the car with a police officer I recognized called Griff walking beside him. Officer Griffin gestured that I should open my window. He leaned in to ask me to follow him to the Rocky Point police station.

"Sure," I agreed.

We left the small hospital where Rosalie's

body had been brought from the beach and turned south on Ocean Avenue. Rocky Point, about a fifteen-minute drive from Portsmouth, included three miles of New Hampshire's eighteen-mile coastline. As we drove, my eyes kept drifting to the dunes, and I wondered if Rosalie's body had been found among the tangled brambles near the street or by the thick wash of seaweed closer to shore. It was just awful to think about, and I couldn't stop.

I waited for Gerry to speak, but he didn't. "Was it her?"

"Yes," he answered, sounding stupefied.

I took a deep breath to suppress some unexpected tears. "How did she die?" I asked quietly.

"Badly." He gazed out of the window at the gold-specked ocean, and after a moment, added, "I guess she drowned. Her face was puffy."

I was sorry I asked.

Still following Griff, I pulled into the Rocky Point police station lot and parked. The station house was designed to match the prevailing style in the affluent New Hampshire seacoast town. It looked more like a cottage than a police station with shingles weathered to a soft dove gray and the trim painted Colonial blue.

"Are you okay?" I asked him.

"Sure."

I nodded, speculating that his dismissive tone reflected a combination of wishful thinking and denial, murmured something empathetic, and watched as he stepped out of the car.

Officer Griffin approached, and told me, "You, too. If you don't mind."

"Me?" I asked, surprised.

"You knew her, right? Rosalie Chaffee?"

"Yes."

Griff nodded. "Come on, then."

Tendrils of anxiety rippled up my back, then down again. I knew nothing about Rosalie's death, but I knew things that I didn't want to talk about, including secrets she'd shared in private conversations. My experiences with the police didn't inspire optimism. Interviews were routinely more intrusive than expected and invariably led to an unwarranted veneer of suspicion.

Feeling powerless and fussy, like a child being sent to the principal's office for an infraction she didn't commit, I followed the two men inside.

CHAPTER TWO

I wondered if Ty would question me himself. Ty Alverez was Rocky Point's police chief and my boyfriend. At least he was the police chief for now.

He'd had an interview ten days ago for a new job, a big one — running the terrorism alert system for northern New England. Homeland Security was setting up a system of early alerts and first responders, and in our area he'd be top dog. I thought there was a good chance that he'd get the offer, and if he did, I thought he'd take it. I didn't know how I felt about that. The job would take him away a lot, to D.C. and to various spots in the three states he'd oversee: New Hampshire, Maine, and Vermont.

I wondered where Ty was now. His car — his vehicle, I corrected myself with a small, private smile, remembering a shared joke about what I was to call his jumbo SUV — wasn't in the lot.

"Follow me," Griff said to Gerry. To me he added, "Have a seat. Someone will be with you in a minute."

"I'll see you later," I called to Gerry as Griff led him down the corridor.

I could guess where Griff was taking him. Room Two, a dismal interrogation room with a cage in the corner for, as Ty put it, unruly guests, was down that hallway. I knew the room — in the past, I'd been the one interviewed there.

I didn't feel like sitting, so I wandered over to the bulletin board and began scanning the notices and warnings. A few minutes later, a female officer I'd met briefly at the annual Rocky Point Police Christmas party, Officer Claire Brownley, came into the vestibule from the other side of the building and greeted me.

"Josie Prescott, right?" she asked.

I nodded.

"I'm Officer Brownley. We met last December. Thanks for coming in. Follow me, please."

She led the way to a small, windowless room. There was a shiny gold numeral one on the door. Inside, I spotted a human-sized cage, similar to the one in Room Two, a large wooden table in the center, and six metal chairs.

Officer Brownley gestured that I should sit, and I chose a chair at the far end with the cage out of sight in back of me. She sat on my left and placed a flip-up notebook on the table, squared up its bottom edge, and smiled at me.

"This shouldn't take long. I understand you knew Ms. Chaffee."

Officer Brownley was about my age and looked Irish with cornflower blue eyes, black hair, and skin so white it looked bleached.

"That's right," I acknowledged.

"Did you know her well?"

"Pretty well. We were friends."

"When did you see her last?"

"Yesterday."

Officer Brownley made a note and nodded. "We'll come back to that. First, tell me about her."

"I don't know," I floundered. "She was nice."

"In what way?"

I paused, trying to think how to describe her. "Rosalie was fun to be around. She had a bubbly, can-do personality. She worked hard, both on her Ph.D. and on writing Mr. Fine's biography. Plus, she was raising her kid sister on her own, yet she always seemed to have something upbeat to say."

"How did you meet her?"

"Through work. Gerry Fine," I explained, nodding toward the distant Room Two where I'd assumed Griff had taken him, "and his wife, Edie, bought several antiques from me. Gerry asked me to help install the paintings and place the decorative items." I shrugged. "I've been in the Heyer's offices several times over the last year or so. Rosalie was in and out a lot — never for long, half an hour here, twenty minutes there, that sort of thing. We hit it off right away." I closed my eyes for a moment, as a jolt of sadness jabbed at me.

"Let me get the picture right. When you were at Heyer's, you were in Rosalie's office working?"

"She doesn't — *didn't* — have a real office," I replied, correcting myself. I paused and swallowed to control my tears. I was determined not to cry. "She had a desk in an old storage closet off of Tricia's little office. Tricia is Gerry's assistant."

"And you were there installing paintings in Mr. Fine's office?"

"Yes, and in Ned's office."

Officer Brownley made a note. "Who's Ned?"

"Ned Anderson, the CFO. Chief financial officer."

She nodded. "Back to Ms. Chaffee. You got to know her at Heyer's?"

"We'd chat while I worked, if she was there. She's really sweet." I felt a catch in my throat as I realized what I'd said. "*Was. She was* sweet."

Officer Brownley nodded again and wrote something down. "Did you know any of her other friends or colleagues?"

"Some."

"Who?"

I told her about Rosalie's ex-boyfriend, Paul Greeley, and a snob named Cooper Bennington. Paul was Rosalie's office mate at Hitchens College, the small, elite private college where Rosalie had almost completed the requirements to earn her Ph.D., and where Cooper was the assistant chair of the department.

When Officer Brownley prodded me for other names, I mentioned a couple of other people that I'd met in passing. I closed my eyes for a moment, wishing the memories of fun times weren't quite so vivid.

Paige. At her age, how can she possibly cope with such a loss? I wondered, agonized at the thought. "Do you know where Paige, Rosalie's sister, is?" I asked, opening my eyes.

"No, why?"

"She's just a kid, you know?"

Officer Brownley nodded. "I don't know exactly where she is, but I know she's with some family friends."

I nodded, but didn't speak.

Officer Brownley cleared her throat. "So . . . you said Rosalie and Paul had dated?"

"Yeah. They broke up a few months ago."

"When?"

"I'm not sure exactly. Fall sometime."

"Why?"

Something my lawyer, Max, told me just before my first formal interview with the police in a murder case a couple of years back came to me. "Don't volunteer information," Max had directed. Plus, I hated the thought of stating something as fact that I didn't 100 percent know to be true. Rosalie had confided that Paul had become possessive, but she never told me that his jealousy was why she broke up with him. Recalling his flirtatious nature, it was easy to imagine alternative reasons — maybe he'd been two-timing her and she caught him. Maybe he'd broken up with her and to save face, she'd lied and said that it was she who'd ended their relationship.

"Josie?"

I met Officer Brownley's curious eyes with

bland insouciance. "I don't know."

"Some memory came to you just then. What was it?" she pressed.

I shook my head. "Just recalling some of the good times. Nothing relevant."

"How'd Paul take it? The breakup, I mean."

"I have no idea."

"Really? Rosalie never said?"

"No."

She paused for a moment, her head tilted, maybe considering whether she believed me or not. "Was she dating anyone else? Cooper Bennington, for instance?"

"No," I replied disdainfully. I couldn't imagine anyone ever, under any circumstances, no matter how rich he might be, dating Cooper Bennington. Privately, I thought of him as Cooper the Condescending.

"Did he ask and she refused?"

"Not that she ever told me."

"You don't like him," she remarked.

I shrugged. "Cooper — well, Cooper's one of a kind."

"In what way?"

"He's a little full of himself, that's all."

Officer Brownley nodded and wrote a note in her book and turned the page. "What did Rosalie think of him?"

Don't volunteer information, I reminded myself. *But maybe it's relevant.* "She didn't like him."

"Why?"

"Professional jealousy."

"In what way?"

"I don't know much about it, but from what Rosalie told me, her research was generating a lot of interest. She'd been invited to present a paper at some conference this winter, and Cooper was pretty resentful about it."

"How do you know?"

I shrugged. "Anyone within a mile or so would have known," I said, remembering the scene.

Cooper was about my age and he wore his dark hair moussed back in a smooth, carefully coiffed wave. His brown eyes were set far back under heavy brows, and he always looked like he needed a shave.

Rosalie had invited me to join her and a few colleagues one Friday in October at Connolly's Pub. "It's good for us to have civilians around," she said, laughing. "Otherwise we take ourselves too seriously."

"When is your presentation slot?" Paul had asked midway through the evening, his eyes drawing Rosalie in.

"Where are you going?" Cooper demanded, obviously annoyed that he didn't know that Rosalie had plans to be absent.

"I've been asked to deliver a paper at February's symposium."

Cooper's eyes narrowed. "On what?"

"My usual. Historical communications."

"We all specialize in historical communications. What's the title?"

" 'How Communication Affects Community Relations During Exploration,' " she stated, then smiled at him with specious interest. "You submitted a proposal, too, didn't you, Cooper? What was your title?"

Cooper finished his beer and smacked his mug on the table. "Derivative topics work well in small symposia — it allows the organizers to develop a coherent theme," he said as he slid out of the booth. "See ya all on Monday."

Officer Brownley nodded, acknowledging the point of the story. "Do you have any other examples?"

"Same sort of interaction over and over again. It was almost as if they took pleasure in needling one another." I smiled. "Cooper once told her she needed approval for something or other, I don't recall what, saying, 'After all, I am the assistant chair of the department.' When he was out of earshot, she snorted and mocked him. 'You need my approval, because I'm the chief cook and bottle washer,' " I mimicked, talking through my nose as Rosalie had done.

She nodded and wrote something in her notebook. "What do you know about her family life?" she asked, changing the subject.

I winced and looked away. Every time I thought of Paige's loss, some small part deep inside of me cringed. So many bits of me had shrunk and curled and died after my mother's death. I'd only been about a year older than Paige was now when I lost my mother to a ghastly cancer death and my life changed forever. Remembering the loss hurt like a bad sunburn, except inside out. I was afraid for Paige. "She lived with her kid sister, Paige," I said. "She's in middle school."

"Just the two of them?"

"Yes," I replied.

"What's she like? Paige?" Officer Brownley asked, recalling me to the present.

"Funny. Smart. She listens a lot. She's a good athlete. She likes ballet." I shrugged.

She nodded. "You said you saw Ms. Chaffee yesterday?"

I shifted in my chair and brushed back some hair. "That's right. We went to lunch." I shrugged. "We had a good time."

"When and where did you go?

"About one. Murray's."

"In Portsmouth?"

"Yeah."

"When was lunch over?"

I thought back. "About two-thirty."

"What did you talk about?"

"Nothing special."

"Like what?"

"We talked about her sister's dancing and how she's pretty serious about it. How Rosalie liked her job but couldn't wait to finish her dissertation and get her Ph.D. How Portsmouth is different from New York City — I used to live there and she's never been. We talked about antiques — how I appraise them and she collects artichokes." I shrugged again. "Like I said, nothing special."

"Artichokes?" Officer Brownley asked, uncertain she'd heard me right.

I smiled. "Artichokes are actually a pretty popular collectible."

"Really? Why?"

"People collect all sorts of things for all sorts of different reasons. But there's a long-standing tradition of integrating vegetables and fruit into designs — textiles, architecture, paintings, sculpture, and so on."

"Still . . . artichokes?" She raised a brow, which I took as a sign of good-natured incredulity.

I smiled again and nodded. "In ancient Greece, they were considered to be an aphrodisiac."

She shook her head, part amazed and part intrigued. "An aphrodisiac," she repeated. "What else is popular?"

"Well, there are trends, of course," I replied, enjoying her reaction. "But it's safe to say that pineapples are pretty consistently in vogue. They were an expensive delicacy in Colonial times, so any hostess who served them to her guests, well, to put it simply, she was putting on the dog. You see pineapples all over — there are renditions in pottery and porcelain, pineapple-shaped door knockers, fence and molding ornamentation, everything. Corn's big too — it indicates a bountiful harvest. And grapes — grapes represent friendship and conviviality."

"Amazing," Officer Brownley said, shaking her head "So, back to your lunch with Ms. Chaffee . . . What else did you talk about?"

I thought back. "We talked about what we were going to do over the weekend. She was taking Paige to Boston to go to the Museum of Fine Arts. She asked if I wanted to join them, maybe stay for dinner afterward."

"What did you say to that?"

"I told her I'd love to — but couldn't. My company runs tag sales on Saturdays. Pretty much, I've got to be on site."

Officer Brownley nodded again and wrote a couple of words in her notebook. She flipped the page and looked up, her guileless blue eyes meeting mine. "Until we know more," she said, "we're treating her death as suspicious. So, do you know if she had any arguments with anyone?"

"No."

"How about business issues?"

"Like what?"

"Does she owe anyone money?"

"Not that I'm aware of." She wrote a few words, and as she did, I asked, "You're saying that she was murdered, aren't you?"

"No, I'm not saying that. These questions are just routine." She paused to look at me. "Any situations at all you're aware of that could have got her in trouble?"

I didn't know what to say. *Never gossip,* my father warned me long ago, when I was about Paige's age and had come home with a tale of seventh-grade deception and betrayal. *Don't spread it and don't listen to it, either,* he said. *Gossip will always come back at you sideways and bite you in the butt.* My mother added, *There's another reason to stay quiet, Josie — gossip hurts.* I took a deep breath, acutely aware that Officer Brownley was waiting for my response. But I still couldn't decide what to do.

When I worked for Frisco's, the famous auction house in New York City, after I'd blown the whistle on my boss's price-fixing scheme, some of my so-called friends had used gossip in its most diabolical form as a weapon against me. They combined innuendo with shunning, and I'd found it nearly impossible to bear. To this day I used my father's final admonition on the subject as my guiding principle: *When in doubt, stay quiet.*

"Josie?" Officer Brownley prompted, wiggling her fingers to encourage me to speak.

She didn't look angry, and I felt relieved.

"She had a secret admirer," I said, looking down.

"What do you mean?"

"Someone was sending her flowers and stuff, signing the cards 'Secret Admirer.'"

"How do you know?"

"She got a bouquet last week at Heyer's, fabulous red roses. I was there. She threw the card away."

"Were the flowers delivered directly?"

"No. Una, the receptionist, signed for them, I think. At least she brought them in to Rosalie."

"Why were they sent to her at Heyer's?"

"I don't know."

"She wasn't there much, was she?"

"No. She spent most of her time at Hitchens. She only came to Heyer's to interview Gerry or to go through business documents that needed to be kept in the building."

"She was writing a book for Heyer's?"

I tried to keep from smirking. "She was ghostwriting Gerry's autobiography."

"He's only about forty, right? Isn't it unusual for someone that age to write an autobiography?"

I shrugged. "I suspect that Gerry thinks people who aspire to business success would enjoy reading about the path he took."

"Would they?"

"God, no."

Officer Brownley smiled appreciatively, but didn't comment. "Back to the flowers," she said. "You're a hundred percent sure that neither Rosalie nor Una gave you any hint about who sent them?"

"Yes."

"Was there any conversation about it? With Una, maybe?"

I thought back. "I can't remember exactly, but I got the impression that the deliveries had been going on for a while."

"What gave you that impression?"

"Well, one thing was that Rosalie told me she'd thrown away *all* the cards."

"Did the flowers always come to Heyer's?"

I shook my head. "No. Rosalie mentioned that she'd given the last bouquet to a student at Hitchens. And there was no way she'd transport them anywhere, even to the trash. She wanted nothing whatsoever to do with them."

"This is pretty incredible. How did she react?"

"She felt as if she were being stalked, and it really freaked her out. Over drinks one night, she quoted some statistics — that something like twenty-five percent of stalkers end up killing their victims."

Officer Brownley leaned back in her chair and then shook her head. "Why didn't she call the police?"

"I asked her that. She said, 'And what, report that I've been getting flowers?' "

Officer Brownley fixed her eyes on mine. "What about you? Why didn't you tell me about this right away?"

I looked down, embarrassed. "She asked me not to tell anyone. I promised."

"Why would she ask you to promise about something like this?"

I shrugged. "I don't know. Except I think

maybe she did know who was sending them. Rosalie was plenty scared. That part is true. But I remember wondering at the time if she knew but couldn't get him to stop."

"Why did you think that?"

"I don't know. A combination of factors, I guess. Her refusal to go to the police. The way she groaned when Una brought them in, as if it were a familiar irritant." I shrugged. "I wish I could be more specific, but I can't. It's just a sense I had."

She nodded. "Thank you for telling me. It's helpful." She wrote in her notebook for a while.

"What else aren't you telling me about?" she asked, smiling.

Her friendly demeanor made her comment inoffensive.

I looked at her straight on and shook my head. *Suspicion isn't knowledge,* I rationalized. And secrets must be kept.

Under the table, out of sight of her penetrating gaze, I crossed my fingers, just in case. In as casual a tone as I could muster, I said, "Nothing."

Officer Brownley cocked her head, maybe assessing whether I was lying, dense, or whether I truly didn't know anything else. "You sure?"

I met Officer Brownley's eyes. "Yes," I said

firmly. "I'm sure."

As Officer Brownley led me back to the vestibule, I allowed myself to relax a notch or two. It felt as if I'd dodged a bullet. Having been involved in two murder investigations in two years, I was relieved that, so far at least, I'd managed to escape the stigma of possessing guilty knowledge this time around.

CHAPTER THREE

Officer Brownley asked me to wait and left me alone.

There was no sign of Gerry, and I wondered if he'd finished before me. I stood by the front counter and waited for Cathy, a civilian admin who was busy typing something into her computer, to look up. I figured I'd ask her whether someone had driven him back to his office, but before she glanced in my direction, Ty appeared from an inside door, saw me, and smiled.

I smiled back, suddenly breathless, and my pulse quickened as it always did in his presence. He was just so damn attractive. He was tall and broad, with dark hair, craggy features, and weathered skin, and he exuded confidence and trustworthiness.

"Hey," he said, lifting the counter panel to join me.

"Hey," I responded.

"I'll walk you to your car."

"What about Gerry?" I asked. "Mr. Fine. He was in with Griff. I drove him here."

Ty nodded. "We'll see he gets a ride."

We walked silently toward my car. My engineer boots clacked against the frozen asphalt. It was growing colder, and I noted that the sun was partially gone. Thick gray clouds were rolling in, and there was a smell of snow in the air.

"Let's walk to the beach," Ty said, directing me away from my car.

"Okay," I replied.

We crossed Ocean Avenue, clambered up the dunes, and skittle-ran down the other side to the beach. The sand was stone hard and snow free. The ocean was turbulent.

Rosalie and I had walked along this very stretch of sand only last autumn. It had been a sunny, crisp October Sunday. Paige and one of her friends whose name escaped me had run ahead poking around for sand glass and unchipped clam shells. I recalled glancing at Rosalie's grave demeanor and thinking that she seemed unnaturally pensive.

"You okay?" I'd asked after a pause.

She'd shrugged. "Man trouble. What else, right?" she'd replied, exhaling loudly with a self-deprecating, frustrated puff of air.

"Paul?"

"Yeah."

"Paul 'Give Me Air' Greeley," she'd called him when she'd first told me about him. "He's getting possessive," she'd said that day on the beach.

"Really?" I'd queried, surprised.

During the several times I'd met him, I'd never spotted any jealousy. On the contrary, he'd flirted openly with every woman in sight, me included. He was drop-dead gorgeous and possessed the gift of charm — an intoxicating combination.

When did I first meet him? I asked myself, thinking back. *Sometime in the fall.* Rosalie had invited me to join her and a few of her university colleagues for a department get-together. One glimpse at Paul and I understood Rosalie's light-hearted nomenclature — "Give Me Air," indeed. Paul Greeley was tall and lean, with a hint of a smile on his face and the promise of passion in his eyes. Everything about his appearance, from his thick blond hair to his well-fitting blue jeans, appealed to me. "Whew," I'd whispered to Rosalie as I sipped my glass of wine. "He's a knockout."

She smiled saucily and licked her lips. "Yeah. What do you expect? He's a firefighter. Haven't you ever noticed? They're *all* gorgeous."

I had observed that phenomenon and we talked about it, comparing notes. "You mean Paul used to be a fireman?"

"No. Current — he's a volunteer. In fact, I think he's some mucky-muck like a deputy chief or something."

"Impressive," I said, gazing at him — he was sizzling.

I'd had a way different reaction to Cooper Bennington. The assistant department chair was obnoxious and easy to dislike. Not only did he think he was better than everyone else, he didn't try to pretend otherwise.

"Well, hello," Paul had said to me that night, his tone a caress.

I recalled the interaction well. He'd looked at me, and I'd felt stripped naked, yet oddly I wasn't upset — I was flattered. Paul exuded charisma.

"Hi," I greeted him, smiling despite myself.

"Rosalie tells me you're an antiques appraiser. So I guess that means that you're as interested in history as we Ph.D. types."

Cooper snorted. "Real historians deal in facts. Antiques appraisers are self-serving and overly reliant on subjectivity."

"Present company excluded, of course," I joked, assuming he was trying to be funny, not rude. I was wrong. He was just a supercilious prig.

"Perhaps," he replied meanly.

Rosalie had nailed it, I thought, when she'd called him an arrogant jerk. I'd met a lot of people like Cooper Bennington when I worked at Frisco's. Most of them came from old money. I tried to remember what I knew about the Bennington family. If I recalled right, their fortune derived from bootlegging. His attitude made me wonder what he'd had appraised that had been valued lower than he'd expected or thought fair.

"Don't mind Cooper," Paul said in response, extinguishing the fireworks with deft kindness. "He can't stand the thought that anyone knows things that he doesn't know. And antiques appraisers know container-loads more things than he does. Makes him cranky."

I'd smiled at Paul then, appreciating his effort to render Cooper's nasty comment benign and irrelevant, and now, my eyes still focused on the surf, I shook my head to dispel the memory. Rosalie was dead. I'd lost a dear friend.

Waves crashed, casting seaweed onto the shore, and the wind was picking up, dotting the ocean surface with frothy whitecaps. A storm was coming. "It looks like snow," I said.

Ty scanned the cloud-shrouded horizon. "Yeah," he agreed, then turned toward me. "I need you to tell me what you know."

"What are you talking about?"

"Officer Brownley tells me you fibbed."

I looked out over the near-black ocean. A gull, gliding low, spiked and dove, then flew away. "I didn't fib."

"What do you know, Josie?" Ty asked as if I hadn't spoken, watching me with professional intensity.

"Nothing."

"Come on."

"Why do you think there's more?"

"Josie," he directed, "now."

"I'm serious — why would you think that?"

"Why do you ask? So you can lie better next time?"

I stayed quiet, a little hurt by his comeback. It wasn't that I wanted to lie, but I certainly wanted to master the art of discretion. Being circumspect is crucial in any business that involves divorcing couples and family members swarming like killer bees during an estate distribution. Also, as I'd learned when striving to avoid the press during the price-fixing scandal in New York, discretion offered the best chance at preserving my privacy. Yet despite years of experience, it seemed that I'd make a lousy poker player. Finally I looked up at him, and said, "I don't lie. You know that."

"Yeah, I know." He cleared his throat, a half-cough. "Still, we think you know something else."

I didn't know what to do. I felt half an inch tall even thinking of betraying a friend's trust. I looked out toward the place where gray sky merged with the black-green ocean.

"Josie?" he prodded.

I met his eyes, and knew I had to tell. *I'm sorry, Rosalie. Forgive me,* I thought. I took a deep breath and spoke. "She confided in me that she'd just sold her first book. She was so excited she said she could burst."

"I don't understand. Why would that have to be a secret?"

"The atmosphere at Hitchens was pretty intense. She wanted to get her dissertation approved and pass her orals before anyone in the department knew of her success. If people found out about the book deal, she was afraid she might be sabotaged."

Ty nodded. "What was the book about?"

"Something about communication during exploration. She didn't want to tell me the particulars, but she couldn't resist sharing the book deal itself."

"Can you remember what she said?"

I nodded. I pictured Rosalie sipping her iced tea, eyeing me with an impish gleam. "If I tell you a secret, will you promise not to tell?" she'd asked, her tone tantalizing.

"Who would I tell?" I'd teased.

"Cross your heart and hope to die?"

An instinct of danger had made me stop joking. I'd tilted my head, considering my options. "Are you sure you want to tell me?" I'd asked softly.

"If I don't tell someone, I'm going to burst!"

I'd smiled then, and said, "Okay. I promise."

And then she'd told me how a big New York publisher was offering her a fat advance to write a book and how the deal was going to change Paige's and her lives in a major way.

"I shouldn't have told you, but it's so fabulous that if I didn't tell anyone, I was just gonna scream!"

"I'm the only one who knows?" I'd asked, pleased to be singled out.

She'd said I was, and I'd felt honored.

I looked up after recounting the conversation and Ty nodded again, stared at me for a five count, then said, "What else?"

I stared at him, undecided. I didn't want to tell Rosalie's other secret. And, I reminded myself, unlike the book deal, I didn't *really* know anything. "I just *hate* to gossip, Ty. And really, I don't *know* anything."

"Understood. You don't *know* anything. That said, tell me what you *think*. Don't quibble."

"I'm not!" I protested. "There's a world of difference between gossip and fact."

He nodded. "Agreed. I promise never to quote you as reporting as fact anything that's gossip."

I gave in to his logic and persistence. *Maybe he is right,* I thought. *After all, it sounds as if this is a murder investigation.* "I think Rosalie and Gerry were having an affair."

Ty nodded as if he wasn't at all surprised.

"Is it true?" I asked.

"I have no idea," he said. "I just needed to know what you *didn't* tell Officer Brownley. What makes you think they were having an affair?

"Lots of small things. Giggles when they were alone in his office that stopped abruptly once they realized I was around. Ditto phone calls she received when we were out where she chatted for a while, then didn't say who it was while looking like a kid caught with her hand in the cookie jar. Once I heard her say 'Geeer-ry!' in that tone, you know, real flirtatious, stretching out the first syllable. 'Geeer-ry!' And I'm not the only one who thinks so. Someone at work said something."

"Who?"

"Ned Anderson," I answered, hating it that I was telling tales. "The chief financial officer."

"What did he say?"

"I hate this, Ty."

"I know you do. It's important, Josie, or I wouldn't ask."

"Was Rosalie murdered?" I whispered, looking north along the deserted beach.

"Josie?" Ty commanded. "What did Ned Anderson say?"

"About what?" I asked, continuing to look into the far distance. I noted that we were exchanging questions, a tactic which, according to Wes Smith, a local reporter, was a tried-and-true method to avoid revealing things you wanted to keep private.

"It's too early to be certain about the circumstances of her death," Ty said, "but I need you to answer my question as if she had been murdered. What did this Anderson guy say?"

51

I sighed. "Part of my hesitation is a 'consider the source' thing. Ned seems to have an attitude about Gerry."

"In what way?"

"Ned is pretty sarcastic in general, and after a particularly obnoxious moment, Rosalie confided that Ned had applied for the CEO position that Gerry got. Evidently, Ned has worked for the company for something like seven years, and he was pretty ticked off that he didn't get the job." I shrugged and looked up at Ty. "I'll tell you, but his comments may represent nothing more than a small-minded, mean-spirited man's attempt at humor."

"Got it. I can tell that you like him a lot."

I smiled a little. "But that's only because you're so insightful."

He smiled back and waited for me to continue.

I took a deep breath, and shivered. The sun was almost completely blocked, and it was frigid. "It was about a week ago. I was in Gerry's office, hurrying to finish mounting a bracket, when Ned came in."

Ned Anderson was around forty, tall and too skinny, with an Adam's apple that bobbed up and down when he spoke, and a receding chin. He was a mass of affectations. He wore a leather duster and cowboy hat, and often, he carried a hand-carved walking stick. I suspected that in his heart of hearts, he thought of himself as the Marlboro man. On this day, he'd tittered unattractively as he stepped into Gerry's office.

"Anyone here?" he asked sarcastically.

"Just us arty types," I kidded.

"Where's my fearless leader?" he asked, his tone offensive, not wry.

"I don't know."

"How about his faithful minion?"

"Tricia? She's at lunch."

"And his sycophant scribe?"

"Rosalie?"

"Yes-s-s-s," he answered as if he was stating the obvious to someone incredibly dumb.

"Haven't seen her," I replied.

"Oooooh," he mocked. "He told me Rosalie was due into the office today for one of their tête-à-têtes and now they're both gone, are they? Together, I wonder?"

Feeling uncomfortable, as if I'd aided and abetted them in playing hooky, I didn't respond. Instead, I turned back to my work.

Ned stood watching me for several seconds, then said, "Well, if you see them, tell them that I completely understand — and would appreciate it if Gerry would call me when he can squeeze a little business into his busy day."

I cleared my throat and met Ty's eyes. "That's it," I told him, and he nodded.

"What else makes you think they were having an affair?"

I hesitated again. "It was the way they looked at each other. I can't explain." I smiled at him. "Like we do. Like they were lovers."

Ty didn't smile back, but his hard, all-business demeanor softened, just a little. He raised his hand to touch my cheek, drawing his index finger slowly along the side of my face, starting just below my ear, following the angle of my jaw, sweeping along my neck until my parka stopped his progress. I leaned into the motion to give him access, closing my eyes. He took his hand away and I looked at him, an electric current racing through my veins. He smiled, and said, "Later."

I nodded but didn't speak.

"About what you were saying. I want to be clear," he said. "You didn't catch them doing the deed on his desk or anything of that nature?"

"No, not at all. That's why it's gossip."

"Okay," Ty said, nodding. "Thank you, Josie."

"Can I ask you something?"

"Sure."

"Officer Brownley told me that Paige, Rosalie's sister, is staying with a friend. Can you get me the number so I can call her?"

"Yeah. I have it inside."

"Can I ask you something else?"

"What?"

I turned up my collar, trying to block the wind that stabbed at my skin and caused my eyes to water. "Should I have told you about Rosalie and Gerry?"

"Yes. Absolutely." He watched me for a moment. "Is there anything else you know or think you know that you haven't told?"

I shook my head, suddenly weary. "No. You've got it all, now."

He smiled again, and suddenly I felt less cold, less anxious, and less guilty about revealing Rosalie's secrets. Basking in the warmth of Ty's love, I felt safe.

As I backed out of my parking space, ready to head back to Heyer's to collect the hardware I'd left strewn about when Gerry and I had rushed out, a patrol car turned into the lot. Griff was behind the wheel, and as he drove by, I saw that Paul Greeley and Cooper Bennington were sitting in the rear. Griff must have left for Hitchens as soon as he escorted Gerry into the interrogation room, I thought. I didn't envy Paul and Cooper the conversations that awaited them.

I wondered what they knew — and what they'd reveal. Then I gasped.

All at once, I remembered that Rosalie kept a diary. We'd shared a laugh about our different perspectives on the subject.

"I can't believe you don't keep a diary!" she'd said earnestly a few months ago. The subject arose because she'd apologized for being late for a lunch date — she'd been writing in her diary and had lost track of time.

"I never have. Even as a little girl, I never wanted to."

"You should try it again," she'd insisted. "Journaling is one of the most important forms of self-expression. And often they're of enormous historical value. Just think if Samuel Pepys hadn't kept his diary."

I acknowledged that the seventeenth-century journal kept by the "everyman," Samuel Pepys, was of immeasurable value to historians. The government official's journal recounted, in thrilling detail, the events of his time — the grisly plague, the Great Fire of London, even England's naval war with the Netherlands, among innumerable other personal and societal happenings.

"But I'm not doing it!" I added with a grin. "I don't like to write, my life isn't that interesting, and I'm way too private to boot."

She'd laughed at that, and exclaimed that we'd just discovered a major difference between us. "It's the exception that proves the rule."

"What's the rule that it's the exception to?" I asked.

"Great minds think alike, of course," she said gaily.

"The truth is that fools rarely differ," I retorted.

She'd laughed again and I'd joined in, and now, driving down the interstate, I pulled to a stop in the breakdown lane and punched the button activating the car's blinkers. *My friend is gone,* I thought, shaken by the memory. *And little Paige is all alone.*

I called Ty and told him about the diary.

"What does it look like?" he asked.

"I don't know. But she carried it with her all the time in her tote bag. She said she never knew when she might have a minute to write."

He thanked me, and told me how to reach Paige.

After a moment spent gathering my thoughts, I dialed the number. A machine picked up. I left a message, hung up, and stared unseeing into space, upset and worried about I wasn't sure what. Finally, my melancholy passed enough for me to drive on, and as I edged into traffic, I wondered if Rosalie's diary would offer any clues as to the cause and manner of her death.

CHAPTER FOUR

Wes Smith, the irritatingly persistent reporter who wrote for the Portsmouth-based *Seacoast Star,* called as I was merging into the traffic heading north on I-95.

"Josie," he said in a tone of intrigue, "you're in the middle of another murder investigation, huh?"

"Hello to you, too, Wes."

"My contact tells me you were just interrogated by the police about Rosalie Chaffee's murder," he said provocatively, ignoring my dig.

"Jeez, Wes," I said, glancing at the dashboard clock, "I only left the station ten minutes ago."

"Thanks," he replied, somehow, through the magic of Wes-think, translating my complaint about police department leaks into a compliment about his investigative skill. "So what do you know?"

I shook my head, resigned to the impossibility of keeping my participation secret. Lots of people knew I'd been at the Rocky Point police station, from police personnel to Una, the Heyer's receptionist who'd watched, big-eyed, as Gerry and I had quick-stepped out of the building. And once Wes got a whiff of my involvement, an innocently phrased question or two would be all that was required to fill in the blanks. I wondered what else he'd learned.

"First of all, I was *interviewed,* not *interrogated.* Second of all, how do you know she was murdered?"

"Confidential source," he said importantly.

"Give me a break, Wes."

"Seriously, it's true."

"Are you sure?" I asked. "She was murdered?"

"Why? Did you hear otherwise?" he retorted, eager for news.

"Last I heard, the medical examiner's report wasn't completed."

"True," Wes acknowledged, "but you know how that goes. The report may not be finished, but they know enough to be able to say that Rosalie was hit over the head and drowned."

I gulped air. "I'm sorry to hear that." I took another deep breath. "Did you know her, Wes?"

"No. You?"

I considered hanging up. It was beginning again. Wes was somehow drawing more information out of me than I wanted to be giving. That I was on-site when Rosalie's boss, Gerry, needed a ride to Rocky Point was pure coincidence, but I could hear Wes now: *It's Josie's third murder,* he'd tell his editor, salivating at the thought of another hot story. His last front-page feature, "Anatomy of a Homicide Investigation," made it clear that I wasn't a murderer, *gee, thanks,* but seeing my name prominently displayed as someone involved in a murder investigation was an experience I wanted to avoid repeating. *Still,* I mused, *Wes is very connected and a reliable source of information.* And, I acknowledged to myself, I was curious.

"Her boss bought some antiques from me," I explained, "and I've been installing them. She was writing a book for him."

"What was she like?" Wes asked, jumping in.

"Nice. She was a great girl. This is all off-the-record, right, Wes?"

"Why?" he whined. "This is just background info."

I cast my eyes heavenward. Wes was so

61

predictable. "Off-the-record or nothing."

He sighed deeply, signaling acquiescence. "Okay, okay. I won't quote you."

"Even if you verify what I say independently?"

"Same as always," he agreed, implying he was being patient in the face of my unreasonableness. "With outside verification, I can use any facts I learn from you, but I still won't name you as a source."

"Okay, then."

"So, what was she like?" he repeated.

I told him what I knew, but not what I speculated, and Wes seemed disappointed that I had no gossip to share. He ended our conversation with a brisk "Talk soon."

Talk soon, I repeated silently, sick at the thought.

During the months I'd been a reluctant whistle-blower and witness in the price-fixing scandal that rocked the antiques auction world in New York, I'd been rubbed raw, first by my boss's betrayal, then by my colleagues' spite and the media's relentless hounding. It was awful. And then it got worse — my dad died. His death sent me reeling, and after breaking up with my boyfriend, I left New York to start a business in New Hampshire. My dad once told me, *If you reach the end of your rope, tie a knot and hang on. And if you can't hang on, move on.* I moved on.

Much to my surprise, I loved New Hampshire. I found it filled with people who value independence and freethinking. The countryside is lush and varied, and the environment is just right to foster my company's growth. I loved Ty Alverez, too, and I was keeping my fingers crossed that our fun and tender relationship was for real. What I didn't need was another murder investigation sucking me into its vortex.

Una, sitting behind the reception desk at Heyer's, tried hard not to sneer as she told me who was waiting in Gerry's office — his wife, Edie. Una's lank hair hung to her shoulders. She wore it parted in the middle, straight and flat against her head. She looked tired most of the time, no surprise since she worked full time and was rearing three kids on her own. I had no idea how old she was. Younger than me, I guessed.

"What's Edie doing here?" I asked, not quite whispering.

"Maybe she needs a new credit card."

I didn't smile because the jab was dead-on. Edie wanted to be "one of the girls," and it didn't seem to register that a wife of a CEO who appropriated her husband's car and driver for midday trips to Boston's tony Newbury Street probably didn't have a lot in common with the company's receptionist, who was up to her ears in debt and trying to juggle the bills so she could buy her twelve-year-old the new sneakers he swore he couldn't live without, and still eat.

I recalled the scornful look on Una's face last Christmas when she told me about the crystal vase that Edie had given her as a Christmas gift. "Just what I need," she said, "an etched glass vase. That'll really help put food on the table."

Edie Fine was a tall woman, almost as tall as her husband, and professionally thin, like a model or a dancer. Her dark hair was cut in a dramatic wedge. She was, it seemed, a fan of cosmetic surgery. Her breasts were high on her chest, perfectly ball-shaped, and large; her face was tautly wrinkle free; and her lips were pout enhanced. She was dressed in the height of fashion, and she wore lots of diamonds all the time.

"Where's Gerry? Do you know?" Edie asked as soon as I stepped into his suite's outer office where Tricia sat quietly, typing.

It was my day for being asked questions I didn't want to answer.

"Have you heard about Rosalie?" I countered.

Edie was breathing hard, and if I was able to read faces at all, she was mad as hell. "Yes, I heard about it just now on the news. It's why I came. Where is he?"

"I don't know for sure. He was at the Rocky Point police station last I saw."

She didn't reply. Her eyes were locked on mine, assessing I don't know what. She turned and walked into Gerry's office, pausing at the double-wide window that overlooked the pond. I followed her gaze. The pond was frozen and covered with a dusting of snow. Brittle-looking grasses swayed in the breeze. I could almost hear the wheels in her mind turning.

"The reporter on the radio said that Rosalie's death might be murder," she said with her back to me. "Is that true, do you think?"

"I don't know," I said. "I don't think the police are done with their tests."

"May I ask you something?" she asked.

She turned to face me, a cheerless smile softening her features. *She knows,* I thought. *She knows about the affair.*

"Sure," I replied, only because I couldn't think of a polite way to say no, dreading her question, wondering what Tricia must think witnessing such a scene.

Edie's chest began to heave and her lips

thinned. "What do you know about their relationship?"

"Nothing," I said, backing away, wishing I had the courage to run. "I don't know anything. If you'll excuse me, I've got to get my tools and stuff."

She lost it. One moment she was in control, and the next her face was contorted. "The son of a bitch!"

Without another word, she spun toward Gerry's desk, grabbed a crystal-framed photograph showing the two of them on a yacht, and hurled it across the room, shattering the frame and denting the wall. She was panting. Shards of glass formed a chaotic pattern on the thick gray carpet.

I whipped around and nearly ran into Ned, the CFO, as he entered Tricia's anteroom. Tricia didn't even look up. She had the gift of working through pandemonium.

"What did I miss?" Ned asked, looking amused, nodding toward Gerry's inner office. "Hello, Tricia. Any blood drawn?"

Neither Tricia nor I replied. I don't know what was in her mind, but from my perspective, I just couldn't bear the thought of enduring Ned's sarcasm. Instead, I moved toward where my tools lay in erratic happenstance. My hands were shaking.

"Are you all right?" he asked me in a

kinder tone.

"Yes," I said softly. I could hear Edie on the phone, but not her words, and I was relieved that she wouldn't be able to overhear us discussing her. "It's Edie. She's kind of upset."

His sneer reappeared. "Ah!" he said knowingly, raising his brows. "The cat was away and the mouse played — and now he's been caught."

Tricia was back at work, pretending he wasn't there. I took her lead and ignored him, and continued gathering items and placing them in my toolbox, uncomfortable in his presence. Ned was like a gnat buzzing near your face, irritating and unstoppable. Rosalie had once remarked that Ned was an effective CFO for the same reason that he was a hateful person — he seemed to delight in ferreting out flaws.

"The grapevine says that you took Gerry to identify Rosalie's corpse," he said. "I gather that it was, in fact, Rosalie?"

"Yes," I answered.

"And?"

"And what?"

"And what did you learn about her death?" he asked.

I shrugged again. "I don't know anything except that she's dead."

"I thought you were dating the police chief."

"He doesn't talk to me about his work," I said, affronted that anyone would think he might.

He glanced at Tricia, then winked at me, his Adam's apple bobbing. "Got it. You can fill me in later."

"I have nothing to say," I insisted.

"It's okay, Josie," he said, crossing to the door, ready to leave. "I won't tell if you don't."

I gazed after him for a moment, then stole a peek at Tricia, still apparently ignoring everything around her. I hoped Ned didn't think I'd just made some sort of pact with him. I exhaled loudly, wanting to be away from all of the emotion. Within seconds, I heard a decisive click as Edie hung up the phone. A moment later, she strode out of Gerry's office and, without looking in our direction or uttering a word, left.

Still trembling from the afterclap of Edie's volcanic eruption and Ned's malicious implications, I asked Tricia if she was okay.

"Certainly," she said, without missing a keystroke. "When I'm at work, I never pay attention to anything but the job."

I nodded, then looked down. My toolbox showed an empty compartment. My screwdriver was missing.

"I think I left something in Gerry's office," I said, stepped inside, and glanced around.

The scratched and pockmarked photograph lay abandoned amidst fragments of glass, another victim of infidelity. Shaking my head, dismayed to have witnessed Edie's emotional outburst, I saw something in the corner, a book, a slim, tan leather volume, upside down, spine up.

I took a step toward it and looked over my shoulder again. I heard nothing and took another step. A red ribbon, the kind that marked a reader's or writer's place, curled toward the wall. I knelt beside the book and picked it up. It was Rosalie's diary. I fanned the pages, seeking out her last entry. Rosalie had written it just before she met me for lunch.

Should I read it? I asked myself. Diaries, I knew, were considered by their writers to be sacrosanct. Surely Rosalie wouldn't want other people knowing her most intimate thoughts. But it was too late for that. As evidenced by Edie's shattering rage, Rosalie's privacy had already been breached. I knew what Ty would say. He'd tell me that it was police business and to leave it alone. I smiled as I realized how Wes would view the opportunity — he'd expect me to photo-copy it for him.

I turned to the door and held my breath to listen closely. I heard the soft hum of electricity and nothing else. I couldn't resist. Feeling a bit like a voyeur, I began to read.

"I'm looking forward to lunch with Josie. She's a keeper!" Rosalie had written. I teared up and looked away to stop from cry-ing, then, after I'd regained control, read on. "Chief is irritating me in ways I never thought possible. Doesn't everyone know that perseverance can easily become stalk-ing? *Hello!* I can't make Chief stop. I've tried logic, begging, *everything!* It's frightening and disturbing. Gerry is nothing but kind and giving. Sigh. Sigh. Sigh. I'm like a silly schoolgirl and I want to twirl and shout with glee and share my love. What to do, what to do?"

Is she saying that Gerry is Chief and a stalker — that he has a Jekyll-and-Hyde sort of split personality? I asked myself, disbeliev-ing. *Or that someone else she called Chief is stalking her?*

I shook my head, confused. I had no way to know.

I took a deep breath and glanced again toward the anteroom. I flipped through the pages, stopping here and there to read.

70

Nothing stood out as hot news — certainly there was no hint of the secret Rosalie had confided to me during her last lunch. In the last two months, mostly she wrote about Gerry. It was hard for me to believe, but Rosalie seemed to have adored him.

The phone rang, and I dropped the diary, startled. I heard Tricia tell someone named Erin that she'd be right down.

"Josie?" she called. "I've got to go to the service center. I won't be long."

I scooped up the book and held it behind my back. "Okay!" I replied, poking my head out into the anteroom in time to see her step into the corridor.

"Where are you going, Trish?" Gerry asked from the corridor, out of sight.

"There's some question about binding your board report," Tricia told him.

Gerry was back! I dashed across the room and placed the book as I'd found it, stretching out the red ribbon against the baseboard. Within seconds, I was back in the anteroom, kneeling by my toolbox, hidden by Tricia's desk. I closed my eyes, waiting for my tumultuous pulse to quiet, thinking that if I stayed out of sight until Gerry was ensconced in his own office, I might get away without speaking to him.

Time passed, seconds probably, but it felt

71

like minutes. I heard nothing. Soon Tricia would return and find me huddled in a corner like a wounded animal. I began to feel foolish. I edged my eye around the corner of Tricia's desk and peeked. From my kneeling position, I had a clear view of Rosalie's cubbyhole.

The door was open and the lights were on. Gerry was standing motionless staring at her desk. I followed his gaze and gaped. Rosalie's old brown leather tote bag, the one she always carried, sat on top of her desk. I fell back on my heels, my brain reeling.

That explained how her diary ended up in Gerry's office. Rosalie must have returned to Heyer's at some point after our lunch and after she took Paige back home — and somehow left her tote bag behind.

This morning, Edie must have breezed into the office and spied it. When Tricia stepped out for a cup of coffee or to use the rest room, I thought, she took the opportunity to sneak a peek. Finding the diary would have only taken moments.

I felt suddenly breathless, desperate to get away. I stood up and took several calming breaths. "Hi, Gerry," I said.

"Jesus, Josie!" he exclaimed, swinging

around to face me. "You scared the shit out of me."

"Sorry. I'm heading over to Ned's office to hang the Sharp," I said, referring to the desert scene that Gerry had just bestowed on him last week.

"It's okay, doll," he replied, grinning. "Good. Go make Ned's day."

His stint at the police station didn't seem to have hurt him any — he didn't merely look none the worse for wear; he looked cocky.

I didn't hesitate — I wanted to be out of there before Gerry spotted the full extent of Edie's destruction. I selected a screwdriver, mounting filament, and level from my toolbox, and eased the painting out from behind the credenza.

The Joseph Henry Sharp oil was exceptional, and a perfect choice for Ned. Last week Gerry had told me to get Ned something special. "Like what?" I'd asked.

"Buy him a beauty," Gerry told me with a wink. "He likes Western art. Ned's got no self-esteem 'cause no one takes him seriously, no matter how much aristocracy he has in the family, but he's a helluva CFO, so this'll give him a boost. Spend fifty, sixty thousand. You know, not too much, not more than you spent on things in *my* office, but enough so he feels the love. You got what I'm saying, doll?"

Quite a boost, I'd thought at the time. The painting was rare. At auction it would have fetched something over $60,000, so Gerry got a bargain when I sold it to him for $55,000.

Ned's office was on the far side of the building, diagonally opposite Gerry's, and almost as large. I nodded to his secretary, a middle-aged woman I knew hardly at all, and stepped into his room.

Ned's desk was positioned kitty-corner to the entranceway, facing both the door and the windows. Two credenzas provided nearly eight feet of flat surface, all of it covered, mostly with stacks of files. At one end was a nice repro of a Remington cowboy.

I scanned the walls, considering where it would be best to hang the painting. In addition to a few simple desert scenes, Ned had an interesting collection of arrowheads mounted on linen and framed in rustic pine; a cuckoo clock in the form of a log cabin, with a grizzly bear that popped out to strike a triangle with a metal rod to mark the time; and a necklace of bear teeth strung on a frayed leather thong, which was probably worth a small fortune if it was real. I approached the necklace for a closer look. While I was admiring the artifact, the bear sounded the quarter hour. I smiled. His clapper struck hard and the brass reverberated.

"Where are you thinking of hanging it?" Ned asked, nodding toward the small oil painting.

My heart skipped a beat — I hadn't heard him come into the room. "It might look good there," I said, pointing at a space on the wall across from the arrowheads, above the cowboy.

He shrugged and I couldn't tell if that meant he didn't like my choice or didn't care. I didn't know him well enough to read his signals. Mostly what I'd observed was that he always had something quick-witted and mean to say.

"Was there someplace else you'd like?" I asked.

"Can't make up your mind, huh? Just like a woman."

"What?" I asked, ready to protest the absurd comment.

"Just joking," he said with a grin that never reached his eyes.

I turned away, irritated. I hated it when people said that. "So?" I asked. "Is that a yes?"

"You're the expert," he said, shrugging and sitting behind his desk. "You tell me."

"Okay, then," I said. "Over the cowboy it is." I wiggled a freestanding coatrack aside. "Nice coatrack," I said. "Ponderosa pine, right?"

"How'd you know?"

I smiled saucily. "After years of experience appraising hundreds of objects, you too will be able to identify wood at a glance!"

"Everyone's got to be good at something," he said dismissively.

I didn't respond to his cutting comment. Instead, I moved his knob-handled walking stick to the far side of the room and began the careful process of measuring.

Ten minutes later, I asked him, "What do you think?"

He looked up and smiled, sincerely this time. "It's a beauty, isn't it?"

I followed his gaze. *Big sky country,* I thought. The artist used a complex layering process to evoke the rough beauty of a land that never seemed to reach the horizon.

"It sure is," I agreed. I looked at the Remington repro depicting a weary cowboy. "You're a fan of Western art, I see."

"Thanks," he said as if I'd complimented him.

"How did you get into it?" I asked, packing up my tools.

He shrugged and smirked. "From when I was a little tyke. I collected those myself," he said, pointing to the arrowheads.

"They're nicely mounted."

His Adam's apple bobbed, but he didn't speak.

"See you later," I said.

As I walked to my car, I called Tricia. "Tricia, it's Josie. A quick question — was Rosalie in the office yesterday afternoon?"

"No, why?"

"Her tote bag is there. On her desk."

"So it is," she said after a short pause. "That's odd, isn't it?"

"Could she have popped in while you were on break?"

"I wasn't gone from my desk for more than a minute or two all afternoon. I was working on Gerry's board report."

"I'll tell the police," I said, thinking that since Rosalie would have had to use her key card to gain entry, the police would be able to tell if she'd stopped by.

"Okay," she agreed. "I'll make sure no one disturbs it."

I told her I'd be in touch, then stared into space for a long time, mystified.

CHAPTER FIVE

I called Ty as soon as I was in my car and got his voice mail. "Ty," I said, choosing my words carefully, "I'm just leaving Heyer's and I wanted to let you know that I saw Rosalie's diary in Gerry's office. Mrs. Fine, Edie, had been there. Anyway, when I left it was on the floor. Also, Rosalie's tote bag is on her desk and according to Mr. Fine's assistant, Tricia, Rosalie wasn't in all day yesterday, but I guess the key cards will tell you for sure. Talk to you later."

I couldn't *not* tell the police what I'd seen, but I figured I didn't have to reveal that I'd read the diary. I felt ashamed, though, as I recalled words my father had spoken years earlier. *Situational ethics,* he'd warned me, *is bull. A lot in life isn't black or white. But for those things that are, don't fall into the trap of rationalization.* I shrugged. *I shouldn't have read it,* I chastised myself, then wondered again how the tote bag had got onto her desk.

Ten minutes later, I pulled into my building's parking lot, looking first at the big burgundy PRESCOTT'S ANTIQUES, AUCTIONS, AND APPRAISALS sign mounted on the roof, then at an old brown van idling near the front door.

As I walked by, I smiled at the driver, a grim-looking young man with long brown hair. He didn't respond, and I couldn't tell whether it was because he didn't notice my greeting or didn't care.

I pushed open the front door, setting Gretchen's wind chimes jingling, the cheery noise mingling with the rhythmic patter of her typing.

A stranger, an unkempt young woman in her midtwenties, stood facing my chief appraiser, Sasha. Sasha was holding a jumbo-sized plastic bag containing something flat and wooden.

"His mother," the woman said, answering a question I hadn't heard.

"Did he tell you where his mother got it?" Sasha asked.

"No. But I think he made some notes. I can look when I get home."

"That would be useful. Thank you."

"Hey," I said to Gretchen.

"Josie," Sasha said, noticing me, sounding relieved, "this is Lesha Moore. Ms. Moore, Josie Prescott, the owner."

"Nice to meet you. What do you have there?" I asked as I walked toward them.

"Whistler's palette," the woman named Lesha answered, sounding irritated, maybe at having to repeat her story. She shrugged with an attitude that matched her appearance. "At least, that's what Evan, my boyfriend, told me."

I nodded and took the plastic bag from Sasha's extended hand. At first glance, the wood looked right. It was probably maple, maybe poplar. It had a rich patina, a golden sheen that comes from generations of use. There were dabs of dried paint along the outer edge, the hues ranging from thunderstorm gray on one end to snow white on the other.

Behind me, Gretchen had succumbed to the lure of gossip and stopped typing. Here, right in our office, stood someone who said she possessed a palette that had been used by one of America's greatest artists, James McNeill Whistler.

I looked at Lesha. Her dirt-brown hair was stringy, and she had the sunken-cheeked, desperate look of a drug addict or an anorexic. I handed the bag back to Sasha, and smiled again. "You're in good hands," I told Lesha. "Sasha's the best!"

"How long is this going to take?" Lesha grumbled, unimpressed.

"Sasha?" I prompted, resisting the temptation to answer for her.

Sasha lacked confidence about everything except art and antiques, and since she was far more interested in things than people, she lacked social and communication skills as well. But since responding to client questions and concerns was part of her job, she had to find a way to handle the responsibility. She had to be able to give information, explain procedures, and soothe ruffled feathers whether I was available or not.

"It depends," she told Lesha. "We need to run some tests."

"What kind of tests?" Lesha demanded.

"On the wood, for instance. And we need to trace the provenance, the record of ownership."

"Why?"

"That's all part of the appraisal pro-process," she stammered. "First we have to authenticate the palette, then we have to assess its value. It's a process, and it takes time."

Lesha sighed clear to her belly. "So . . . how long?"

"A few days to a few weeks," Sasha said, visibly hating that she had to deliver news that Lesha would probably perceive as bad.

"No way a few weeks," she announced, almost stomping her foot. "Forget about it!"

"I understand," Sasha said calmly, doing a good job, I thought, of conveying empathy without backing away from her reasoned estimate. She handed Lesha the plastic bag.

Lesha stood with her hands on her hips, pouting as she weighed her options. "Okay, okay," she said, accepting our terms without enthusiasm, "but hurry."

"We'll do our best." Sasha turned to Gretchen, and said, "Would you please give Ms. Moore a receipt for the contents of this bag?"

Gretchen prepared the paperwork, including taking and printing some digital photos that she had Lesha sign, all while Lesha paced impatiently. Gretchen's striking emerald eyes opened wide, appreciating the drama. As Lesha angrily pushed open the front door to leave, Sasha reminded her to look for the notes about the palette's history.

Lesha brushed Sasha off with a quick "Yeah, yeah," and half ran to the waiting brown van. I watched through the window as the driver, the man with long hair, said something to her and she answered by shaking her head. He left rubber as he peeled out of my parking lot.

"Whew. What's her problem?" I asked.

"I don't know. She seemed angry," Sasha answered.

I shook my head and raised my eyebrows to convey mystification. "Who's Evan?"

"Evan Woodricky. Her boyfriend. She said he died of some blood disease and left the palette to her in his will."

"That sounds fishy."

"Really?" Sasha asked, surprised.

Sasha had many gifts, but judging people's sincerity wasn't among them. She was literal and trusting, but at least she knew her limits. Thankfully, she was never defensive. Unlike most people, who, in my experience, either never thought about their abilities to read people at all, or had a wildly inflated notion of their capabilities, Sasha knew herself well. She also knew that while she would never excel at managing client expectations or picking up on exaggerations or misstatements, she could improve.

"Check the provenance — and the authenticity — carefully," I warned.

"I will." Picking up the plastic bag, tilting it to catch the dim natural light, she asked, "Do you think it's maple?"

"Probably."

Sasha placed the bag containing the palette gently on her desk and began to jot notes on a pad of lined paper. No doubt she was listing avenues of research and questions that needed answering.

"So, what else is going on?" I asked Gretchen.

"Everything's under control," she answered. "Eric's preparing for Saturday's tag sale."

"Good. I'll be in my office," I said, and pushed through the inside door that opened into the warehouse.

As soon as I started up the spiral stairs that led to my private office, Gretchen's voice crackled over the PA system. "Josie," she announced, "Ty's on line one."

Upstairs, I sank into my desk chair, swiveled to face the window, and punched the button labeled *1*.

"Hey," I said.

"Hi, there. So . . . tell me about the diary and the tote bag. Start with the diary. Did you see it in Edie's hands?"

"No."

"What did you observe?"

Anguish, I thought. "I saw her in Gerry's office."

"What did she say?"

84

"She asked if Gerry and Rosalie were having an affair. I told her I didn't know."

"Then what?"

There was no point in keeping quiet. "Ty, she went crazy," I said softly. "She picked up a photo from his desk and hurled it against the wall."

"And?"

"And then she talked on the phone for a minute and left."

"Where was the diary?"

"I saw it later. After she was gone. I think she threw it. At least, it was against the wall as if it had been thrown."

"Did you read it?" he asked.

I shut my eyes. "I glanced at it," I confessed.

There was a pause. "What did you do with it after you read it?"

"I put it back where I found it."

"Well, let's hope it's still there," he said coldly. "Hold on, okay?"

I opened my eyes and shook my head. He was right. I should have called the police right away, as soon as I realized what the book was. If Rosalie's diary was missing, it was my fault.

Ty came back on the line. "What about the tote bag?"

"She always carried it, Ty. She called it

85

her mobile office."

"Did she keep the diary in it?"

"Yes. She carried it with her all the time."

"Did she have the bag at lunch?"

"Yes. Absolutely."

"Okay, thanks for telling me." He paused, then cleared his throat. "There's one more thing. A business issue."

"Okay," I said, tensing immediately. No matter what our relationship, if a police chief said he wanted to talk about business, probably the news wasn't good.

"I wanted to let you know that I've asked Officer Brownley to follow up with you."

My heart sank as memories of last year's horrible gala flooded my mind. A woman had died in my auction venue during a charity event my firm was sponsoring, and the police had been inexorably suspicious, sarcastic, and uncaring. *No doubt Ty has told Officer Brownley about our conversation on the beach,* I thought, *so now she thinks I'm a liar.* "Oh, God," I objected. "I don't want to talk to her again. What does she want?"

"Just what you think she wants."

To hear more about Rosalie's affair with Gerry, I thought, flashing on Edie's unbridled explosion. "Why can't you be the one to question me?"

He paused for several seconds, too long,

and I wondered if I'd irritated or offended him.

"Will you be cooking tonight?" he asked, completely ignoring my question, "or would you like to go out for dinner?"

"Ty!" I protested.

"Come on, Josie, give me a break. Sorry the arrangement doesn't suit your personal preference."

"Thanks for being so sensitive."

"I wanted to give you a heads-up. I've done that. Give me a call later, okay?"

He hung up with a sharp crack, and holding the receiver, staring at the phone, it felt as if I'd been slapped.

When you're at work, no matter how upset you are, put a smile on your face, and get down to business, my father told me years ago. *Don't wear your heart on your sleeve.* Yet how could I *not* be emotional? I was upset about Rosalie's death, I shrank from the thought of having to talk to Officer Brownley again, and I was hurt and confused by Ty's tone. I forced myself to put my distress aside and called Paige again.

Whoever answered the phone called her name and in a minute I heard a sad "Hello?"

"It's Josie."

"Hi, Josie."

"I'm so, so sorry, Paige."

87

"Thank you."

I'd been polite like that when my father died. I recognized the cadence — she was in shock, coping, but not assimilating much. "I wanted you to know that if I can do anything to help, you let me know. You can stay with me. Or I can drive you places. Or cook you dinner. Whatever you need, I can do."

She sniffed. "Thank you," she repeated, her voice wavering.

"Write down my phone numbers, okay?"

"Okay. I've got a pen."

I had her read back both my work and cell phone numbers, and after we were done, I sat, staring into space. *Don't think of the police. Or Ty. Or Rosalie. Focus on work,* I chided myself.

I scanned the piles of papers and files on my desk awaiting my attention. Nothing appealed to me. I didn't feel like looking at my accountant's latest report, reviewing Sasha's draft of catalogue copy for an upcoming auction of perfume bottles, or reading a salesperson's proposal to upgrade our inventory control system. I sighed and walked to the window.

Branches on my old maple shimmied in the strengthening breeze. The sky was thick with steel gray clouds. Instead of dealing with paperwork, I considered going home and cooking. When feeling blue or anxious, I turn to the cookbook my mother created for me when I was thirteen, just before she died, finding motherly comfort in its handwritten pages.

I returned to my desk, and I was halfway through my accountant's good news report — it was official, December's tag sale's bottom line was up a healthy 11 percent from a year ago — when Gretchen called to tell me, "Officer Brownley on line two."

"Hi, Josie," she said, sounding not the least bit irritated. "I understand Chief Alverez told you that I need to talk to you some more."

"I'm glad to help if I can."

"Thanks. I'm going to be in your neighborhood in an hour. Will you be there?"

"Yes."

"Good. See you then."

As I sat staring at my maple tree, I thought about Rosalie, and only then did panic start to rise. What could Ty and Officer Brownley possibly think I knew that I hadn't already told them?

CHAPTER SIX

The tag-sale room was a shacklike structure attached to the right side of the warehouse. When I'd first bought the old factory, the room had been rickety and unused. I brought it up to code but left it plain. I figured customers would be more likely to expect bargains in an underdesigned venue than one that was stylishly decorated.

I spotted Eric as soon as I stepped into the room. It was Thursday, so he was overseeing the setup for Saturday's sale. I wished I could think of a less labor-intensive approach to merchandising than taking all of the unsold inventory down after each week's sale and restocking the tables as the weekend approached, but it was the only way I'd ever found to keep the displays looking fresh. And as the sales figures proved, my strategy was working.

Barely out of his teens, twig thin, and earnest, Eric was my warehouse guy, overseeing everything from facility management to inventory. I'd recently promoted him to supervisor, and he was doing fine, but he was a reluctant leader, filled with self-doubt and continually expecting failure.

"Stagger the glasses," Eric instructed a temp, a white-haired woman who was new to us, moving pieces of Depression glass-ware into position as he spoke. "Put one over here and another over there. Don't just line them up."

"Oh, I see," the woman replied, sounding excited to receive direction. "Shall I do it that way with all of the sets of glasses?"

"Yeah," Eric told her. "And let me know if you have any questions, okay?"

I glanced at her name tag as I approached and said hello to them both. Her name was Cara. I wondered if she wanted a permanent job. I liked her attitude and we could always use part-timers interested in working the tag sale regularly.

"Hey, Eric," I said. "How's it going?"

"Slowly," he half whispered as we walked toward the far door. His face was lined with worry. "We have two new temps. They don't know how we do things."

I nodded. "Maybe we ought to think of hiring another part-timer, someone who can work every week. Cara looks good," I said, nodding in her direction.

"She seems okay," Eric agreed.

"Let's see how she does on Saturday."

With a final glance around the sparsely filled tables, I left him to the task and made my way to the main office. Fred, wearing his signature rat-pack cool suit and tie, was hanging up his topcoat.

"Any luck?" I asked.

He shook his head. "Twentieth-century repro of an eighteenth-century print," he said matter-of-factly, delivering the news that not only was the art print not incunabulum as I'd hoped, it wasn't even an original.

"Well," I said philosophically, "I guess the tag-sale inventory just got a boost."

"Yeah. It's a beauty, though. We shouldn't price it too low."

"No, go ahead and price it the same as the others. For some lucky buyer it'll be a real find," I said.

The tag-sale pricing policy I'd set when I first opened Prescott's was simple: Everything was to be priced fairly, even on the low side, and occasionally we slip in a significant bargain to reward good shoppers, create buzz, and encourage customers to continue their hunt the next time they come through.

Last Saturday, I'd walked by a middle-aged woman holding a pink fluted Victorian bride's basket just in time to hear her whisper to a younger woman, maybe her daughter, "Lillian, look at this — it's only fifty dollars!"

"Wow!" the young woman exclaimed. "It's beautiful!"

They were right, it *was* a bargain. At auction I'd expect the nineteenth-century object to fetch more than a hundred dollars. But we weren't currently building collections of glassware, except cobalt pieces, so I decided to let it go for a song. With any luck, they'd tell everyone they knew about their stellar find.

Fred nodded, opened his portfolio case, and extracted the art print.

Sasha, watching him, twirled a strand of her lank brown hair. "Look at this, Fred."

"What is it?" he asked, squinting through his square-shaped black-framed glasses.

"The client said it's Whistler's palette."

Fred stopped cold and stared at the bag with laserlike intensity. "Really?"

"That's what she said. Josie and I think the wood looks right, but who knows?"

"What's the history?" he asked.

"She got it from her boyfriend who died a few weeks ago. The boyfriend got it from his mother."

"How do you plan on authenticating it?" he asked.

Confirming an antique's pedigree, an important part of the appraisal process, was often tough and sometimes impossible. Without letters of agreement, receipts, or bills of sale, how do you know that an object wasn't stolen or that its history wasn't misrepresented? We use diaries, business records, oral histories, and official records to document ownership and association, and we double- and triple-check everything. A good appraiser needs to be part hound and part detective, smelling out clues that can be followed up methodically.

"Lesha's looking for the paperwork that she thinks will provide some history. I'm going to wait until I hear from her," Sasha said.

"You ought to start analyzing the palette itself," Fred argued. "Don't just wait for her."

"I will, but not a lot. We might learn things from her that would make our work more efficient," she responded.

Fred and Sasha were an anomalous pair. Fred was New York City street smart. Sasha was 100 percent small-town trusting. He had a solid education but relied more on his years of experience and razor-sharp instincts. She had a Ph.D. in art history but no common sense. He was self-assured; she was timid. He was acerbic; she was refined. But they shared key qualities: They were both curious, knowledgeable, systematic, precise, and honest. Their conflicts were intellectual, never personal, and together they found creative ways to solve stubborn problems. They were a great team. *Lucky me,* I thought.

"I seem to recall that Whistler had some unusual work habits," I remarked. "If I remember right, he used extra-long brushes so he could stand far away from the canvas. Maybe you could see if he did anything funky with his palettes."

"I'll get started on it right away," Sasha said.

"What's up next for you, Fred, now that the print is done?" I asked.

"I'm pecking away at the Samuels estate."

I nodded again, and allowed myself a private *Atta girl.* Morehead Samuels, a well-known collector from Toledo, had accumulated four M. W. Hopkins paintings, eight pieces of Hungarian pottery, and more than two dozen artifacts from the whaling industry, an eclectic mix of valuable objects. When he died, his executor, a lawyer in

Ohio, having read a profile of Prescott's in *Antiques Insights,* a trade journal that had written us up a few months ago, contacted me to handle the appraisal of the entire estate. His decision to choose us, a relatively new appraisal firm — and further, one that was neither local nor New York City–based — caused quite a stir in the antiques world, and I was proud as all get-out. It was an exciting project and, potentially, a reputation-building one.

Paul Greeley pushed open the front door, and out of the corner of my eye, I saw Gretchen sit up straighter and smile. He sure was good-looking, but it was more than that. He had intelligent eyes and lots of laugh lines and he carried himself with unconscious sangfroid.

"Well, hello," Gretchen said. "Can I help you?"

He spotted me. "Josie," he said, fake-shooting me with his index finger. He favored Gretchen with a smile, then turned to me. "Got a sec to talk business?"

"Sure. Come on in. We can go to my office."

I led the way through the warehouse to the spiral staircase that gave access to my private office.

"I hope we can grab a cup of coffee

sometime, and tell uplifting Rosalie stories," he said.

"Sounds good. There are lots of them." I gestured that Paul should sit in one of the two yellow Queen Anne wing chairs, and I took the other. "You mentioned business?"

"I need your help in finding a perfect birthday gift for my mother."

I smiled. "Sure. What does she like?"

He smiled back and I felt my heart skip a beat. He had a certain something that made it easy to relax in his presence. Yet I felt wary as well, sensing that he wanted more than I had to give, and that he wanted it too quickly. It was as if I were in danger of being drawn into a sticky web of his making.

"Nothing," he said. "That's what makes it tough."

I laughed. "Well, I've always liked a challenge. Tell me more."

He made a face. "There are two problems. One, she has everything she needs or wants. Two, she has unpredictable taste."

"Jeez. Okay. Does she collect anything?"

"Nope."

"What's her house look like? I mean how is it decorated?"

He gazed around. "Like this. Beautiful and substantive." He looked at me. "Just like the room's owner."

I felt myself blush and wondered if he was flirting with me or negotiating, figuring that if he buttered me up, I'd lower the price.

"Thank you," I said, my tone neutral. "She likes eighteenth-century decorations, then?"

"Is that what this is?" he asked, looking around again.

"Mostly."

"I guess. I'm no expert."

"Did you have anything in mind?" I asked.

"No," he said, smiling again. "I'm content to leave the decision in your capable hands."

I continued to ask questions and get unhelpful answers, then I asked him for his budget. After a little more conversation, I mentioned a spectacular Louis XVI mustard pot, a cobalt glass jar enclosed in a covered silver stand. I'd been planning on including it in an auction of cobalt glassware later in the year, and felt a momentary pang at suggesting it to Paul. Any antiques dealer will tell you that it's harder to buy than sell, so it's always a temptation to keep back the best stuff.

"It sounds exactly right," he said.

"Come on, then. Let's take a look at it."

I led him to the back of the warehouse where the cobalt objects were stored. Walking through the dimly lit warehouse, I was keenly aware of his masculine presence. He smelled of some aftershave or cologne, fresh and clean, like a mountain meadow on a warm spring day. When I glanced over at him, he was smiling down at me, and I found myself responding, and looked away. I reached for the mustard pot.

I showed him the three hallmarks on the base, plus another near the top rim. I rubbed the silver lovingly — I could almost feel the richness of the metal. It was a terrific piece in astoundingly good condition. The glass bowl was original, and even the hinge worked smoothly.

"Sold," he said, looking at me, not the mustard pot.

"Okay, then," I said, and headed for the front office, glad to be back among other people.

I had Gretchen write up the sale. Paul thanked me for the help and told me that he was going to follow up on that cup of coffee.

I watched as he got situated in his old BMW. If I, in our casual encounters, found him shiveringly attractive and hard to resist, I couldn't even imagine what Rosalie's experience had been like. *Is he genuine?* I wondered. *Or does he use his good looks as a coin of the realm, counting on women's panting enthusiasm to get what he wants?*

As I turned away from the window, Gretchen said, "So . . . is he single?"

"Yes," I replied, smiling. "He is."

She tilted her head and smiled, a flush of pleasure brightening her ivory complexion and adding extra sparkle to her eyes. "You don't say."

"You want his number?" I asked.

She tapped the bill of sale and grinned broadly. "I've already got it."

Gretchen and Paul, I mused. They sure would make a dazzling-looking couple, but I didn't want to encourage Gretchen too much. For all I knew, Paul was a suspect in Rosalie's murder.

CHAPTER SEVEN

Officer Brownley pushed open the front door and the four of us — Sasha, Fred, Gretchen, and I — froze, creating a small tableau. The only sound was the jangling chimes. As they began to quiet, I stepped forward, and my movement seemed to release us all from our momentary immobilization.

"Officer," I said, smiling, "come on in."

I introduced her around.

"Is there somewhere we can talk?" she asked.

My heart began to thud at her question, memories of past encounters with the police quickening my pulse. I had nothing to hide, but I'd learned the hard way that innocence wasn't always a sufficient shield.

"Sure," I answered. "My office."

As I headed toward the stairs, I fought a rush of despair. I'd spent countless hours last year in a kind of limbo, a place where

101

the police acted as if I were guilty, where they'd almost accused me of things openly, and where I'd felt diminished and defenseless and weak. Today, even though Officer Brownley was polite and pleasant, it felt as if I were being led back into hell. As I stepped into my office, Dante's words came back to me: *Abandon hope, all ye who enter here.*

"Chief Alverez filled me in," she said. "So I know that you think Rosalie was having an affair with Mr. Fine."

"I'm sorry I didn't tell you," I said, embarrassed.

"Perfectly understandable," she replied, waving it away. "But it *is* important to our investigation that you tell us everything, whether you want to or not."

"Okay."

"And now, with her diary and tote bag surfacing at Heyer's, well, I'm really trying to nail down Ms. Chaffee's movements yesterday, and I'm hoping you can help. You said you saw her for lunch."

"Right," I acknowledged.

"When she left the restaurant, where was she heading?"

"To pick up Paige at ballet. I don't know what she did after that."

"Did you walk out of the restaurant together?"

"No. Rosalie went to the ladies' room."

"Are you certain that you don't remember anything that could give us a clue as to what she did next? Like 'I've got to make a phone call,' or 'I need to check something with Mr. Fine,' or 'I have to stop at the grocery store on my way home'? Nothing like that?"

I thought back to our conversation, then shook my head. "Sorry, but no. Can I ask you something? From your questions I gather Rosalie didn't go to Heyer's?"

She paused, then said, "That's right. According to Heyer's security, her key card wasn't used yesterday." She paused again. "If you had to guess, where do you think she went after she picked up Paige at ballet?"

"Maybe she decided to hang out with Paige. Or to work from home so Paige wouldn't be alone."

"What makes you think that?"

"It's all speculation — but it's still school break, and I'm guessing that Rosalie might have wanted to spend as much time with her as she could. One thing that Rosalie really liked about her situation was that she had a lot of flexibility. If she wasn't actually teaching a class at Hitchens or interviewing

Gerry Fine at Heyer's for the book she was writing, she could work from anywhere."

She nodded. "Where else? Where else might she have gone?"

She wants me to guess that she and Gerry met for a tryst. I had a startling thought — *maybe they had.*

"I don't know," I repeated. "After lunch, I came back here, to my company. I didn't see or speak to Rosalie again."

Officer Brownley observed me for several seconds. It was disconcerting. Finally, she said, "Thank you. I appreciate it. Did she say anything about her experiences at Hitchens College?"

"Yesterday?" I asked.

"Anytime."

"Sure."

"What?" she asked.

I shrugged. "She was eager to finish her dissertation. She was ready to get on with things — her professional life. She was hoping to get a teaching job at a small college somewhere warm."

"Where was she applying?"

"I don't know. She didn't say. I may be wrong, but I got the impression she was several months away from applying."

Officer Brownley nodded. "Can you think of anything out of whack?"

"Like what?"

"Like a day last week when she should have been at Heyer's, but wasn't. Or some time when she should have left work to go home, but didn't. Or a time she shouldn't have been at school, but was. Did she do anything that made you wonder where she was or *why* she was where she was? Ever?"

I nodded, thinking. In the time I'd known Rosalie, I'd become somewhat familiar with her schedule. She taught a seminar called Communication Challenges During Explorations at Hitchens on Tuesdays and Thursdays. She made a point of being home to be with Paige by five-thirty each afternoon, and Heyer's was midway from Hitchens to her house, so her meetings at Heyer's were almost always late in the day. Yet as I searched for an aberration, I realized that her schedule wasn't at all complex or confusing, which meant that anyone who wanted to find her would have an easy time doing so. She was juggling a lot of balls, but she was a creature of habit. Her class schedule and office hours were public knowledge. Even her appointments at Heyer's were known within the company — everyone at Heyer's used the same electronic calendar program. When Tricia entered an upcoming meeting between Gerry and Rosalie into the system, everyone from Una, the receptionist, to the guys in the mailroom would know about it right away.

"The only thing I can think of is that her schedule was fairly predictable and public," I said.

"Tell me what you mean," she requested.

She made several notes, nodding as I explained.

"What about this affair she was having with Fine?"

"What about it?"

"Did you read about it in her diary?"

I looked away, momentarily stunned that Ty had told her I'd read the diary. *Of course he told her,* I thought. *It wasn't our secret.* "Yes," I said. I met her eyes. "Did you find it at Gerry's office?"

"Yes. Fortunately, it was there, and it was intact. We got the tote bag, too."

I looked down, grateful to be spared the lecture I knew I'd earned. "I'm glad. I know I should have called you sooner. I'm sorry."

"Do you know what was in her bag?"

I thought for a moment. "Usual stuff — a notebook and a wallet. Her calendar, keys, a cell phone, a makeup case, and lots of pens." I shrugged. "I don't know what else."

She nodded. "What's your sense about Mr. Fine and Ms. Chaffee's relationship?"

she asked. "Were they serious?"

"I have no way of knowing."

"I know Ms. Chaffee didn't talk to you about it, but what's your intuition telling you? Not for quotation, just your feeling about the situation. Was he planning on leaving his wife?"

I paused. I could feel Officer Brownley's unrelenting gaze on my face. I looked up.

"Really, I don't know."

Officer Brownley nodded. "I believe you, Josie." She stood up and handed me a card. "I know she was a good friend of yours. I'm sorry for your loss."

"Thank you."

"You think of anything else, you call me."

I told her I would, then walked her out and stood in the doorway as she made her way to her car. As she moved to step inside, she turned and waved. It was cold.

I waved back.

It had started to snow, and there was a thin dusting of powdery flakes on the ground. As I watched, I thought of Officer Brownley's questions about Rosalie's predictable schedule. *My schedule is predictable, too,* I thought, and prickly bumps joggled up my arms. I stepped back inside and closed the door. I wasn't afraid, exactly, but I didn't feel safe, either.

CHAPTER EIGHT

Eric knocked softly until I looked up. He stood just outside my office, with a worried expression on his face.

"I'm sorry to interrupt you," he said, "but I saw this girl through the window. She was standing in the snow. She's pretty young, I think."

"And?"

"She wasn't lost. She wants to talk to you."

"Me?" I asked, surprised. "Who is she?"

"Paige Chaffee."

I was close to speechless. "Where is she now?"

"I left her downstairs with Gretchen," he said.

"Good thinking. You can bring her up."

Eric clambered down the stairs; I stood and walked toward my window. It was only three-thirty, yet it was almost dark. I watched as snow streamed down, big flakes accumulating quickly. Already an inch or more coated the branches on my old maple tree.

I turned when I heard Eric's clomping step followed by a softer patter. Eric appeared in the doorway next to a tiny blond pixie. She was conservatively dressed in clean, well-fitting blue jeans and a crewneck sweater with an Oxford-collared shirt peeking out, and she looked younger than twelve. Her boots were lemon yellow knee-high rubber galoshes. She wore a blue parka, unzipped. She seemed to be sizing me up at the same time that I was observing her.

"Here she is," Eric announced by way of introduction.

"Hi." I walked to meet her and give her a big hug, holding her close for several seconds.

I indicated that Paige should take one of the yellow wing chairs and I sat across from her in the other one. She was thinner than Rosalie, but their shared heritage was evident in their prominent cheekbones, wide-set brown eyes, and shiny hair. "I'm just so sorry, Paige. Your sister was so special."

She nodded, cleared her throat, and said, "Thank you."

"Do you want to take your coat off? Can I

get you something to drink? Do you like tea? We have hot chocolate, too."

She slid out of her jacket and let it fall to the floor, her expression glum. "Nothing, thank you."

I wondered what family she had left, if any. Now that Rosalie was dead, was she all alone in the world? Listening to her solemn voice, another little part of me withered.

"Are you okay?" I asked.

"I need help," she said.

I nodded. "Okay. What kind of help?"

"I'm staying with my friend's family. So I don't have to go into foster care, you know?"

I hadn't thought of that. *Poor Paige.* "That's good."

"My cousin Rodney is coming on Saturday. He's my nearest relative. The person they appointed — the court, I mean — as my temporary guardian called him."

"You don't sound happy about that."

"I'm not."

"How come?"

Tears seeped from the corners of her eyes and she palmed them away. "Rodney wants to take me back to California."

I nodded. We sat in uneasy silence.

"Rosalie hated him," she said.

"Do you know why?"

"Not exactly."

"Sounds scary."

"I don't want to go with him."

"I don't blame you. It's a terrible situation."

"I can't let him go through everything, but I don't know how to stop him."

"What do you mean?" I asked.

"Rosalie said you were an appraiser. Right?"

"Yes, that's right."

"She explained about what you do. She said you make a list of things and figure out what they're worth."

I nodded. "That's a good description."

"That's what I want. Before Rodney can steal anything."

"What do you think he might steal?"

"I don't know. That's why you need to do your appraising right away. Before Rodney gets here on Saturday. That's why I came. So you have time."

She was becoming increasingly agitated. I could hear it in the quavering of her voice and see it in the shaking of her hands. I understood. When my mother died, I'd had my father. When my father died, I'd been unable to put a coherent sentence together for a week. That was seven years ago, and I still missed him every day.

As I watched, she tucked a strand of wispy

hair behind her ear. She was breathing too quickly, almost hyperventilating. I wondered when she last ate.

"Is there something in particular you're worried about — an object that you know is valuable?"

"Yes, but I don't know what it is."

"What do you mean?"

"Rosalie didn't tell me." She picked at her sleeve, maybe pulling pills, though none were visible from where I sat. She lifted her eyes and stared at me. I sensed her concern — she wanted to tell, but was afraid to do so.

"If I can help you, Paige," I said, meaning it, "I will."

She nodded, but didn't speak. By any standard, Paige was too young, too inexperienced, and too vulnerable to assess whether she should confide in me.

"You won't tell?" she asked, sounding absurdly young.

"I won't tell unless I have to. But I can't know what I can do to help you, or what I can't do, until I know what we're talking about. I can't promise to never tell, but I can promise that I won't gossip about it just because."

Another minute passed before she spoke, and when she did, I had to lean forward to catch her words.

"Rosalie said we were rich, and when I asked what she meant, she said we owned something that was priceless, but she didn't want to sell it — she wanted to donate it to a museum. She was just waiting until she got tenure. Then she said we'd be set and we could go ahead and donate it."

"And she never told you what it was?" I asked.

"No. She told me that loose lips sink ships and it wasn't fair to ask someone my age to keep a secret like that. She was wrong! She could have trusted me. I told her so at the time."

"I don't think she meant that she couldn't trust you, Paige," I said. "It sounds like she was operating on what's called a need-to-know basis. Do you know what that means?"

Paige shook her head.

"It's a military term that means that people aren't given information unless they have a *need* to know it. You didn't *need* to know, so she didn't tell you."

"Except that she was wrong. I did need to know. You just asked me what it was and I can't tell you." She bit her lip and looked away.

"Point taken. Maybe she loaned it to a museum. That would be a safe place for it."

She shook her head. "She would have told me."

I nodded. She looked down at the carpet, a Persian in red and gold, as if she were trying to determine if it were genuine or not. It seemed hard to believe that Paige wouldn't know more about an object her sister described as museum quality, yet I couldn't imagine why, once she'd made up her mind to confide in me, she'd want to withhold that key fact.

"Maybe it's a desk," she added.

"What kind of desk?"

"Old. Rosalie got it from our mom when she graduated college. I don't remember much about it, but I know it was really special."

"Where is it now?"

"I don't know. I don't think Rosalie told me."

I nodded. Lots of heirs in the midst of tumultuous grief and unexpected decision-making responsibilities lost track of details, even of their routine schedules. That a twelve-year-old girl in Paige's circumstances would forget about an object she hadn't seen or thought about in years would be a norm, not an exception — her mind was full. It was possible that she might remember something more about it or its location in the coming days and weeks.

"So will you help me?" she asked after a few seconds, without looking up.

I considered the obstacles to my saying yes. She was a minor with a court-appointed guardian. "Why did you just show up here?" I asked, struck by the oddity of her unexpected arrival. "Why didn't you call?"

"Because it's too hard to explain on the phone. And I need to let you into the house. I have the key."

She waited for me to respond with an expression like Oliver Twist's when he was asking for more food — game, but without much hope.

"How did you get here?" I asked, stalling.

"I hitchhiked."

"You're kidding!" I exclaimed. "That's so dangerous! Really, Paige, don't do that ever again! Call me and I'll make sure that you get to wherever you want to go, okay?"

"Okay," she agreed, her tiny voice barely carrying across the short span that separated us.

Rosalie had talked about living on the West Coast, although she'd never mentioned a cousin named Rodney. Her conversation had revolved around her childhood, when she and Paige had lived with their parents in Santa Monica. They'd lived in a big house with a swimming pool and a gazebo for barbeques and parties, and life had been good. Then their parents were killed in a car crash near San Diego when Rosalie was twenty-eight and Paige was just eight.

"Yeah, it was tough," she'd acknowledged in response to my shocked dismay on hearing of the tragedy. "But I was old enough to become Paige's guardian, thank God. Can you imagine how much worse it would have been if I hadn't been able to take charge of her?"

Paige, orphaned four years ago, had been lucky enough to have a big sister who loved her and who cared for her. Now, it seemed, she was utterly alone.

I shook off the memory, and looked at Paige. She was watching me, waiting for my reply.

I had to help her. I couldn't leave her adrift with a court-appointed guardian and a much-hated cousin from California. I forced a smile, aiming to convey self-assurance and dependability. "Of course I'll help you. Don't worry, Paige. We'll find it — whatever it is."

CHAPTER NINE

With Paige's permission, I called my lawyer, Max.

Max Bixby was kind and smart; protective yet flexible; a rock of stability and reliable good sense that I depended on for far more than his legal acumen. I could picture him leaning back in his big black leather office chair, wearing a brown or green tweed jacket with a color-coordinated shirt and bow tie. Knowing Max was on my side made it easier to face all sorts of frightening and confusing events.

"Josie!" he said when I had him on the line. "How's tricks?"

"I'm fine, Max. But I have a kind of, well, unusual situation here."

"Okay, shoot," he said, shifting seamlessly from casual chitchat to business.

"Have you heard about Rosalie Chaffee's death?" I asked.

"Only from the news. Why?"

"I knew her. We were friends."

"Terrible what happened."

"Horrible," I agreed. "Just unbelievable." I glanced at Paige, feeling conspicuous and uncomfortable discussing her situation in front of her. She'd walked across the room and faced the window. The snow was blowing hard against the near-black sky. "I don't know if it was discussed on the news, but Rosalie had a sister, Paige."

"No, it wasn't. But I'm aware of her because Paige is in the same class as my eldest, Andrea. Andrea has mentioned her — she says that Paige is a good sport and a nice girl. I don't think I've ever met her myself."

"She *is* nice. She's right here with me in my office."

"Really? Why?"

"Well, she's asked me to do something and I thought I ought to call you about it."

"Tell me," he instructed.

"It seems that there's a cousin named Rodney who's coming from California to take charge of her. Until then she's staying with a friend's family. To avoid foster care."

"Good."

"Yeah, except that Paige says that Rosalie hated Rodney."

"Not good."

"And Rosalie told her they were rich, that they owned something good enough to merit being donated to a museum, but she — Paige, I mean — she doesn't know what Rosalie was referring to. So, anyway, Rosalie mentioned what I do to Paige, what an appraiser does. Paige wants an appraisal done before Rodney gets into town."

"Pretty savvy move for a kid."

"Yeah."

There was a long pause while Max considered the circumstances. I heard a winter bird call something, then an answering caw-caw, then silence.

"Paige will have had an attorney appointed by the court."

"She only mentioned a guardian."

"I can make a couple of calls and find out."

"Should she hire you to represent her? To protect her rights. I don't know the legal wording, but if you represent her, you can authorize the appraisal and maybe even check out this Rodney guy, right?"

"The court might allow it. I have some experience in family court. At twelve, most courts would entertain the notion that she should be allowed to have an attorney of her own choosing," Max reasoned. "Let me get the lay of the land and get back to you, okay? It shouldn't take too long."

We hung up and I swiveled to face Paige. She still stood by the window, so I spoke to her back. "Max is going to find out if you already have a lawyer. He thinks the court probably appointed one for you. He'll call me back."

She turned toward me and nodded. "Thank you."

"I had another thought," I said. "The people you're staying with . . . they might be worried, you know? What do you think about calling them?"

She shrugged. "I don't need to. No one's there. They work, and my friend's still at swim practice."

"Still. I'd feel better. I'll call if you want and leave a message. Okay?"

She told me their name and number. As expected, no one was home. I left the message, telling them who I was and that I'd see that Paige got back to their house safely.

When I finished, I buzzed down and asked Gretchen to bring up some hot chocolate. "Are there any cookies or anything around?" I asked.

"Are you kidding? We *always* have cookies!"

"Good. Bring a few, will you?"

"None for me," Paige said when I'd hung

up the phone.

I shrugged. "I hope you'll nibble on one. Even if you don't feel hungry, you've got to eat."

Gretchen brought up a tray, her eyes big with curiosity.

"Here you go," she said, a smile in her voice, placing the tray on the butler's table near the wing chairs. "Can I do anything else?"

"No, thanks."

Paige and I sat in companionable quiet while waiting for Max's call. I was pleased to see her eat two cookies and finish her entire cup of hot chocolate. *At least she has some food in her stomach,* I thought, *and some real milk from the hot chocolate.*

Gretchen buzzed up to tell me that Max was on line one.

"Arthur Bolton has been appointed to represent Paige," he said, "and I don't think it's necessary or desirable for me to interfere with the court's arrangements. I reached him just now and he was appreciative of the information I gave him about the need for an appraisal. Since he's familiar with your work, he's comfortable asking you to proceed. He'll be calling you within the hour to direct you to conduct a formal appraisal, one for which you should bill the estate.

Rosalie apparently died intestate, so all of her possessions will pass to Paige. That means they'll be held in trust for her until she's eighteen. Mr. Bolton agreed that it's prudent to catalogue all assets before any outside interest comes into play — for instance, Rodney."

"That's great. Thanks, Max. What about Rodney?"

"He agrees that a full background check should be conducted before a minor is turned over to an unknown person."

"This is all good news, then."

"Yes. I know his work — Bolton's competent and thorough."

"I'll tell Paige."

"Please also tell her how impressed I am with her. Not many adults would have acted with the presence of mind she's shown."

"That's really true, isn't it. I'll tell her you said so."

By the time I'd filled Paige in and explained that I could start the appraisal in the morning, her lawyer, Arthur Bolton, called and officially authorized me to act.

We agreed that I'd stop by his office by nine the next morning to pick up a letter of authorization and the keys. Paige had returned to the window and stood leaning against the frame, peering into the far distance, a picture of loneliness and despondency.

"May I speak to Paige, please?"

"Certainly," I replied, and called Paige to the phone.

"Hello," she said. "Uh-huh . . . okay . . . let me get a pen. . . . I'm ready . . . okay . . . school and work, right . . . the house, and car, and her health club . . . Yes, at Heyer's . . . okay . . . okay . . . Thank you."

She handed me the phone, and said, "Mr. Bolton said I should tell you that Rosalie used the corporate health club at Heyer's. Even though she wasn't a regular employee she got to use the facilities. She has a locker there."

"Thank you. You should think about other places she might have kept things, but right now, with this snow, I better get you to your friend's house. Okay?"

She nodded, looking and, if I knew anything, feeling wretched. I could imagine at least some of what she was going through. As an only child of doting parents, their deaths had been horrible for me. The sharp sting of loss had faded, but not the just-below-the-surface ache. And there was another legacy of losing too much when I was too young to cope with the turmoil — an always-present anxiety that loss was my lot in life. Although I rarely spoke of it, I lived with a constant low-level concern that occasionally metamorphosed into fear, that it was, in fact, my affection for someone that caused the loss. I knew it wasn't true, but knowledge isn't always enough to overcome irrational worry. To this day, it's hard for me to let myself feel and show love.

Once, when I was having trouble committing to a college boyfriend, my father said, *You can't control how you feel, but you can control how you act. Never make decisions based on fear, only hope.* Since then I've tried to follow his advice, with mixed success. Fear, I've learned, is a deeply entrenched enemy of hope.

Paige, at twelve, had already experienced more fear than many people had to face in a lifetime. Perhaps, I thought, if I could find Rosalie's treasure, Paige could rediscover hope, and from hope might come courage.

CHAPTER TEN

Gerry called as I was shutting down my computer.

"Gerry? Did he say what he wanted?" I asked Gretchen, when she buzzed up to tell me he was on the line.

"Nope! He just asked for you."

I glanced at Paige standing near the door, her parka zipped, ready to go. "Would you come up here and get Paige? Keep her company in the office until I finish with him."

"I'm on my way!"

Almost immediately, I heard the tap-tap of Gretchen's French heels against the concrete floor on the warehouse level, and I said to Paige, "I've got to take this call. I shouldn't be too long."

"Is that the man Rosalie's writing the book about? Mr. Fine?"

I nodded. "Did you know him?"

"I met him once. At the Heyer's company

summer picnic. It was nice of them to include us because Rosalie wasn't a regular employee."

Gretchen stepped into the room. "Hi, Paige! Follow me!" Gretchen said. "Let's go downstairs. I found some yummy candy!"

As soon as they started off, I picked up the receiver. "Gerry?"

"Josie? Is that you?" he asked in a different tone than I was used to, more intense and less friendly. For the first time I heard nothing jovial in his voice.

"Yes. Sorry to keep you waiting."

"Did you see Edie?"

"When?" I asked, delaying the inevitable.

"Today. When she threw the picture."

"Yes, I saw her. She was upset."

"How did Rosalie's bag get here?"

"I have no idea."

"Damn it. And now the cops have it — and her diary."

I didn't respond.

"What did you say to Edie?"

"About what?" I asked.

"About Rosalie and me."

"I told her the truth, that I had no idea."

"Was anyone else in the room when she let loose?"

"No. But Ned came in just after."

"Shit. Did he see her do anything?"

"No."

"Thank God for small favors, huh?"

I shut my eyes. *What a miserable beast of a man,* I thought. *Talk about blame the victim.* I didn't respond.

"What about Tricia?"

"She was there."

"Una too, right? She would have seen her both coming and going. Did Edie say anything to her?"

He was consulting me as if I were an ally in his attempt at damage control and I resented the heck out of it. "I think Una saw Edie leave when she was still pretty upset, but I don't know for sure."

"That's just great," he said sarcastically. "Anyone else around?"

"Not that I know of."

"I can't believe Edie left the diary just lying around. Did you read it?"

"Yes." *So there,* I thought. *Now he knows that I'm aware of his affair with Rosalie.*

"Damn. Why'd Rosalie have to keep a damn diary anyway?"

I was stunned at his narcissism. He didn't seem upset about Rosalie's death, just put out that he'd been caught having an affair. I didn't reply.

"More to the point, why did you tell the police about it? All you did was make a bad situation worse."

Screw you, I thought. "I've got to go," I said, matching his icy tone. "Someone's waiting for me. 'Bye."

I hung up, shaking my head. *What a sleaze,* I thought.

Downstairs, I scooted everyone out early so none of us would be driving during the worst of the storm. Paige and I trudged through the ankle-high snow to my car.

Driving was treacherous. The snow was falling faster than the plows could clear the roads, and even the interstate was a mess.

"Look," Paige said, pointing.

A car had slid off the pavement and was lying askew in the median gully. "It's bad out here, all right. Take my cell phone and call 911, okay? Tell them the location of the car. Just south of exit seven, heading north."

Fifteen long minutes later, I pulled to the curb in front of a nice-looking Colonial on the outskirts of Portsmouth. Paige was ready to jump out, but I insisted on walking her into the still-empty house. The answering machine stood on a small telephone table in the front hall. A red numeral one was blinking — evidently my message was still unlistened-to.

"Brrrrr," I said. "It's cold."

"I can turn up the thermostat," Paige said, stepping around the corner into the living room.

"Where is everyone?" I asked.

"Mrs. Reilly works in Boston," Paige explained, "and is always late. Mr. Reilly gets home around five-thirty or six."

"What about your friend?"

"Brooke? She's on the swim team. She practices every day."

"Are you okay here alone?"

"Uh-huh."

" 'Cause you can come home with me," I offered.

"That's okay. My stuff is here, you know? Thanks, though."

"You want company? Because I could stay."

"Thanks, but I sort of just feel like reading, you know?"

I nodded. "You have my cell phone number. You call me anytime, okay?"

"Thanks."

"I'll call Mr. Bolton after I've done walk-throughs everywhere — probably tomorrow afternoon." I patted her shoulder, wishing I could do more, and left. I sat in my car with the engine running and watched the Reilly house for a minute, tracking Paige's progress as she turned on lights, then drove a block away and stopped to call Ty.

"Hi," I said. "I'm heading home."

"I'm sorry I snapped before, Josie."

"I'm sorry, too. And talking to Officer Brownley was fine. She's actually very nice."

"Good. Listen, there's something we need to talk about."

"What's that?"

"I got offered the job."

My heart began to beat extra fast. I focused on a distant street sign, partially covered with snow. The flakes were smaller than before and swirling in the gusty wind. The temperature was dropping — I was sitting in my car in the middle of a blizzard. I still didn't know how I felt about his taking a position that required so much travel. *And what if it leads to a promotion that takes him to Washington permanently? My business is established in Portsmouth. I can't follow him.*

"Congratulations," I said, knowing it was the right thing to say.

"Thanks. We've got a decision to make."

I smiled, pleased at his use of the word "we." "Yeah. A big one."

"Listen . . . according to the weather, we're in for a real nor'easter. We can make a fire and talk about it. Why don't you come to my place?"

Going to Ty's was an easy decision. His

big, masculine contemporary was way more comfortable and homelike than my small rental. He had a Jacuzzi tub and two fireplaces, one in the master bedroom. Ty told me to use my key to get in, and that he'd be home by seven-thirty at the latest.

Even with a stop at the grocery store to buy the ingredients for Beef Wellington, salad, and mashed potatoes, I was ensconced in Ty's kitchen by six-thirty. By seven, I'd changed into the pair of comfy sweats I kept stashed in a spare closet, rolled out the dough, and was sautéing mushrooms for the roux.

An old Chet Baker recording was playing in the background, and I was sipping a guavatini as I stirred the gently bubbling mixture. What I could see of the meadow that stretched from the rear of Ty's house to the woods that marked the boundary of his property was all white. There was no sign of life. It was a good night to be inside.

My cell phone rang, startling me. I grabbed it from the counter where I'd placed it so it would be at hand. "Hello?"

Silence.

"Hello?" I said again.

I heard breathing on the line, and a sudden echoing bang.

"Hello? Who is this, please?"

Silence except for the breathing, then a click — he, or she, hung up. Maybe it was a wrong number, I speculated. Shrugging, I turned back to the stove, gave a final stir to the mushroom mixture, and readied the beef for the oven.

My mother's instructions called for sealing the dough's seams with a lightly beaten egg. *Apply the egg liberally, Josie,* she'd written in her precise handwriting. *It adds a golden sheen and delicious richness, too!*

I heard stomping, and momentarily panicked, then peeked out of the kitchen door window. It was Ty, ridding his boots of snow. I hadn't noticed the sound of his vehicle driving up, nor had I heard the garage door opening or closing, but there he was, reminding me that snow muffles sound. He became aware that I was watching him and smiled, and I smiled back, feeling the familiar, welcome jolt of electricity.

Later, after he'd changed into jeans and opened a bottle of Smuttynose, he leaned against the back wall of the kitchen and watched as I chopped vegetables for the salad.

"So," I said, "what are you thinking?"

He shrugged. "It's a pretty good opportunity."

"Yeah." *He's going to take it,* I thought.

"But."

"Exactly. But. Fifty percent travel, right?"

"That's what they say." He drank some beer. "What do you think?"

I continued chopping, and chose my words carefully. When I'd been offered the plum job at Frisco's, right out of college, my dad had been unwaveringly encouraging. I'd been the one to express concern about whether I could handle the responsibility, not him. And I'd been the one to express dismay at moving from Boston to New York, not him. Instead of articulating reservations, he'd conveyed confidence in my abilities and reassured me that he'd visit New York frequently. His attitude had been a gift, sending me off into the unknown without worrying about the home front. I wanted to offer Ty the same level of support that my dad had offered me.

"The job sounds perfect for you. And it's flattering as all get-out that they asked you so quickly. You only interviewed ten days ago."

"Well, they're looking to fill these new positions ASAP. I was a good fit, that's all. I mean, yeah, it's flattering, but not all that much, actually. Mostly, it's right place, right time, you know?"

I continued chopping. "You underrate

133

yourself. They need skilled and experienced leaders and they recognized those qualities in you."

"Thanks," he said, ever taciturn. After a moment, he added, "What don't you like about the job?"

"It's dangerous — but so is being a police chief." I shrugged. "Surprise, surprise, I hate the thought of how much travel is required. I'll miss you like crazy."

I glanced at him. He wasn't looking at me. He was looking down, his handsome, rough-hewn features in repose. He could have been deciding what TV show he wanted to watch for all his demeanor revealed about his thoughts. Then he looked up and smiled, and I smiled back and returned to chopping.

Ty came up behind me and encircled me with his arms, softly kissing the back of my neck. His breath was hot and erotic. "Me, too," he whispered.

He took the knife and placed it on the cutting board. He slid his hands up my arms to my shoulders and turned me around, and using an index finger, tilted my head back so our eyes met. After several seconds, he leaned down and kissed me. It was a long kiss, intimate and comforting and knee-weakening, and for that sweet and searing moment, I thought of nothing.

But then the euphoria passed and I pulled away. I looked up at him and touched his cheek. "You should take the job," I said. "We'll work it out."

He nodded. "Yeah, that's what I thought, too. It'll be a big change and —"

Ty's police scanner crackled and he stopped talking to me and listened to a report of an accident on Ocean Avenue. Almost immediately, his phone rang and he answered with a brisk, "Alverez."

"Okay," he said. "I'm on my way."

"Is everything okay?" I asked as he flipped his cell phone closed.

"There's a three-car pileup on Ocean," he told me.

"Injuries?"

"Yup. EMS is en route. I've got to go to the scene."

"Damn! Kiss me again before you go."

He brushed my lips with his, and then he was gone.

The lights flickered twice, and then before I had time to register that the electricity might go out, the house went dark.

I gripped the counter's edge and waited for my eyes to adjust to the blackness. The cloud cover was complete; I couldn't discern a thing. I side-stepped to the built-in desk where I knew Ty kept a flashlight.

It was eerie. Concentric circles of white light shimmied on the tile floor as I sidled along the kitchen's perimeter to the wall phone. I pushed the buttons for Ty's cell phone and he answered before I heard it ring.

"Ty, the lights went out."

"I heard on the news there are widespread outages. Are you okay?"

My eyes lit on the oven — an electric oven, now dark. "Absolutely. But the Beef Wellington will suffer."

"I need a generator," he said, not for the first time.

"Probably a good idea," I replied, thinking of the generator back at my place. My former landlord, Mr. Winterelli, whose niece, Zoë, was now my landlady, my neighbor, and my friend, had installed it at the back of my little house about six months before he died. I'd never used it, but it was enormously comforting knowing it was there.

"What would you think about going to your place? The driving is bad, but nothing is impassible. I think the snow is letting up a little."

"Good idea. I'll leave now."

"I'll let you know when I'm on my way."

Using the flashlight, I found an insulated container Ty kept in a high-up cabinet and eased the baking pan containing the partially cooked beef inside. Outside, bundled up, I placed it on the front seat, and turned on the motor. While the car heated up, I swept away the several inches of built-up snow, then backed out of the driveway.

Crawling along, seeking out familiar landmarks to help me stay on the road, I drove through whiteout conditions toward the interstate. Finally I made it to the relative safety of the recently plowed highway with its overhead streetlights.

According to a local radio station broadcasting from Hitchens College, we could expect the storm to last until dawn the next day, maybe longer, depending on whether the wind let up enough so the hovering storm could move offshore. They were predicting two feet of snow by morning. Power lines were down from the combination of heavy snow and wind. More than 7,500 customers were without electricity.

All at once a car appeared in back of me, tailgating. I was momentarily blinded by its headlights reflected in my mirror, and I gasped and swerved. My car begin to fishtail, and quelling a spark of panic, I followed my dad's oft-repeated instruction to steer into the spin, and almost right away, I felt the tires regrip. My heart was hammering against my ribs.

I looked back through the rearview mirror and saw that the car had retreated, thank God. Once I was firmly back in control, I began to shake and pant, my typical reaction to a crisis handled well. I got off two exits farther up, and it took concentration and care to slow down and navigate turns without skidding. I made a right off the secondary route, only minutes from home, and noticed a car in back of me signaling a turn, too. I wondered if it was the same car that had come up on me so suddenly on the interstate. I hadn't noticed it since then, but I wasn't certain that I would have — my focus was on the road in front of me. I looked back several times, but I couldn't identify anything about it, not even its shape. It was just a big dark blur.

I fought my way up the hill, turned to the left with the following car still in sight, then pulled into my driveway a quarter mile down the road. I noticed lots of lights on at Zoë's house, a reassuring sight in the too-dark and lonely night. *Maybe,* I thought, *I'll go say hey to her so I won't have to be alone.* The car that had been in back of me drove past and disappeared.

I hate coming home to a dark house, so I always leave a light on upstairs in my bedroom and I glanced at it now, relieved to see its welcoming golden glow. I turned off the wipers, then the engine, and sat for a moment, listening to the engine clicking quiet and then to silence. Within seconds, the windshield was thickly matted with snow, cocooning me, but I didn't feel safe. I felt raw with emotion.

With a sigh, I stepped out into knee-deep drifts and struggled up the steps to my house.

I got the beef into the oven and nibbled on leftover salad while Vivaldi's *Four Seasons* played softly in the background. I decided not to call Zoë. I wanted to take a hot shower, wrap myself up in my favorite pink chenille robe, and read *The Black Mountain,* a favorite Rex Stout mystery, while I waited to hear from Ty.

After my shower, I decided to sit in my rarely used living room. I turned on the walkway lights so I could watch the storm, curled up in a club chair with my book, sipped lemony tea, and occasionally peered outside to watch the snow fall in slanting twirls.

A car slowed, then stopped, shielded by the high hedge that separated my house from the street. I could see it, but barely. The hedge was as tall as a man and thick, the kind of denseness that occurs when bushes are carefully groomed for generations. Mr. Winterelli had nurtured his garden like an adored child.

Ty, I thought, hoping it was his oversized SUV that had come to a stop by the hedge. I couldn't imagine who else would come visiting on such a night. The vehicle backed up. Was someone lost? Maybe they were trying to take advantage of the light cast by the pole-mounted lamps that illuminated my walkway to review their directions or read a map.

It wasn't Ty's car.

I couldn't identify much about it in the thickly falling snow, and I couldn't see the driver at all. It appeared to be a medium-sized, dark-colored sedan. The car plunged into darkness — someone had turned out the headlights.

I felt my pulse speed up, and, keeping my eyes on the car, patted the air, then the table, found the lamp and pushed the button to turn off the light. Standing, I made my way to the porch to turn off the outside lights. I flipped the switch and the night went black. It was as if I were suddenly alone in the world — me and the nameless somebody in the barely seen car by the hedge.

Allowing my eyes to adjust, I returned to the living room and sidled up to the window. I shielded my eyes, hoping to see better. No luck. All I saw were shadows on the snow, dots of black on a gray background, parts of the hedge against the snow-covered yard, the barely perceptible shape of a dark car and none at all of the driver. I waited for the headlights to come back on, but they never did.

"Who are you?" I whispered.

After a few minutes, I returned to my chair and sat in the dark until, finally, I saw the car, its lights still off, glide away. It seemed to move stealthily, like a predatory animal in the night.

CHAPTER ELEVEN

Around nine-thirty, I gave up waiting for Ty and ate. He called close to midnight, just as I was getting settled under my feathery duvet.

"Things were worse than I expected. One of the injured passengers died, and the car that started the crack-up fled the scene."

"A hit-and-run?" I asked, shocked.

"Yup. Luckily someone got a pretty good description of the car and we got him. He was drunk."

"That's awful."

"Yeah."

"Are you on your way now?"

"About ten minutes away. I'm pretty hungry."

"There's leftover lasagna and the Beef Wellington. Which sounds good?"

"I don't know. I'll forage when I get there. You go to sleep."

As I nestled into bed, my thoughts drifted

to Paige. I hoped she was sleeping tight, but I doubted it. I was worried about her.

I slept fitfully and awakened unrested. I'd fade into sleep, then wake up with a jerk as if something had intruded into the quiet — a noise or a touch, but I never heard anything and no one except Ty was nearby. He slept solidly, seemingly undisturbed by my fretfulness. At seven, my alarm went off and Ty turned over. He'd asked me, when he'd finally come to bed after two, to wake him at eight. Relieved the night was over, I got up, showered, and stood, sipping coffee, by my kitchen window.

The snow had stopped sometime overnight, earlier than expected. Plows had banked the snow waist-high beside the old stone walls that marked various property lines. From the side window, I had an open view to the horizon. The dawn glowed with luminous possibility.

Eager to get going with Rosalie's appraisal, I hurried through my morning routine, reset the alarm for Ty, shrugged into my coat, and pulled on my boots. As I stepped onto the porch just after seven-thirty, I nearly bumped into Paul Greeley looking as delicious as ever.

"Caught in the act!" he said with a lopsided grin.

"What in the world are you doing here at this hour?"

He wore a loose-fitting burnt orange corduroy jacket. It didn't look as if it would be warm enough, but it sure looked good on him.

"I wanted to ask you something, but you look like you're in a hurry."

"I am. Sorry about that. Is it important?" I asked.

"Important, yes. Urgent?" He shrugged. "No. Rosalie's dead, so there's no urgency there. I came to commiserate about her is all. Let me buy you breakfast."

"I just ate. Thanks, though."

"You can keep me company while I have breakfast."

His tone was cajoling, his manner seductive, yet there was something about him that polarized as it magnetized. That I was drawn to him was undeniable, but at the same time, inexplicably, a warning bell gently chimed inside of me.

"Sorry," I said. "I've got an appointment."

"Just my luck. Can I delay you by one minute at least? I want to ask you something."

"Sure," I replied.

"How about if we go inside to get out of

this wind?"

It was bitterly cold, but I didn't want to invite him in. "Tell me here."

"Please?" he coaxed.

I smiled and shook my head. "You only have forty-five seconds left."

"You are so beautiful," he whispered.

I swallowed and my heart began to thump. He was standing too close to me and I didn't like it.

A recent memory came to me. Only a month ago, a porcelain expert named George had asked me out to dinner. He was good-looking, funny, and smart, and if I hadn't been involved with Ty, I would have accepted his invitation in a New York minute. I made a point of telling him why I was saying no. I wanted him to know that under different circumstances my answer would have been an enthusiastic yes.

I had a different reaction to Paul. He too was good-looking, funny, and smart, and when I looked into his eyes, I felt myself begin to melt — he was incredibly sexy. But then my brain kicked in and, for reasons I couldn't explain, I just wanted to get away.

"I'm sorry, but I've really got to go," I said, stepping back, bumping into the shingles near the front door. I felt trapped.

His smile faded. "I'll give you a call, okay?"

"Paul, you know that I'm involved with someone. Seriously involved," I said.

"Still? He's one lucky guy."

I moved to the side and took two steps to get near the porch railing, and in the open air, I felt less threatened. "Thanks."

"Okay, then. I'm going to stay in touch. I should warn you . . . I don't give up easily!"

Like Rosalie's secret admirer, I thought with a shiver. I watched as he walked toward his car, its black finish stippled and streaked by spewed-up rock salt. He pulled out with a jaunty wave. I reached back to tug the doorknob, just to be certain that I'd locked the door, and there, perched against the threshold, was a clear plastic bag containing a square white envelope. I stared at it for a long, frozen moment, my mouth agape.

"You okay?" Zoë called.

I turned. My neighbor stood on the porch, a plastic-encased newspaper in hand.

"Yeah. I guess."

"What is it?" she asked.

"An envelope in a plastic bag," I replied. "Someone left it here."

"Who?"

Paul? I wondered. "I don't know."

"You look completely freaked out. Are you

sure you're okay?"

No, I thought. "Sure. It's just weird, is all," I said, more to reassure myself than her.

She paused as if she were considering whether to believe me or not, then smiled, and said, "Come for dinner tomorrow?"

I smiled back. Dinner at Zoë's was always zany fun, a noisy jumble of kids, food, games, and wine. "I need to check with Ty, but yes. Thanks."

"You sure you're okay?" she asked, observing me closely.

I shrugged. "I'm okay. I've been better, but I'm okay. Really."

She nodded. "You need something, you call."

"Thanks, Zoë."

She stepped back into her house and I picked up the plastic bag and got settled in my car. As the engine warmed up, I took the envelope out of the bag, and looked at it carefully. The word JOSIE was written in block print. I slit it open with my finger and, with some trepidation, extracted the contents. It was a greeting card. The art on the front was a Van Gogh landscape. I turned it over and saw that it had been produced by the Metropolitan Museum of Art.

Holding my breath, I opened it. The pre-printed message read: THINKING OF YOU.

Below it, someone had penned, also in block print, FROM YOUR SECRET ADMIRER.

I tossed it aside as if it were scalding. "Oh, my God," I whispered, shock and terror washing over me in waves.

Paul, I thought. *I caught him in the act of placing the card and he deftly turned it into a request for a date.* I began to hyperventilate. *Paul, who, according to Rosalie, became possessive. Paul, who'd looked at me like a bear looks at honey.*

I dug my cell phone out of my purse and punched the button to speed-dial Ty. Rosalie's reaction of fear and contempt when she received her secret admirer's offerings no longer seemed over the top.

"Ty."

"Are you okay?" he asked sleepily, hearing something worrying in my tone.

I took a deep breath and scanned the snow-covered meadow. I saw nothing out of the way. "Someone left a card on my porch."

"What kind of card?"

"A greeting card in a plastic bag."

"Tell me," he instructed, and after I said it was signed "secret admirer," he interrupted me.

"Where are you?"

"In the driveway."

"I'll be right down."

I couldn't think. I could barely breathe. I was so scared I thought I might faint. *Paul,* I thought. *He killed Rosalie, and now he's set his sights on me.*

Two minutes later, Ty stepped onto the porch. From his backseat, he selected a plastic evidence bag and approached the passenger-side window. I lowered it.

"Show me," he said by way of greeting, and I pointed at the card, envelope, and see-through plastic bag that sat where I'd tossed them, on the passenger seat.

He used a pencil, eraser end out, to gingerly lift the items, one at a time. He studied the card for several seconds, holding it in his gloved hands by its edges.

"I'm assuming you don't know who sent this, right?" he asked.

"I think maybe it was Paul Greeley."

His expression gave nothing away. "How come?"

"When I stepped outside this morning, he was on the porch."

"Why? Did he say?"

I nodded, feeling awkward. "He asked me out."

Ty's eyes narrowed. "Why in person? Why at this hour?"

"He said he wanted to take me to breakfast and exchange Rosalie stories."

"Do you believe him?"

I shrugged. "I don't know."

He nodded. "No one rang the bell?"

"No. When I picked the plastic bag up, I noticed it was icy cold, though. So it had been on the porch for a while."

"We don't know that. Plastic would get cold quickly in this weather."

"I guess," I acknowledged.

"Did anyone call?"

I remembered the wrong number call I'd received while I was cooking at his house last evening. I looked up at him. "I got a call. I thought it was a wrong number." I recounted the details.

I found the number in my cell phone's log. It was a 207 area code — Maine. He wrote the number down and asked if anything else had happened. "Anybody else surprise you by appearing at your door? Any oddball calls at work? Anything?"

"No," I replied, shaking my head.

"Have you noticed anyone hanging around? Anyone following you?"

"Maybe," I managed, and swallowed, and told him about the car that had seemed to be following me last evening and the one that had stayed so long by the hedge. *Oh, God*, I thought. *What's going on?*

"What did it look like?"

I shrugged helplessly. "I don't know. Black. Or dark-colored. Medium-sized. A sedan, not an SUV, a pickup truck, or a van. But I know that description isn't terribly helpful."

He pulled his notebook from his inside coat pocket and wrote something down as I spoke. I watched him, trying to get a read on his thoughts. I couldn't. He was, as he always is, self-contained, and his countenance revealed nothing.

"Am I in danger?"

He paused. "What's your day look like?" he asked, ignoring my question.

"I'm going to check in at my office, and then I need to appraise Rosalie's possessions, which Paige's lawyer, Mr. Bolton, has hired me to do."

"Give me a minute, okay?" he asked, gesturing that I should stay put.

He stepped onto the porch, squatted by my front door, then stood up and systematically surveyed the entire area, the porch, the yard, the street, and the woods beyond.

"What are you looking for?" I called.

"Footprints, tire marks, anything that might help us ID the guy who left the card."

I looked through the rearview mirror. Tire marks crisscrossed the road by the hedge.

It's hopeless, I thought.

"Okay," Ty said, "I'll be back in five minutes."

He hurried into the house. While I waited for him, I looked out over the meadow. Prisms refracted in the snow, dazzling and distracting me. It was a perfect winter day — the air was clean and crisp. *One of God's days,* my mother would have said.

I turned my attention back to my secret admirer. *Who but Paul would do such a thing?* I asked myself. It had to be someone known to both Rosalie and me, and no one else seemed to fit.

If Gerry had sent Rosalie cards on the QT, pretending they were from a secret admirer as subterfuge, she would have been pleased, not creeped out. And she wasn't. She'd been genuinely repulsed. *No,* I thought, *not Gerry. But wait! Maybe Rosalie hadn't known that the cards and flowers were from Gerry. Maybe he was building it up as a huge surprise for her.* I shook my head, realizing that there was no way of knowing. Frustrated, I asked myself, *Who else do I know who knew Rosalie?*

I'd met some men at Hitchens College events, I recalled, but no one in particular stuck in my memory besides Paul — except Cooper the Condescending. In Cooper's ideal world, he'd never have to interact with anyone he considered beneath him, which was nearly everyone. I smiled as I recalled my father's assessment of the Boston Brahmins: *The Lodges talk only to the Cabots,* he'd mimicked, recounting the old adage, *and the Cabots talk only to God.* I stopped smiling. Toward me, Cooper had never even been courteous, let alone amorous. Impossible, I concluded.

Unless I just can't tell, I realized.

Ty reappeared, buttoning his coat, and gestured that I should lower the passenger-side window. "We just got a call from Bolton, the lawyer," he said. "Because of the manner of Rosalie's death, he decided to request a police observer. Officer Brownley will stay with you throughout the appraisal."

I nodded. I hadn't expected an official escort, but once he told me about it, I realized what a good idea it was. With an objective official observer, the not-yet-met, but nonetheless reviled Rodney could never claim that I was lying about Rosalie's possessions. "Good."

"I'm heading to the station. You okay?"

"Yeah, thanks. I've been thinking — can I read Rosalie's diary?"

"Why?"

"In case there's a reference to the object

Paige referred to."

"When we read it, we'll let you know if there's anything remotely related to a missing item."

"It might not be that simple."

"I can't just let you read it."

I nodded. "If I can't find something, I'll ask again."

"And if we notice anything relevant, we'll tell you."

"Fair enough."

Ty slid behind the wheel of his vehicle. I closed my eyes for a moment, willing myself to be calm and strong. When I opened them, Ty was gone. I looked over my shoulder and saw that he'd pulled out and was waiting for me to lead the way, but for that one stunning moment, it was as if I were totally alone in a frozen landscape, bare and exposed.

Ty soft-beeped his horn and waved as I turned off the interstate and he continued on toward Rocky Point. I waved back.

I parked near Prescott's front door and hurried into the tag-sale venue. Standing by the door, I scanned the displays to gauge Eric's setup progress. The glassware display was charming. Eric had draped white table-cloths over cardboard boxes to create a multilevel merchandising field. Spotlights that ran along ceiling tracks showed off the sharp edges of etched crystal, the rich whiteness of milk glass, and the translucent luster of blue lace Depression glass. With retail prices ranging from $5 to $35, no item was especially valuable, but all were in excellent condition — we never offered broken or chipped objects for sale — and most would find homes quickly.

I noticed that Eric had moved a fake fireplace that we used as decoration throughout the winter to the wall farthest from the outside door and surrounded it with fireplace accessories — andirons, pokers, and the like. It was an effective display, and I made a mental note to acknowledge his efforts.

Plastic tubs full of art prints stood ready for customers to flip through; black velvet-lined cases held miscellaneous pieces of gleaming sterling silver flatware; and a collection of old tourist postcards from the 1940s, encased in plastic sleeves, littered a long table, scattered for easy viewing. Boxes were stacked on empty tables and the floor. Eric and his team had made progress, but they still had a lot to do.

Satisfied, I left the tag sale for the main warehouse area. I packed up one of our video cameras along with its related gear, filled in the checkout log my insurance required, and wrote Gretchen a note, letting her know that I was riding with Officer Brownley and would be in touch.

CHAPTER TWELVE

The house Rosalie had rented was a two-story square quasi-Colonial on Hanover Street not far from a mini strip mall. There was room for one car to park in a narrow driveway, and based on the snow-covered shape, a car, presumably Rosalie's, was in the space. Officer Brownley wedged the patrol car up against the snow-packed curb. A small patch of lawn at the front of the property was blanketed in two feet of snow. No one had shoveled the path, so, with Officer Brownley following close behind me, I struggled to the front door. By the time I got there, my jeans were wet from above my knee-high boots to midthigh. I shivered.

It was an ordinary house in a middle-class neighborhood with no indication of affluence inside or out. Outside, I noticed that the shingles needed repainting. Inside, I saw that the furniture was well-used, mismatched hand-me-downs.

Standing just inside the front door, I recalled the time I'd asked Rosalie where she lived. It was last winter, the first time we'd gone out for lunch.

She'd laughed. "A low-end rental fit for a poor grad student. Consider yourself lucky — I'll never invite you over, so you'll never have to see it."

I shook off the memory as I removed the lens cap from the video recorder. "Have the police taken anything?" I asked Officer Brownley.

She pulled out a pocket-sized spiral-bound notebook and found the page she wanted. "Some photos and her computer. It was a laptop, a Toshiba," she said.

"Can I find out if there's a file on the laptop that might mention her possessions? Lots of people keep an inventory."

"I can ask," she said, and made a note.

"Thanks. What kind of photos?"

"Why are you asking?"

"If they were art shots — professional photographs — they may have value and I need to include them in the appraisal."

"Nothing like that. We only took some snapshots."

Following the protocol I'd established for all Prescott's appraisals, I recorded everything as I walked slowly through the house, room by room, creating a permanent video record annotated with my spoken observations. Officer Brownley trailed along.

The living room was decorated in early Americana with hooked rugs and Colonial-print fabrics. A quick once-over revealed nothing special except what appeared to be a machine-sewn nineteenth-century American flag framed in brick-colored wood. I counted twenty-three stars, configured in irregular straight rows on what seemed to be dark blue wool. There were thirteen stripes. From what I could tell, both the stars and stripes appeared to be made of either muslin or cotton.

There was an artichoke-shaped toss pillow on the sofa, artichoke-shaped finials on the lamps, and four reproduction artichoke botanical prints lined up on the back wall.

"I see what you mean about artichokes," Officer Brownley remarked.

I nodded. "Yeah."

In a small office off to the side, a scarred wooden desk was covered with papers. An unlocked two-drawer file cabinet was packed with neatly labeled Pendaflex folders and manila files. I flipped through — there were paid bills, school records, and old tax forms. We'd need to review everything to see if some letter or document of value was mixed in with the rest. For the recording, I listed what was visible and called out the names of the labeled files.

On a corner of the desk was a tall, skinny red leather album. Pasted into the first page was a 1940s-style Valentine's Day card. Using a fingernail, I gentled it open. "To my darling," someone had scrawled above the printed verse that promised everlasting fidelity, then below it, "With all my love, Chief."

Chief! I thought, recalling the diary entry. *Who is Chief?*

On the next page snapshots of a country cottage were pasted at a jaunty angle next to a heart-shaped gift card reading, "Here's my heart, don't break it." There were restaurant receipts; several cards, also signed by "Chief"; bits of ribbon and gift wrap; a neon-bright pink dried maple leaf; and the remnants of several colorful balloons. Someone, presumably Rosalie, had tracked several weeks' or months' worth of fun and romantic activities with the person called Chief. There was no indicator of whether the scrapbook was current or not.

"I'm taking the album in for examination," Officer Brownley said in a tone that brooked no argument.

Fingerprints, I thought. *Maybe DNA evi-*

dence as well. "I'll need a receipt and I want to record all the pages first."

"I'll write you out a receipt, no problem. Why do you want to record the pages?"

I shrugged. "Ephemera. Some of it might be valuable."

"What's 'ephemera'?"

"Printed material. Usually it refers to everyday items made of paper — things like newspapers, flyers, post cards, theater programs, and," I said, gesturing toward the scrapbook, "greeting cards."

Officer Brownley nodded and held the pages open with the tips of her fingernails as I recorded each two-page spread, detailing what I saw for the audio recording.

I watched as she slipped the album into the same kind of plastic evidence bag Ty had used to protect the greeting card I'd found on my porch, and sealed it up. Seeing the bag brought back the shuddering fear I'd felt when I'd first discovered it. I focused on my breathing as Officer Brownley wrote out a receipt.

"Who do you think 'Chief' refers to?" she asked.

"No idea."

I continued my work. Three wooden chairs circled the desk, a small television sat on an ancient stand, and a floor-to-ceiling bookcase was packed with books. I recorded everything, spotting nothing of interest. The books were mostly scholarly texts mixed with some novels and slim volumes of poetry. In the business we refer to them as reading copies, jargon for books that, no matter how well loved they may be, have little or no resale value.

With a final look around to confirm that I'd recorded everything, I walked into the kitchen. High up near the ceiling, someone, presumably Rosalie, had painted a playful border of angled artichokes intermingled with letters. I walked to the middle of the room and tried to make sense of it. Nothing. I slowly turned full around, recording it, seeking a logical explanation. *W* was the first letter on the front wall, followed by *GT-SERH&.*

The letters *XCYXSJUW* appeared on the wall that abutted the dining room, then *GN-FTJFEJ* . . . then *QSBPHIBO,* and then I circled back to *WGTSERH&.*

Could the letters be a kind of shorthand? I wondered. *W.G. could be the initials of a friend, someone Rosalie was fond of from California, perhaps.* I shook my head. *I can make anything up. Did it mean anything that two of the series ended with an ampersand?*

Nah. Maybe she picked stencils at random. I shrugged and took it in again, slowly this time, focusing on what it could mean. *It's a code,* I realized in a flash.

"What do you make of it?" Officer Brownley asked, surprising me. She'd been so quiet, I'd forgotten she was there.

"I don't know. A code maybe."

She stared in puzzlement at the jumbled letters. "What kind of code?"

I twisted my head as I scanned the letters and considered her question. "I need to think about it."

Continuing my survey, I recorded the artichoke-topped canister set to the left of the sink on the old red Formica counter. There was a decent etched glass vase and a book called *Making Cheese at Home* displayed on a small easel near the stove. Three pink Post-it Notes sticking out from the tops of pages caught my eye and I opened the book to the places they marked — the title page, a recipe for a hard Italian cheese, and instructions on whitewashing the walls of a cheese cellar.

The book had been autographed by the author. The inscription read, *For my friend and fellow cheese lover, Rosalie, with fond regards, M.,* followed by the author's full name, *Michelle Grover.* I replaced the book and continued my recording. The only other items on the counter were a toaster oven and an old-fashioned, much-used mixer. The dishes and glassware were chipped and mismatched. The flatware was stainless and cheap to begin with. The bowls, pots, and pans were old and of no value.

"Basement next," I told Officer Brownley.

"Okay."

The steps creaked. At the bottom of the stairs, I paused to look around. In the dim light cast by a low-wattage, dangling lightbulb, I could see enough to know that the stone-walled cellar was empty except for asbestos-covered pipes, an ancient boiler, and a small water heater. It smelled musty. I moved quickly, recording the near-barren space as I checked for doors that might lead to inner rooms. I found none and left, relieved to be aboveground.

"Nothing down there," I remarked.

"Where next?" Officer Brownley asked.

Using my thumb, I gestured toward the second floor. Upstairs, I opened drawers and cabinets, examined closets, and looked under beds. I climbed the narrow staircase that led to the attic, recording everything, everywhere. There was nothing remarkable except that in one of the bedrooms, probably Rosalie's, the bedspread featured a pattern of artichokes in baskets, a fabric no doubt intended for kitchen use. *She sure was hipped on artichokes,* I thought.

I took one last spin through the house to be certain that I hadn't missed anything, packed up the files and papers in boxes I'd brought along, then led the way outside. The rush of cold air was a relief. I was glad to be out of there.

After stowing the boxes in the patrol car, Officer Brownley and I used our arms to brush the snow from Rosalie's car trunk. I located the proper key and opened it.

Inside was standard winter gear — a shovel, a roll of paper towels, and a bag of kitty litter for traction in snow. The glove box drew a blank, too. I pulled out the car's operating manual, a small ice scraper, a bottle of hand sanitizer, loose napkins, and a map of New England.

As I closed the car door and locked it, I began to feel dispirited. I'd invaded Rosalie's privacy, and I'd found nothing of significant value. The best object was the flag, and I doubted it was worth more than a few thousand dollars. Yet I didn't believe that nothing of value existed. I'd known Rosalie long enough to believe that she just wouldn't have lied to her sister. Either the object was in another location or I'd missed something.

I wished I had the scrapbook in my possession, but comforted myself that I'd carefully recorded every element, and had confirmed that the inscriptions and verses were readable. *Who,* I wondered again, *is Rosalie's Chief?*

"Gretchen!" I said, when she answered with her cheery greeting. "It's me."

"Oh, hi! Are you done already?"

I glanced at the clock on the car dashboard — I rarely wear a watch since it always seems to get in the way when I work — and saw that it was only ten-thirty. "Yeah, that wasn't too bad, was it? Less than two hours."

"Well, we've been busy!"

"Oh, yeah? How so?"

"That girl, Lesha? She stopped by with a letter giving someone Whistler's palette as a gift."

"Interesting. What else?"

"Someone came by with a truckload of furniture to sell."

"What kind of stuff?"

"I don't know. Fred bought the lot of it. He's right here. Do you want to talk to him?"

"No, just ask him if there's anything

special. I'll hold on."

"Fred — Josie wants to know if any of the pieces you bought today were special." Her voice was muffled, but I could still make out the words. I couldn't hear Fred's reply, but in a few seconds, Gretchen came back on the line.

"He doesn't think so," she said. "A davenport of unknown origin."

"Sofa or desk?"

"Desk."

I wondered what shape it was in. Even davenport repros could have significant value if they were well made and in good condition. The desk style is delightful — first designed, it was thought, by Captain Josiah Davenport in 1790 for his use on a trans-Atlantic journey, the original had been produced by a maker named Gillows. Over the centuries the term *davenport* has evolved to refer to any small desk with multiple storage compartments. I wondered what the one Fred had purchased looked like and fought an inclination to get him on the phone and ask. "Tell him I'll catch up with him later."

"Will do!"

"Rosalie had an office at Hitchens, so I'm going to check it out."

"You know where *I'll* be!" she said, a tinkle

of laughter in her voice.

I slipped my phone into my bag, shut my eyes, and leaned back, trying to relax. I could feel the tension in my neck and shoulders, as if strips of steel had replaced muscle. My thoughts flitted from wondering what Wes, the *Seacoast Star* reporter, was learning from his sources to hoping that Paige was staying strong, and from trying to figure out my secret admirer's identity to worrying about the unwanted attention I was receiving from Paul. I lifted my shoulders and lowered them several times, but the stone-hard tension remained.

Whistler's palette came into my mind. I could picture the artist painting, daubing his long brush. *Sasha should learn about Whistler,* I thought, *before she focuses on the wood. We don't even know if he used a palette! Or if he had some work habits that, if discovered, would shed light on the palette's authenticity.*

I opened my eyes and watched as we passed thick stands of conifers dotted with snow.

My thoughts strayed to Edie Fine. Was it possible that this wasn't the first time Gerry had strayed? Perhaps it wasn't the sexual aspect of their affair that enraged her, but the emotional intimacy they evidently shared. From what I read in Rosalie's diary, Rosalie was over the moon about him. Edie might be inured to her husband's philandering, but the thought of his actually loving a stunning young woman like Rosalie was a whole different kettle of fish. Suddenly I realized that it didn't matter whether Rosalie and Gerry had *actually* been involved or not — the relevant fact was whether Edie *thought* they had. And *when* she first reached that conclusion. Perception, I knew, trumped reality.

I closed my eyes again, frightened and troubled. It was completely plausible that Edie had known of the affair for days or weeks. And considering her volatile temper, I had no trouble believing that if she thought Rosalie was out to steal her husband, she would have killed her.

What I didn't know was how good an actress Edie was. But then I remembered a day last fall — I'd been on my way out after doing some work in Gerry's office and Edie put on quite a show. She'd leaned up against the front counter in a faux-relaxed stance, chatting with Una and me.

"What do you girls think?" she asked. "Would an avocado green sweater work with brown slacks? Or do you think it would be better with black?"

It was a pathetically transparent effort at gal talk, and both Una and I knew it. Edie didn't give half a hoot what either of us thought about fashion. It was a moment out of central casting, in which Edie was playing the CEO's perky wife, the one the entire staff admired. We knew it was a sham because we'd witnessed her past tirades. She was neither warm nor kind. She was manipulative, insensitive, and judgmental.

The question remained: Could she have staged a fit — yelling and throwing things to create the illusion that she had just learned of her husband's betrayal — to set the stage for a later denial in case she needed to prove that she had no prior knowledge? I knew the answer — hell, yes. If she was Rosalie's killer, she would act her heart out.

Rosalie's office at Hitchens was in Webster Hall, an ivy-covered building located on the far side of the campus overlooking a small summerhouse. A mountain of snow heaped at one end of the horseshoe-shaped parking lot blocked the western view. When Officer Brownley and I turned into the lot, I saw only three cars. The new semester hadn't yet begun.

Inside, an old-fashioned directory was

mounted on the wall. Small white plastic letters nestled in black rubberized grooves. Rosalie's listing read R. CHAFFEE 308.

"There it is," I said, pointing.

It was cold and still. Our footsteps echoed on the marble flooring. The staircase was huge, probably twelve feet across, with banisters as thick as a man's thigh. On the first landing, Officer Brownley and I paused to take in the vista.

Stiff grass and a tangle of winter-bare bushes circled the summerhouse and flanked what was probably a meandering walkway stretching a hundred yards or more to the north before disappearing into a stand of birch. Nearer to the building, covered with a blue tarp, was a huge stack of wood, three cords or more, I guessed. I wondered where the fireplace was and whether it was on as large a scale as the stairway. Looking east, I saw an endless stretch of thick, dark evergreens.

"That's quite a view," I remarked.

"Yeah," Officer Brownley agreed.

The place was eerily quiet.

Rosalie's office was located halfway down the third-floor corridor on the right. The door was locked. Shapes, probably a desk and chair, were visible through the wavy frosted glass. I knocked, just in case. There

171

was no response.

Using one of Rosalie's keys from the ring Mr. Bolton had given me, I entered with Officer Brownley on my heels. The room was small, about ten by ten. Its one window faced the summerhouse. The office was set up for two people, with a pair of desks back-to-back jutting out from the outside wall. A series of narrow cabinets were positioned on either side of the window, and bookcases filled the remaining wall space. Everywhere I looked, journals, books, and papers were stacked haphazardly.

A framed photograph of Rosalie and Paige stood on one of the desks alongside an artichoke-shaped paper clip holder.

"Is it normal for a student to have an office?" Officer Brownley asked.

"I think so when you're a Ph.D. candidate with teaching responsibility."

I began recording.

"Excuse me," a man said, sounding outraged.

I spun around and bumped into Officer Brownley, who was also turning to confront the newcomer.

It was Cooper the Condescending. He looked petulant.

"Who are you?" Officer Brownley commanded.

"I'm the assistant chair of the department," he answered, sounding shocked that anyone didn't know he held such a lofty position.

"Your name?"

"Dr. Cooper Bennington." He turned to me. "We've met before, haven't we?"

I was livid that he didn't remember me. When I'd met him last fall, he'd insulted me by implying that antiques appraisers were neither professionals nor historians, and now he didn't even recall doing so! "Yes," I said, matching his tone. "I'm Josie Prescott."

His face revealed that he couldn't quite place me — *the bastard.*

"And I'm Officer Brownley here on official business."

"What official business?" he asked, turning back to Officer Brownley, ignoring me.

"We're here to inventory Ms. Chaffee's possessions."

"By what authority?"

"The lawyer representing her heirs."

"Let me see your authorization."

I handed him the letter Mr. Bolton had provided and he read it carefully, his skepticism apparent.

"I'm going to check this out. Step outside, please."

"No." Officer Brownley turned to me. "Ms. Prescott, please continue." To Cooper, she added, extending her hand, "The letter?"

Cooper tried to stare her down, finally gave up, and slapped the paper into her hand. He stormed away.

"Whew!" I exclaimed once he was gone.

Officer Brownley shook her head, unimpressed. "Guys like that —," she said, then cut herself off.

"What?" I asked.

"Give me a royal pain."

I smiled, liking her more than ever. "You are obviously a woman of stupendous insight. He has, one might say, an exaggerated idea of his own importance."

"Yeah. That too."

I switched on the video recorder, quickly canvassed the bookcases, then swung toward the desk and memorialized the scattered papers. Under Officer Brownley's watchful eyes, I rearranged papers so that they all were recorded, pausing only when I discovered a spiral-bound document entitled "Methods of Communication During the Lewis and Clark Expedition: An Analysis of Ways and Means." The author was Rosalie Chaffee.

"Oh, my God!" I exclaimed.

"What is it?" Officer Brownley asked.

Of course, I thought. *Lewis and Clark. That explains it!* "This must be a draft of Rosalie's dissertation."

"Does it matter?"

Oh, does it ever! I silently shouted, maintaining a poker face. I didn't want to share my conclusion until I'd checked it out, even though I knew I wasn't wrong. It felt as if the tilting earth had righted itself, and everything now made sense. *Artichokes.*

CHAPTER THIRTEEN

"Cooper tells me you're raiding my office."

It was Paul Greeley, and his tone was conversational, as if he and I were sharing a silly little joke. I laughed despite myself. His allure was irresistible even as my internal warning system whirred loudly. *Who said a killer can't be charming?* I reminded myself. With the memory of finding the greeting card fresh in my mind, I was extra glad that Officer Brownley was there.

"Raiding? Hardly," I replied.

"Good. I still haven't had any coffee, so I'm not yet prepared to stop a pillaging intruder, even one as, how shall I say, *petite,* as you."

I felt myself blush. *Think business,* I told myself. A book straddled the crack between the two desks, and I picked it up to ask, "Is this yours? Or Rosalie's?"

He stepped forward and guided my hand to rotate the book so he could read the spine. His touch electrified my hand, and I caught myself breathing shallowly, exhaling more than I was inhaling.

"It's mine," he said. "But you can have it if you want."

"Thanks," I said, "but no thanks." I replaced the volume and prepared to begin recording again.

Paul squeezed my arm near my wrist and didn't let go when I tried to pull back. "Is she with the police?" he asked in a undertone meant just for me, jerking his head in Officer Brownley's direction.

"Yes."

"Siccin' the cops on me already?"

Before I could deny the charge or introduce them, my cell phone rang. Recognizing Ty's number on the display, I felt a sudden slash of guilt, as if I'd been caught doing something wrong.

"Excuse me," I said, and turned my back to them, hoping for a semblance of privacy. "This is Josie."

"It's me," Ty said.

"Hi."

"How's it going?"

"Good. We're making progress."

"Anything yet?"

"I'm not sure. How about you? Any news for me?"

"About the card and envelope? I'll have the preliminary lab report later today. I'm not optimistic that there'll be any forensic evidence. But you never know."

"Really? That's a disappointment."

"Early days. We'll see what the test results show."

I couldn't think of how to respond knowing that Officer Brownley and Paul Greeley both stood within easy earshot. "I'm in Rosalie's office at Hitchens. Can I call you in a while?"

"Sure."

After we signed off, I turned to find both Officer Brownley and Paul watching me. "So, Officer, shall I finish up?"

"Yes."

"Am I in the way?" Paul asked, and I wondered if he was being sarcastic.

"I think I'm okay," I told him. "Did you two meet one another?"

They hadn't, and I performed the introductions. Officer Brownley, I noted, seemed utterly unimpressed with Paul's smile.

He kept his eyes on me the whole time. He was impossible to ignore, and equally impossible to deal with. I wished he'd go away, and I felt weak and embarrassed that in spite of everything, I remained aware of his appeal.

"That's it," I told Officer Brownley when I was done.

I packed up my gear and Rosalie's papers and gave a final wave to Paul as we left. Throughout, he continued to observe me with a smile that conveyed all sorts of possibilities, but I found it disconcerting, and not the teeniest bit enthralling.

I wanted to return to my office, and Officer Brownley wanted to check in at her station house, so we agreed to meet at the Heyer's reception desk at three.

She dropped me off, and inside, I was greeted first by the soft tinkling of Gretchen's chimes and second by Sasha's expression of relief.

"Oh, good!" Sasha said. "I'm glad you're here."

"What's up?" I asked.

"Lesha dropped off this letter, and I was hoping you'd look at it." She handed me a plastic-covered document.

Miss Stephanie Milhouse
210 E. 36th Street
New York, NY 10016

July 17, 1959

Mrs. Donald Houston

119 Ellison Road
Newton, MA 02159
Dearest Mari,

Thank you to you and Don for a wonderful vacation. Everyone at work is admiring my tan!

I'm so pleased that you feel the magic working! You're so talented that you deserve all the success Whistler's palette can bring you. Take good care of it!

So I'll look for you next Thursday — around five, right? I have the tickets, so we're all set.

Love,
Steph

"What do you think?" I asked.

She shrugged, twirling her hair. "It's on Southwick paper. . . ."

I nodded. Southwick Paper Company had been around forever.

"If it's counterfeit, it's well done," I said. "Very detailed."

"I agree. The content has the ring of authenticity."

"What will you do now?" I asked.

"Check out the paper stock."

"What's your instinct tell you?"

"It's a definite maybe."

"Keep me posted!" I said, smiling. "Remember to look into Whistler's work habits, too. I mean, we don't even know if he used a palette."

She nodded. "I'll see what I can find out." She sat down at her computer, her attention immediately directed to the challenge. Her intelligence and concentration were apparent in everything she did, and I found myself excited imagining what she might discover.

I skipped checking in with Fred or Eric because I was eager to follow up on my idea about artichokes, but before I could begin my research, Gretchen called up to tell me that Wes Smith was on line one.

I thanked her, and hesitated as I reached for the phone. I could ask Gretchen to take a message, but I knew what the message would be — an urgent request to return his call. *Should I or shouldn't I?* I debated. I didn't want to talk to him, yet I very much wanted to know why he was calling. I waged a quick internal battle between prudence and curiosity, and curiosity won.

"Wes?"

"You didn't return my call," he complained.

"I'm fine, thanks. You?"

"Ha, ha. I'm okay. Why didn't you call back?"

I sighed. He was hopeless. "I didn't get a message."

"I left it on your cell phone," he said.

"When?"

"About a half an hour ago."

"That's not very long, Wes. Give me a break. I haven't even turned it on in the last half hour."

"Okay, then. Listen," he said, lowering his voice. "I have news. And a question for you."

"For me? Why me?"

"Not on the phone," he said conspiratorially.

"I don't have time today, Wes. If it's important, tell me or ask me now."

"It's about how Rosalie Chaffee died. Don't you want to know?" He sounded offended.

"Of course I do. Tell me."

"Not on the phone," he repeated.

"Why not?"

"I can't risk compromising my confidential sources by discussing the situation on the telephone," he said haughtily.

"Then we're at a standstill. I just can't get away right now."

He sighed dramatically, as if I'd let him down, then went on, "Let me ask you something — can you identify wood by sight?"

"It depends. Sometimes. Why?"

"The murder weapon. You're an important resource. We need to talk," Wes repeated, his voice low and intense.

My worry meter spiked. I didn't know what he was talking about, but his intensity and conviction came through loud and clear. I did a quick calculation. "Four o'clock," I told him. "I can meet you in Rocky Point at four."

"Great!" he exclaimed. "At the regular place? The dune?"

I pictured the sandy hill where we'd met so often in the past. "Same place," I agreed. "It's private."

I swiveled toward the window. The snow on my maple's branches was softening. I looked out, past the church spire, into the distant woods. I shivered. *What in heaven's name does Wes want?* I wondered. I shook off my vague worry and turned back to my computer. I entered "Lewis and Clark" and "code" and "artichoke" in the search engine and got 759 hits. It took about five seconds to confirm my dim memory of a college history lesson.

President Jefferson had adapted a poly-alphabetic coding system so Lewis and

Clark could communicate with him secretly. According to most experts, the coding system was first created in the sixteenth century by the French mathematician Blaise de Vigenere.

I shook my head as I read, amazed. It was hard to picture life without computers, let alone life without telephones. Back then, if you wanted someone to know something, you either went there yourself and told them or you arranged for the message to be delivered — and there was no postal service in the vast frontier Lewis and Clark explored.

President Jefferson's system was intended to allow Lewis and Clark to communicate urgent information in a timely manner, but as near as anyone can tell, it was never used — they were unable to spare a man to carry messages.

I could easily envision Rosalie playfully using the president's coding system. I was willing to bet big money that I'd just discovered the answer to the mystery of the tilting letters in Rosalie's kitchen, and the irony wasn't lost on me. Rosalie was a communications expert, and her field of expertise was communicating while exploring. How amusing that she would choose a system to encrypt her message that in

	a	b	c	d	e	f	g	h	i	j	k	l	m	n	o	p	q	r	s	t	u	v	w	x	y	z
a	b	c	d	e	f	g	h	i	j	k	l	m	n	o	p	q	r	s	t	u	v	w	x	y	z	&
b	c	d	e	f	g	h	i	j	k	l	m	n	o	p	q	r	s	t	u	v	w	x	y	z	&	a
c	d	e	f	g	h	i	j	k	l	m	n	o	p	q	r	s	t	u	v	w	x	y	z	&	a	b
d	e	f	g	h	i	j	k	l	m	n	o	p	q	r	s	t	u	v	w	x	y	z	&	a	b	c
e	f	g	h	i	j	k	l	m	n	o	p	q	r	s	t	u	v	w	x	y	z	&	a	b	c	d
f	g	h	i	j	k	l	m	n	o	p	q	r	s	t	u	v	w	x	y	z	&	a	b	c	d	e
g	h	i	j	k	l	m	n	o	p	q	r	s	t	u	v	w	x	y	z	&	a	b	c	d	e	f
h	i	j	k	l	m	n	o	p	q	r	s	t	u	v	w	x	y	z	&	a	b	c	d	e	f	g
i	j	k	l	m	n	o	p	q	r	s	t	u	v	w	x	y	z	&	a	b	c	d	e	f	g	h
j	k	l	m	n	o	p	q	r	s	t	u	v	w	x	y	z	&	a	b	c	d	e	f	g	h	i
k	l	m	n	o	p	q	r	s	t	u	v	w	x	y	z	&	a	b	c	d	e	f	g	h	i	j
l	m	n	o	p	q	r	s	t	u	v	w	x	y	z	&	a	b	c	d	e	f	g	h	i	j	k
m	n	o	p	q	r	s	t	u	v	w	x	y	z	&	a	b	c	d	e	f	g	h	i	j	k	l
n	o	p	q	r	s	t	u	v	w	x	y	z	&	a	b	c	d	e	f	g	h	i	j	k	l	m
o	p	q	r	s	t	u	v	w	x	y	z	&	a	b	c	d	e	f	g	h	i	j	k	l	m	n
p	q	r	s	t	u	v	w	x	y	z	&	a	b	c	d	e	f	g	h	i	j	k	l	m	n	o
q	r	s	t	u	v	w	x	y	z	&	a	b	c	d	e	f	g	h	i	j	k	l	m	n	o	p
r	s	t	u	v	w	x	y	z	&	a	b	c	d	e	f	g	h	i	j	k	l	m	n	o	p	q
s	t	u	v	w	x	y	z	&	a	b	c	d	e	f	g	h	i	j	k	l	m	n	o	p	q	r
t	u	v	w	x	y	z	&	a	b	c	d	e	f	g	h	i	j	k	l	m	n	o	p	q	r	s
u	v	w	x	y	z	&	a	b	c	d	e	f	g	h	i	j	k	l	m	n	o	p	q	r	s	t
v	w	x	y	z	&	a	b	c	d	e	f	g	h	i	j	k	l	m	n	o	p	q	r	s	t	u
w	x	y	z	&	a	b	c	d	e	f	g	h	i	j	k	l	m	n	o	p	q	r	s	t	u	v
x	y	z	&	a	b	c	d	e	f	g	h	i	j	k	l	m	n	o	p	q	r	s	t	u	v	w
y	z	&	a	b	c	d	e	f	g	h	i	j	k	l	m	n	o	p	q	r	s	t	u	v	w	x
z	&	a	b	c	d	e	f	g	h	i	j	k	l	m	n	o	p	q	r	s	t	u	v	w	x	y
&	a	b	c	d	e	f	g	h	i	j	k	l	m	n	o	p	q	r	s	t	u	v	w	x	y	z

actuality had proved useless.

I printed out what was commonly referred to as President Jefferson's Artichoke Matrix.

I transcribed the characters that I'd recorded earlier that day: *WGTSERH&XCYXSJ UWGNFTJFEJQSBPHIBO.*

The only unknown was where Rosalie's message began. Without that information, all using the matrix would accomplish would be to exchange one set of jumbled symbols for another set of jumbled symbols. I shrugged and decided to sequence the characters as I had written them down. I had to start somewhere.

I copied them into the middle row of a three-row grid, with the word *artichokes* written over and over again in the top row. Then I found the first letter of *artichokes* on the *x* axis, across the top of the artichoke matrix, and followed the column downward until I found the first letter of the encoded message. Then I followed that row all the way to the *y* axis, the first column of letters, and filled in the square with the corresponding character. In this case, starting with the *A* along the *x* axis, I found the *W* of the encoded message near the bottom of that column. The *W* was situated next to the letter *V* on the *y* axis. I continued decoding the next few letters until it became apparent that my guess as to where I should start was wrong.

a	r	t	i	c	h	o	k	e	s	a	r	t	i	c	h	o	k	e	s	a	r	t	i	c	h	o	k	e	s	a	r
w	g	t	s	e	r	h	&	x	c	y	x	s	j	u	w	g	n	f	t	j	f	e	j	q	s	b	p	h	i	b	o
v	p	&	j	b	j																										

I turned back to the small video monitor and viewed my recording again. *What could I have missed?* I asked myself. Rosalie must have left a clue about where to start. I observed nothing.

I counted the characters per wall — there were eight on each, thirty-two total. I decided to experiment by starting with the first character that appeared at the left-hand corner of each wall, a logical assumption, I thought, since it followed the English reading pattern of left to right.

The wall facing the front read: *WGT-SERH&.* The wall facing the outside on the right read: *XCYXSJUW.* The back wall contained the letters *GNFTJFEJ.* The characters over the door that led to the dining room were *QSBPHIBO.*

A truck rumbled by, breaking my concentration. I glanced at the time display on my computer. It was almost noon.

All I knew so far was that the message *didn't* start with *WGTSERH&.* I tried beginning with *XCYXSJUW.*

a	r	t	i	c	h	o	k	e	s	a	r	t	i	c	h	o	k	e	s	a	r	t	i	c	h	o	k	e	s	a	r
x	c	y	x	s	j	u	w	g	n	f	t	j	f	e	j	q	s	b	p	h	i	b	o	w	g	t	s	e	r	h	&
w	l	e	o	p																											

"Leopard!" I said aloud, and continued.

a	r	t	i	c	h	o	k	e	s	a	r	t	i	c	h	o	k	e	s	a	r	t	i	c	h	o	k	e	s	a	r
x	c	y	x	s	j	u	w	g	n	f	t	j	f	e	j	q	s	b	p	h	i	b	o	w	g	t	s	e	r	h	&
w	l	e	o	p	b	f	c																								

I sighed and started again, this time beginning with *GNFTJFEJ*.

a	r	t	i	c	h	o	k	e	s	a	r	t	i	c	h	o	k	e	s	a	r	t	i	c	h	o	k	e	s	a	r
g	n	f	t	j	f	e	j	q	s	b	p	h	i	b	o	w	g	t	s	e	r	h	&	x	c	y	x	s	j	u	w
f	w	m	k																												

"No way," I said, frustrated. " '*Fwmk*' isn't possible.' " At least not in English. *What if it's a double code,* I wondered, where after decoding it you still had to take another step, reading it backward or using every other letter or something? I shrugged. If that's the case, I'd have to find a professional cryptographer.

I got up and stretched and had some water, then prepared another three-row grid. The last series read: *QSBPHIBO*.

188

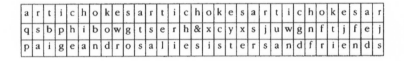

a	r	t	i	c	h	o	k	e	s	a	r	t	i	c	h	o	k	e	s	a	r	t	i	c	h	o	k	e	s	a	r
q	s	b	p	h	i	b	o	w	g	t	s	e	r	h	&	x	c	y	x	s	j	u	w	g	n	f	t	j	f	e	j
p	a	i	g																												

"Paige!" I exclaimed.

I resumed my decoding of the message.

a	r	t	i	c	h	o	k	e	s	a	r	t	i	c	h	o	k	e	s	a	r	t	i	c	h	o	k	e	s	a	r
q	s	b	p	h	i	b	o	w	g	t	s	e	r	h	&	x	c	y	x	s	j	u	w	g	n	f	t	j	f	e	j
p	a	i	g	e	a	n	d	r	o	s	a	l	i	e	s	i	s	t	e	r	s	a	n	d	f	r					

"Wow!" I whispered, hurrying now.

a	r	t	i	c	h	o	k	e	s	a	r	t	i	c	h	o	k	e	s	a	r	t	i	c	h	o	k	e	s	a	r
q	s	b	p	h	i	b	o	w	g	t	s	e	r	h	&	x	c	y	x	s	j	u	w	g	n	f	t	j	f	e	j
p	a	i	g	e	a	n	d	r	o	s	a	l	i	e	s	i	s	t	e	r	s	a	n	d	f	r	i	e	n	d	s

Paige and Rosalie. Sisters and friends. I picked up the phone to call Paige.

"Yes, I know," she said when I had her on the line and reported the message. "After she put it up, she showed me how to figure it out."

"Sounds like fun."

"Yeah," she said in her tiny voice. "It was."

After telling her that I'd just begun the appraisal, and would be in touch soon, I hung up the phone. I spun toward my window and looked out toward the distant woods, frustrated and disappointed. I'd had such hopes that Rosalie's code would provide a clue about her treasure.

I remembered the boxes of Rosalie's folders and papers I'd left downstairs. I'd ask Fred to go through them one by one. So far, it was my best shot at finding something of value.

CHAPTER FOURTEEN

As Officer Brownley and I walked into Heyer's together, I told her about the message I'd decoded in the kitchen.

She shook her head, but didn't comment.

Una, at her regular position behind the chest-high reception desk, looked at Officer Brownley, openly curious, and I introduced them as we signed in, but didn't explain the purpose of our visit. Instead, I turned to Officer Brownley, and said, "This way."

I felt Una's eyes on my back as we made our way down the hall, an odd sensation, and as we rounded the corner that led to Gerry's office suite, I looked back.

She raised her eyebrows and mouthed, "What?"

I raised my shoulders to convey uncertainty.

"Tricia," I said as we stepped into her office, "have you met Officer Brownley? She's investigating Rosalie's death."

Officer Brownley looked around, taking in the wood paneling, soft lighting, oil paintings, and thick rugs.

"How do you do?" Tricia said. "If there's anything I can do to help, please let me know. Rosalie was a remarkable young woman."

"Thanks. Someone will be talking to you about her soon."

To me, Tricia said, "Gerry thought that under the circumstances we ought to lock Rosalie's office. He asked me to give you the key."

"Sounds smart," I agreed, accepting it.

Gerry was on the phone, his voice booming. We could hear him clearly. I stuck my head into his office and nodded hello. He smiled at me as if we were old friends, and waved me in. When he saw Officer Brownley, he nodded politely, and gestured that she should join us.

We stood there, unable to avoid listening to his side of the conversation with someone he called, "Dougie, Dougie." He was leaning back, and he looked like he was having a ball.

He winked at me. To avoid eye contact, I shifted my gaze to the picture window in back of him. As he spoke, I watched a big brown bird circle and glide until it disappeared from view, and then I tried to estimate how far the trees were from the building.

"Dougie, Dougie," Gerry said, "you can't be missing deadlines, not if you want to play in the big leagues. . . . Tell me in one sentence what the problem is. . . . Fair enough. I'll tell you what, I'll give you until tomorrow noon, how's that? . . . You betcha! . . . No can do, nope, nada, not a chance. . . . Dougie, Dougie, come on now, be realistic. . . . Sounds like a plan, my man. . . . Okay then . . . *Mañana*."

He punched the button to disconnect the call, sat forward, and said, "Sit, sit. Tell me what's going on."

I looked straight at Gerry as I introduced Officer Brownley. His eyes were guarded, no longer warm and encouraging. "I'm here to inventory Rosalie's things. For her sister's lawyer."

"Helluva thing," he said, standing up. "When you're done with the appraisal, you okay with finishing the installation?"

"Sure," I said. "I should have time in between things and for sure next week, if that's all right."

Gerry clasped my arm, gave a squeeze, and said, "Josie, doll, whatever's good for you is good for me."

I edged away. His touch wasn't improper, but it made me super-uncomfortable. I was tempted to tap him on the arm, and shout, "Cooties, no touch back!" the way we did in grade school.

"Are we interrupting?" Ned asked in an irritatingly coy tone, entering the office just ahead of Edie. He smirked, and I nearly stamped my foot, I was so annoyed. He sounded like a twelve-year-old with a dirty mind.

"What was *that* about?" Edie asked wrathfully.

"Nothing!" I exclaimed.

"Girls, girls!" Gerry interjected, chuckling. "Edie, doll, you know you have nothing to be jealous about. Josie here is just a good ole girl doing her job. She's wearing her appraiser hat."

Edie wasn't mollified. She'd heard it all before, yet astonishingly, she wasn't mad at him, she was mad at me. In fact, she looked like she wanted to kill me. *She thinks he's putting the moves on me,* I thought, *and she's worried.* I wished I could reassure her that I had no designs on her husband, but there was nothing I could do or say that wouldn't simply fuel her wrath. Her viper-like expression was terrifying.

"An appraisal?" Ned said with a nasty

sneer, and I could almost hear his unspoken, *Is that what they call it these days?* He turned to Officer Brownley, extended his hand, and said, "Hello, there. I'm Ned Anderson, the CFO."

I mumbled, "Excuse me," and nipped out of Gerry's office into the anteroom. Officer Brownley followed close behind and was standing beside me near Tricia's desk as I unzipped the video carry case.

"What's up, Ned?" Gerry asked, his booming voice audible through the open door.

"I need a few minutes to go over some numbers."

"Not today, I'm afraid. I gotta run. I've got an appointment."

Seconds later, Ned stepped into the outer office. "Well, that was fun, don't you think?" he said to me.

"Gerry," Edie said, in an arctic tone. "I just heard a news report naming you as a suspect in Rosalie's murder. Is it true?"

"Edie, sweetheart, we'll talk more tonight. Not now." He strode through the anteroom and down the corridor, a man on a mission. "See ya later," he called to no one in particular.

Edie followed close on his heels, and after

a moment, I exhaled, relieved that they were gone.

"Tricia, can he fit me in tomorrow? He's such a busy man," Ned scoffed.

Tricia didn't rise to the bait, although I wouldn't have blamed her a bit if she had.

It was awful to see Gerry treat Edie with such cavalier disregard. And I knew the truth about his urgent departure. He wasn't going to a business meeting as he'd implied. He was off to his regular appointment at the tanning salon.

"We're here to look through Rosalie's things," I explained to Tricia. "My firm's been hired to appraise everything." I pointed to Rosalie's little cubbyhole and spoke to Officer Brownley. "This is — *was* — Rosalie's office."

She nodded and watched as I began the recording process. I flipped through the jamboree of papers and files, and all of the reference books stashed in a cabinet mounted over the desk, and I found nothing personal. There were neatly organized notes of conversations she'd had with Gerry, along with related documents like copies of his birth certificate and school report cards.

There were only two personal items — a

recent photo of the two sisters on a sofa with bowls of ice cream raised in a mock toast to someone out of sight and a porcelain artichoke on top of a pile of folders and papers — a makeshift paperweight.

When I was done, I locked the door and gave Tricia the key.

The entire process took less than fifteen minutes.

Officer Brownley followed me to the health club, located on the lower level overlooking the pond. I showed my letter to the woman on duty. She was tall and thin, sinewy and healthy looking with a mane of red hair and an easy smile. Her name tag read MANDY.

"Her locker's over there," she said as she pushed open the door to the women's changing room. She pointed. "Number eight. Do you have the key?"

I pulled out the ring and held it up. "You tell me. Do you recognize it?"

"Everyone brings her own padlock. Could be that one, though," she said. "Or this one. Those are about the right size."

The padlock came off easily. Officer Brownley was right next to me when I swung open the door. A blue cotton robe hung on a hook at the back. Dirty white sneakers and sky blue flip-flops sat on the floor. There was a toiletry kit on a shelf. I took it to the counter, and as I extracted the contents one by one — shampoo, conditioner, mascara, foundation, powder, and eyeliner — a bulge on the bottom caught my eye. I touched it gently. Something hard had been placed under the satin liner.

"What is it?" Officer Brownley asked, watching me.

"I don't know. Some kind of bump." Using a fingernail, I peeled back the fabric and gaped. "Look," I said, pointing to a key under the cardboard bottom.

Before touching it, I recorded everything. Then I removed the key and compared it to the others on the ring — it didn't match. It was an ordinary-looking brass key, a house key, maybe.

"I just thought of something," I said, picking up the key ring. "Have we used all the keys on the ring?" I slid each one around the metal circle as I recounted its use. "Front door, car, file cabinet, this locker . . . look! These two are extras," I said, indicating a standard-sized silver-colored key and a small brass-colored one.

"So we have three that we don't know what they go to, right? The two on the ring and the one you just found."

"Right. I bet this one goes to the back

door of her house," I said, wiggling the unused standard-sized key on Rosalie's key ring. "I didn't try it because we were already inside. I didn't think of it."

She nodded. "But we should. We need to know what all the keys open."

"Agreed."

"What do you think it goes to — the one you just found?"

Our eyes met and I shook my head. "I don't know . . . maybe a friend's house — in case the friend locked herself out."

"Not real convenient." She shrugged. "How about the other one?"

"Another padlock?"

"We have no way of knowing without testing them. Let's go to the house and check them out."

I took one final look throughout the locker, added the new key to the ring of Rosalie's keys, and thanked Mandy, the attendant, on the way out.

I couldn't imagine what lock the key fit or why Rosalie had felt it necessary to hide it away. *A man,* I thought. *There's got to be a man involved. Maybe she and Gerry had rented an apartment somewhere. A private place, just for the two of them. What else could it be?*

CHAPTER FIFTEEN

Climbing the stairs that led to the lobby, I said, "I just need to check something about next week's schedule with Una."

"I'll wait outside."

When Officer Brownley was out of sight, I walked over to Una's station. I did want to let her know my schedule, but mostly I wanted to hear the scuttlebutt. Una always knew the skinny on everyone and everything.

Her desk was tucked behind a chest-high, mottled gray granite counter faced in walnut. Her chair was positioned toward the front so she could track people's comings and goings. "Hey," I said as I approached. "How you doing?"

"Okay. How about you?"

I shrugged. "A little upset, to tell you the truth."

Una nodded and made a face. "Me, too."

"I'll be coming in next week sometime to

finish the installation, so I'll see you then."

"Good. So," she asked, lowering her voice, "how come you're here with that police officer?"

I decided that there was no reason not to tell her the truth, so I explained that I'd been hired to appraise Rosalie's estate. Then, to shift the focus from me, I asked, "Have you heard anything?"

"Who tells anything to the receptionist?" she replied with a self-deprecating chuckle.

Maybe, I thought, *if I pose specific questions, I'll get more information.* "Have you talked to the police?"

"Yes. Twice. Mostly they asked about the flowers. From Rosalie's secret admirer."

"What did you tell them?" I asked, the image of the greeting card that had been left on my porch vivid in my memory.

"I figured out that she'd been getting them for about three months."

"October?" I asked, counting back from January. "They started in October?"

"As near as I can remember," she said, nodding, "the first bouquet came just before Halloween. I remember because Rosalie made a joke that it was probably a warlock sending them as some kind of Halloween prank."

That was about the same time she and Paul

broke up, I realized, *and in all probability, just about when she and Gerry got started.* "What did you say?" I asked Una.

"I said that if she was right about it being a warlock, I had a really good guess about who it was — my ex."

I laughed, picturing Rosalie as she joked with Una. "Do you think she had any idea who it was for real?"

"No, and it drove her crazy, not knowing."

"How about the florist?" I asked. "Were you able to help the police determine where the flowers came from?"

"Yeah, but I'm not sure it was helpful. There were, I don't know exactly, but about half a dozen deliveries here, and the flowers were sent from different places."

"Like where?" I asked, curious.

"Taylor's, for one, here in Portsmouth, near Patty's Pantry. They have beautiful flowers."

I nodded, recognizing the name of the restaurant on Route One. "Where else?"

"Lillie's Garden in Rye, Floral Vision in Dover, and Blossoms in Greenland," she listed, naming three nearby New Hampshire towns.

"You have a good memory!"

"Not really," she replied, laughing. "The

police pestered me into remembering, and now I'll never forget."

I smiled. "So some of the florists were used more than once?"

"That's right."

"Any online vendors?"

"If so, I didn't notice," she said, shaking her head. "How about you? Did Rosalie ever say anything to you about them?"

"Just that time you brought them in when I was there. She got mad."

Una shook her head again. "Who can blame her?"

"Absolutely. At first, though, I thought it was kind of cute."

"Ick."

"I know," I acknowledged. I could no longer imagine how I ever could have thought it was cute.

"Are you ready to hear something awful?" Una asked, sounding disgusted. "Gerry told HR to begin searching for a replacement."

"You're kidding! Rosalie just died — she hasn't even been buried yet."

" 'Shame on you, Josie, for not understanding the urgency of the situation!' " she said in an altered voice, her eyes dancing. "Gerry is too important to let the book languish. Just ask him. He'll be glad to tell you all about it."

I smiled and shook my head. "Amazing. Well, listen, I better get going. You take care, okay?"

Outside, I paused to take in a deep breath of the winter-fresh air. All of Heyer's walkways and most of the parking lot were cleared of snow, leaving only small patches of black ice and a thick coating of rock salt. As I picked my way to my car, I noticed that Officer Brownley had pulled up next to the exit and sat with her flashers on, talking on her cell phone. A man I recognized as a sales manager jogged toward his car, a worried look on his face. I waved to him, but he didn't see me. Edie sat in her BMW. She looked enraged and coiled tight, like a snake poised to strike. I slipped into my car, scrunched down, and looked away, relieved that she hadn't seen me.

Officer Brownley spotted me in her rearview mirror, killed her flashers, and pulled out onto the street. I followed close behind.

As we turned onto I-95, I called Gretchen. "Hey," I said. "Anything going on?"

"Sasha has news," she said, barely able to contain her excitement. "Let me transfer you."

"Sasha," I said, "are you about to make my day?"

"Well, no, but I'm not going to ruin it."

"Fair enough. What do you have?"

"The Southwick paper is good."

No wonder Gretchen was excited. Authenticating the palette Lesha had left us had just cleared its first hurdle. "Tell me," I said.

"They call the paper Momentous — it was introduced in nineteen fifty-six."

"When did they discontinue it?"

"They didn't. It's still produced."

"Which means we have neither confirmation nor refutation."

"Exactly. It's not bad news."

"Does Southwick have any way of identifying it? Codes woven into the fiber or something?"

"No. I asked, of course, but I wasn't surprised that they don't mark it. Most of the stock is sold in small lots packaged with envelopes as résumé kits. You know what I mean . . . a hundred sheets of paper and fifty envelopes, that sort of thing. It's not used for archival purposes or anything like that."

"Oh, well. Anything on Whistler's work habits?"

"Not yet."

"Okay. Let me take another look at the letter when I get back to the office."

"I'll put it on your desk if I leave before

you get here."

"Thanks. Anything else going on?" I asked.

"Fred has some not-so-good news."

"Pass me over." After Fred said hello, I said, "Hey, I hear you have bad news."

"Not really bad, per se, just not good."

"I guess this is the day for it. What do you have?"

"The davenport? It's a modern-day repro."

"Darn."

"Yeah. It's sold through the Winslow Reproduction Furniture Web site for six hundred ninety-five dollars."

"So it's not junk," I commented, reacting to the price point. Winslow was known for selling midrange furniture.

"No, but it's not an antique," he said, bridling with contempt.

I discounted 25 percent of his negativity — Fred was an antiques snob. "What's its condition?"

"A couple of nicks and a major scratch."

"How would you price it for the tag sale?" I asked.

He paused. Fred was a superb appraiser, but he had almost no merchandising experience and even less innate sense. His instinct was to jack up the price on those objects he considered especially important and undercharge for those items he held in contempt or simply didn't care for. I was trying to train him to be more objective and thus more commercially savvy.

"I don't know. Fifty dollars, maybe."

"Only minor damage, right?"

"Yeah. Except for that one scratch, which is pretty noticeable."

"I'm thinking more than that — maybe two-thirds off the original price would be fair. Maybe two forty-nine, two twenty-four, something like that."

"Really? That much? It's not even a collectible."

I considered how to explain not just about pricing this piece but the overarching concept. My motive was selfish — the more nuts-and-bolts responsibility my staff could handle, the more I could direct my energy to growing the business. Delegation, for me, was the hardest thing to be good at. *Get good at it,* my father had instructed me. *Be generous with your knowledge, confirm your staff's understanding, and continually remind yourself that not everything needs to be done perfectly.*

"There are two factors to consider," I explained, sounding more patient than I felt. "First, since we don't carry many desks, we don't have a track record on how to price it. And if we don't know what the market will bear, it's probably better to start higher and be able to reduce the price if it doesn't sell quickly than leave money on the table by pricing it too low in the first place — and, worse, to never even know we've done so. Second, two-thirds off is a great deal. I mean, think about it — a sixty-seven percent discount for a nearly new desk is a heck of bargain in anybody's book."

"But earlier you told me not to price the art print repro too high. What's the difference?"

"Good question, Fred. Basically, we have two kinds of customers, users and investors. By pricing art prints all about the same, the users, the people who buy art prints to frame and hang in their homes, know that when they're in the market for that sort of item, they can come to us and find a wide variety of good pieces fairly priced. The investors know that occasionally they'll find a gem, so they keep returning. The davenport doesn't fit into either customer model. Since we don't normally display much furniture at the tag sales, we don't attract either users or investors. Think about it — we're not a used furniture store, which would attract users, and we don't stock enough furniture to attract investors. When we do have a piece for sale, almost by definition it's unique; therefore, it can be priced on its own merits. Does that make sense?"

"Yeah, it does, actually," he replied, sounding surprised that he understood something about business.

"Good. As a general statement, among objects we carry on a regular basis, it's better for us to price a great piece too low than a mediocre piece too high. Among objects we don't usually have in stock, it's better for us to price it too high than too low. It's complex, I know."

"Yeah," he agreed.

From his tone of voice, I could tell he meant it in spades. To be fair, I agreed. I'd need to repeat the underlying theory of pricing strategy many times before it got assimilated, I knew, but reminded myself that it was just part of running a business.

As soon as I hung up, my cell phone rang. I didn't recognize the number.

"This is Josie."

"Josie?"

It was Paige and she was crying.

"What is it, Paige? Are you all right?"

All I heard was snuffling. I felt the world slow down as I entered crisis mode, the place where I seem able to have a three-hundred-and-sixty-degree awareness and cope well. "It's all right, Paige. Take your time. I'm here."

"I'm sorry," she said, her voice muffled with tears.

"No problem. Can you answer a few questions?"

"Yes," she said, her voice barely audible.

"Are you okay — physically, I mean?"

"Yes. It's not that." Her crying swelled into sobbing, then backed off to a whimper. "I'm sorry," she said again.

"I can tell you're really upset, Paige."

"Yes."

"Can you tell me why?"

Officer Brownley had turned off the interstate, and was heading toward the Chaffee house. I ratcheted up the fan another notch. As the sun sank lower in the sky, the air became increasingly bitter.

"I didn't know who else to call."

"I'm glad you called me."

More crying, then, "It's Mr. and Mrs. Reilly," she said, referring to her friend's parents. "I overheard Brooke."

I felt my lungs contract. I wasn't getting enough oxygen. Whatever she was about to reveal was going to upset me. I could smell it. "What did you hear?" I asked calmly.

"They're canceling a weekend trip. Because of me." I heard mortification in her voice, then harrowing, racking weeping. Her voice, when it came again, was wispy and cracked. "They're going to forfeit their deposit somewhere."

It was futile to explain that the Reillys probably didn't care about losing a deposit, that they were, no doubt, glad to be there for Paige. This wasn't about money; this was about pride. Paige felt like a burden.

You'll be fine, Paige, I thought of saying. *Give it time. It's okay. Go ahead and cry. Don't mouth platitudes,* I told myself, dismissing the words of reassurance that flooded my brain. Well-intentioned words that conveyed no truth and therefore offered no succor. *If you want to help her,* I told myself, *well then, roll up your sleeves and do something.* The answer came unheralded.

"How about if you come and stay with me?" I said.

There was sudden silence.

"I mean it, Paige. You're more than welcome."

More silence except for the sound of her breathing. Officer Brownley signaled the turn onto Hanover Street.

"I can come get you," I said.

Snuffling, then some more heartfelt crying.

211

"What is it?" I asked.

"What will I tell Brooke and her folks? They've been so great to me."

"Tell them the truth. I begged and begged and finally you agreed to stay with me for a couple of days. You're taking turns and you'll be back on Monday."

A tearful gulp. "Thank you, Josie."

"Pack up, kiddo. I'll be there in an hour or so."

Poor Paige, I thought. I ended the call, and softly pounded the dashboard in testimony to my frustration.

When we got to Rosalie's house, I parked in back of Officer Brownley's patrol car and turned off the engine, relieved to have a tangible task to distract me from anxious musings about Paige.

CHAPTER SIXTEEN

"Shall we go around back?" I asked Officer Brownley. "Or through the house?"

"Around is probably quicker," she replied.

I led the way, pushing through the heavy snow. Tall trees dotted the small yard, and forsythia bushes ranged along the wood-slat fence that encircled the property, wild and unpruned. *It must be spectacular in springtime,* I thought, picturing the head-high bushes thick with delicate blossoms.

The only section of the perimeter without forsythia was a small hill in the far back corner. I glanced at Rosalie's neighbors' yards, visible through chinks in the fence. All the property within sight was flat. "That's odd, isn't it?" I asked, pointing toward the sharply rising embankment.

"Land sometimes does that," Officer Brownley said, shrugging.

"So abruptly?" I asked.

"It happens."

I bet it's man-made, I thought. *Probably for sledding.* Another wave of sadness washed over me as I considered the charming hominess of the effort. I wondered if Rosalie had built it for Paige as a surprise or whether Paige had helped.

The loose key we'd found in the toiletry kit didn't fit the back door, but the standard-sized key that had been on the ring when Mr. Bolton handed it over did. Officer Brownley and I looked at each other, and I shrugged.

"If you find a lock I don't know about, give me a call," I said.

"It'd be best if you let me make a copy of the keys."

"You know I can't do that without permission. Talk to Mr. Bolton."

Officer Brownley wasn't happy with my response, but nodded philosophically.

"I'll send you a copy of the appraisal when it's done," I said, not to placate her but to bridge the awkward moment. "Mr. Bolton said I could."

She smiled a little. "Thanks, Josie. You spot anything, you let me know, okay?"

I called Wes, told him I was running late but en route, and headed toward the shore. The sparkling sun shimmered low over the forest to the west, and the smooth surface of the ocean was flicked with gilt. Vermillion- and russet-colored clouds streaked the sky. "Red sky at night, sailors' delight. Red sky at morning, sailors take warning," I murmured, remembering the rhyme my father had taught me long ago. Tomorrow would dawn another clear, sunny day.

As I passed the Rocky Point police station, I saw Ty's vehicle parked near the front door. For a fleeting moment I considered stopping to say hey, but didn't. If he asked me why I was in Rocky Point, I'd either have to lie or admit I was meeting Wes. Ty wasn't above feeding tips to the press when it had the potential to help his investigation, but it galled him that I might work with the media, too.

From my perspective, my approach was smart and self-protective: If I was going to be quoted, I wanted to know it. And if I was able to satisfy my curiosity along the way, I saw no harm in it. From Ty's standpoint, it was foolhardy. What I perceived as prudent, he perceived as irresponsible, and maybe even dangerous.

Wes was waiting for me at the top of the dune, standing with his back to me in snow that reached almost to the top of his knee-high gaiters. He was bundled into a navy blue pea coat that pulled tautly across his shoulders, and I wondered if he'd gained weight since he'd bought the coat or was wearing an extra sweater to combat the frigid weather.

"Wes!" He didn't respond, and I figured that the waves rolling into shore masked my arrival. "Wes!" I shouted. No reaction.

I gave my scarf an extra turn around my neck, flipped up the hood of my parka, and scampered up the snow-covered sand to join him. "Hey, Wes," I said breathlessly. A blast of wind blew my hood back. "Tell me why I'm here. It's freezing!"

He turned to face me, and I could see that his cheeks were chapped and red from the dry cold and stinging salt air. "I thought you wanted to meet somewhere private."

"Yeah, but I also wanted to live through the experience."

"Ha, ha," he said.

"Let's go sit in my car, okay?"

He lumbered after me as I pigeon-stepped through the snow down the slope. Once we were in the car, with the seats pushed back as far as they would go and the heat pumping, I twisted around to face him. "So?" I asked.

"I got news. And then a question."

"Okay," I replied warily.

"Looks like Rosalie was murdered for sure." He lowered his voice. "Before she drowned, she was hit on the head."

"It's so awful," I whispered.

"Yeah," he agreed. "So, here's the thing. She died between nine and ten o'clock at night — the same day you guys had lunch."

I shook my head and squinted through a break in the dunes toward the ocean. The water looked inky dark in the gathering dusk, and endless. "How can they be so sure about the time?" I asked. "It was cold that night. Wouldn't that affect their calculations?"

"Yeah, but they can figure it out based on stuff like how digested the food in her stomach was, the temperatures of the water and air, and the tidal patterns. Stuff like that."

"Tidal patterns!" I said. "I hadn't thought of that."

"Yeah. They calculate she entered the water at or near the Rocky Point jetty. They think she was hit with something wooden, then fell or was thrown into the ocean and got pretty banged up hitting rocks on the way down. They're pretty sure that she was unconscious when she hit the water."

His description was painfully vivid. "And she washed ashore with the incoming tide," I whispered, sickened at the picture Wes had painted. I closed my eyes, trying to block the image of Rosalie, her soft blond hair splaying out, as she tumbled from the Rocky Point jetty into the glacial Atlantic Ocean, then arced her way to the seaweed-strewn beach.

I opened my eyes. "How do they know she was struck first? Couldn't her injuries have resulted from hitting the rocks?"

"There were wood splinters in her scalp," he said matter-of-factly. "That's why I asked you about wood on the phone."

The specificity of the image was chilling, and I closed my eyes again. *Splinters,* I thought, shivering, not from the cold this time. I opened my eyes. "Wouldn't splinters wash away in the current?"

"Not when they're embedded," he said.

"I guess," I acknowledged, grimacing at the thought, picturing the Rocky Point jetty littered with nature's detritus. Branches from nearby trees blew onto the beach during storms and were bleached by the sun and tossed by the tide for months or years, ending up as white-gray, satiny smooth driftwood. "But still — she could have fallen on a piece of wood, right? And ended up with splinters? There's lots of driftwood at the Point."

"They said there's a protective coating — varnish — on the splinters, which means it's extremely unlikely they came from driftwood."

"Varnish!" I exclaimed, seeing his logic.

"Yeah. Let me tell you what I know," Wes said. He scanned his paper and found the note he was looking for. "It was an alkyd varnish with some polyurethane added to it."

"That's common," I said.

"How do you know?"

"I evaluate wood and wood treatments all the time. I know stuff like that. And they don't know what kind of wood it is?"

"No. How can they tell?"

"Depending on the size of the splinter, they may be able to tell by microscopic examination. I mean, oak looks way different from cherry, for example. If they can find the object they think was used to hit Rosalie, like a baseball bat or something, they could even do a DNA analysis and match the splinters to the specific weapon."

"DNA in wood?" he asked, sounding astonished. "You're kidding!"

"It's called botanical DNA. The test was developed to catch tree poachers. It's expensive, but it's possible." I glanced at the dashboard clock. It was after five-thirty. I needed to leave soon to collect Paige. "What else did they find?"

"Besides the algae and other ocean stuff, nothing. There were no signs of struggle. No bruises on the backs of her arms as if she'd tried to ward off a blow — nothing like that."

I closed my eyes again as Wes spoke, shaken by the haunting and fearsome image he conveyed. *What would drive someone to take a chunk of wood and strike Rosalie?* Taking a deep breath, I opened my eyes again and looked north. It had grown too dark to see anything, but I knew the Point was there, a mile or so up the beach. Composed of boulders lodged together, the Rocky Point jetty stretched due east from the high tide line a hundred feet or so out into the ocean and rose about ten feet above the surf at low tide, a monolith designed to protect, not kill. The rocks were irregularly shaped and algae-slick, difficult to navigate during the day, and treacherous after dark.

"Why?" I asked Wes.

"Why what?" he asked.

"Why was she there? What possible reason could there be for Rosalie to be on the jetty at nine o'clock on a January night? It doesn't make any sense."

"I don't know. Any ideas?" he countered.

The car was becoming overly warm and I lowered the settings, loosened my scarf, and unzipped my jacket. In the weak glow from the small map light, I could see his eyes as they bored into mine. I was witnessing a diligent reporter working a source — me. "I have no idea."

Wes shifted position to face me full on. "You know how I said I wanted to ask you something?"

"Uh-huh."

"Here's the question — if you were me, what would you do next?" he asked.

I shrugged. "When in doubt, start with motive."

"Love, hate, fear, money, right?"

"Plus jealousy," I said, thinking of Edie. *And maybe Paul Greeley,* I thought, wondering once again how he took the breakup of their romance. Even Cooper the Condescending was a possibility. From what I could see, he felt as passionate about his work as Edie did about her marriage. *If either of them had been thwarted, well, who knows what might have occurred. And don't forget Rosalie's secret admirer,* I reminded myself. *Who is now inexplicably* my *secret admirer,* I thought with a shudder. I looked into both side mirrors and the rearview mirror seeking out I knew not what. The road in back of me was empty. The world was still.

"Who's jealous?" Wes asked, zeroing in on my comment.

His question made me realize that Wes didn't know about Rosalie's affair with Gerry or, apparently, her brief romance with Paul. Or of the professional jealousy I sensed emanating from Cooper.

Evidently, Wes's police source wasn't revealing everything. I considered whether to tell him what I suspected. I was in a quandary again, experiencing the same rippling discomfort I'd felt just before I'd told Ty what I knew. *Since I've told the police, it's no longer secret,* I rationalized. *Ty will be mad as all get-out if I tell — but I want to know things, and in order to get information, I have to provide information.* Wes and I had our own sort of quid pro quo.

Plus, I knew that Wes had contacts and tactics that the police couldn't match. Charge card records, for example. The police couldn't access them without a search warrant, but from past experience, I knew that Wes could — and would. Curiosity won out. "Well," I said, "actually, there are a few people for whom jealousy might apply."

"Who?"

"Promise me we're off the record."

"Josie!" he protested.

"Promise."

"All right. Same as always." He sighed. "Who?"

I nodded, satisfied. "Her boss at Heyer's, Gerry Fine, and his wife, Edie. A guy I heard she was dating for a while named Paul Greeley. Another guy in her department at school named Cooper Bennington. And maybe someone else."

"Tell me."

Taking a deep breath to soothe myself, I stared through the windshield into the night to avoid Wes's penetrating gaze. I explained what I speculated about her affair with Gerry, what I'd observed of Edie's anger, what I'd heard about Paul Greeley's possessiveness, what I'd experienced of Cooper's sanctimony, what I knew about the book deal, what I inferred about her secret admirer, and how I'd seen her diary and tote bag in her office. I stuck to the facts, but I suspected my opinions came through loud and clear. Gerry was lower than pond scum; Edie was pathetic, explosive, and unpredictable; Paul was too smooth; Cooper was cutthroat; having a secret admirer was beyond scary; and Rosalie wouldn't have voluntarily let that tote bag out of her sight.

Wes was a good listener. As I spoke, I could feel the force of his attention. When I finished, he cleared his throat. "I get the jealousy thing with Gerry and Edie, and with Paul. But why would this Cooper guy want to kill Rosalie?"

"She was becoming well known in her field, a pretty rapid ascent for a newbie. But because she didn't have her Ph.D. yet, she was vulnerable to attack, so she was playing things pretty close to her vest. And if he got wind of her book contract, forget about it. It would be ugly for sure."

"You think he got angry enough to kill?" Wes asked incredulously.

"Clearly you've never been around academic types," I remarked, thinking of the several betrayals I'd witnessed during my tenure at Frisco's. Top scholars at the height of their careers had backstabbed their colleagues without hesitation and, sometimes, even without significant cause or benefit. I shook my head to dispel the depressing memory.

"Why didn't you tell me all this before now?" he said, sounding simultaneously impressed and peeved.

"I shouldn't be talking to you at all."

"Yes, you should," he replied confidently. "This is what I was hoping for — some dirt to get me started."

The thought that Wes took what I'd told him as dirt made me feel ashamed. "I didn't tell you as gossip, Wes."

"I know. You meant it as a good thing."

He's impossible, I thought. *He'll never understand my ambivalence.* I kept my eyes toward the front, knowing that second-guessing myself was useless. I could only hope that I'd done the right thing.

Wes scanned his notes. "Do you think Edie Fine could have done it? A woman?" he asked.

"Sure. She had a weapon. A woman can swing a baseball bat or something like that with no problem. And those rocks are slick, so it wouldn't have taken much for Rosalie to topple."

"My source tells me Rosalie was struck by someone taller."

"How can they tell?"

"The blow aimed down."

I thought about what Wes said, trying to picture the attack. "I bet they referred to the angle of the blow, not the height of the perpetrator, right?"

"How'd you know?"

I shrugged. "Logic — maybe Rosalie was squatting or leaning over when she was struck. They wouldn't be able to determine height — at least I shouldn't think they could."

"Fair enough," Wes acknowledged. "What else?"

I thought some more. "Maybe you could see if any of those people have an alibi."

"I'll check everyone out." He paused, then asked, "You have a funny look on your face. What are you thinking?"

"I don't understand how Rosalie's tote bag got into her office at Heyer's."

"She must have gone back to the office."

"She didn't. Apparently her key card wasn't used and she couldn't have got in without it."

"All security can be breached," he said dismissively. He slipped the paper back in his pocket and began to button up his jacket, preparing to leave. "I have a little news. Rosalie hung out with her sister for a while at their house, and then she left, driving herself. That was about six-thirty. According to my police source, Rosalie told the sister that she was meeting a friend, she didn't say who." He opened the door and a blast of wind-whipped cold jolted me. As he stepped out, he turned back to face me. "I betcha it was Gerry." He gave a sprightly wave good-bye.

I wondered what Rosalie thought about in the seven or so hours before she died. *A lifetime can occur in seven hours,* I told myself. *You could fly across the country.* As soon as the thought came to me, I wondered whether Paige's despised cousin Rodney had done just that. If he'd known of Rosalie's treasure, maybe he would have thought that the trip was worth the effort.

CHAPTER SEVENTEEN

I was put through to Mr. Bolton right away.

"Any news?" Paige's lawyer asked.

"Nothing so far," I replied. "There's a nice American flag that might have some value."

"Valuable enough to be Rosalie's treasure?"

"Probably not."

"Hmmm," he ruminated.

"Paige called me," I said, changing the subject. "She's going to stay with me for the weekend."

"What? Why?"

I explained about the Reilly family's weekend plans, and Mr. Bolton grudgingly allowed that it was all right that she stay with me. "I conducted a background check on you, of course, before authorizing the appraisal. I'll call them."

"What about Rodney?" I asked, swallowing my consternation. Background checks were common enough in the antiques appraisal business, but I'd never gotten used to what felt like an unwarranted intrusion.

"We're still looking into things."

"That sounds ominous," I remarked, thinking that since Mr. Bolton's check of me had taken less than an hour, the multi-day check of Rodney didn't bode well.

"No news is no news," he responded.

"Paige isn't going to want to live with him."

"We'll cross that bridge when we get to it. Certainly nothing will happen until Monday in any event. Speaking of which, I need to talk to Paige about her sister's funeral. I expect the body to be released next week."

I shook my head. *Life is just so damn unfair,* I thought. "I can bring her to your office on Monday."

"That makes sense. I assume she won't be going to school. How is two?"

"We haven't discussed it, but I'm guessing she wouldn't want to go back at least until after the funeral. Two's fine. There's another thing," I added.

"Yes?"

"The police took Rosalie's computer. Sometimes people keep asset listings in a word processing or spreadsheet program. Plus there might be an electronic address book that would lead me to places she might

229

have stored things. I asked Officer Brownley if she'd check, but I thought I ought to follow up with you, too."

"Good thinking. I'll get you an answer."

Mr. Bolton gave me his home phone number and told me to call if I needed him. I promised that I would. To try to dispel my growing discontent, I slipped in an old Linda Ronstat CD and drove the rest of the way to the Reilly house singing along with her heart-melting rendition of "Blue Bayou."

Paige must have been on the lookout for me because as soon as I slowed to a stop in front of the house, she was out the door, loaded down. She had a backpack slung over one shoulder and wobbled under the heft of a duffel bag. She was so small.

I popped the trunk and helped her wrestle the heavy duffel bag inside.

"You okay?" I asked.

"Sure."

I patted her shoulder through her puffy parka. As we drove, I kept trying to think of innocuous questions I could ask to put her at ease, but nothing came to me, and we rode in silence for the fifteen minutes or so it took to get to my house. I pulled into the driveway, turned off the engine, and pressed the button that opened the trunk.

"Frankie, give me a break, okay?" I heard Zoë say as I stepped out of my car. I turned to look.

She was half inside her house, talking to someone on the porch. Under the golden gleam of the overhead bulb, I recognized trouble in the rigid stance and grim demeanor of an angry young man. He was maybe eighteen. He wore jeans and a leather bomber jacket. Stenciled on the back in a Gothic font was BITCHES STAY CLEAR.

"Yeah, right," he snarled, spun around, leaped off the porch, and charged down the street, disappearing into the darkness.

"You okay?" I called to Zoë.

"As okay as I can be with a loser cousin in residence."

"Since when?"

"Since this afternoon. His mother, my aunt, threw him out — no surprise since he's a complete bum. He has nowhere else to go, so he shows up on my doorstep. Lucky me."

"Poor Zoë," I commiserated.

"Another day, another problem. You okay?" she asked, squinting in the darkness.

"I'm good. This is Paige Chaffee, come to stay with me for the weekend."

"Hey, Paige. Do you like kids?"

"Sure," Paige replied, confused.

"Wonderful! You're hired!"

"Huh?"

"As a babysitter! Let's talk tomorrow. We're still on for dinner, okay?"

"You're a one-and-only, my friend," I said, laughing. "Yes. Paige and I will be there."

"And Ty?"

"I think so," I said, embarrassed because I'd forgotten to ask him. "I'll let you know."

"Okey dokey. See ya!" Zoë said, and I heard the storm door click home as she stepped back inside.

I let us in, shed my coat in the entryway, hanging it on a hook I'd mounted near the door, and held out my hand for Paige's. It was iceberg cold inside, a disadvantage of being the first person home, which since I live alone, I always am. I turned up the thermostat, then removed my boots, snuggling my feet into my pink fuzzy slippers, told Paige to leave her things in the hall and to follow me, and headed into the living room.

"Come on in. Have a seat." I pointed toward one of the two club chairs in the room. When she was settled, I sat too.

"Are you hungry?" I asked her.

"Not really. But I know I should eat something."

"When do you normally eat?"

232

She shrugged. "Whenever."

I nodded. "I'll rustle something up in a while. But you should feel free to raid the fridge anytime, okay? Then what do you want to do tonight? Do you like TV? Movies?"

She shrugged. "Sometimes. And reading. I like music, too. I've got an iPod in my bag."

After an awkward moment of extended silence, Paige said, "If it's all right, I'd like to go to my room."

"Of course," I replied. "Follow me!"

I led the way to the underdecorated guest room and got her settled, finding towels, showing her where the bathroom was and telling her I'd call her to dinner probably in about an hour. She thanked me with a tremulous smile as she closed the door.

As I walked down the steps, I felt like crying.

I sipped Bombay Sapphire on the rocks as I stirred leftover egg noodles to keep them from burning. Chicken Dijon was in the oven on low, reheating.

I called Ty to tell him about Paige and to ask him about his schedule.

"I'm running late," he said. "You and Paige should go ahead and eat dinner."

"Okay."

"I'll call you when I'm leaving."

"Excellent! But probably you should go home," I said. "With Paige here and all. Assuming your electricity is back. 'Cause if it's not, of course you can stay here."

"From what I hear, it is. I'll call you anyway, just to say hey."

"Okay. Good. And tomorrow, Zoë's asked us for dinner."

"Great. I shouldn't have to work too late." He cleared his throat. "So . . . are you okay?"

I paused, listening for sounds that Paige was out of her room before answering. All was quiet.

"I'm okay. Kind of blue, but okay. I'm glad Paige is here. I'm glad there was something I can do for her."

Ty asked how she was holding up, and I talked a little about how vulnerable she seemed to me. He listened to my description, then said, "Don't magnify it, Josie. Considering what she's going through, it sounds to me like she's doing fine."

"Projection," I commented, laughing a little. "I'm projecting my angst onto her. Jeez. You're some smart fella, aren't you?"

"Well, I don't know about that. But I've seen more people who've lost someone they loved to a violent or unexpected death than you have, that's for sure."

"I'm going to tell her about my dad."

He paused for a minute, thinking. "So she'll know you understand?"

"Exactly."

"It'll probably do you good to talk about it, too."

When we were done, I refilled my drink and called Paige to dinner. Hearing Ty's perspective helped me feel less upset about Paige's depression. His point was well taken — *of course* she was depressed.

We ate in companionable semisilence, sitting in my comfortable, warm kitchen. I asked her questions about her classes and favorite subjects and her taste in music, food, clothes, and movies. Poor Paige did her best. Throughout the ordeal she answered every question put to her calmly, smiled politely when appropriate, and at the end, nearly knocked over her chair in her rush to help me clean up, her brown eyes moist, yet distant. Her sadness was manifest, and the entire experience left me feeling excruciatingly powerless, but because of Ty's observation, less worried about her than I might otherwise have felt.

I leaned against the kitchen counter, screwing up my courage to tell her why I could empathize so completely. "Paige?"

"Yes."

"My dad was murdered."

She placed the dish she'd been rinsing in the sink and looked at me. I nodded. "It's been seven years," I said.

"What happened?"

I shook my head. "It's too tough for me to talk about the gory details. Isn't that something? After seven years, it still hurts. I can share my feelings, and I love telling people about him, but I just don't seem able to describe the events surrounding his death."

She nodded and turned back to the sink. "I can understand that. The facts are beside the point."

"Exactly. Does it matter whether he was shot or poisoned or run over? No. What matters is that he's gone."

"And no matter how he died, you've got a hole left inside of you."

"Yeah," I agreed.

"Does that mean the hole stays with you forever?"

I shrugged. "Some days are harder than others. It's like a wound that's healed except for a tender spot or two."

Paige finishing rinsing a pan. As she dried her hands, she said, "Everyone wants me to talk about Rosalie."

"Do you want to?"

"Not really."

"How come?"

"It makes me cry."

I nodded. "Maybe you'll feel differently someday."

"Did you want to tell those stories right away when your dad died?"

I recalled my zombielike demeanor in the immediate aftermath of his death. I'd gone through the motion of living for weeks, ignoring questions and people I hadn't wanted to interact with or even to acknowledge.

"No, not right away. At first, I developed stock answers to unwanted questions. If someone asked what happened to him, like you just did, for instance, I'd reply that I was certain that they understood that it was just too awful for me to talk about." I shrugged. "Almost no one asked a follow-up question after that."

"Some people did?" she asked, appalled.

"Some did, yes. People are curious and some people are just plain rude."

"What did you do?"

"I remember one person I worked with. She said, 'Wow, if you can't talk about it, it must be just horrible. What happened?' " I smiled. "Isn't that funny? Sort of, anyway."

I shrugged again. "I told her, 'Thanks for understanding.' Believe it or not she tried rephrasing the question a couple of more times before she gave up."

Paige averted her gaze. "I've been worrying about what I should say to people when I'm back at school. If they ask, I mean."

I wondered if Paige would be joining Rodney in California. *Maybe it would be better for her,* I thought, *to start fresh in a new location, a place where she could heal at her own pace and not be forced to respond to unwanted questions.*

"I think it depends on how much you're comfortable revealing. Just because people are curious doesn't mean you're obligated to answer their questions."

She shrugged. "I've got to think about it."

"When you're ready, you can practice on me. I'll pretend to ask you impertinent questions so you'll be ready to field them." I paused for a moment to gather my thoughts. "Talking is good, Paige. It helps you clarify your thoughts and feelings. But it's also important that *you* get to decide if and when and to whom you talk."

She nodded. "That makes sense."

"Anyway, if you ever want to talk," I added, "I'm always available to listen."

She nodded, and after several seconds,

whispered, "Thanks. Maybe later."

We were quiet for a few moments. "I have an idea — let's watch a movie," I said.

"Okay."

"Have you ever seen *The Turning Point?* It's one of my all-time favorites."

"No. What's it about?"

"Two ballet dancers."

Paige and I were getting settled onto the sofa when Ty called to say a quick good night.

"Electricity's on," he said.

"That's good news."

"I love you, Josie."

I smiled, inside and out. "Me, too."

"Ready?" I asked Paige after we hung up.

She nodded. "Ready."

I found myself enjoying Paige's reaction to the movie as much as I did the film itself. She leaned forward every time a dance sequence came on screen, her attention riveted.

At the end, I stood up and stretched. "What do you think?" I asked.

"I loved it," she answered breathlessly.

We talked about the movie for a while — how friendship is complicated, how competition changes everything, and how ballet requires such a high level of discipline.

Later, after Paige went to bed, I stood in

the dark and looked out the front window. The house was too quiet, and in the silence, noisy thoughts crowded my head. Thoughts of Rosalie and her secret admirer. Thoughts of Ty's new job and Paige's depression. Thoughts of the greeting card left on my porch and car following me. And always one thought, terrifying in its intensity and impossible to dispel — there was a killer on the loose.

CHAPTER EIGHTEEN

Paige was sitting in the kitchen listening to her iPod when I stumbled in around six the next morning to make coffee. Her hands were folded in her lap, and her eyes were focused in the far distance, over the meadow, past the thick knot of maples and pine trees, toward Ty's sprawling contemporary. She said hello, her mind a million miles away.

"Want some OJ?" I asked.

"Thanks."

I poured the juice and told her I'd make breakfast after I started coffee. I kept half an eye on her as I scooped coffee grounds into the maker. The phone rang, and, startled, I spilled coffee grounds onto the counter.

"Damn," I said, and grabbed the phone. "Hello?"

"It's me," Ty said.

"Hey." I tucked the phone under my chin

to free my hands and finish preparing the coffee. "You're calling early."

"It's Saturday. You start early."

" 'Tis true," I replied.

"You got a sec?" he asked.

"Not really," I replied, glancing at the wall clock. "I'm making breakfast for Paige and me. Then we gotta go."

He cleared his throat. "Actually I'm calling you in my role as police chief."

My heart skipped a beat as I flipped the toggle to start the coffee. "I'm all ears," I said, trying for a light tone.

I snuck a peek at Paige. She was sitting with her back to me, staring through the window. I followed her gaze and saw acres of pristine white snow, then forest. The sky was brilliant blue with fluffy clouds. I edged into the hallway.

"We're following up every lead." He cleared his throat. "I'm telling you because it's police policy to keep victims apprised of our progress."

"Thank you."

"So I wanted to let you know that there are no fingerprints on the greeting card or envelope."

I heard a whoosh and looked toward the coffeemaker. Brown liquid dripped into the pot.

"No surprise," I said, disappointed none-theless.

"No. But we think there's probably a con-nection to Rosalie's secret admirer."

"How come?" I asked, and closed my eyes, braced for bad news.

"One of the shops that delivered the flow-ers is a hole-in-the-wall, cash-only, short-memory sort of place. The others are fully automated. Which means they can tell us how they got the orders. All of the orders came by phone. In every case, the caller used disposable cell phones. They're un-traceable."

"With a two-oh-seven area code?"

"Yeah. Actually, one number was the same as the one used to call you last night."

I felt disassociated, as if I were listening to a discourse on investigative techniques. The information was too frightening to process. "Jeez."

"Yeah," Ty agreed.

"You said they can't be traced, right?"

"Right. If they're on, we can locate them. We keep trying, with no luck. By now they're probably in a landfill somewhere, you know?"

"Wow." A new, terrifying thought occurred to me. "What about if someone calls one of the stores to place an order?" I glanced at

Paige, still sitting in unquiet repose. "To me, I mean?"

"They call us. We've issued an alert."

"What if he calls a new place — one he hasn't used before?"

"It's a general alert. They'll call us, too." His tone softened. "By the way, I assure you that I won't be sending you any flowers in the near future."

"Shame on you."

"I'll hand deliver them. But I'm being serious here, Josie," he added. "In case some slip through and you think they're from me — they're not."

"Got it."

"Tell your staff, okay?"

"Tell them what?"

"If a flower delivery arrives, confirm where the flowers are being sent from. That's all. No one on your staff should make an issue of anything — they shouldn't try to delay the delivery guy or imply there's a problem. Just confirm where they're from and call Officer Brownley."

"Okay," I said, my heart fluttering. "Can I ask you something?"

"Sure."

"If the orders were placed by phone, how did he pay for them?"

"Or she. We're dealing with a husky-voiced individual. The flowers were purchased using prepaid credit cards."

"What are they?"

"They're mostly used by people who are trying to establish credit or have bad credit. They're cash and carry, which means they can't be traced."

"Wow," I said, trying for a light tone, "who knew? But you'd still have the person's name, right?"

"The name he — or she — used was Pat Smith. Even if it's the secret admirer's real name, which I doubt, there's no clue as to whether it's a man or a woman. I've checked — there are more than six thousand Pat Smiths in the country. And there's no indication that Rosalie ever knew anyone by that name."

I felt dazed. "This is pretty scary."

"I want to stress that we know what we're doing and we're damn good at it."

"Okay, then."

"There's more. My new job. They've asked me to come to a meeting in D.C. on Monday."

I sat down on a bench I'd placed near the front door. "And?" I asked.

"I said okay."

"Really," I said because I couldn't think of anything else to say. "How long will you be gone?"

"A few days, I guess. But they asked us to block out the entire week, so who knows."

"Do you know what you're meeting about?"

"Canadian border stuff."

It's such an important job, I thought. I stood up and made my way back into the kitchen. Paige looked up and I raised a finger signaling that I'd only be a minute more.

"You know I wouldn't go if I thought you were in danger," he said.

"I hope you're right," I said, forcing myself to sound chipper. A thought came to me about the nature of hope. *We believe what we want to believe,* my father told me. *And usually, we want to believe there's hope.* "You know that famous saying about hope?"

"Which one?"

" 'Hope springs eternal in the human breast.' "

"Alexander Pope, right?"

"Right. You get my point?"

"No. Or rather, yes, of course I do. But you meant it flippantly, as if your safety was based on hope and a prayer, not reasoned thinking and good police work."

"How about this one: 'A hope beyond the shadow of a dream'?"

"That's good, but even less true. Who

wrote that?"

"Keats."

"We're taking good care of you, Josie. Claire Brownley is a damn good cop."

I believed him, though I didn't know why. I felt the tautness in my shoulders loosen and the sharp pain in my chest ease, just a bit. "Okay, then. I'll trust in police smarts, not mere hope."

"Do you love me?" Ty asked.

"Yes, I do."

"I love you, too."

We hung up and I stood for a moment, clutching the phone to my chest. I was reassured, but just a little. It felt as if I were adrift in the ocean in a small boat during a raging thunderstorm, threatened by roiling waves and lightning strikes. Everything was out of my control, from Ty's new work schedule to Paige's sadness to my secret admirer's intentions.

It was irrational, I knew, but as I stared into the shadows, I felt my nemesis was drawing closer.

"Can I ask you a question?" I asked Paige as we finished scrambled eggs and toast.

"What?" Paige asked.

"You know the photograph of you guys eating ice cream?"

"Uh-huh."

"Who were you looking at? The photographer?"

"Yes."

"Who was it?"

"Paul. Paul Greeley."

I nodded. "Thanks. So . . . we'll go in about a half hour, okay?"

"If it's all right, I just want to stay here," she said quietly.

I insisted, telling her that she could sit in my office and read or listen to music to her heart's content, but I wasn't comfortable leaving her alone in my house. "I have errands today, but there's always someone around at Prescott's. We send out for pizza on Saturdays, so you'll have people to eat with."

"All right," she said unenthusiastically.

Thinking of the desolate days and nights following my father's death when I was inconsolable and unable to be around people, I added, "I understand your wanting to be alone. But it's important that you don't become isolated. You need to be around people, and to let those of us who care about you do things to help you."

She nodded and didn't say another word the whole way to Prescott's.

Gretchen was already at her computer

when we arrived. "Paige is going to spend today with us," I said.

"Super!" Gretchen said warmly, and handed me a pink message sheet.

Mr. Bolton had called to report that the police found no inventory or address book on Rosalie's home or work computers, that the police had her address book — an actual book — and would let me know if the names led to anything related to my appraisal. I shrugged philosophically. It would have been helpful to have the inventory, but we'd do fine without it.

I got a stoic Paige settled upstairs on the love seat. I noted that she was reading Agatha Christie's *And Then There Were None*. Downstairs again, I communicated Ty's instructions about calling the police if flowers were delivered. Gretchen listened, concerned.

"Are you in danger?" she asked.

"No," I assured her with more confidence than I felt. "It's just a precaution. Fill in Sasha and Fred, all right, in case you're not in the office when they're delivered — *if* they're delivered."

"Okay," she said, and copied Officer Brownley's phone number on Post-it Notes that she pressed onto everyone's computer monitor.

"Thanks," I said, and headed over to the tag-sale room where Eric was stretched out under a table.

"Hey, Eric," I said. "What are you up to?"

"Loose screw," he replied, his voice muffled.

A moment later, he pushed himself out from under and slipped the screwdriver into his tool belt as he stood up. "The table was kind of wobbly. It's okay now."

"Excellent! How's Cara doing?" I asked, nodding toward the new white-haired temp.

"Good. She's a quick learner."

"I've got my fingers crossed." I scanned the room. It looked ready for our nine o'clock opening. "Well done, Eric."

He shook his head, embarrassed in the face of praise.

Upstairs again, I glanced at Paige, sitting with her legs tucked under her, reading, and turned my attention to Lesha's letter. It sounded credible, but then I looked at it from a technical perspective.

The font was Courier, typical for typewriters of the 1950s, but then I spotted an oddity — the letters were in perfect alignment. *It was printed on a computer,* I realized. Every letter was equally dark and dense.

No way could a typewriter have produced such perfect text. I remembered using my mother's old Smith Corona. No matter how hard I punched the *M* key, the impression was never as dark as the other letters and the *S* tilted to the left.

I was about to call down to see if Sasha was in yet when I saw another flaw and gaped. *How could I have missed it?* I asked myself. *There were no zip codes in 1959!* I shook my head, shocked at the author's chutzpah.

To confirm my memory, I Googled "zip code" and "history." I was right, zip codes started in 1963, four years after the letter had allegedly been written. I shook my head and thought the situation through.

Just because the letter is a phony doesn't mean the palette is a phony, too, I realized. It could be that when Sasha asked if there was any documentation about the palette, Lesha thought she'd give the appraisal a helping hand by creating the letter. It wasn't unheard-of for heirs to try to goose an object's value by falsifying documents.

Yet, having met Lesha, it was hard to believe that she'd written such an articulate and plausible letter. Which made me wonder more about Evan. I called down to the office. Gretchen answered merrily.

"Is Sasha there?" I asked.

"Taking off her coat as we speak," she said.

"Would you ask her to come up?"

I swiveled toward my window while I waited. Glittering sunlight lit up the bare maple.

"Hi," Sasha said as she stepped inside my office.

Anxiety was evident in the way she spoke that one word, a not unexpected reaction to an unanticipated summons from me. Insecurity always led her to assume the worst. I introduced her to Paige, then handed her the letter.

"It's a phony," I told her, and explained why.

"I could kick myself! I can't believe I missed it!" she exclaimed, aghast at her oversight.

"I know. I had the same reaction."

"At least we discovered it before the appraisal. It could have been worse."

"What now?"

Sasha shook her head, still focused on the letter. "I'd say we're back to the beginning. For all we know, Evan wrote the letter and when Lesha presented it she sincerely believed it was genuine."

"Do you think so?" I asked her.

"I don't know."

"I don't know either. But it wouldn't surprise me to learn that Lesha knew it was fake when she gave it to you."

"The whole situation is shocking, really," she said, dismayed.

"Yeah," I agreed. "You had Fred confirming the addresses in Lesha's letter, right? You should pull him off that job."

"I will. I'm so sorry," Sasha repeated, twisting her hair.

I shrugged. "We all missed it, Sasha. It's why it's good we have lots of eyes looking at things. Fill Fred in, okay?"

She nodded.

"We still have to research Whistler's work habits because the palette could be genuine even if the letter isn't. If you're having trouble tracking information down, I can probably find someone who can help us."

"Okay. I'll let you know."

I asked her to get Fred started on Rosalie's papers. "I need him to look for any reference to anything of value, any place other than her known locations where she might be storing objects or additional papers — anything that might help identify assets."

She nodded.

"Tell him to keep the papers in order in case someone else wants to look at them, okay? Also, please coordinate with Fred to cover the instant appraisal booth. I'll try and do at least an hour or two, but realistically, I don't know how much I'll be able to pitch in today."

Sasha paused at the door to apologize again about failing to recognize Lesha's letter as a fake, and when I reassured her that it was okay, she thanked me for my understanding. Sasha took enormous pride in her appraisals, and I knew that this miss would rankle.

I gazed out the window as I considered the situation. Rainbow sequins prismed off the snow-covered roof of the church across the way.

Who wrote the letter? I wondered. *Lesha? The angry guy in the pickup? Evan?* Suddenly I realized we were taking Lesha's assessment of how she came into possession of the palette at face value. We didn't even know if she stole it, and if so, from whom. Had Evan ever owned it? Had she ever been, in fact, Evan's girlfriend? Had he left a will? My mouth opened as shock registered. Was he even dead? And assuming he was, we didn't know what killed him. Lesha had called it a blood disease. A blood disorder that kills could be anything from leukemia to septic poisoning to AIDS to poison.

I Googled "Evan Woodricky" and "New Hampshire." I found no local Evans. I searched again, this time looking for an Evan Woodricky anywhere in the country, and got three hits. One was into heavy metal bands, another was looking for tactics for growing tomatoes in rocky soil, and a third was on a nine-month assignment teaching English as a second language in Brazil. I shook my head and tried Googling Lesha's name. Nothing. I picked up the phone and called Wes Smith, my best source.

"I was going to call you later today," Wes said. "I got news."

I looked over at Paige. She seemed absorbed in her book, but even so, I didn't want to talk to Wes in front of her.

Losing a parent when you're between ten and twenty is the worst thing that can happen to a child, my father told me the day of my mother's funeral. *At that age, you're old enough to understand the magnitude of your loss but too young to handle it well. Be gentle with yourself, kiddo. You're in for some tough times.* I'd wept at his words, raging against the fates, bitter and unforgiving, cursing God and the doctors and cancer. I carried the scars of that loss with me still.

"I can't really talk."

"Me, either. Let's meet. When?"

I looked at the time display on my computer monitor. It was almost nine. "An hour?" I asked, thinking that would give me time to check out the tag sale before I met him.

"An hour's good. Where?"

"How's the Portsmouth Diner?" I asked.

"Done. See ya," he said, and hung up.

My adrenaline began to flow. Wes didn't make idle boasts. If he said he had news, he did. I could hear it in his voice. Something in his tone conveyed that he didn't just have information, he had answers.

Chapter Nineteen

Not wanting to leave Paige alone in my office, I brought her downstairs and asked Gretchen, "Where are you with the mailing?"

"About halfway through stuffing the envelopes."

Every six weeks or so we sent a promotional mailing to everyone in our customer database. Our next special was for Valentine's Day: On the Saturday before Valentine's Day, everything at the tag sale that was heart shaped or red would be 10 percent off.

"Can I draft you to help Gretchen?" I asked Paige.

"Sure."

"Great! Pull up a chair."

Once Paige was settled in and working, folding flyers in thirds, text side out, and inserting them so that the colorful graphic was visible as soon as the envelope was opened, I headed to the tag-sale shack.

"Do you know how to ice-skate?" I heard Gretchen ask as I was leaving.

"Yeah. I love it. How come?"

"Donna Marie Braun — did you see her in that movie, *After the Springtime?* Oh, my God, isn't she gorgeous? Anyway, she was in Aspen over Christmas skating, and her skates were pink with white polka dots! Isn't that just adorable?"

As I passed out of earshot, I smiled. Gretchen's comforting chatter reassured me that I was leaving Paige in good hands.

I entered the tag-sale room and glanced around.

Inventory was strong. One new acquisition was sure to go fast, a collection of bronze animal bookends. They were only about twenty years old, and as such, they weren't antiques, but they were fun, attractive, and at only fifteen dollars a pair, they were priced to move.

I pulled into the Portsmouth Diner's parking lot just before ten and was settled in a booth near the back when Wes came in.

"You first," Wes said as soon as he slid into the banquette.

"Hi, Wes. How are you?"

"Good, good. Whatcha got?"

"I'm fine, thanks."

"Ha-ha. So?" he asked, wiggling his fingers to speed me up.

I sighed. Wes was, as my mother always said about people who didn't adhere to the standards of common civility, "something like something I don't know."

"Can you find out for me if and how someone died?" I asked.

"Sure. Who died and why do you want to know how?"

"It's in connection —" I broke off as the waitress arrived.

I ordered coffee and a fruit salad, and shook my head as Wes ordered a double side order of bacon and a Coke.

"What kind of breakfast is that?"

"What do you mean?" Wes asked, surprised.

"Bacon and Coke?"

He shrugged. "I like bacon and Coke."

"God, Wes."

"Forget what I eat. Tell me about the dead guy," he said.

I sighed. "As part of an appraisal I'm working on, I've run into . . . well, a situation. . . . I'm following a 'something's fishy' hunch." I described the circumstances, including the fake letter. "I also need to know whether Evan left a will, and if so, whether Lesha's the beneficiary of the palette."

"Got it," he said, taking notes on a sheet of paper. "Can you e-mail me a copy of the letter?"

"Why?"

"For the article. My editor loves exhibits."

"What are you talking about, Wes?"

"I need the letter for the article," he said in a tone indicating he thought I was pretty slow on the uptake. "This is bonzo stuff . . . a young man dead in the prime of life . . . his greedy girlfriend . . . a bogus letter . . . a fortune at stake. . . . I'm telling ya, my editor will love it. Have you decided when you're going to call the cops? I'll want to have a photographer there for the takedown."

"Bonzo?"

"I don't know where it comes from. Maybe I made it up. Bonzo . . . it means great."

I shut my eyes and took a deep breath. Wes sounded depressingly eager to be in for the kill. "First, you tell me about Evan," I said sternly, opening my eyes. "Then we decide whether to involve the police."

"Josie!" he griped. "Time is of the essence. I'm up against a deadline."

"Forget it, Wes."

The waitress brought my coffee and his Coke.

"I'll talk to my editor about delaying," he said, "but I don't know. He's pretty much a hard-ass."

"This isn't a negotiation, Wes. Jeez. You print a word, even an implication, about this, and you'll *never* see that letter. *Never, ever.*"

"And if I hold off?" he asked, looking absurdly young and hopeful as he sipped his Coke.

"Maybe."

He made a face and lost the attitude. "Why *wouldn't* you report it to the police?"

I explained that a falsified letter didn't prove either that the object was counterfeit or that Lesha was the perpetrator of the hoax. "It could have been her boyfriend, or someone else who wrote it."

"How do you decide if you *should* report it?"

I shrugged. "Learning about Evan's death — or whether he's alive — will help."

He eyed me with a speculative gleam. "You decide to bring in the cops, I'm your *first* phone call, right?"

"Yes, that's fair. I can do that."

He double-knuckle-tapped the table, satisfied. "Great. Why don't you e-mail me the letter now so I'm ready? Just for my records."

Give Wes an inch, I thought, *he'll try for a mile.* I shook my head. "No," I said. "What's *your* news?"

He sighed, acquiescing, Wes-style. "I checked everyone's alibi the night Rosalie died."

"And?"

"Unclear. Gerry Fine was at a business dinner followed by a business after-dinner drink."

"Has it been confirmed?"

"So it seems. I mean, the police have Gerry's charge receipt for dinner and they have a cash receipt for the lounge." Wes scanned his notes. "He ate with a vendor from Indianapolis named Petrie who says he went back to his hotel right after dinner."

"So who did Gerry have the drink with?"

Wes grinned. "Apparently, when the police asked that question, Gerry winked and said he can't remember the guy's name."

Rosalie, I thought. "Which restaurant did he go to?"

"The Miller House."

"Nice place," I said.

The Miller House was an elegant, tasteful, and expensive restaurant located in a renovated eighteenth-century Colonial. Ty had taken me there to celebrate our first anniversary.

"Where was Edie?"

"Home the whole night, alone."

I shook my head. "Something's rotten in Denmark."

"Why do you say that?" Wes asked.

"Edie would have joined the business dinner."

Wes shrugged. "She and Gerry both say that he often has business dinners without her."

I nodded. "That sounds pretty solid."

"They're married."

I nodded, his point taken. Not only could Edie not testify against Gerry but I could easily envision her lying to protect him — or, I corrected myself, her way of life. "So . . . what do you think?"

Wes nodded. "The police aren't buying it a hundred percent either. I mean it might be true, but it can't be verified. She joined him for some dinners, but not all. There's more — are you ready for a shockeroonie?"

"I'm braced," I replied, amused.

"It seems that someone tried to call her later and she didn't pick up. She told the police that she heard the phone ring, but didn't feel like talking to anyone, so she let the machine answer it."

"That could be."

"It's possible," Wes agreed, shrugging. "Probably not, though."

"Why do you say that?"

"The limo driver who brought Gerry home reported that Edie's car wasn't in the driveway where she always left it."

"Really? What did she say to that?"

Wes grinned. "That her car was in the garage."

I shrugged. "So?"

"So the driver said she doesn't use the garage. She likes going in through the front door, not the kitchen entrance."

I smiled. That sounded like the sort of thing Edie would do. She'd want her jazzy BMW on display for the neighbors to envy, and for sure she'd think that people like her *only* used the front door.

"What did she say to that?"

"It's hard to believe, but from what I hear, she looked down her nose at the police officer and asked if he was accusing someone of her background of lying."

I laughed. "I can see her saying it as clear as day," I replied, enjoying Wes's amazement.

"Is she really like that?"

"Yes."

Wes shook his head derisively. "Anyway,

Paul Greeley was at a lecture at Harvard," he said.

"Proven?"

"Nope. He had an e-mail exchange with the organizer and clearly stated that he *planned* to attend, but it was open to the public and more than a hundred people were there."

The waitress slid a plate heaped with bacon in front of Wes and a parfait glass full of fruit in front of me. "Want more coffee, dear?"

"Yes, please." To Wes, I asked, "How do you follow up with something like that?"

"The police up here ask the police down there to see if they can find someone who saw him, but you know how that goes," Wes said, crunching bacon.

"No. How?"

He shrugged. "Unless he stood out for some reason, like he got into a hot discussion with the speaker or something, it's more than likely no one would notice him. People were focused on the podium, not one guy out of a hundred."

"I don't know. He's pretty noticeable."

"In what way?"

I smiled, remembering a word my friend Katie had once used to crush me at Boggle. "He's haptic."

"What does that mean?"

"Touchable. I think it's a science word that implies the person has a predilection for the sense of touch, but I was using it in a, shall I say, nonscientific way. Let me put it this way — he's sizzling."

"Yeah, whatever. No one notices anyone no matter what unless there's some drama."

"Come on, Wes, that's silly. Lots of people notice things! Especially good-looking people of the opposite sex."

"I'll prove it to you. Shut your eyes."

I did as he said. "Now what?" I asked.

"Describe someone you noticed here in the restaurant."

I thought about it, and was taken aback at how little I recalled. "There's a woman in a pretty striped sweater sitting at the counter."

"What does she look like?"

"She's got brown hair, I think." I opened my eyes. "Wow, I see what you mean. I noticed the sweater, not the woman. And not much else." I surveyed the diner. There were maybe twenty people scattered at tables, booths, and the counter, and I hadn't registered anyone in particular.

Then I saw Ned Anderson standing at the counter waiting for a take-out order. I almost didn't recognize him. Instead of a business suit, he was wearing his traditional leather duster over a Western-style shirt and Levi's topped by a wide-brimmed hat. His brown alligator cowboy boots sported half-inch heels. He leaned on his walking stick with his chin up and his chest out as if he were a king surveying his loyal subjects, not a customer in a diner watching a short-order cook flip pancakes. His royal demeanor reminded me of a painting I'd seen years ago in London's National Gallery of Napoleon leaning against his scepter, his pride and entitlement evident in the tilt of his head and cast of his eyes. From the profile, Ned seemed to have no chin at all, and his Adam's apple looked twice as big as from the front.

As if he could feel my eyes on him, he turned and looked at me. He smiled, pocketed his change, picked up his to-go bag, and said something to the cashier. I looked away.

"What are you looking at?" Wes asked.

"Ned Anderson."

Wes's eyes fired up. "Where is he?"

"By the cash register."

"Introduce me, okay?" he asked with a reporter's zeal.

Before I could reply, the waitress came and handed me a note. "That fellow asked that I give you this," she said, nodding in

Ned's direction.

"Thanks."

I accepted a folded piece of cheap note-pad paper, opened it, and read: *Didn't want to interrupt. Got a sec to talk? Ned*

To Wes, I said, "I'll be right back."

"What's up?" he asked, his news antenna activated and on full alert.

I shrugged. "I have no idea."

I slid out of the booth and joined Ned where he was waiting by the entryway.

"Josie!" Ned said as I approached. "Fancy meeting you here."

"Hi, Ned."

"I was just thinking of you."

"Why's that?" I asked, not really wanting to know.

"Today's your tag-sale day, right?"

"Every Saturday, yes."

"I was thinking I might stop by and take a look. Do you have any Western art?"

I thought about that. "There may be some art prints, I'm not sure. Maybe a couple of pieces of Indian jewelry — silver and turquoise, Hopi, I think."

"How can you run a business without knowing your inventory?" he asked, pretending to be shocked.

"I'm pleased to report that we turn our inventory pretty darn quickly."

"All the more reason to know it. I bet your employees are robbing you blind."

What a misanthrope! I thought spitefully. "Thanks for the tip," I said, wishing he hadn't asked to talk to me.

"Busy with the new appraisal assignment?"

"A little," I said, purposefully vague.

"And talking to a reporter? Aren't you a busy bee."

"Do you know Wes?" I asked.

"Only by his writing and photograph." He leaned forward and whispered, "Are you giving him a scoop?"

I stepped back. "Hardly."

"Are you going to be at your tag sale today?"

"In and out."

"Maybe I'll stop by."

"You'll have to let me know if you find anything. 'Bye," I said, turned, and returned to the booth quickly, wanting to get away before he could make another nasty remark.

As I slipped into the booth, Wes commented, "So that's Ned Anderson. How come you didn't bring him over?" He sounded hurt.

"Give me a break, Wes."

Wes and I watched Ned pick his way through the icy parking lot to his midnight blue Volvo.

"So, where were we?" I asked. "I remember — you'd just finished proving to me that trying to prove that Paul Greeley was at that Harvard lecture would be an exercise in futility."

"Right, right," he said. "They'll try and nail it down, but . . ." He flipped a hand.

"What about Cooper?"

"At Hitchens, working."

"Anyone see him?"

"Only early on. No one saw him — or his car — after eight."

"So let me get this straight — of Gerry, Edie, Paul, and Cooper, only Gerry's alibi has been verified."

"I don't know about verified. Seconded is more like it."

"What do you mean?"

"The restaurant and lounge were busy. Yes, Gerry was there for dinner with the vendor guy. His charge receipt gives the timing and his driver confirms that he took him from work directly to the restaurant and directly home afterwards with no stops in either direction. Yes, the bartender and waitress noticed him in the lounge later. But he paid cash for the drinks and no one remembers seeing him leave, and his driver says he doesn't remember exactly when he drove him home, so the timing is up in the air." He shrugged. "Maybe it's true. But as alibis go, none of them are worth much."

I looked out of the plate-glass window into the far distance, trying to make sense of Wes's information. I'd expected to leave with answers, and instead I had more questions. The waitress refilled my coffee cup without asking.

"If you were me, what would you do at this point?" Wes asked.

"I'm still curious about how Rosalie's tote bag ended up at Heyer's."

"According to my source, the police don't know. They tested the bag and everything in it for fingerprints, and found only Rosalie's. Except for the diary — that had Edie's prints on it, too — and yours."

I nodded and looked down, ashamed.

"What did she write about?" Wes asked, never one to miss an opportunity.

I shook my head.

"Josie!"

"Forget it, Wes. What about the tote bag itself? Were there any prints on it?"

Wes sighed loudly, disappointed. "Only smudges. What else do you want to know?"

Consider the basics, I reminded myself. What did I actually know about Rosalie? She was, by my observation and by all accounts, a good sister, a fun friend, and a hard worker. And she clearly enjoyed men.

She'd been with Paul for a while, and recalling the tiger's *gggrrrr* she'd playfully growled when describing him to me the first time we'd seen each other socially, she was a hottie. She was with Gerry when she died. Had there been other men as well?

When Officer Brownley had asked if Rosalie had been involved with Cooper, I'd dismissed it out of hand. Now I wondered if it could have been true. My nose wrinkled. *Not in this lifetime!* I thought. But I'd said the same about Gerry.

"Have you run into any references to someone named Chief?" I asked.

"No. Who's Chief?"

"I don't know. Maybe an ex-boyfriend."

"Tell me," Wes instructed.

"There's nothing to tell. I ran into a reference to someone named Chief, that's all."

"Where?"

"It doesn't matter."

"It might. Where?" he pushed.

I cocked my head, thinking about what, if anything, to reveal. I decided that the scrapbook, which I'd seen in the course of my official work, was fair game, but not the diary.

"Rosalie kept a scrapbook," I said. "There

272

were a couple of cards from someone who signed his or her name 'Chief.' That's all I know."

"How did you get to see the scrapbook?" Wes asked, sounding as if he resented what he perceived as an investigative coup.

"I'm doing a comprehensive appraisal."

He nodded. " 'Chief,' huh? No other clues to his identity?"

"Not that I know of."

I turned again to look out the window. It was streaked with salty residue. "I'm trying to understand what's going on, Wes. Nothing makes sense to me — there seems to be no pattern to anything."

"Specifically . . . what sticks out in your mind?"

"I don't know." I thought about Wes's question as I picked at a sad-looking chunk of honeydew melon, then shrugged. "Have the police learned anything else about the splinters?"

"They've sent samples somewhere for analysis. Nothing yet."

"Have you heard any speculation on why she was at the jetty in the first place?"

"No." Wes spoke the word as if he hated admitting that there was something he didn't know.

"You said Paige didn't know where Rosalie went?" I asked. "Doesn't that seem weird?"

"Not necessarily. Rosalie gave the age-old answer to avoid telling. She said she was 'out with friends.' "

I couldn't help smiling. The mere thought of Wes, who was about a dozen years younger than me and so naive when it came to women he'd had to ask *me* where to take a girl to dinner, recounting an age-old answer as if he were a grizzled old wise man, was a laugh and a half.

"What else would you ask if you were me?"

What else? I repeated silently. *We know almost nothing. We know the manner of death but not the means or whether it was murder or manslaughter. We know the likely motive — jealousy. Or was it? What about Rosalie's treasure?* I asked myself. *And as for opportunity, everyone, it seemed, had — or might have had — opportunity. What else do we need to know?* My mind was a blank. I looked at Wes and shrugged. "You know what I think?"

"What?"

"I think the smartest thing I can do right now is to get back to my tag sale."

CHAPTER TWENTY

As I merged with traffic on I-95, I noticed a boxy, dark-colored sedan two cars back that seemed to be pacing me. If I pulled out into the passing lane, it did, too. When I returned to the middle lane, it followed suit. My worry meter whirred onto medium alert. The car looked similar to the one that had been close when Paige and I drove through the snow, but I hadn't got a good enough look to know for sure. *It looks the same as the one that idled by my hedge, too,* I realized, and the thought spawned bristly apprehension.

I tried to see who was driving, but from such a distance, and at such a speed, I couldn't. I couldn't make out if there was a front license plate, let alone determine if it was registered in New Hampshire. The reflecting sun dazzled me and made my eyes tear.

I tried to lose him.

I quick-zipped into the passing lane without signaling, slammed my foot onto the gas, passed three cars in seconds, and as an exit ramp approached, confirmed that the lanes next to me were clear. I spun the steering wheel hard to the right and slowed as if I intended to get off the interstate.

The car mimicked my actions. *What do you want?* I silently asked him, then I shouted the words aloud. "Tell me! What do you want?"

I cruised past the exit and considered my options. I didn't feel threatened exactly. The driver didn't tailgate or try to intimidate me by pulling up alongside me or dashing in front and slowing down. I wanted him to go away, but not until I discovered his identity. *If I can lead him onto surface roads where we'd go slower,* I thought, *I'll have a better chance of identifying the car or the driver, or both.* I sought out a reference point, trying to calculate how far it was to the next exit. I recognized a minimall visible through the leafless trees. *About three miles,* I thought.

I glanced at the rearview mirror. The car had disappeared. *Has it slipped back? I* considered and scanned the highway. *No.* I looked ahead and there it was, far ahead of me and speeding up. While I was busy planning an exit strategy, the other guy up and got himself out of Dodge. *Damn,* I thought. I began to wonder if the whole situation was only my imagination at work. *Maybe,* I told myself, *it's just a false alarm.* But as soon as I had the thought, I discarded it. It *wasn't* a false alarm. Speeding ahead that way was a clever ploy by someone determined to scare me while avoiding exposure. Impulsively, I hit the accelerator. *Two can play at this game.*

I gained on him, pulling closer as I carefully weaved through the morning commuters. Soon I was going seventy, then seventy-five. My car was older and smaller, and I was struggling to keep up, and as I pushed toward eighty, it felt too risky to continue the pursuit. Instead, I tried to memorize the car's shape, seeking out distinguishing features, but I couldn't.

The entire vehicle was smeared with mud and salt residue. At first the car appeared black, but sometimes, when a glint of blinding sunlight hit it, it looked dark green, and then a moment later, navy blue. Even the car's brand and logo were masked, and despite concentrating hard, I couldn't make out a single digit of the license plate, but it was definitely a New Hampshire tag. The person driving was huddled over the steering wheel. He — or, I realized, with a start, for all I knew, *she* — wore a watch cap, pulled low; unstylish, wraparound sunglasses; gloves; and a thick, dark overcoat.

A minute later, I gave up. Watching with impotent frustration as the car disappeared around a bend, I tried to think what I should do next. As the crisis passed from the initial, critical phase to the assessment phase, I started breathing fast. The car was long gone, and I had no meaningful description. Paralyzing fear enveloped me.

I parked around the side of my building, near a stand of birch. My hands were shaking from the aftereffects of the panic-fired episode, and my mind was churning with agitated thoughts.

There were three people whose identity was unknown: the person in the car I now thought of as my stalker, the secret admirer who'd left me a greeting card, and Rosalie's murderer. I shivered. *Was one person responsible for all three acts?*

I leaned my head against the steering wheel.

Something exploded on the roof and I jerked upright, then sank down, hunched over, my mouth falling open, looking everywhere at once and seeing nothing but the unplowed expanse of my back parking lot and the impenetrable forest beyond. Another explosion rattled the back window. I ducked, scooting sideways to the passenger's side, and rolled onto the floor under the dashboard. I hit my head and scraped the side of my hand. My heart was thumping so furiously it felt as if it were trying to escape my chest. I had no idea why, but it was clear that I was under attack. I couldn't swallow and I could barely breathe. I clenched my eyes shut and tried to think how to escape. There was no way out.

Another bursting thump. And another.

Time passed.

I kept my head down, huddled in a ball, with both feet jammed under the seat.

Is the attack over? I wondered. With no way to tell whether my unknown, unseen enemy was gone or merely regrouping, I stayed where I was, unable to think of anything to do to save myself.

Three more shocks punched the car in quick succession, then there was another letup, longer this time, and after what felt like an hour but was probably only a few minutes, I opened my eyes, elbowed my torso high enough to peek, and saw star-bursts of snow scattered on the rear window.

I shut my eyes, then opened them again. I'd panicked because someone had chucked snowballs at my car, I thought, embarrassed. I hoisted myself up onto the seat and sat for a while longer, taking deep breaths, and then I was fine. I spent a minute rubbing and stretching my limbs to help my blood flow.

Squatting backward on the front seat, I had a clear view of most of the parking lot, and I saw two teenage boys horsing around, running and jumping, and hurling snowballs at each other. Probably their parents were shopping at the tag sale.

I reviewed the time line. Just before the first strike, I'd rested my head on my steering wheel, so they hadn't seen me. They thought the car was empty, and they were just having fun, probably competing over which of them could hit it from the greatest distance.

I remembered something my father told me when I was in college. I'd been struggling to maintain a decent grade in a required course on statistics. After my dismal showing on the midterm exam, my father said, *When you have clear evidence that you're not able to accomplish something on your own, stop pretending that you're more talented, experienced, or skilled than you are, and get help.* I signed up for tutoring, worked like a dog, and nailed an A on the final. Achieving that A was among my proudest accomplishments.

I remained ambivalent about whether the car that had frightened me had, in fact, been following me. Deciding to err on the side of caution, I called Ty. He was unavailable, I was told, and I wondered whether he was interrogating someone, and if so, whom.

The engine had been off for a long time, and I became aware of the encroaching cold. I needed to either turn on the heater or get inside. I leaned back against the headrest for a moment, watching streaks of pale clouds floating high in the bright blue sky. I heard a high-pitched squawk close by, then saw a gray-white bird swoop and rise and fly away. Glancing in the rearview mirror, I saw two cars enter and one leave the lot.

Tag-sale day was well under way. *Time to get to work,* I told myself. I called Officer Brownley and got her voice mail. I left an awkward-sounding message half apologizing for having no information to share but wanting to alert her to a possible stalking event. The message sounded convoluted and stupid to my ear, and I wished I hadn't called.

After another minute, girding myself to put on my professional face, I got out of the car and trekked over crusty snow toward the front.

Paige was licking her fingers as I entered the office. The pizza had arrived.

"You're kidding!" she said to Gretchen, her eyes alight with pleasurable interest.

"I'm not either! It's true."

"I don't believe it!" Paige said, laughing.

It was a delight to hear Paige laugh, and the joyous sound drew a smile from me. "What don't you believe?" I asked.

"The pizza diet!" Paige said.

"What's that?"

The Teenager's Best Way to Lose Weight, Gretchen quoted.

"For real?"

"Absolutely."

"I'm with Paige. It sounds hard to believe," I remarked, scooping a still-warm slice of mushroom pizza out of the box.

"I just read about it in *Celebrities Up-Front.* Twenty-two percent of teenage actresses use it as their number-one form of weight control," Gretchen said earnestly.

I knew that Gretchen's addiction to gossip, celebrity and otherwise, wasn't all that unusual. Lots of people enjoy the innocent pastime of keeping up with other people's doings. But it never ceased to amaze me how much of it Gretchen believed.

"Go figure," I said to avoid an argument.

Gretchen stood up and smoothed her skirt. "Not that it hasn't been fun discussing strategies for maintaining our girlish figures," she said, vamping a little, winking at Paige, "but I've got to relieve Eric."

"Thanks, Gretchen," Paige said shyly.

"Oh, please, are you kidding me? I'm the one who should be thanking you." To me, she added, "Paige finished stuffing the envelopes." She smiled at Paige. "When you're done eating, come and join me at the cash register if you want. You can help bag."

"Okay, thanks."

"Gretchen's just great, isn't she?" I asked after she'd gone.

"Oh, yes! She's *so* nice. And *so* funny!"

Listening to Paige recount Gretchen's gossip-addicted discourse, I realized that I, for whatever reason, had assumed the mantle of protector. Gretchen was all about fun. I didn't feel jealous exactly, but I was aware of wishing that Paige would interact with me with the same joie de vivre that I'd just witnessed in her exchange with Gretchen.

After we were done eating, I brought Paige

to the cashier's station. I needed to relieve Sasha in the Prescott's Instant Appraisal booth. Sasha, in turn, would rotate into the front office to cover the phone while Gretchen was at the cash register.

I stepped in through the waist-high door and sat behind the desk, and turned to greet the first person in the queue. "Come on in," I said to an attractive, fifty-something woman. She had intelligent eyes, short, wavy gray hair, and an easy smile. As I welcomed her, I kept one ear and half an eye on the activities and people milling about on the sales floor. "I'm Josie Prescott," I said to the woman sitting across from me.

"Hi. I'm Barbara Evans."

"Welcome. Let's get a look at your object. What do you have?"

"A vase."

She handed me a lovely ivory-colored ewer, hand painted with pink and red flowers, and stamped LIMOGES on the bottom.

"How did you come to own it?" I asked as I peered inside, and slowly rotated it, examining the entire surface.

"It was my mother's. She got it from *her* mother, my grandmother, who always said it was hand painted."

I noted some minor paint flecking on the

spout and rim and a hairline crack along the bottom.

"Yes, that's true." I smiled to mitigate the impact of my next comment. "But it's not unique — or even, I'm afraid, particularly rare."

"How do you know?"

I pointed to the barely visible line that ran along the handle and spout. "Do you see this?" I asked. "It's a seam. It indicates that the pitcher was manufactured using a mold."

"Which means it was mass produced," she said, understanding the implication.

"Exactly. The Limoges region of France has been a major porcelain exporter for more than two hundred years. A lot of the work done there is mass produced."

"What's this one worth?"

I stroked the satiny finish. It might not be rare, but it was certainly lovely. "I would expect it to bring about thirty dollars at auction."

"Thirty dollars!" Barbara exclaimed. "I can't believe it! That's all?"

"It's worth more than that to you, am I right?" I asked, smiling.

She laughed. "Are you kidding? To me, it's priceless. . . . I'd never sell it!"

"You think of your mom and grandmother

every time you look at it, right?"

"Exactly."

"Lucky you."

"Thank you," she said, her tone serious and thoughtful. "That's very kind of you."

Barbara Evans stood up and shook my hand, and cradling her grandmother's vase like a baby, she left the booth.

The next person in line, a tall old man with a cane, stepped forward.

"Hi," I said. "I'm Josie Prescott."

"Hi. Melvin Isaacson."

"Welcome. What did you bring today?"

With a trembling hand, he rested his cane against the table and extracted a folk art cabin cruiser from a large canvas boat bag and rested it on the table.

"Wow!" I said. "It's a beauty."

It was a good size, about eighteen by twelve inches, and crudely carved out of walnut. It gleamed from careful polishing. The maker's mark read: MISTY MISS, REGISTERED STATE OF MAINE, 1824, JOSIAH DRAKE.

"Look inside," he said proudly.

I squinted, trying to see through the tiny windows. The interior was accurately rendered. There was a miniature captain's chair and steering wheel, benches and drop-down tables, a brass railing, and light fixtures. It was charming. I examined it carefully, seeking out signs of rot, insect infestation, cracks, or other damage, but there were none. It was a magnificent example of American folk art, in stellar condition.

"What do you know about it?"

"Not much of anything. My wife found it in her aunt's attic about a month ago. We had to clean it out after she died. We never saw it before."

"How about her husband?"

"She was a maiden lady."

I nodded. "Give me a minute," I said, and turned to the computer.

I brought up a browser and logged on to one of the many proprietary sites we used to keep current with prices. I knew that folk art was popular right now, and in our region, maritime artifacts were always popular, but I didn't know the name Josiah Drake, nor did I know whether cabin cruisers held any special allure. The sites I consulted gave me significant information, but of a general nature, and I had a hunch that this object was special and worth more research.

Mr. Isaacson waited patiently as I searched three separate sites and IM'd Shelly, a former colleague from my Frisco days. Shelly had remained neutral during the meltdown that followed the whistle-blowing debacle, a far kinder reaction than that showed by most of my so-called friends. While Shelly and I were no longer close, she called on me periodically for tips on how to approach off-the-wall appraisals and was always accessible when I needed specific information likely to be in her head or at her fingertips. Since I knew that Shelly was more likely to go somewhere without her purse than without her BlackBerry, I figured there was a good chance that I could reach her immediately. I crossed my fingers that she was online.

She was.

Condition? she IM'd back in response to my succinct description of the boat.

Near mint. Crude carving. Signed.

Crude, folk art crude? Or crude crude?

I smiled. I could hear Shelly's diction in the question. *Folk art crude,* I replied. *Let me send you a photo.*

Cool.

Mr. Isaacson happily agreed to the taking and e-mailing of photos, and within a minute I'd sent four shots off via e-mail; in another minute, Shelly was back with a reaction. *Nothing on Drake. Great-looking boat. Your thoughts as good as mine.*

I signed off. "It's a beautiful piece," I

started, "but Josiah Drake isn't known as a folk artist."

He snorted. "So you got to be famous to be of value?"

"No, but I don't want to mislead you. It helps."

"So where does that leave us?"

"With a fabulous example of craftsmanship, probably American made."

"How much is it worth?" he asked, eyes narrowed, ready to argue.

"About two thousand dollars."

"Really? That's not nothing." A slow grin transformed his face. "You think a museum might want it?"

"Absolutely."

"Which one?"

We discussed his options and he shook my hand, satisfied and eager to discuss with his wife donating the boat to a Maine maritime museum in her aunt's name.

"If you're thinking of donating it, probably you want to get a formal appraisal. For tax purposes."

"Makes sense."

As Mr. Isaacson made his way out of the booth, I glanced around.

Fred was showing off the davenport repro to a young mother, her baby asleep on her shoulder. Paige was helping Gretchen wrap a pair of glass candlesticks in bubble wrap.

As a young man stepped into the booth ready for his turn, Sasha approached.

"It's Ty," she whispered. "He's on the phone and he says it's urgent that he talk to you."

I met her worried eyes. "Can you sit in for me?" I asked, then said, "Excuse me," to the young man before heading to my office at a full trot.

"Officer Brownley had me listen to your message," Ty said.

"I felt kind of stupid leaving it," I confessed, still breathless from my run across the warehouse and up the spiral stairs to my office. "I really had nothing to say."

"No, you did the right thing. You didn't recognize the driver?"

"No."

"Tell me about it in as much detail as you can remember."

I described the cat-and-mouse chase I'd had with the other car.

"Was it a BMW?" he asked when I was finished.

"Could be. You know I'm pretty lame when it comes to cars. All I can tell you is that it was a kind of boxy sedan and definitely dark in color."

"Did you think to look for the name of the car? You know what I mean — sometimes there are chrome numbers or letters."

"I tried, but I couldn't see anything," I said, then added, "Can I ask you something, Ty?"

"Sure. What?"

"Who do *you* think is following me?" My throat constricted as I spoke and I ended up choking and coughing. "Sorry," I managed, and took a sip of water from the bottle I keep on my desk. *Fear,* I thought. *Fear'll kill ya.*

"It's too early to say. We have to keep looking for something that points to someone in particular. Everyone involved seems to drive a dark sedan, for instance, so your description doesn't help us narrow the field — or expand it either."

"Figures, huh." I brushed hair out of my eyes. "Ty?"

"What?"

"I'm kind of scared. What should I do?"

He was quiet for a moment. *Why?* I asked myself. *What does he know that he doesn't want to reveal?*

"I've arranged for extra patrols," he said, his tone subdued. "And you know to call at the least sign of anything. Don't wait, don't hesitate, don't delay. Let us help you."

"Okay," I said quietly. "But it sounds like there's not much you, or I, can do."

"We're looking into lots of different things, Josie."

Suddenly I was having trouble breathing. "Do I need to hire Chi again?" I asked, referring to the bodyguard I'd employed last year.

"I have no reason to think so. Tonight, I'll take a look around and touch base with the night duty officer."

"Okay, then," I replied, trusting the system, trusting Ty.

"See you around six-thirty?"

"Perfect."

After we hung up, I sat at my desk for a while, feeling weak. I felt lucky and grateful to have Ty in my life. I took a deep breath and picked up the phone to call Zoë and tell her that Ty would be at dinner.

CHAPTER TWENTY-ONE

Paige sat cross-legged on the love seat, leaning over her backpack, rustling around for something. I was at my desk, a stack of photographs in front of me.

"Paige?" I asked.

"Yes?" she replied, looking up.

"I wanted to let you know that Ty, Chief Alverez, is coming with us to Zoë's tonight."

"He is?" she asked, immediately wary. "Why?"

"He's a friend of mine," I replied, leaving the explanation simple. "You've met him, right?"

She nodded. "Twice."

"About Rosalie?"

She nodded again and looked down at the carpet. "He told me what happened to her. Then he talked to me about her later."

Suddenly my eyes welled and until I blinked the tears away, I couldn't speak. After a moment's silence, I said, "I'm going to do some work. Are you okay?"

"Yeah. Is there any way I could check e-mail?"

"Sure. You can use my computer. I'll switch places with you."

Ten minutes later, I interrupted Paige again. "I hate to bother you, but I could use some help."

"Sure."

"Come here for a sec."

She came and sat next to me on the love seat.

"These are images of your sister's scrapbook. I know it might be painful for you to look at them, but do you think you could? You might recognize something that could provide information about places she hung out, people she knew, that sort of thing."

She nodded, her eyes big and somber.

"The video captured every two-page spread. Gretchen printed them out."

With trembling fingers, she accepted the stack of photographs. She bit her lip as she turned the photos over, one at a time.

"I remember when she went to this movie," she commented, tapping the ticket stub.

"Who did she go with?" I asked.

"I don't remember. Maybe I never knew."

"It's okay," I said, nodding encouragingly.

"Who's Chief?" she asked.

"Good question. I don't know."

"Maybe Paul," she said. "I don't really remember, but I think maybe Rosalie used to call him Chief."

"That's right — he's a volunteer fire-fighter, right?" *Deputy chief.* I hadn't made the connection, and now my heart began to pound at the thought. *I need to tell the police.*

She nodded and resumed her review. "I remember this," she said, pointing at a postcard from a North Conway ski lodge. "I stayed with the Reillys when she went away for the weekend. That was last November."

"Who'd she go with? Did she tell you?"

"A 'hot date,' she said," Paige repeated, unembarrassed at the quote.

She turned to the next photo. "Oh!"

"What is it?" I asked.

She pointed to an image of a frilly coaster with the initials TMH monogrammed in the center, and said, "That's from Rosalie's favorite restaurant. She took me there once."

"Do you remember its name?"

"The Miller House. It was nice, but Rosalie said it wasn't a sister sort of place. It was a dating place." Paige rolled her eyes. "She went there a lot."

"Who with?" I asked.

"Everyone. I mean, everyone she dated. This was the place she liked best for dinner."

I nodded, and said, "Keep looking."

She began turning sheets again. "Oh, look!" Paige said, and gulped. She began to cry.

"What is it?" I asked, handing her a tissue.

She wiped the wetness, swallowed hard, and patted her eyes. "This bit of ribbon. It was from my Christmas gift to her last year."

"What did you give her?"

"Some note cards with artichokes on them. Rosalie liked to send handwritten notes."

I nodded. "Me, too."

When Paige was done, with no additional revelations to offer, I thanked her. She said she was done with e-mail and dug out her iPod, her expression glum.

I returned to my desk and swiveled to look out my window and cast my eyes north. The Miller House, where Gerry had eaten the night Rosalie was murdered, was located in Maine. *Just like those disposable cell phones, the ones that were used to call me.* I glanced at the time — it was after two, the tail end of lunch, a slow time for a restaurant. Within a minute, I had a plan.

I went to Hitchens's Web site, navigated to Rosalie's department's home page, and eventually found what I was looking for, photos of each teaching assistant. That took care of Rosalie and Paul Greeley. Cooper's photo was on the faculty page. I found Gerry's photo on the Heyer's home page — *no surprise since he's such a narcissist,* I thought.

It was tougher finding a usable image of Edie. I finally located a pretty good three-quarter profile of her from their yacht club's newsletter and, indulging a last-minute brainstorm, decided to add another attractive female, Una, into the mix. I was able to extract her image from a group photo on the Heyer's Web site, from a page titled "Company Fun."

Using Photoshop, I cropped them, sized them to match one another, and printed them out. Slipping my handiwork into see-through plastic sleeves, I told Paige, "I've got to go out for a while. I'll be a couple of hours, probably. You can hang with Gretchen downstairs, okay?"

Gretchen was in the front office typing. "Hi," she said, with spurious cheer.

From that one word I could sense that something was wrong. "You okay?"

She made a comical expression. "I just asked that fellow, Paul, for a date and got shot down," she told me.

"You're kidding!" I exclaimed.

"Always the way," she said, resigned.

"He's nuts."

"Thanks."

Paul's got to be crazy, I thought. Why a man wouldn't pursue an attractive, sweet young woman like Gretchen was beyond me. In fact, I didn't understand why men didn't *flock* to Gretchen. And if it mystified me, it must have completely baffled her.

I stepped outside and paused, looking around. Since I wasn't stupid, foolish, or in denial, it was only prudent to check for anything amiss near and between the parked cars before I ventured off the stoop. *Nothing.*

There were three dark-colored, boxy sedans amongst the dozen or so vehicles parked near the tag-sale entrance. I shook my head, surprised to realize how many cars look similar to one another — and to the one that had been following me.

None of the three was streaked with salt or covered with mud, but neither had any of them been freshly washed, and I suspected none of these was the car that had chased and frightened me.

Sitting in my car, I called Officer Brownley and left a voice mail about Paul maybe being the man Rosalie had called Chief.

A voice inside me, one that I didn't want to listen to but couldn't quiet, kept questioning my ability to cope. A cloud bank momentarily blocked the sun, darkening my view, and shivers ran up and down my arms and back.

Driving along the secondary routes and then onto the interstate, I kept alert for anomalies, and saw nothing untoward. I looked over my shoulder. Was someone there watching me, far enough away that I didn't see or sense him — *or her,* I reminded myself — yet close enough to track my movements? It was a terrifying sensation, and one that I couldn't seem to shake.

The Miller House was located in Eliot, Maine, not far from the bridge that connected New Hampshire to Maine. Walking up the flagstone pathway from the big parking lot, where I parked reassuringly close to the front door, I admired the mature landscaping and freshly painted white siding. Inside, I was greeted by the aroma of cranberries mixed with something else, cinnamon maybe.

Sensory branding, I thought. I'd just read an article about it. Big-name retailers were using carefully crafted scents to foster brand awareness and develop customer loyalty. I'd been toying with the idea of trying it out at Prescott's.

A smiling hostess in a dimity print shirt-dress greeted me. "May I help you?"

She was probably on the shady side of forty and looked smart and sassy, like the kind of broad who'd tell an apologetic drunk that he had more excuses than a pregnant nun and to call a taxi and get on home to sleep it off.

I turned on my most disingenuous smile, a thousand-watter. "I don't know . . . I have a kind of off-the-wall question. I hope you'll bear with me."

"Sure," she said, intrigued.

"I'm an antiques appraiser, and in the course of an estate appraisal, I've come across something that I think comes from your restaurant. If so, and if I can connect the dots, I might be able to locate some more of the owner's possessions. Also, it's possible that you might be able to help me figure out who she was hanging out with. And that may lead me to more of her things as well."

"That sounds pretty complicated."

"Yeah," I acknowledged. "Here's the thing. I have two extra keys. I don't know what they go to. If I can find *that* out, then I may discover that she has more objects for me to appraise."

"I'm not really following you."

"I'm not doing a good job of explaining." I sighed. "It's a coaster."

"What is?" she asked, becoming impatient.

"The item that told me she'd been here. Do you still use those monogrammed doily ones?"

"Yes, certainly."

I nodded. "That's what I found in her scrapbook. So I know she had at least one special meal here."

A couple walked past us on their way out, and thanked the hostess for a lovely lunch. The dining room was empty.

"Who?" she said.

"Rosalie Chaffee," I said, and showed the hostess the photo I'd brought along.

Her eyes flew to my face. "That's the dead girl."

"Yes."

"I told the police everything I knew," she said.

"Which was what?"

"Why do you want to know what I told the police?"

I looked at her intelligent eyes. *When in doubt,* my father instructed me, *tell the truth. People don't expect it, and it sets you apart as a winner.*

"I'm trying to help Rosalie's sister, Paige. She's only twelve. Oh, golly, I haven't even introduced myself." I extended a hand. "I'm Josie Prescott."

She shook it and seemed to relax a bit.

"And you are?" I asked.

"Betty Murphy."

"Nice to meet you, Betty. I've been hired by the lawyer representing the estate, and the sole beneficiary is Rosalie's sister, Paige, who as I said, is only twelve. I have a letter here that explains my role. Let me show it to you." I reached into my tote and extracted a business card and Mr. Bolton's authorization letter. "Here," I said, handing her the letter.

She read it carefully and handed it back. "I'm glad to help. Rosalie was one of my favorite customers."

"She came here often?"

"Yes. At least once a week. Sometimes more."

"Who'd she come with?"

"Various people."

"She was here the night she died, right?" I asked, taking a flyer.

302

"Right. She came in for a drink."

I can't believe it! I thought, and then I could. I'd asked the question just because, and hadn't really expected to receive confirmation that she'd been at the restaurant. "Who with?" I asked.

"Gerry Fine of Heyer's Modular Furniture. The police had me look up his charge receipt. He had a business dinner first — he used his company charge card."

Rosalie was here with Gerry on the night Rosalie died — and the police knew it. "Had she been here with him before?" I asked Betty, knowing the answer would be yes.

"Yes," she said. "Very often. She and Mr. Fine often had business dinners here."

Yeah, right, I thought. *Business dinners, my caboose. Gerry got his company to pay for his meals with Rosalie.* Somehow that made the whole affair sleazier than ever. *What a cretin,* I thought.

"Did Rosalie ever come here with other people?"

"Sure. She was a regular guest."

"Did she ever come with him?" I asked, showing Paul's photo.

"Yes," she said, nodding. "But not for a while."

"You have a good memory," I remarked, smiling.

303

She blushed, pleased. "It's part of my job to remember guests. And of course, the police have just asked the same questions."

"When was the last time you saw him?" I asked, holding up Paul's photo.

"I went through the charge receipts for the police. Paul Greeley, right? The last one from him was in October."

"How about him?" I displayed Cooper's photo. "Do you recognize him?"

She took the plastic sleeve and looked at his photo for a long time, tilting her head, concentrating. "He doesn't look familiar to me."

I nodded. "How about her?" I asked, showing Edie's picture.

She cocked her head, thinking. "I don't think so."

"This one?" I asked, handing her Una's photo.

"Now, this is one the police didn't show me . . . yes," she said, tapping the plastic with her finger. "I've seen her. But not with Rosalie."

"Who with?" I asked.

"Mr. Fine."

Gerry had been involved with Una! It took a heavy dose of willpower to keep my astonishment from showing on my face. "When was that?"

"Hmmm . . . a couple of times last summer, maybe? I think that's right — I remember one night she wore a red strapless dress." She looked at me and smiled. "It looked very good on her."

I nodded. "Would you remember if —" I started, interrupted by a man who clomped into the anteroom.

"Hey, Betty," he called. "Christ Jesus, it's as cold as a witch's tit out there."

"Marcus," Betty scolded, "what are you thinking of, wearing only that light jacket?"

"I was only going from the house to the car and from the car in here!"

"You're going to catch your death of cold! Let's get you a little something to chase the chill away."

"Smart woman," he said, and she laughed and escorted him into the lounge.

"I'll be right back," she called to me over her shoulder.

I stood there, distilling Betty's revelations. *Gerry lied about not having seen Rosalie the night she died, and since the police questioned Betty, they knew it, too. Plus, Gerry had, apparently, been having an affair with Una until Rosalie entered the picture,* I thought, shaking my head. *And poor Edie.* I bet that Gerry stayed with her because it was cheaper than divorcing her. *What a heel.*

305

It was one thing to fall in love with another woman and be unable to resist Cupid's arrow. It was another to behave like an eighteenth-century rake. Gerry didn't care about anything or anyone but Gerry. As I stood, waiting for Betty, I tried to figure out why Edie stayed. *Does she love him or does she feel trapped?* My guess was that she was as self-centered as he was and cared only about protecting her lifestyle.

Words my father spoke in response to my gushing report about a college friend who'd gotten engaged to the son of one of the nation's richest men came to me. *Marry a man for his money, Josie, and you'll earn every penny.*

I shook off the sick-sad thought and instead gazed around the anteroom. From where I stood by the hostess podium to the kitchen, running floor to ceiling, there were scores of two-by-two-foot gated cubbyholes — individual wine storage units. I felt my heart lunge. The unit in front of me had a brass plate next to the lock that read, "Jim Thornapple." On the unit to the left, the brass plate read, "Lisa and Matt Freidman."

"Marcus, you're a piece of work!" Betty chided, chuckling as she returned to her hostess station. "Sorry," she said to me. "Where were we?"

"No problem. I was about to ask if Gerry ate at the restaurant often."

She considered the question. "Besides the times with Rosalie, maybe once a month. Some larger business dinners — you know what I mean. Six or eight people — department heads, sales people, that sort of thing. But one-on-one dinners with other people? Not all that often. No other women, if that's what you mean."

"Change of subject — did Rosalie have one of these individual wine units?" I asked, crossing my fingers that I'd found the answer to at least one of Rosalie's extra keys.

"No." She looked at a unit on the side wall. "But Gerry Fine does."

I turned to her, astounded. "May I see if one of the extra keys on Rosalie's ring fits his unit?"

"Customers don't have keys."

"But there are locks." I pointed to a nearby unit's ornate iron lock.

"It's their wine, but we keep the keys."

It makes sense, I thought. "I see. Did Rosalie ever come here with anyone I *haven't* asked you about?"

She thought some more. "I can't answer that. I mean, not lately that I know about. But she was here a lot. And keep in mind that I don't work every day, although it feels

307

like I do!"

I smiled, acknowledging her mild joke. "Anything else you can think of that I should ask you to help jog your memory? Any altercations? Any situations?"

She considered that, then slowly shook her head. "Nothing comes to mind."

"You've been very helpful," I said, and extended my hand. "Thank you."

"Rosalie was a great girl. You let me know if I can do anything else, okay?"

I assured her that I would, and as I turned to leave, I saw Marcus, leaning over the bar punctuating the air as he made a point about something to the bartender. The cold outside was brutal and I scrunched up my coat, protecting my neck. All I wanted was to get to my car.

Gerry is the nexus, I thought.

Both Edie and Una knew they'd been replaced by a younger model. With Edie's vituperative tongue, and Una's status as a single mother on the edge, I wondered how they'd taken the rejection.

I considered each woman's personality and attitudes. Edie was hypersensitive, always alert for snubs and perceived offenses. Her anger was defensive; she struck out protectively, shredded by jealousy. Una seemed content with her day-to-day life, but she made no secret of her difficult financial situation, and I knew from my own experience that Gerry was generous to people he cared about or needed. It wasn't a stretch to suppose that when they'd been together, he'd helped Una pay her bills. And now that they were apart, he didn't.

I shrugged. With a little imagination, it was easy to assign motives to anyone about anything. Yet I couldn't help but notice that for someone as well liked and admired as Rosalie, there sure seemed to be a lot of people who might have wanted to kill her.

CHAPTER
TWENTY-TWO

Wes called as I was driving back to my office.

"I got a dead Evan Woodricky," he said, all business.

"Tell me."

"Hampton Beach. Two weeks ago. OD."

Hampton Beach was a coastal town south of Portsmouth. "Wow," I said.

"Got a pen?"

"Give me a sec. I'm in the car." I pulled off to the side of the road and turned the flashers on. "I'm ready."

Wes rattled off a Hampton Beach address and I noted it in my book.

"That's his mother's place. He shared an apartment with some friends in Salem. From what I hear, it was a real dump," Wes said, and told me that address, too.

"What did he OD from?" I asked.

"Smack."

"Heroin?" I said, to confirm that I understood. *Heroin in New Hampshire?* I asked myself. I shook my head. *Everything is everywhere.* "Did he leave a will?" I asked Wes.

"No way to tell. It hasn't been submitted for probate," Wes said, "but that doesn't mean anything. It could be that it's a small estate being handled privately by some lawyer. Or it could be that it hasn't been submitted for probate *yet.*"

"Was there a police investigation of the death?"

"Why?" Wes asked, jumping on my question. "Ya thinking foul play?"

"No, no. I don't know anything, I'm just asking."

"They always conduct an investigation in situations like this. In this case, he was a known junkie, so they probably didn't dig all that deep. He had two arrests in the last year alone."

"Do you know his roommates' names?" I asked.

"Yup, I got it right here. Lesha Moore and Sam Dixon. They're junkies, too."

Lesha, I thought, nodding. *And Sam was probably the nasty-looking guy in the pickup.*

"Thanks, Wes," I said. "I owe you one."

"You betcha. You got anything for me now?"

"No."

"Okay, then. See ya."

I called Gretchen.

"It's me," I said. "Is everything under control?"

"Yes. Paige is great — she's helping me put on the labels for the mailing."

"Terrific. Listen, ask Sasha or Fred to pack up the palette we're investigating, will you? Whistler's palette? I need to show it to someone. I'll be there in about twenty minutes. I'll call when I'm closer and someone can run it out to me."

"Okay."

"Also the letter Lesha brought."

"Got it."

"And tell Sasha that I'm checking something out — to hold off on her research until I get back to her."

"Will do."

An hour later, with the palette and the letter in hand, I parked half a block away from Evan's mother's house, trying to decide on my opening line.

Mrs. Woodricky lived about three blocks from the ocean in a weathered bungalow with pretty blue shutters. The porch had a much-used, much-loved look about it, even in the dead of winter. There were tarp-covered chairs and tables; window boxes

312

wreathed with evergreen garlands; and a hammock frame bolted to the ceiling, the support chains dangling and swaying in the frigid breeze. A sprig of birch twigs and berries adorned the front door, an after-Christmas decoration.

I took a final look in my mirrors. Nothing. I didn't want to bother Mrs. Woodricky, but I needed information that only she could provide — if she was willing to do so. I sat in my car for a few minutes, wishing I could skip this part. I knew that there was no good way to ask a grieving mother about her dead son's possessions. I also knew that I had no choice, it was part of the appraisal process, and it had to be done.

I tramped up the unshoveled sidewalk to the house and climbed the steps. From the porch, looking east, I could see a sliver of ocean between the houses, and as I watched, three-foot waves broke with violent claps, sending sprays of white froth into the air toward the shore. Then the wave ebbed and another one broke, splayed forth, and slipped away. It was hypnotic. Finally, I turned away, clacked the shell-shaped brass knocker, crossed my fingers that Mrs. Woodricky would be home and willing to talk to me, and waited.

The door swung open and a woman of

sixty-plus asked, "Yes?" She wore a plaid blazer and forest green slacks.

"Hi. Are you Mrs. Woodricky?"

"Yes. May I help you?"

Her eyes were gray and watery, and I wondered if she had allergies or had been crying a lot. She wasn't wearing any makeup, and there were brown spots near her nose and on her cheek. She looked worn-out and in-the-bone sad.

I took a deep breath. "Hi, I'm Josie Prescott. I'm an antiques appraiser and I have reason to think you can help me authenticate an object."

"Me? I don't have any antiques."

"It's about an artist's palette. James McNeill Whistler."

She stared at me, her eyes moist and soulful. "Who are you?" she whispered. "What do you want?"

I forced myself to stay focused. "It may have been your son's."

She tipped sideways as if pushed and clutched the doorframe.

"Are you all right?" I asked. "Can I help you to sit down or something?"

"Evan?" she asked. "You knew Evan?"

"No. But I may have something that was his — Whistler's palette."

She nodded. "Yes, Evan had it."

"Really?"

"Evan was a good artist. Very talented. Everyone said so."

A sudden gust of wind blowing off the water pierced my skin, and I shivered. It was cold on the porch — killing cold.

"May I come in and explain? I promise I won't take long," I asked.

She didn't reply, but she stepped back, allowing me to cross the threshold. I pushed the door shut and glanced around. The living room was to the left, furnished with a traditional sofa and two club chairs. All three pieces were upholstered in a turquoise-and-mauve flowered print. A big flat-screen TV dominated one corner. To the right was the dining room. A round oak dining room table with four ladder chairs were positioned under a simple brass chandelier. A matching sideboard was against the outside wall. A vase of orange berries sat in the center of the table.

"Come on in." She led the way into the dining room, placed her hands on the top of one of the chairs, and indicated that I should sit. "I'm sorry," she said, "but I don't remember your name."

I took out a business card and handed it to her. "I'm Josie Prescott."

She accepted the card but didn't look at

it. Instead, she dropped it on the table in front of her, keeping her eyes on me as if she were afraid I was an apparition, that if she looked away, I'd disappear.

"What is it you want?" she asked.

"My company, Prescott's, has been asked to appraise a palette. We were told it was Whistler's by the woman who brought it to us — Lesha Moore. Do you know her?"

She recoiled as if I'd slapped her, and from the look on her face I could tell that she loathed Lesha. "Yes," she said, unable to disguise her revulsion, "I know her. *She* has the palette? Is that what you're telling me — that *she* has it?"

"She told us that Evan willed the palette to her."

She shook her head. "No way. Evan didn't leave a will."

"Are you sure?"

She shrugged. "Of course I'm sure! I have all his things."

"Here?"

"No. They're at my brother's. I asked him to go to Evan's apartment the same day he died and pack everything up. I didn't want that girl touching any of his things."

I nodded. "I want to be sure I heard you right. Evan did own Whistler's palette?"

She nodded. "Yes. It was mine and I gave

316

it to him. And if she gave it to you, it's stolen and I'm calling the police right now."

"Fair enough — but the palette I have may not be Evan's. Maybe it's a fake."

Mrs. Woodricky nodded. "That sounds like Lesha."

"Could you explain to me how it came into your possession?"

"Sure, I'll tell you. Then you can explain it to the police."

I was about to learn the secret of Whistler's palette — it was a heady moment.

She rubbed aimless circles on the well-oiled wood tabletop.

"It came from my mother, Mari Houston."

I reached into my tote bag, found Lesha's letter, and handed the plastic sleeve to her. "Are you familiar with this?"

"What is it?" she asked, looking bewildered.

"Lesha said it was Evan's."

She read the letter slowly, shaking her head. "This is crazy," she said when she was done.

"In what way?"

"Well, it's sort of right."

"What do you mean?"

"My mother *was* Maribelle Houston, she *was* called Mari, we *did* live in Newton, and she *did* get the palette from her best friend,

Stephanie Milhouse." She tapped the plastic several times. "But I've never seen this letter."

I nodded. "The letter's not genuine, but it sounds like it couldn't have been written without Evan's help."

"I'm ashamed to say that —"

She broke off abruptly, stood up, turned her back and stood for a minute, her arms hanging by her side, her hands curled into tight, tense fists. She whipped around, nodding, a decision made, sat back down, and looked at me straight on. "Evan was troubled, but never would he have done something criminal like faking this letter."

I nodded, struggling to think of what else I could say. I decided to come back to business, not wanting to push, but needing to know. "You said your mom got the palette from her girlfriend?"

She looked up, her eyes alive with memory. "That's right. My mom and Aunt Stephie — I grew up calling her Aunt Stephie — were friends from when they were nothing-old. I always knew she was related to Whistler through her mother's side of the family, but it was never anything we spoke about, and I couldn't tell you how I first learned of it. It was just part of who Aunt Stephie was, you know?" She sighed and idly thumbed the tabletop, her eyes drifting down. "When I was young, my family spent summers at the Cape. My mom took painting classes at a studio in Hyannis every year. Sometimes she took watercolor, sometimes oil, sometimes life drawing. She just loved that place." She shook off a thought and pointed at an undistinguished oil painting of a marina.

"She wasn't very good, but she sure loved it," she said, gazing at the painting. "Aunt Stephie used to join us at the beach for her two-week vacation every year." She turned and looked at me. "She was secretary to an important man in finance, I don't remember his name. Anyway, she did live on East Thirty-sixth Street, in New York just like that letter said. Murray Hill, the neighborhood was called. I visited her once."

"When did she move to New York?" I asked.

"After high school. She went to secretarial school in Manhattan."

"When did Ms. Milhouse give the palette to your mom?"

She frowned, concentrating, then tapped the letter again. "I guess it would have been just about then. The late fifties or early sixties."

"Were you there when she handed it over?"

Mrs. Woodricky smiled. "Was I ever! It was a wonderful moment. My mom nearly fainted with pleasure. It was summer, and Aunt Stephie took the train to Boston like always, and from Boston she took the ferry to Nantasket. We picked her up there and went, right away, to Paragon Park. It was an annual tradition."

"What's Paragon Park?" I asked. I'd grown up in the Boston area, too, but I'd never heard of it.

"It was an amusement park. Oh, it was fun!"

"Then what would you do?" I asked, smiling.

"We'd have lobster rolls and fried clams at the Clam Shack. And then we'd drive down to Hyannis." She sighed. "That night, once Aunt Stephie unpacked, she told my mom she had a secret, and my mom told her she couldn't, that they never had secrets between them. I can see Aunt Stephie's face as clear as day. She was smiling just like the Cheshire Cat."

She shook her head. I waited for her to continue, but she didn't. She just stared into space, lost in her memories. After a while I asked, "Then what happened?"

"My mother and Aunt Stephie were laughing about what her secret could be and then she ran into her room and came back out with the palette. She handed it to my mom and said that she just knew that the magic would transfer."

She shook her head and tapped the plastic sleeve again. "Just like in the letter. It's nauseating that Lesha would fake a letter like this." She pushed it away as if it were poison.

I nodded, thinking that it was more likely that her drug-addicted son wrote the letter, probably to help him sell the palette and get money for drugs. I'd bet that when he died, Lesha just capitalized on the opportunity. For appraisal purposes, it didn't matter. I knew the letter was a fake. What I didn't know was whether the palette was bogus, too.

"Would you know the palette by sight?" I asked.

"I'm not sure," she said, thinking. After a few seconds, she raised her eyes to mine. "Yes. Yes, I would."

I extracted the plastic bag containing the palette and slid it across the table. Mrs. Woodricky picked it up.

"This isn't Evan's palette," she said, pushing it across the table. "I mean, this isn't

Whistler's palette."

I nodded, not surprised. "How do you know?"

"Ours has a scorch mark — here," she said, tapping a spot near one side. "We figured someone who used it at some point smoked and a cinder fell on it." She looked at it again, and I followed her eyes. "The wood looks right." She looked up at me. "Do you know how Whistler arranged his paints?"

"No. Do you?"

She shook her head. "No. But I know he did it in some certain way. Evan researched it. He really thought he could absorb Whistler's genius if he followed his routine. It sounds stupid, but it was real to him."

"Thank you for the information. You've been very helpful. May I ask you one more question?"

"Of course."

"Do you know where the real palette is now?"

"It must be in one of the boxes at my brother's place."

I nodded. "Would you ask your brother to check? I don't mean to add to your grief, but it would be very helpful to know that the real palette is extant."

"I'll ask him. I want to know, too."

I stood up, palette and letter in hand, preparing to leave. "Will you call me and let me know whether your brother finds it?"

"All right." She stood up and we walked toward the front door. "What are you going to do?" she asked, nodding toward the palette.

"I don't know yet."

Mrs. Woodricky nodded. I could see ridges of tension along her chin and neck.

"You should call the police," she said. "If you do, tell them to call me," she said. "I'll be glad to talk to them."

What she meant, of course, was that she'd be glad to do Lesha whatever harm she could, and having met Lesha, I didn't blame her a bit.

CHAPTER
TWENTY-THREE

Gretchen was so keyed up she could barely contain herself. "Josie!" she exclaimed as soon as I was inside.

"What?" I asked, hanging up my coat.

"They arrived!" She stepped aside to reveal a breathtaking bouquet of two dozen wine-colored roses in an etched glass vase.

I felt the blood drain from my face. The floor seemed to tilt and I grasped the lip of Gretchen's desk, glad for the feel of solid wood. *Don't panic,* I told myself. "Did you call Officer Brownley?" I asked calmly.

"Yes."

"What did she say?"

"Not to touch them and she was en route. She was calling from Durham, so she said she'd be about half an hour."

I nodded, my eyes held fast by the crimson nightmare. *When you can't think of what to do, breathe,* my father instructed. *Stop, think, breathe.* I took a deep breath, and then another.

"There's a card," Gretchen reported.

"We'll wait for Officer Brownley." I took another deep breath and felt the world begin to right itself. "Who brought them?"

"A delivery guy. From Floral Expressions."

"When?"

"About fifteen or twenty minutes ago."

While I was carefully checking my car's mirrors, I thought bitterly, *my secret admirer had been ordering flowers. The son of a bitch.* I hated the flowers, and hated the man who'd bought them for me.

"They're really unbelievable looking," she commented, wanting, in typical Gretchen fashion, to accentuate the positive, a personality quirk that made her a delightful employee, but was as irritating as all get-out now.

I took a step back and pressed my hips and shoulders into the outside wall. I was unable to look away from the flowers. I closed my eyes and forced myself to breathe, then opened them. "Where's Paige?"

"Upstairs, reading," Gretchen said as her wind chimes jingled.

Officer Brownley entered the office carrying an empty cardboard box. She saw me, then the roses.

"Have you touched them?"

"No," I replied. "Gretchen said there's a card."

Officer Brownley stepped forward, spotted it, snapped on plastic gloves and edged it out of the green plastic trident where it was lodged.

I watched as she gently eased the card out of the envelope, mindful of fingerprints. She held it up so I could see it. The message, pencil-written in all-capital block letters, read:

YOU'RE MORE BEAUTIFUL THAN THESE, THE MOST SPECTACULAR ROSES AVAILABLE. I KNOW WHERE YOU LIVE. I KNOW WHERE YOU WORK.

LOVE,
YOUR SECRET ADMIRER

"It's so completely creepy," I whispered. I turned to face her. "I thought the florists were on alert. Ty said they weren't supposed to deliver flowers to me without calling you first."

"They weren't. Human error. The florist had a new employee."

"Human error," I repeated, stunned. If

not for a new employee, the police might have the man responsible in custody.

"We've already recontacted all florists within fifty miles to reiterate the warning and instruct them about training their staffs."

"Does the florist have a record of when the order was placed?" I asked.

"Yes. The flowers were ordered in person by someone who dropped off the vase and the card. The order was placed just after the store opened, around ten this morning."

"Was the florist able to identify the customer?" I asked.

"Yeah. A guy who looked like a homeless bum handed the clerk an envelope and the vase, and left. The instructions and card were in the envelope. Along with cash."

"A dead end," I said.

"Not necessarily. Patrols are out now, looking for the homeless man. We have a description."

I nodded and glanced at Gretchen, her eyes big with interest, then looked carefully at the vase. "The vase," I said. "It's unusual."

"In what way?"

"It's etched glass."

Officer Brownley made a note, then, still wearing plastic gloves, carefully braced the vase in the box, using padding she'd brought along.

As she was heading out the door, Gretchen handed me a message. Ty had called to say he'd be at Prescott's about six and we were to wait for him before leaving.

Heading up the steps to my office, I held on tight to the railing. The entire situation felt surreal to me, as if I were an actor in a play I hadn't read. I paused on the upper landing and looked out over the warehouse, breathing deeply.

"Hey, Paige," I said as I stepped inside.

"Hi." She looked up from her book.

"I've got to go back to the tag sale. Ty is coming here around six, so we'll be leaving then. Are you hungry? Thirsty? Bored?"

"I'm okay."

"Really?"

"I've been having trouble concentrating."

"How come?" I asked, sitting next to her.

"Mr. Bolton."

"What about him?"

"I'm scared about the meeting. I've never had a meeting with a lawyer. I'm not going to know what to say and I don't know how to pay him."

"Since he's your lawyer, you can tell him anything. It's called a privileged communication."

"What should I tell him?"

"Well, that depends on what he asks you, of course. But you should tell him the truth."

"Do you know what he's going to ask me?"

"I know a couple of things. He's going to ask you about Rosalie's funeral."

Paige began to cry. Soon, silent sobs racked her slender frame and she seemed to sink deeper into the love seat, almost disappearing into the folds of the pillows. I sat beside her and touched her shoulder, prepared for an embrace that never came. I kept my hand in place until the sobs abated.

"I don't think I can," she whispered, her hands covering her eyes, rocking to and fro, to and fro. "I just don't think I can."

"Can you tell me? So I can tell him?"

"Okay."

Asking a twelve-year-old about her sister's funeral was about as horrific a task as I could imagine. I took a deep breath and jumped in. "Did Rosalie ever tell you anything about her wishes?"

"No."

Of course not, I said to myself. *Rosalie was only thirty-two when she died.*

"How about your parents? Do you know where they're buried?"

She nodded but didn't speak.

"Where?" I asked.

"California."

"What part?"

"Santa Monica."

"Is that where you lived?"

"Yes."

"Near where Rodney is now?"

She nodded again.

"We can ask Mr. Bolton what he thinks about having Rosalie buried near your parents."

"Okay."

She spoke so softly, I could barely hear her.

"That way, if it ends up that you move out to stay with Rodney, you'll be nearby."

"I don't want to."

"I know," I said lamely.

"Can they make me?"

"I don't know. We can ask Mr. Bolton. I know he was doing a background check to make sure Rodney wasn't a criminal or anything."

Paige began to cry again, making little mewing sounds, and I felt my heart crack in tiny pieces all over again. I slipped my arm over her shoulders, and her tremors radiated up my arm. After a long minute, her crying grew quieter, then stilled.

"Do you know why Rodney and Rosalie

had a falling-out?"

"Not really. Something about money."

Money, honey, I thought. "So what we're deciding is that you want to talk to Mr. Bolton about burying Rosalie in California, near your parents. And about where you're going to live."

"You'll go with me?" she asked, uncovering her eyes for the first time, her voice cracking.

"Yes. Absolutely," I replied, patting her arm. "Paige, I'm so sorry you're in this situation."

She began to cry again, and this time she leaned into me and let me hug her. I rested my chin lightly on top of her head and held her until her convulsive weeping slowed.

"I'm sorry," she whispered, choking on the words.

"You have nothing to be sorry about," I said, meaning it.

She began to cry again, softly this time, and then she sat up and wiped her wet cheeks with the side of her hands. "I miss her so much."

I nodded. "And you probably will forever."

"Like my folks."

"Yeah. Do you miss them as much now as when they first died?"

"Sort of, but it's not the same."

"Like me. Missing my parents has gotten less sharp, but the hurt is always there."

"How do you handle it?"

"I cook."

"Really?" Paige skewed around on the love seat to face me.

"Yeah. Tomorrow I'll teach you how to make Jerry's Chicken. Jerry was my grandfather."

Paige looked at me, one wounded soul to another. "Thank you, Josie."

Fred called up. "I've got something," he said.

"What?" I asked.

"Maybe a motive for murder."

CHAPTER
TWENTY-FOUR

I escorted Paige into the tag-sale venue, then crossed the concrete expanse into the main office.

Fred handed me a sheet of fine stationery, letterhead from a Boston-based attorney. It was dated a month before Rosalie's death. From reading the letter, I gathered that Rosalie had inquired about a colleague's unauthorized use of her unpublished primary research in an article he had submitted for peer review. While the lawyer agreed that the use of her research was clearly inappropriate, the gist of his opinion had to do with the complexity of assessing and proving damages. Attached to the letter was a copy of a cease-and-desist demand that the attorney had sent at Rosalie's request to the offending colleague, Dr. Cooper Bennington.

"Wow," I said softly. *Professional jealousy was an understatement,* I thought. *With Ro-*

salie dead, might Cooper do more than use her research? Might he claim it as his own? "Any sign of a reply from the accused or his attorney?" I asked.

"No."

That must have made for some tense departmental meetings, I thought. *But good for Rosalie. It was a ballsy move to stand up for herself that way.*

I tried to assimilate the meaning of what I'd just learned. *Cooper had a reason to kill Rosalie,* I thought. *A powerful one. Not only would he be likely to avoid a charge of plagiarism but he might be able to claim her research as his own. If Paige hadn't requested an appraisal, he might have gotten away with it.*

I nearly gasped as I remembered something else. *Rosalie called him Chief.* I shook my head. It's true, I thought, but it couldn't possibly be relevant. She referred to him as the chief cook and bottle washer. But her tone had been disdainful and the references to Chief in the scrapbook were adoring, not ridiculing.

I shrugged helplessly. I couldn't go back in time to figure out what had been in Rosalie's head when she spoke those words, but I did know that Cooper Bennington had one heck of a solid motive for murder. *I'll tell Ty about Cooper tonight,* I thought.

"Make me copies of those papers, okay? I'll take them with me."

"No problem."

"Good work, Fred," I said.

"Thanks." He flung his arm backward indicating three boxes. "There's still a lot to do."

"Yeah, well, keep at it. The faster we get through it, the better."

I found Sasha working the floor in the tag-sale room and reported what I had learned from Mrs. Woodricky.

"We'll have to call the police," she said, stricken.

"Maybe." I shrugged. "I want to think about it some more. If we need to report it, we'll call them on Monday."

"It's awful, what Lesha did."

"Yeah."

I took another turn in the Prescott's Instant Appraisal booth, and afterward when Sasha relieved me, I weaved my way through the dollhouse display to talk to Cara, the new temp.

"Hi, Cara. How's it going?"

"Good. This is a marvelous business you have."

"Thanks."

"May I ask you something?"

"Sure," I said, immediately on guard. Her question might appear innocuous, but my experience is that if someone feels the need to ask permission to inquire about something, the question is often unwelcome.

"Is that Paige Chaffee?"

I glanced at Cara, but she wasn't looking at me. She was gazing beyond the cashier stand, toward the stool where Paige sat.

"Yes. Do you know her?"

"No, but I knew Rosalie a little. I recognized Paige from her photo on Rosalie's desk at Heyer's. How is she holding up?"

I shrugged. "About how you'd expect."

Cara turned to face me. "I only met Rosalie once, but we really hit it off." She smiled and added, "Desks."

"Desks?" I repeated.

She nodded. "I met Rosalie last fall when I was temping at Heyer's. I was admiring Mr. Fine's office suite — it's so elegant, and she told me that yours was the inspiration — all those marvelous antiques. Anyway, I mentioned my antique desk, or maybe she mentioned hers first, I don't remember. Regardless, one thing led to another and we discovered that we had them in common."

"Rosalie talked about an antique desk?" I asked, aiming for a neutral tone, not wanting to reveal my tingling excitement. Cara had unknowingly provided independent confirmation of the desk Paige had alluded to as "special."

"Yes. But what's most remarkable is how we acquired them. My grandfather chose one for me based on *my* personality, and her mother did the same for her based on *her* personality. Until I met Rosalie I thought my grandfather was the only person who'd ever done such a thing." She shook her head. "Rosalie and I had a good laugh over the different styles they picked. Her mom bought her a secretary from the Regency period, very delicate and feminine. My grandfather chose a big, sturdy rolltop for me. He said that I always had a lot going on so I needed a big desk, and since I wasn't the neatest girl around, he picked one with a lid that closed so I could hide my mess."

"That's charming, isn't it?"

She laughed. "Not really! Not when your own grandfather calls you a slob!"

I smiled. "Did Rosalie tell you where hers was?"

"Isn't it at her house? I just assumed —" she said, breaking off as Eric joined us.

"We sold the set of milk glass bowls," he said proudly.

"Good job," I told him, then turned back to Cara. "You were saying that you just assumed her desk was at her house?"

"That's right. I use mine all the time. We only spoke that one afternoon."

I nodded. "Thanks. I'll see you both later."

"Would you let me know about the funeral?" Cara asked as I moved away.

"Sure. You can call us anytime after Monday. Gretchen will know."

Eric followed me, and when we were some distance away, indicated with a nod of his head toward the side wall that he wanted me to stop.

"What do you think about Cara? Should we offer her a permanent job?"

"It's up to you." I smiled. "You're the boss."

"Me?" he asked, worried at having to voice an opinion. He swallowed awkwardly. "I don't know."

"Sure you do. Did she make any mistakes today?"

He shook his head.

"Did she comment on whether she liked the work?"

"Yeah. She said she loved it and hoped we'd call on her again."

"What's the downside?"

"We just met her on Thursday. We don't

know much about her."

"Fair enough. What could you do about that?"

He shrugged. "I don't know."

I nodded. "You could tell her that we'd like to consider offering her a permanent position and have her fill out our job application. Then we can check her references. Gretchen can help you with the paperwork."

"That's a good idea! Should I talk to her now?"

"How about taking her aside after we close?"

We finalized the details, and I was pleased to see him walk away with a bounce in his step.

As I went to rejoin Fred, I had a thought about Rosalie and her Regency desk. She hadn't intended to stay in New Hampshire once she finished her degree, so it was logical that she'd rent a furnished house and leave her good stuff somewhere else. The question was, where?

I found Fred, elbow-deep in Rosalie's papers.

"Have you found any reference to a place where Rosalie might have stored anything? Somewhere large enough for furniture?" I asked.

He pushed up his glasses and shook his

head. "Nothing so far."

"Let me help go through the paperwork."

"Sure."

He hoisted a still-sealed box containing files and folders stuffed with papers I'd collected from her office at Hitchens. There was a sheaf of notes about communication models that we'd need to examine in more detail, drafts of proposed presentations, and an accordion file holding unpaid bills. Apparently Rosalie had paid her bills while she was at work.

Recalling that Officer Brownley had asked whether Rosalie owed anyone money, I looked into the dated slots one by one. She'd scheduled her next car payment for the tenth of January. Renters' insurance was due on the eighteenth.

"Holy cow!" I exclaimed, extracting a sheet from the slot labeled *28*.

"What?" Fred asked.

"Looks like I found a storage room."

Evidently Rosalie had rented a storage room, unit ten, at a place called Tim's Storage, located on Tenth Road in Rocky Point. I felt my heart begin to race in anticipation of finding the desk, which was maybe the museum-quality antique that Rosalie had told Paige existed. Regency period furniture was in fashion, and good examples with interesting associations could demand hundreds of thousands of dollars.

I knew you wouldn't lie to Paige, I thought. *I just knew it.*

I dialed the number of Tim's Storage right away. A gruff-sounding man answered on the second ring sounding as if I'd interrupted him. I wondered if it was Tim.

"Hi," I said. "How late are you open?"

"Six o'clock."

Darn, I thought, my eyes on the Mickey Mouse clock on Gretchen's desk. It was after five-thirty. No way could I get there before six. "How about tomorrow?" I asked.

"Same. We open at noon on Sundays."

"Can you tell me anything about unit ten?"

"Like what?"

"Like when the owner last visited."

"Who is this?" he retorted, instantly suspicious.

I didn't blame him. I could have kicked myself for asking such a direct question. "My name is Josie Prescott. I'm an antiques appraiser based in Portsmouth. Never mind." All I'd done was put him on the defensive, and I couldn't think of how to explain the situation over the phone. "I'll stop by and explain why I'm asking."

He grunted something, and I took it to

mean that he doubted I could explain my interest to his satisfaction.

"Who are you, please?" I asked.

"Tim."

"Hi, Tim. Will you be there tomorrow?"

"Yup."

After I hung up, I stared at the phone, debating whether I needed to report my discovery to the police. *Yes,* I thought. *I'll tell Ty tonight.* Wanting to cover all bases, I also called Mr. Bolton.

At six, I said good-bye to the staff, and left Sasha in charge of closing. At 6:05, I waved hello to Ty as Paige and I hurried across the parking lot to my car.

As we pulled into traffic, my cell phone rang. I slipped in my earpiece and looked at the number on the display — it was Wes.

"Hey, Wes," I said.

"I've got info," he said, his tone low and mysterious sounding.

"What?"

"Not on the phone."

"I have no time, Wes. It's got to be on the phone."

I glanced back and saw Ty two car lengths back. It was reassuring to have him nearby.

"Josie!" Wes whined.

I shot Paige a look to see if she was listening, but I couldn't tell. She was leaning back, her head turned, staring out of her window. "I just can't, Wes. I'm betting that whatever you tell me will be in the morning edition — am I right?"

"Of course!" he replied, shocked at my suggestion that he would be a laggard when it came to reporting the news.

"So I promise not to reveal what you tell me until tomorrow morning."

He sighed deeply. "It's about the murder weapon. They've finished the test, the one on the wood. It's apple wood. Does that suggest anything to you?"

Apple wood, I thought. I glanced at Paige again. She couldn't help but hear my comments, but as near as I could tell from her expression, she wasn't listening in particular. "Not really," I said to Wes. "It's everywhere around here."

"Yeah." Wes sighed. "So I expected a call today. What about Whistler's palette?"

Finally something I could talk about in front of Paige. "It's not genuine."

"So it's fraud?"

"Well, attempted fraud, anyway. I still need to do some research." Saying it aloud grounded me. I didn't want to call the police on Lesha if she was a victim of Evan's deceit.

343

"How come?"

"I'm not convinced that the woman who asked us to appraise it is in on the scam. It's possible that the con was set up by her now-dead boyfriend, and that he gave her the palette and letter before he died. She may think she has the genuine article, and if he told her it was hers, she may think that she has the right to sell it."

"Even without a will?"

"If he gave it to her *before* he died, whether he had a will or not is irrelevant. I don't know . . . I just want to arm myself with as much knowledge as possible before I decide what I should do."

"Makes sense . . . but don't forget, I'm your first phone call."

"Once I've decided how to handle it," I agreed, "I'll call you first. I promise."

"Okay, then," he said, and was gone.

Apple wood, I mused. New Hampshire had acres and acres of apple orchards. Gnarled limbs sometimes ended up at the beach, where, over the years, they weathered into gray driftwood. *But that doesn't explain the varnish,* I thought, and shook my head.

Ty parked in front of the tall hedge and I pulled into the driveway. The little light I always left on in my bedroom glowed, welcoming me home. Ty opened the door with the key I'd given him more than a year earlier and flipped the switches that lit up most of the ground floor.

"It's good to see you again, Paige," Ty said.

"Thank you." Her voice was barely audible.

"I want to change into sweats," I said, referring to my usual at-home attire. "See you guys in the living room in five minutes, okay?"

"Would it be all right if I lie down before we go to Zoë's?" Paige asked. "Just for a few minutes."

"Sure," I said. "You want something to nibble first?"

She shook her. "I'm just tired."

"Okay. Go on ahead. But it won't be for long — I figure we should leave here in about half an hour. Is that okay?"

She nodded.

As I stepped out of my dirty jeans and sweater and into comfortable, warm sweats, a picture of Ty came to me. In my mind's eye he was relaxing on the sofa with a beer in his hand and his legs resting on the coffee table, ankles crossed, frowning at the news. *I love you,* I thought, sending the vibe downstairs.

When I walked into the living room, I saw

that Ty had closed the drapes and was sitting on the sofa just as I'd envisioned, a bottle of Smuttynose in hand. He muted the TV.

"Hey," he said. He placed his beer on a copy of *Architectural Digest* and stood up.

"Hey," I said, approaching him.

He tucked my hair behind my ear, leaned down, and kissed me.

"Would you make me a drink?" I asked.

"Sure. What's your pleasure?" he asked as he led the way into the kitchen.

I thought for a moment. "A guavatini."

I sat at the table and watched as he mixed the guava nectar with vodka and swirled the shaker.

"I've got some information," I said.

He handed me the glass filled to the brim with the frothy orange-pink mixture, and I repeated Cara's story about the desk, then handed him stapled copies of the letter and attachments documenting Cooper's alleged plagiarism and Rosalie's storage unit.

"What's all this?"

"Paperwork suggesting a humdinger of a motive for Cooper Bennington to have killed Rosalie and evidence that she maintained a storage unit in Rocky Point."

He read through everything, nodding periodically, then called Officer Brownley and filled her in. From what I gathered, listening to their brief conversation, there was some reference to Cooper in Rosalie's diary that was related to the lawsuit and they decided that Officer Brownley would reinterview him in the morning. My curiosity was fired up.

"There's a storage unit, too," he told her. "Yeah . . . Josie found it in her papers . . . Tim's, you know the place, off Madison. . . . I don't know, let me ask her." He turned to me. "How long has she had the unit, do you know?"

"No."

"I assume you want to check out the storage unit tomorrow, right?"

"Yes."

"I want Officer Brownley to accompany you."

"Sure. I already spoke to Mr. Bolton about it."

He nodded and arranged for Officer Brownley to pick me up at my house at noon. I'd ride with her to Tim's Storage.

"I want to tell you something that Rosalie wrote in her diary," he said when he was off the phone, "because it might be relevant to items you find — or, more to the point, items that *should be* there. About two months before she died, Rosalie wrote that she caught Cooper nosing around her office. She saw him sitting at her desk with drawers and files open. What seemed to really gall her was catching him red-handed with a photocopy of her journal pages."

"Her diary?"

He shrugged. "That's all we know. What do you think? When she wrote 'journal,' did she mean 'diary'?"

"I don't know. In some contexts, the words are synonyms. I know she referred to her entries as 'journaling,' so maybe. It might help if I could read the actual entry."

He shook his head. "That's all it said. Have you found any photocopied journal pages?"

"Not that I'm aware of. I'll ask Fred." I shook my head, dismayed. I looked at him, and as always, his striking brown eyes revealed nothing. "Cooper going through Rosalie's desk is unbelievable! Trying to steal her work is . . . is . . . wicked!"

"Yeah. I don't mind admitting that we're looking forward to talking to him about it."

His matter-of-fact words sent shivers up my spine. *Couldn't happen to a nicer guy,* I thought spitefully.

I finished my drink and at ten to seven, I ran upstairs and knocked on the guest room door. "Ten-minute warning, okay?"

"Okay. Can I wear jeans?" she asked through the door.

"Jeans will be fancy. I'm wearing sweats."

"I'll be down in a few minutes."

Downstairs, I discovered Ty leaning against the wall, grinning.

"What is it?" I asked. "You're smiling."

He didn't reply. Instead, he came to me, set down his beer, and enveloped me in his arms, hugging me for a long time, rocking just a little.

"Wow!" I said when he let me go. "What's that about?"

"I love you."

"Hot damn!" I said, and standing on tippy toes to reach, I kissed him.

Chapter
Twenty-Five

Three-year-old Emma tugged on my arm. "Josie!" she screeched, jumping up and down. "Want to see what monkey bear did?"

"Sure, sweetie. In a sec. First, meet Paige. She's staying with me for a couple of days."

"Hi," Paige said, smiling.

"Want to meet monkey bear?" Emma asked her.

"Okay."

"Monkey bear climbed a chair. Come."

"And this is Jake," I said, waving to Zoë's six-year-old son.

"Come look at monkey bear!" Emma insisted, tugging the hem of Paige's sweater.

"Sure," she said, extending her index finger. Emma gripped it in her pudgy little hand. "Do you want to come, too, Jake?"

"Not to see monkey bear. He's stupid. I have a truck that can back up."

"Really? Show me."

"Monkey bear! Monkey bear!" Emma sang.

"We can do both," Paige said diplomatically.

Zoë chuckled. "Nice to see you, Paige. Welcome! Throw your coats over the banister — you know the routine. And you haven't met my cousin Frankie. Frankie, this is Josie, Paige, and Ty."

We all said hi, but he didn't speak.

Frankie had slicked-back black hair and acne and he looked surly. When he turned to walk away, I saw the back of his T-shirt. It read:

Ass
Grass or
You Pay the Gas
Nobody Rides for Free

Jake was clamoring for attention, and I told Paige that she could follow the kids into the front room. Emma tugged her finger and laughed. Jake insisted that she watch his truck back up first.

"Oh, God, Frankie, change your shirt," Zoë said.

"Me?" Frankie protested, whipping around. "What the fuck's the matter with my shirt? Haven't you ever heard of free fuckin' speech?"

"Frankie, please," she said, then half smiled, trying to take the sting away, and repeated her request. "Please?"

"Fuck you."

"Ty?" Zoë asked, turning to face him, her hands on her hips. "Help."

Ty met her troubled gaze and nodded.

"Frankie," Ty said in a restrained, rational tone, "no one's looking for any trouble here."

"Better fuckin' not be."

Ty stared at him for a five-count. "Would you do me a favor, Frankie? Go up and change your shirt, okay?" he said, his tone deeper and more menacing.

"Who the fuck you think you are?" Frankie asked ferociously, his ugly little button eyes blazing a warning.

Ty placed his arm on Frankie's shoulders, an apparent gesture of camaraderie, then slid his hand back and pincer-gripped his neck. "Let's talk about it, just you and me, okay?" Ty said, and hustled Frankie up the steps to the second floor.

"Zowie! I've never seen Ty like that," Zoë whispered, big-eyed.

"You've never worn a disrespectful T-shirt," I countered.

"I guess not. But I'm plenty disrespectful

all the same."

"No, you're not. You're irreverent and outrageous, but you're always respectful about it."

She laughed and shook her head.

I waggled the bottle of guava nectar I'd brought, and she said, "Excellent! Let's make a pitcherful." She poked her head into the living room. "Hey, Paige! Are you a Coke girl? Ginger ale? Apple juice?"

"Ginger ale, please," Paige replied.

"Apple juice for me!" Jake called. "I can help!"

"Thanks, Jake. How about Emma?"

"She's with monkey bear," Jake explained, as if that was responsive.

Jake dashed ahead into the kitchen. Five minutes later, after Jake and I delivered their drinks, including an apple juice for Emma, I asked Zoë about dinner. She stopped shaking the cocktail mixer and looked over my shoulder. I turned around. Frankie was wearing Ty's sweatshirt.

"Frankie here agreed with me that with women and kids around, he really shouldn't be wearing shirts with sayings like that, right, Frankie?" Ty said, entering the kitchen in his corduroy shirt, the cuffs rolled up.

Frankie looked shell-shocked. I looked

carefully at his neck, but didn't see any marks.

"Sure," he said.

"He's going to get some more appropriate duds tomorrow."

"Right," Frankie agreed.

"And he's going to watch his language."

"Uh-huh."

"So, tell me, Frankie, you're from Boston, right?" Ty asked as if the altercation had never occurred. He accepted the beer I handed him.

"Yeah," he replied.

"You a Bruins fan?"

"Sorta."

"So what do you think of their chances against the Penguins?" Ty asked, leading Frankie to the small table off to the side of the kitchen.

Frankie started to answer, and Zoë resumed shaking the guavatinis. "Wow!" she whispered. "Way to go, Ty!"

"See if it lasts," I replied in an undervoice.

"It's got to. Forget that *I* don't want to see that BS, but I don't want him near the kids unless he cleans up his act." She poured our drinks, cocked her head, listening, then said, "I think I'll go check on them. They're awfully quiet."

Guavatini in hand, I joined Ty and Frankie

at the table. The transformation seemed incredible. Frankie was almost animated talking about hat tricks and penalties, and he didn't curse once.

Zoë entered, Emma on her hip. "The natives are getting restless. Time for food!"

"What can I do to help?" I asked.

"Nothing! You're a queen to me. Paige agreed to babysit tomorrow. You know what that means?"

"What?"

"I get to go to the mall without my darlins'. Woo-hoo! Hot time in the old town tonight! Zoë's going shopping!"

"That'll work out for Frankie, too," Ty said.

Frankie looked down at his hands. I noticed he chewed his nails.

Zoë shifted Emma to a new position and gently rubbed her back. She looked over at Frankie, then back at Ty, and her expressive face revealed her thoughts. She understood that Ty wanted to be certain that Frankie got to go shopping.

"Right. You can do your thing, Frankie, and I'll do mine. We can hook up later for some pizza or a burger. Sound good?"

He nodded. "Sure."

Later, after we were home again, with Paige upstairs in bed, Ty came to me and tilted my chin up so our eyes met full-on, and then he hugged me. I shut my eyes and buried my head in his chest, feeling cherished and protected. After a long while, I opened my eyes and turned my head, and among the dozen or so vases I kept on top of my kitchen cabinets, I saw one made of etched glass. "Oh, my God," I said.

"What?" he asked, pulling back to see my face.

I pointed to it. "Look. An etched-glass vase."

"What about it?"

"The roses that were delivered today — they were in an etched-glass vase."

"Officer Brownley mentioned it. She's checking it out."

"I just remembered something," I said.

"What?"

"Una, the receptionist at Heyer's. Last month, Edie gave her an etched-glass vase for Christmas. She was upset and I can't say I blame her. She needs money, you know, not glassware."

Ty nodded, thinking about what I said. "Did you see it?"

"No, she just told me about it. When I was signing in, you know? We often chat. I don't remember what I said, exactly. Something neutral, I think, about how I liked etched glass as well as cut glass." I shrugged. "I was trying to make her feel better about a gift she didn't want.

"There's something else that may be relevant. I don't know." I looked at him. "You know how Mr. Bolton told me to track down every place Rosalie might have kept things?"

"Yeah."

"Well, I identified a coaster from Rosalie's scrapbook as coming from The Miller House restaurant," I explained. I met his eyes and hoped mine revealed as little as his did. "I went there."

"Why?"

"Paige insists that Rosalie had something of great value, and I haven't found it — and I have two extra keys, one of which Rosalie hid away as if it were valuable. I figure the key's got to go somewhere."

His eyes hardened. "What would a key fit at The Miller House?"

"Those wine-storage units, maybe. Also, I thought that maybe I'd learn about other people Rosalie was friends with." I shrugged again.

"So did you learn anything?"

"Well, Gerry has a wine-storage unit. And customers don't get keys or store anything there except wine they buy from the restaurant, but I learned something else. Gerry took Una to dinner there a few times, I'm guessing until Rosalie came into the picture."

"What?" he asked, his tone so brusque, I winced.

"Betty, the hostess, said that Una had been a dinner guest of his more than once last summer."

"Last summer? And Una has an etched-glass vase," he said, thinking.

"Yes."

"Given to her by Gerry's wife, Edie."

"Apparently."

"And you don't know who else has one?"

"I don't know, but if that was this year's gift to Gerry's employees, maybe a lot of people." *If so, did she keep one for herself?* A memory came to me. "Rosalie has one. I saw it in the kitchen, next to a book on making cheese. It wasn't an antique, but it was nice. I'm pretty sure it's the same style."

He nodded again. "What else did Betty say?"

"She said that Rosalie went there a lot with whatever guy she was dating." I thought for a moment, then shrugged. "That's all, I think."

He reached for his phone and he gave Officer Brownley a long list of questions to ask of and about Una, Edie, Gerry, and The Miller House. After he was off the phone, he said, "Besides going to Tim's Storage, what are your plans tomorrow?"

"I don't know. I told Paige I'd teach her to make Jerry's Chicken, so I need to go to the grocery store."

"I'll tell Officer Brownley to take you."

"Really? Are you saying that running around town is a risk?"

He shrugged. "No. I don't think there's any danger. But there's no sense taking chances."

My heart started beating at his carefully measured words. "Well, I won't be going out to the jetty after dark, I can tell you that," I said, trying to lighten the mood.

Ty smiled. "I always knew you were a sharp cookie."

"Seriously, Ty . . . that last message was pretty darn creepy — 'I know where you live. I know where you work.' " I shivered as I remembered the dark sedan that had followed me more than once. "Do you think you'll ever catch him — or her — whoever's been following me? And the secret admirer?"

"Yes," he replied, his tone reassuringly confident. "I'm waiting for some forensic test results."

"Like what?"

"Like various things." He smiled again. "Come here."

And I walked into his arms and closed my eyes and felt completely safe. After a short reprieve from worry, I leaned back and touched his face. "I love you," I whispered.

"Me, too," he murmured.

I tucked my hand inside his left arm and walked him to the door. "You gave Frankie money for clothes."

"He's just a kid," he said.

"You're a good man, Charlie Brown."

"Aw, shucks."

"Are you going to miss me while you're away?" I asked in a sleepy soft voice, suddenly exhausted.

"More than you know."

"Want to know if I'm going to miss you?"

"No."

"What do you mean, 'no'?"

"If I ask, you might tell me you're not going to."

"I am," I said, yawning.

"You are what?"

"Going to miss you."

He kissed the top of my head, and left. I stood by the door watching until his SUV rounded the corner and then I stood some more, wondering if the fear that held me in

360

its grip was based on fact. It felt as if someone was out there, after me, threatening, powerful, hidden, and yet inching ever closer. I checked that all the doors and windows were locked, then hurried up the stairs to bed.

Chapter
Twenty-Six

Melting snow dripped from the gutter and roof, and the meadow visible from the big window over the sink seemed to undulate as snow liquefied in the early January thaw. I was glad for the temporary reprieve from the numbingly cold and long New Hampshire winter.

Paige came downstairs just as I was finishing mixing the batter for blueberry pancakes.

"Hey," I said. "How are you?"

She shrugged. "Okay."

Her eyes were puffy and sort of red and her skin was pasty white. My heart cracked a little. I poured two glasses of orange juice and walked through the slanting yellow sunlight that spilled across the floor to the table and sat down.

I patted the chair next to me, and said, "Come and join me. Have some juice."

"Okay."

"I don't know about you, but I hate Sundays."

"You do?" she asked, surprised.

I shrugged. "Without family, it's hard."

Paige nodded and turned away, looking out toward the meadow, and sipped some juice. "Rosalie and I always spent Sundays together."

She began crying, tears spilling over and running down her cheeks.

"I'm so sorry, Paige," I whispered, and got her some tissues.

As I rubbed her shoulder, I stared out the window. Everything in sight was white, blue, or green. White snow, blue sky, and green conifers. Sometimes there was brown, but not today. No deer streaked across the meadow, nor was there wind that allowed bare limbs to show. Everything was still. After a while, Paige's tears slowed and she grew quiet and finished her juice.

"What do you do about Sundays?" she asked.

"Keep busy."

"Doing what?"

I shrugged. "Fun things that absorb my mind, not just my hands." I smiled. "I cook. I read. I work. I go to museums or movies or plays."

Paige nodded, listening hard.

"Want to know the things I *don't* do?"

"Sure. What?"

"The worst things for me are to go for a walk alone, or listen to ballads, or crochet, or knit — anything that lets me spend too much time thinking in isolation is bad. Not 'bad' bad, if you know what I mean." I paused, trying to find the words to express my thoughts. "I mean, thinking is good, but not when I'm feeling sad and lonely — then it's brooding, not thinking."

Paige nodded. "I understand."

"Do you still want to babysit today? 'Cause I'm sure Zoë would let you off the hook if you're not up for it."

"No, I'd like to do it. It's just what you said. It'll keep my mind occupied, not only my hands."

"Okay, then. You're going at eleven?"

"Yeah."

"I have an errand, and then I'll go grocery shopping, but I should be home by about three or four."

"Okay."

"You've got my cell phone number if you need anything, right?"

"Uh-huh."

"Zoë will have lunch for you, but I'm thinking we should have a nibble in the late afternoon. You know, something light, 'cause

Jerry's Chicken takes a while to cook."

"Okay."

"What's your favorite snack?"

"I don't know."

"Are you a carrot and cucumber sort of girl? Potato chips? Cookies?"

"Anything."

"Paige!" I objected, laughing a little. "Stop being so agreeable! I want to know *your* favorite."

"Pizza."

"Done! What kind of pizza? Thin crust like we had at the store yesterday? Deep dish? What toppings?"

She smiled shyly. "My favorite favorite is Pizza Quickies."

"Yum. How do you prepare it?"

"Sauce and cheese. Plus fresh tomatoes. And sometimes Rosalie added a green thing on top — an herb, but I forget its name."

"Basil?"

"Yeah, that's it! How'd you know?"

"It's yummy and it goes great with toma-toes. What kind of cheese? Do you remem-ber?"

"I'm not sure. One came in little pieces in a plastic bag and the other one we shook from a can."

"Mozzarella and parmesan. Sounds delish." I nodded. "Okay, then. We got us a plan."

I heard a thump as a clump of wet snow fell from the roof. I watched the drips for a moment, then got up to cook breakfast.

"I just realized that I don't know if you're a churchgoer," I said. "I'd be glad to take you if you want."

She shook her head. "I'm mad at God."

I cocked my head. "Maybe you want to go to church and tell God how you're feeling."

She shook her head. "No, thank you."

"If you change your mind, let me know."

"I won't. I haven't been to church since my parents died."

"What did Rosalie say to that?"

"She said that I shouldn't be mad at God, that He took them because they were so wonderful and He needed them in Heaven. I don't know if she believed it or just thought it was one of those things you have to say." Paige shrugged. "I'm just plain mad."

I hugged her then. And she hugged me back. And later, she ate three pancakes.

Just before eleven, Paige went next door to Zoë's to babysit. I wanted to talk to Shelly, my New York appraiser buddy, before Officer Brownley came to get me.

It was a good time to call. It wasn't so early that I'd wake her, nor so late that I'd miss her. Shelley was a die-hard party animal, typically booked to the teeth every nonworking moment. As far as I knew, it was she who invented the disco nap, an after-work two-hour-long snooze intended to allow her to club-hop long into the night and still show up at work on time and perform at peak level. I also knew that she never skipped Sunday brunch at the Water Club.

"Shelly!" I said when she answered. "It's Josie. From New Hampshire."

"Jesus, Josie! What time is it?"

"It's almost eleven. I wanted to be sure and catch you before brunch. Aren't you awake yet?"

"God, no. Hold on. Let me throw some water on my face."

I giggled and thanked her, then glanced at the clock to time her. Two minutes later, Shelly was back on the line. *Not bad,* I thought.

"So what's up?" she asked.

"Whistler's palette. What do you know?"

"Nothing."

"You're a twentieth-century American art

367

expert," I protested. "You must know something."

"I don't know everything about everything, but I'm flattered that you think I do. You should talk to Aaron."

"Aaron Goldmark? Why?"

"Aaron's Ph.D. dissertation was on Whistler. Hold on. I'll find his number for you."

I heard rustling, then Shelly said, "Got a pen? If you call him now, you've got to promise not to tell him you got his number from me."

"God, Shelly, you are a hoot!"

"I miss you, too, Josie. How is it up there in the frozen tundra?"

I turned to the window. Rainbows of refracted light streaked across the pristine meadow. "Sunny and beautiful."

"Isn't it like a gazillion degrees below zero?"

"Shelly, you really have to get out and about more. It's gorgeous up here. And no, it's not a gazillion degrees below zero. We're above freezing already today."

"Oh, joy! You should come for a visit," Shelly said. "There's a new country place in the Village. We can go line dancing."

I loved line dancing, and was good at it, and it pleased me that Shelly remembered. "One of these days," I warned her, "I'll turn up on your doorstep wearing cowboy boots."

"You got it, girlfriend."

"You need to come visit me, too," I told her.

"Josie, you're a peach, but I don't like the country. I don't even like the suburbs."

We chatted for another few minutes. She told me about her recent promotion, our former boss's efforts to rehabilitate his reputation after spending time in prison for conspiring to fix prices, and a new club in Tribeca. I told her about my company's expansion, my growing friendship with my neighbor and landlady, Zoë, and Ty's new job. She didn't mention if she was dating anyone, and I didn't reveal that Ty's likely travel schedule worried me.

I always enjoyed our conversations, and as I hung up, I realized that I missed her. I wondered if the dilution of our friendship was inevitable or whether I could have done something to prevent it.

I eyed Aaron Goldmark's phone number. I didn't know him all that well, but I decided that there was no time like the present, and dialed. A woman answered and I heard her call, "Aaron! Aaron?"

He got on the line. "Hello?"

"Aaron," I started, "this is a blast from

your past. It's Josie Prescott. We worked together a couple of times when I was at Frisco's."

"Josie!" he exclaimed. "It's been years! Good to hear from you. How are you?"

After a couple of minutes of catching up, I told him that Shelly said he was the man to ask about Whistler.

"I don't know about that, but I'll tell you whatever I can. What do you need?"

"I have a palette that's alleged to be Whistler's, but apparently isn't. But a real one may exist. So I have a few questions, if I might."

"Yes, please," he said, his interest fully engaged.

"First of all, Whistler used palettes, right?"
"Yes."

"Poplar or maple?"

"Typically, but not exclusively, maple."

"How did he arrange the colors?"

"Lead white in the center, with browns and grays ranging out."

"Always?"

"Always. This is exciting. How did the palette come into your hands?"

I promised to tell Aaron everything as soon as I was at liberty to do so. After I hung up, I sat with the phone in my hand, picturing the fake palette. There were smudges of gray at one end and white at the other.

Mrs. Woodricky had said that Evan was a devoted fan of the artist. If that was true, and he'd laid out the paints, he would have gotten it right. The case against Lesha just got stronger.

CHAPTER
TWENTY-SEVEN

Outside was a mess. The melting snow had nowhere to run off, so pools of ice-cold water stood everywhere. My knee-high waterproof boots got a workout as I slogged through ankle-deep puddles to Officer Brownley's car, looking and listening purposefully. Nothing registered as trouble. It was a relief to slide into the passenger seat. I was glad to see that someone I knew was on my side.

"That legal thing with Cooper Bennington is something, huh?" I said as we drove away.

"Yeah. Makes me wish I knew more about Ms. Chaffee's research, you know?"

"You and me both. What's your next step?" I asked.

"I'm meeting with him later today."

"He'll deny everything."

"Probably. But I have calls in to Rosalie's lawyer." She shrugged. "With the right questions, maybe we can get him talking. And if that doesn't work, we'll hire a communications expert to analyze who stole what from whom, how, why, and when — if they did."

As we approached the industrial-looking building with the orange and purple TIM'S STORAGE sign near the door, Officer Brownley slowed to a near crawl, then pulled to a stop in front of the corrugated steel facade.

Out of the sun, it was bone-chillingly cold. The building was a prefab windowless metal structure half a block long. The office was the size of a storage room, and the utilitarian metal had been painted canary yellow. It was freezing, nearly as cold inside as out.

A stocky man of about fifty, wearing a dark plaid flannel shirt and jeans, entered the office from an inner door.

"Are you Tim?" I asked.

"Yup."

"I'm Josie Prescott. We talked on the phone yesterday."

Officer Brownley stepped inside.

He glanced at her, then back at me. "Hi, Claire," he said.

"Hi, Tim. How's it going?"

"It's going."

I showed Tim the authorization letter. "We

want to look at unit ten, please."

He took his time reading it. "This isn't a court order," he observed.

"No," I acknowledged. "But according to the lawyer, that paper should be good enough."

Tim scratched his ear as he assessed my words. "You think so? I'm not so sure 'bout that. This is a sensitive business, and my customers seem to have pretty damn inflexible ideas about privacy." He handed back the letter.

"I represent the heir to her estate."

"I haven't acknowledged that she *is* a customer."

I took a deep breath. "Assuming she rented unit ten," I said, meeting his eyes full on, "her heir wants us to examine the room."

"So you say. Even assuming she's the renter, I don't know she's dead."

He wasn't buying it and I couldn't think of any way to persuade him.

"Hold on," I said.

I got my cell phone from where it rested at the bottom of my bag, called Mr. Bolton, who asked me to put Tim on the line. The two of us stood and listened, mostly to Tim's grunts.

"Murder?" Tim asked, and eyed me. "Uh-huh . . . Yup . . . Nope — last time? That'd be last Wednesday. . . . That's right. . . . Yup . . . Nope . . . Didn't say . . . Nope . . . Didn't see anything . . . Sure, if they want to . . . Okay."

He handed me the phone. "Mr. Bolton?" I asked.

"Yes. I'm here. It seems that Ms. Chaffee visited her room last week."

I wondered why. Was it a regular visit, had she added something to the room, or had she taken something away?

"Can we go in?" I asked Tim.

Tim shrugged and led the way down a long corridor. Our steps echoed in the metal chamber. He stopped in front of a padlocked blue metal door with the numeral *10* stenciled on it in white. I tried the smaller of the two still-unused keys, and it worked. Tim swung the door open revealing a metal-walled room, about five by seven, topped by a heavy-gauge wire mesh screen.

There in the center stood an English Regency-style secretary. It featured satin-wood inlay and splay feet, a style popular in the first decade of the nineteenth century. I raised the slant top and counted six small drawers and two cubbyholes, each inlaid with satinwood. An ornate leather-cornered blotter covered the writing surface; an empty, sterling silver ink stand nestled in a rounded indentation; and leaning against the side was a square envelope.

I uncapped my video camera and described the desk as I recorded it from every perspective. When I was done, I reached for the envelope.

Officer Brownley said, "Wait — don't touch it."

I stopped midreach and nodded. "Can you see what's inside?"

"I'll try." She pulled on plastic gloves and used the eraser end of a pencil, just as Ty had done earlier, to lift the flap. She slipped the card from the envelope. She tilted it so I could read it along with her.

It showed an illustration of a smiling young woman in a gown and mortarboard standing at the top of a hill, arms thrown up to the sky in a celebratory V. Inside was printed *Congratulations! You did it!* Below, in a feminine script, someone had penned, *Rosalie, Dad and I are so proud of you. This desk reflects our view of you — elegant, hardworking and ladylike. Enjoy it, my dear, dear daughter. Mom.*

"Nice, huh?" Officer Brownley said.

"Way nice," I agreed, fighting tears. "Sensational."

"Is this the valuable thing you were looking for?"

"I don't know. Let me take a minute."

I kneeled, and used the small flashlight I kept hooked to my belt when I worked to examine the underside. Faintly, in the far corner, I saw a maker's mark. I didn't recognize it, but I wasn't an expert in Regency furniture, so that didn't mean anything one way or the other. We could look it up. Wearing plastic gloves Officer Brownley handed me, and following her warning to be careful, I opened drawers and searched for secret panels, not unusual in desks from this period, but didn't find anything. The dovetail construction lent credibility that the piece was genuine.

I turned to face Officer Brownley. Tim looked on, interested. "It appears to be in excellent and original condition. But unless there's something special about its provenance or association, it's not all that valuable, and I doubt that we'll find anything special."

"Why?" she asked.

I shrugged and gestured toward the card. "From the tone of her mother's comments, I think she would have mentioned something like that, don't you?"

"What do you mean?"

"Rosalie was a historian. So if the desk

had been owned previously by a famous historian or someone she admired or something, it's likely she would have written about it." I shrugged again. "It's an educated guess based on how people often act, but that's all it is, you know? There's a maker's mark so we can do some more research on it."

"If you're right, how much do you think it's worth?"

"Unless there's something special about it that comes out when we do the research, I'd be surprised if it would sell for more than five thousand dollars. It's an attractive desk in terrific condition, but it's not unique."

She nodded. "We'll examine it for forensic evidence — then what will you do with it?"

They'll seek out fingerprints and anything that might provide DNA, I thought, *in case they need it for later testing.*

"We'll bring it back to my company and begin the appraisal process." I paused. "When can I get it?"

"Chief Alverez says this is top priority, so we'll do our work today. We'll examine it here, collect our samples, and turn it over to you."

"Okay, then." I turned to Tim. "You're open until six, right?"

"Right."

We settled on five-thirty for me to send a truck. I'd need to disturb Eric on his day off, but if I got it to the warehouse today, Sasha could begin the appraisal first thing in the morning.

"You said you saw her last week. Did she take anything away with her?" I asked as we walked back toward the office.

"Nope. She just signed in and out."

"So if she took something away, it must have been small enough to fit in her bag."

"Yup."

"Can I get a copy of the contract?" Officer Brownley asked.

"Sure. I guess she won't be complaining any."

We followed Tim to his office. I stood and watched as Officer Brownley examined a slender manila file and asked for photocopies of various documents.

We thanked Tim and left. As we rode to the grocery store, I called Eric. I apologized for bothering him on a Sunday and told him what I needed him to do. He assured me that he had the time and could get the desk, no problem. I reminded him to reset the alarm on his way out, and he promised he would. I trusted him completely, but he was young.

I didn't know about Officer Brownley, but I was white-hot curious. If the desk wasn't Rosalie's treasure — and I didn't think it was — the valuable object she'd talked to Paige about was still missing.

CHAPTER TWENTY-EIGHT

Officer Brownley came inside my house with me. "I'd like to take a quick look around."

"Sure," I said, immediately fretful. "But how come?"

"An excess of caution."

Her tone betrayed her concern. "Do you have any information that I don't have?"

"No." She helped carry groceries inside, and then said, "I'll be back in a minute."

I had just placed the package of English muffins near the stove when she entered the kitchen. "All clear," she said.

"Thanks." I met her deep blue eyes, which sent a reassuring message of calm. She didn't look worried, and her confidence transferred itself to me. "Want a cup of coffee or something?"

"No, I'm going to take off. Don't hesitate to call if you need anything, okay?"

"I won't."

"When do you want to leave tomorrow?"

"About seven-thirty. I want to get in early."

"You have outside appointments?"

"Yes."

"Chief Alverez asked me to have someone accompany you when you went somewhere."

They didn't know if I was in danger, but they obviously thought I might be. "Okay," I said, hiding my anxiety as best I could.

"Anything happens," she stressed, "you call me right away."

"You're on my speed dial."

She smiled then and left.

"Jake knows a lot about trucks," Paige told me. "And Emma's very good at tumbling."

Paige sat at the kitchen table as I thumbed through the leather-bound, handwritten cookbook my mother had given me shortly before her death, when she was only forty. I found the entry labeled *Jerry's Chicken.*

"Sounds like you had a good time. Or at least a time that helped counteract the onus of Sundays."

She nodded. "It helps to think about other people."

Out of the mouths of babes, I thought. "Yeah."

Jerry's Chicken had been created by my

grandfather, my mother's father, Jerry Keas, who was an onion guy. He loved growing them and he loved eating them. He also loved cooking with them and he invented this recipe.

It's not easy to make, my mother had written all those years ago. *Don't try it unless you have the time.* With Paige by my side, I was looking forward to taking the time. Cooking was, to me, a major stress reducer, and by sharing the recipe, and the experience, with Paige, maybe she'd take away a memory that would offer a respite from tension in the dark days sure to come.

I set aside the book. "You ready to cook?" I asked.

"I guess. I don't know much."

"I sure hope you know how to make pizza!"

She smiled shyly. "That's easy."

"What do we do first? Toast the muffins?"

"No. First you preheat the oven. Plus, you don't toast the muffins, you bake them."

"Got ya."

"We always covered the cookie sheet with aluminum foil. Helps with cleanup."

"Good idea."

We lined the sheet and preheated the oven. While I watched, she spooned ready-made pizza sauce onto the muffin halves in a pretty spiral pattern.

"Do you spread it out?" I asked.

"No. It'll spread on its own when you cook it. You don't want to use too much or the muffins get mushy."

I nodded. "Now what?"

"The cheese."

"I thought we'd grate fresh parmesan instead of using the stuff in the can."

I showed her how to hold the grater.

"Have a nibble," I told her.

"Yum."

"Is it better?"

"Way better," she said, smiling.

I watched as she sprinkled the part-skim mozzarella and dribbled the parmesan.

"I love cheese," she said.

"Me, too."

"Do you want to use fresh basil? I got some at the store."

"First the tomato."

"I got these." I handed her a tub of grape tomatoes. "The others just looked awful."

"Tomatoes in January in New Hampshire," she acknowledged. "Hopeless. That's something I miss about California. The fruit and vegetables are better." She examined the grape tomatoes I'd handed her. "These will work fine. We can slice them in thirds, the long way."

After the tomatoes were in place, she tore the basil into strips and crisscrossed the surface. "That's it," she said as she slid the cookie sheet into the oven.

"Want some ginger ale?" I asked.

"Sure."

As I poured, I told her, "I found Rosalie's desk."

"Really? Where?"

"In a storage unit near Hitchens."

"Wow! Is it the treasure Rosalie told me about?"

I shook my head. "I don't think so. I'm sorry, Paige. It's a fine piece of furniture. But it's not hugely valuable, I don't think."

She sighed and looked down. After a moment, she asked, "What else was in the storage room?"

"Nothing. Except for a note from your mom to Rosalie when she gave her the desk and an inkstand for an old-fashioned quill pen. Those were on the desk."

She nodded. "Now what?"

"We'll appraise the desk starting tomorrow — and the inkstand, although I don't think it has much value either. And I keep looking."

"Can I see it?"

"Sure. We'll go to the office first thing."

The timer rang. She slid the pizza muffins

onto a cooling rack.

"Am I right in assuming you don't want to go to school until after the funeral?" I asked.

She nodded. "If it's all right."

"Of course. Is there anything else you want to do tomorrow?"

"Sometimes I go to ballet on Mondays. There's an open class for advanced students at five."

"Would you like to go tomorrow?"

She nodded.

"I'll see you get there. And to the Reillys afterwards."

"Thank you," she said, her voice so small I could barely hear her.

"Or you can continue to stay here. I love having you."

She smiled tremulously. "I hate being trouble."

"You're no trouble, Paige." I reached out and patted her hand. "You're a delight."

She teared up and winked the wetness away.

"We can decide tomorrow," I said.

"Okay."

We ate the gooey-delicious pizza and chatted, and as the sun sank low on the horizon, we agreed that half a muffin was just enough to carry us through until dinner.

Ty called as Paige was peeling the aluminum foil from the cookie sheet, and I stepped into the living room for a semblance of privacy.

"I'm here," he said. "It's a nice place. In Georgetown."

"I like Georgetown."

"Come on down."

I laughed. "What time do you start tomorrow?"

"Eight."

"That's about when I'd get there."

"Yeah, I guess that's about right." He paused. "I just spoke to Officer Brownley."

"So you know about the desk."

"Yeah. You think it's anything?"

"No. I mean, it's a great desk, but it's not museum quality, not by a long shot."

"So you keep hunting."

"Exactly. And since we're talking business, there's something else I'd like to ask you about. I know it's not your jurisdiction, but I'm not sure what to do about a possible attempt at fraud." I filled him in about Whistler's palette.

"And this Lesha Moore wrote the letter?"

"Not clear. I think it's more likely that Evan wrote it before he died," I replied, and explained my thinking.

"And the palette?"

"That had to be her. Evan would never have placed the paints in that order. But he might have bought an old palette intending to pass it off as Whistler's without telling her the palette *wasn't* the real one."

"But she's the one who actually submitted the phony palette for appraisal and possible sale, right?"

"Yes, but she might have thought the palette was genuine. Evan might have been the brains behind the scheme and died before he could execute it. My guess is that *he* faked the letter *and* acquired the palette."

"Where's the real palette?"

"Probably boxed up in his uncle's house."

"Why wouldn't he have used the actual Whistler's palette?"

" 'Cause Evan was a junkie but he also was an artist, and even if he wasn't painting for a while, he would have protected it. It was, to him, priceless."

"If it was the real deal, how much would Whistler's palette sell for?" he asked.

"Lots."

"Hundreds, lots," he asked, "or thousands, lots?"

"I don't know. Probably hundreds of thousands," I replied, "maybe more. One of his palettes is in the Smithsonian."

He whistled. "Attempted grand larceny

for sure, then. Okay, since your business is located in Portsmouth, this is their call. I'll fill them in and let you know how they want to proceed. In the meantime, keep everything intact. Don't return anything to Lesha."

After we said good-bye, I stood at the front window for a moment staring out into the night. The moon had risen early and streaks of silver light illuminated the empty world. *To silver light in the dark of night,* my father often toasted. He died before I could ask him where the toast came from. *Maybe he coined it during a moonlit night like this,* I thought.

I returned to the kitchen and asked Paige whether she was ready to start cooking dinner.

"Yeah," she said, smiling a little. "It's fun with you. Rosalie and I mostly tried to do it quickly."

I swallowed hard to keep from crying. Her compliment meant more to me than she could know. I could almost hear my mother telling me I'd done well.

"Excellent. First, we'll caramelize the onions."

"They're big," she said, watching as I hefted two onions.

"Vidalias," I explained. "They were my

389

grandfather's favorite."

My mother had adored her father, a grandfather I'd never met. "He encouraged me to read," she'd explained to me. "I was only eight when he started me on Mickey Spillane." I repeated the story to Paige as I supervised her cutting the onions into paper-thin slices.

"Who's Mickey Spillane?" she asked.

"A mystery writer. The book covers were kind of racy, so her mom, my grandmother, didn't approve."

"What happened?"

I smiled, recalling my mother's face as she told me the story. "My grandfather gave my mom a flashlight so she could read under the covers at night and her mom would never know."

"I love that!"

"*And* he kept her in batteries."

What a guy, I thought, wishing for the thousandth time that I'd known him. An only child of parents who were only children of older parents, I'd never met a relative, and as far as I knew, I had no family at all.

Eric called around seven, to say that the pickup was complete. "And," he added, "I remembered to set the alarm."

"You're the best!" I told him, meaning it. "Thank you."

I turned my attention back to the recipe. We whipped up a nutmeg-laden white sauce, layered Fontina cheese and the onion slices in a lacy pattern on butterflied chicken breasts, sautéed them, and served them over a bed of rice pilaf with a spinach and avocado salad with dried cranberries dressed in a tarragon white wine vinaigrette.

"The secret to salad," I said, drizzling salad dressing, "is to dress less and toss more."

"I've never had anything like this," Paige said. She looked utterly unimpressed.

"You don't have to eat anything you don't like. There's plenty of English muffins so you can always make more pizza."

"I'll try it." She paused, then added, "Rosalie would eat anything, like my dad, but I've always been kind of picky, more like my mom."

"Well, there's no pressure here," I assured her. "You eat what you want."

"Thanks."

She didn't much like the salad, but she did like the chicken and rice, and more to the point, she tried everything, which I told her was pretty darn impressive for a twelve-year-old.

After dinner, she asked to check e-mail and while she was busy at the computer, I found myself unable to settle down. I paced. Cooking with Paige had succeeded in distracting me, but the diversion was over, and my amorphous fears had returned.

Is my secret admirer out there tonight? I asked myself, trying to see into the shadows. I shook my head, confused and troubled. I couldn't stop thinking about Rosalie.

If Rosalie did in fact have drinks with Gerry the night she died, where did she go afterward? Since her car was in her driveway, covered with snow, she must have driven herself home and then gone out again. According to Wes, Gerry's driver reported that Edie's car wasn't visible when he drove Gerry home. Could Gerry have followed Rosalie to her place and then driven her somewhere else, trusting his limo driver to keep her presence secret?

I scrolled through my phone's stored numbers until I found Wes's cell phone number, and pushed the recall button. It went to his voice mail immediately.

"Wes," I said, "it's me, Josie. I have a question — you know that Gerry had drinks with Rosalie, right? The night she died, they were at The Miller House. Here's my question. She drove herself to the restaurant and home again. I know because Paige said Rosalie went out, yet the next day we found her car snowed in. So she must have gone out again later, with someone else doing the driving. Do you know who that someone else could be? Call me, okay? 'Bye."

I flipped the phone closed and looked out toward the hedge, half expecting to see a boxy, dark-colored car. I stood up and stretched, ready to head upstairs when my cell phone rang. *Wes,* I thought, *returning my call.*

It wasn't. The display showed a 207 area code.

"Oh, no," I whispered.

I was unwilling to answer it, yet unable to put it down. The ringing stopped, and still I stared at it. In less than a minute, the envelope icon appeared. There was a message.

"Josie," a voice said as if the speaker were breathlessly exhaling and barely enunciating words. "You need to stop. Stop, Josie." The voice changed and became icy cold and stone hard. "Or you'll be sorry." The words were indistinct, but the underlying emotion was palpable and terrifying. I played it again.

What am I to stop? I wondered. *How can anyone know what I'm doing?* I walked closer to the window and stood in dappled moonlight. I forced myself to breathe deeply, trying to subdue my electrified anxiety. Then, after a moment, I called Officer Brownley.

"I'm sorry to disturb you."

"Not a problem. What's going on?"

"I got another call — a message — and it was pretty disturbing."

"In what way?"

"He — or she — spoke."

"Saying what?"

I closed my eyes, embarrassed. I repeated the message, feeling awkward.

"Did you recognize the voice?"

I thought for a moment. "I don't know about the voice, but last time there was a sound."

"What kind of sound?"

"A clang."

"What was it?"

"I don't know."

"You saved it, right?"

"Yes," I replied, closing my eyes.

"Call me back on your landline, okay?"

"How come?"

After a pause she said, "So I can listen to the message."

"Okay." I hung up.

All at once, I had a terrifying thought. Was Officer Brownley telling me the whole story? Was it just that she wanted to listen to the message? Or was it that someone was listening in to my phone calls and she wanted me off that line? I stared at my cell phone. The 207 caller might have heard my message to Wes. What else might he — or she — have heard? I closed my eyes and leaned against the wall for support, fighting panic.

I opened my eyes and dialed her number again from my regular phone.

"First, give me the number," Officer Brownley said when we were reconnected.

I read off the numbers to her. After I was done, she said, "Hold your cell phone near the receiver and play it for me."

I did so, and she had me hit replay so she could listen to it again.

"How was that?" I asked.

"Good enough for me to get an idea of what you're talking about. You said you didn't recognize the voice, but did it sound like the same caller as before?"

"I don't know. I think so."

She paused for a moment. "You okay?"

"No," I replied. "I'm scared."

"I understand. I'm going to call your local precinct and request extra patrols."

"I thought you and Ty already did that."

"We did. I mean extra-extra patrols."

"Thanks." I swallowed. "Someone is listening in to my calls, aren't they?"

After a chillingly long pause, she said, "Maybe. We'll check it out."

I tried to quiet my too-quick breathing without success. I stood off to the side of the window, out of direct view of anyone outside. Methodically, I looked through the hedge, seeking out something, anything, that would explain my accelerating apprehension, but again I saw nothing. I circled the house, watching, waiting at each stop for something to move or catch my eye, my breathing growing faster, not quieting down as I'd hoped. Someone was trying to scare me and it was working. I was worn to the bone with feeling helpless, and I knew that the only antidote for fear was action.

CHAPTER
TWENTY-NINE

"You're going to think I'm a scaredy cat, but I don't want to stay here tonight," I told Paige.

Paige, standing in candy-striped flannel pajamas, said, "How come you're scared?"

I didn't want to reveal the details, but I couldn't think of how to avoid it. "I got a frightening phone call." I shrugged and tried to smile. "I think it would be prudent to stay somewhere else tonight."

"Okay."

"You don't need to be worried," I assured her, wondering if it was true. "I've alerted the police and they don't think there's any danger." I shrugged. "As I said, I'm a scaredy cat."

She smiled. "Me, too."

I smiled back. "So let's pack up and head to Ty's."

"Is it okay for us just to show up?"

"Yeah." I smiled again. "That's what

friends are for. He's not there, but I have a key."

I kept clothes and various grooming items at his place, so I had no need to pack, but Paige did. She was, presumably, returning to the Reillys' tomorrow, so she needed to bring all of her stuff with her tonight.

Paige packed in ten minutes flat. Together we swung the heavy duffel bag into the trunk and loaded everything else into the backseat. I didn't wait for the car to warm up; I just took off, and kept checking the mirrors to see if we were being followed. We traversed back roads thick with packed snow and shimmering ice, and when we arrived, I was confident that we were alone and safe. My eyes still on the move, I used the remote device that I kept in my glove compartment and parked in Ty's garage. I exhaled, feeling as if it were the first clear breath I'd taken in a while, inordinately relieved that my car was out of sight.

Once we were inside, I reset the alarms that guarded the house and property, turned on lights, turned up the thermostat, and showed Paige to the guest room.

"I'm kind of keyed up," I said. "I'm going to watch some TV. I know it's late, but in case you want to join me, you're welcome."

"I'd like that," she said. "I know I couldn't

sleep either."

I got her busy in the kitchen microwaving popcorn and, using Ty's landline, called him on his cell phone. I didn't want to use mine. The thought that someone might be listening to my calls completely terrified me.

The call went to his voice mail and, trying to keep it light so as not to worry him, said, "It's me. I'm crashing at your place with Paige tonight. No biggy, but another crank call came in and I just plumb don't want to be at my house, so here we are! I told Officer Brownley all about the call. Talk to you soon. 'Bye."

I considered waiting until morning to call Officer Brownley and tell her where to meet me, but then I remembered that the extra patrols she'd arranged would need to be redirected.

"I hope this is the last time I'll talk to you today," I joked.

"Not a problem. Actually, I was just going to call you."

"How come?"

"You first," she said.

"I'm at Ty's. I just got too scared to stay at my place. He has an alarm system, so I feel safer here."

"Fair enough, but you should have called and let me or a local patrol car escort you."

"Yeah, probably. But it didn't even occur to me."

"Well, I'm glad you're there." She paused. "Josie? Don't hesitate to call me. Anytime. Even if you think it's silly. Okay?"

The compassion and caring evident in her words and tone brought unexpected tears to my eyes, and for a moment, I couldn't speak. "Thank you. That means a lot." I cleared my throat. "So why were you going to call me?"

She cleared her throat. "Keep in mind, I'm no expert, but I asked someone who is. Basically, someone sends a short message to your phone, that, unbeknownst to you, creates a three-way call. He or she simply listens in."

Unconsciously, I stepped back until my thighs touched a chair. I sank into it. "You're kidding," I said.

"No. It's easy if you know what you're doing. There's a little reprogramming involved, but not much. It seems the three-way call is activated by *your* phone, so they're alerted when you're on the phone by their own phone ringing."

"But wait! If it's initiated by *my* phone, the three-way call charge will be on my phone bill."

"Right. Except we already know the phone

numbers involved — the disposable cell phones."

My heart-pounding terror faded, replaced by righteous outrage. "I feel violated."

"Yeah. Obviously, you shouldn't use your cell phone until we sort this out."

Paige came into the room bearing a huge bowl of buttery popcorn.

"Got it," I said, forcing myself to sound competent, not panicked. "Thank you."

"Anything else?"

"Nope! You've given me plenty to think about. See you in the morning."

As I replaced the receiver, Paige asked, "Are you okay?"

I shrugged. "I won't lie to you, Paige. This is an anxious time."

She nodded, but didn't speak.

"Do you know how to make a fire?" I asked, eager to busy my hands and mind.

"No. Is it hard?"

"Not if you cheat."

She giggled. "What do you mean?"

"We use a Duraflame log, and stack wood on it. You can't fail."

I deputized her to hand me logs and showed her how to crisscross them so oxygen could flow. She observed the process with interest, and within minutes, we had a crackling fire.

Paige sat beside me on the sofa, clutching her knees to her chest as we watched a rerun of one of her favorite TV shows, *Project Runway*. I was pleased that she was animated as she voiced her opinions, but I knew that her grief and shock would return, catching her unawares, and casting her adrift once again. But for now at least, she was having some fun, and I was, too. But my neck and shoulders were aching with tension, and my pulse wouldn't quiet.

Ty called at six the next morning.

"I just got your message," he said. "Sorry I missed you last night — I crashed out early."

"No problem," I replied drowsily.

"Are you awake?" he asked.

"Not really."

"I need you to try to focus. It's important."

"Later. Right now I'm in your bed, and you're not here."

"Officer Brownley is going to take your cell phone and give you a disposable one. She needs to take yours for audio analysis."

"Uh-huh. She told me."

"Make sure you don't give out the number of the disposable one she'll be bringing you. It's important."

I sat up, pushing aside the duvet, fully awake. "Jeez," I said. "But if I call someone, they'll know my number."

"No, they won't. It's unlisted. Their phone ID display will read 'private caller.' "

"Okay."

"She said she's meeting you at seven-thirty. What's your day look like?"

"I'm taking Paige to see her lawyer at two and maybe to ballet at five. And if there's time, I want to run over to Heyer's and do some work on the installation."

"In terms of the disposable phone she'll be giving you, I'll know the number and she will, and no one else."

"What should I do about calls that I might get on my real phone? You know how much I use it. It's my primary number."

"Short term, check your voice mail, and tell us if any more calls like this come in. Long term, you'll get the phone back eventually." He cleared his throat. "By the way, I like the idea of coming home and finding you in my bed."

I lay back down. "I was wondering if you were going to respond to that comment," I said, fishing for a compliment.

"Oh, yeah, and as soon as possible, I'll prove it to you."

"Excellent," I said, smiling, closing my

eyes, relishing the moment.

An hour and a half later, Paige and I were in the car en route to my office, with Officer Brownley following close behind.

The threat that seemed so dire last night seemed less frightening this morning. And I was as eager as all get-out to tell Fred about the photocopied pages from a journal and to look at Rosalie's desk in the light of day.

Fred, his tie loosened, looked up as we entered Prescott's. Fred was a night owl, so it was surprising to find him at work at seven-thirty on a Monday morning.

"Fred!" I said. "What on God's earth are you doing here at this hour?"

He glanced at his computer monitor to check the time. "I'm almost done."

"You've been here all night?"

"Yeah." His black, square-framed glasses had slid down and he pushed them back.

I wanted to pepper him with questions, but hesitated. He'd been working on Rosalie's papers, and I didn't want to create an awkward situation with Paige.

"Have you met Paige? Rosalie's sister."

"No." He stood up and said, "Hi."

"Hi," Paige replied.

"Any news about the all-night project?" I minijerked my head toward Paige and grimaced, hoping he would interpret my signal correctly.

"Those papers you wanted me to sort through?"

Appreciating his discretion, I mouthed, "Good job." Then aloud, I said, "Yeah." To Paige, I added, "I'll just be a sec."

"No problem," she said, ever patient, and sat down on one of the guest chairs and pulled out her iPod. Melancholy seemed to shroud her, simultaneously insulating her from pain like a protective cloak, yet also rendering her heart-wrenchingly vulnerable.

"I still have about a third of a box to go through," Fred said.

"You sure you're not too tired?"

He shrugged and stretched. "It shouldn't take more than a few hours."

"Have you found any photocopied journal pages?"

"What kind of journal?"

"I don't know."

He paused, reflecting. "Nothing like that, I don't think."

I nodded, then turned to Paige. "Ready?"

"Sure." She stood up.

"Follow me," I told her, swinging my arm over my head in a show of fun bravado, and led the way to the warehouse.

Rosalie's desk was in the new-inventory

area, swaddled in protective padding. I carefully unwrapped the quilted fabric, and when the desk was revealed, Paige exclaimed, "I remember it!"

Under our bright lighting, the red-dark patina of the mahogany almost glowed. "It's a beauty," I said. "Your mom had wonderful taste."

She smiled a little at my words and circled the desk.

I noticed residue from the police examination, powder and something a little sticky. Using a clean white cotton rag that we bought by the bagful, I wiped everything clean. I spotted no variations in the finish, which might indicate refurbishing and is almost certain to diminish value.

As Paige looked on, I continued my examination.

I slid each drawer out and examined every surface. Using a handheld spotlight, I illuminated the underparts of the desk. The wood was cracked, but no more than I would expect in a two-hundred-year-old piece of furniture. In dealer's parlance, it appeared "dry and untouched."

"Would you hand me the camera on that shelf?" I asked Paige.

I photographed the faded maker's mark, then turned my attention to the blotter. It appeared permanently affixed. It was thin, and the fleur-de-lis pattern etched in gold on the four corner pieces was a perfect match for the silkwood inlay on the slant top and drawer fronts. I wondered if the blotter had been fabricated to match the desk and was, in fact, period appropriate, or someone had commissioned it at a later date. As I ran my finger along the edge, I asked Paige if she knew.

"My mom had it made for Rosalie's birthday."

"Do you remember when?"

She nodded. "About a year after Rosalie's graduation, I think. She got the blotter for her next birthday."

I eased my fingertips under the front edge and felt it give and I lifted it. A standard business-size envelope was centered under the blotter. It was labeled *Paige.* Its presence told me that the police hadn't looked under the blotter.

Paige reached for the envelope.

"You can't touch it," I told her. "We need to call the police."

"It's mine," she protested.

"I know. But the police need to test for fingerprints and stuff. Then you can read it."

She didn't speak, but I could tell from the

tension in her jaw that she was angry. I walked half a dozen steps to a wall phone and, from memory, dialed Officer Brownley's cell phone.

"It's Josie. I found a letter to Paige in the desk."

"Where?" she asked, sounding astounded.

"Under the blotter."

After a long pause, "Have you touched it?"

"No."

"Thanks, Josie. I'm on my way."

"Will you have to take it? Can you examine it here? It's addressed to Paige."

Another pause. "Tell her I'm sorry, but we will need to take it. We'll be sure and let her know what it says as soon as we can."

I hung up and repeated Officer Brownley's response.

Paige stood up, her arms crossed in front of her, her eyes icy.

I bit my lip. I knew I'd done the right thing, the only thing under the circumstances, but still — it must be awful for her to see the communication and be prohibited from reading it.

"Come on," I said, and took her back to the office.

She sat with her lips pressed together and her eyes down, listening to music. I asked

Fred for some papers to sort. He handed me a stack from the files in Rosalie's house, and while we waited for Officer Brownley, I systematically reviewed each one. I found nothing of interest. Half an hour later, just as Gretchen and Sasha were arriving, Officer Brownley arrived. Accompanied by Paige, I led her to Rosalie's desk.

"We didn't think to look there," Officer Brownley remarked when I showed her where we found the letter.

I nodded. "Can you see if the envelope's unsealed? If so, maybe we can at least read the letter now."

Wearing plastic gloves, she flipped it over. The flap was tucked in snugly.

"We need to let the trace-evidence people examine it intact," she said. "I'm sorry."

I nodded. Paige didn't respond at all, but she looked angrier than ever.

Officer Brownley slid the envelope into an evidence bag, promised to keep us posted, and left.

"How long will it take?" Paige asked once she was gone.

"I don't know."

"Josie!" Gretchen's voice crackled on the intercom. "Fred wants to show you something."

"Let's go," I told Paige.

As soon as we stepped inside the office, Fred handed me a collection of hand-written notes in a manila folder, and said, "I found it just this way."

I nodded and opened the folder. The notes were written on steno-pad sheets, the top of each page frayed where it had been ripped from the notebook. I read:

Private Richard Windsor

- *recruited Kaskaskia, 1803*
- *living in Sangamon River, IL???*
- *joined L&C, Camp Dubois, 1 Jan 1804*

More than two hundred years ago, I thought, *about the same time as a British carpenter was building Rosalie's desk.* I continued reading.

DOB — unknown
POB — unknown
Woodsman, hunter
Q:

1. *Where was he from? (And when born?)*
2. *Where did he learn to read and write?*
3. *Formal schooling? (Records kept?)*
4. *Church records?*

5. Harrison Bros. records?

His date and place of birth were unknown. So, too, it seemed, was his background. Rosalie's notes went on for several pages. I was reading a scholar's research. Evidently, Private Windsor was a member of the Lewis and Clark expedition. I wondered why she was interested in him more than any of the others. I skipped to the end.

Peabody Museum — Harvard
Nat'l Park Service — Oregon???

"Take a look at this," Fred said. "It may relate to the same thing."

He handed me a typewritten letter of agreement documenting the sale of a book called *The Private Journal of Private Richard Windsor.* The letter was dated March 4, 1981. Sarah Chaffee bought it from someone called Hayden Furleigh for $4,000, a huge sum for any but the rarest books back then, and still a substantial chunk of cash. I got an adrenaline rush. *Bingo!* I thought. Rosalie was right — potentially, the journal was of incalculable value. I glanced at the last entry I'd read:

Peabody Museum — Harvard

Were those two museums that housed documents Rosalie wanted to consult? I wondered. Or were those two possible buyers of the journal?

I turned to Paige. "Who's Sarah Chaffee?" I asked.

"My mother. Why?"

"Who's Hayden Furleigh?"

"My aunt. Rodney's mother."

"Hayden and your mom were sisters?"

"Yes. Why?"

"We're going through your sister's papers, and there was a reference to them. Do you know anything about your aunt?"

"Not much. We didn't speak to that side of the family."

"I thought the breach was between your sister and Rodney?"

"I don't think so. I think they inherited it. I don't really know. Except that whatever it was about had something to do with money."

"Fair enough," I said, thinking that maybe Rodney would be able to shed some light on the issue.

"Good work, Fred. Outstanding. Is this everything? Are you done?"

"Yup."

"Put everything in the safe, okay?"

"Will do."

"And then go home!"

"Yeah," he agreed, stretching.

I didn't want to say anything to Paige until I had my hands on the journal, but I was so energized I could hardly contain myself from hooting and kicking up my heels. It looked like we'd identified Rosalie's secret treasure. Standard operating procedure for a scholar would be to photocopy the journal to protect the original from wear and tear or harm. Assuming Rosalie had followed this protocol, where were the photocopied pages? And where was the original journal?

We'd need to go through every book on every shelf to see if she'd disguised the journal by slipping it into an ordinary dust jacket, a simple way to camouflage it from casual observers. I shook my head. From her own journal entry it was obvious that Rosalie hadn't considered Cooper a casual observer. On the contrary, her assessment was that he was a thief. I wondered if he was a murderer, too.

My next step was to be certain we hadn't missed the photocopy, but before I could ask Gretchen to get teams to Rosalie's office at Hitchens and her house to pack up all of the books and remaining paper materials, the phone rang. It was Officer Brownley.

"I need to fax you the letter."

"Sure." I gave her the number.

Almost immediately, the fax machine whirred and clicked and a sheet of paper rolled out.

Dear Paige,

If you're reading this, something's happened to me. Not that I expect anything to happen to me, mind you, but you know me — I like to be prepared.

So, kiddo, here's the scoop: We own a rare journal. Actually, calling it rare doesn't begin to describe it — It's darn close to priceless. I had to take it out of storage because Cooper was sniffing around. He saw a receipt from Tim's where I was storing it and — surprise, surprise — got his own unit. I nearly fainted when I ran into him there! Knowing how much he wants to get his hands on it, I could just see him sneaking in a pair of bolt-cutters to break in and steal it. Anyway, the purpose of this note is twofold.

First, when you're old enough, sell it. I hope a museum will buy it, but if you get a higher bid from a private collector, take it! I'm too romantic for my own good and it was a romantic notion to donate it. It's appropriate to sell it, sweetie, so don't hesitate. It'll set you up for life — college, travel, everything. Talk to Josie Prescott. You know who I mean, right? My friend, Josie. She's as honest as the day is long and will guide you in selling it for the best price.

Second, here's where I put it — not ideal because of the harsh weather conditions, but at least it's safe: DZYNVMRL&X.

Love you to bits, Rosalie

I took a deep breath and handed it to Paige. "Here."

Paige read it slowly, then gave it back to me and sat in statuelike silence, rivulets of tears running down her cheeks.

Tears welled as I read her tribute to me, and I closed my eyes for a moment, willing myself to regain control.

"It sounds just like her," I said after a moment.

"Did Cooper kill her?" she whispered.

"I don't know, but you can bet the police are checking into it."

I called Officer Brownley. "I've read it," I

415

told her.

"Obviously we're following up on Cooper's storage unit. My question to you is, do you or Paige know what those letters at the bottom mean?"

"Probably it's the same code as in the kitchen. The artichoke code."

"That's what I figured. Can you decipher it for me?"

"Sure. I'll call you back."

As I hung up, I asked, "Do you want to decode it, Paige?"

She shook her head. I patted her shoulder, and said, "I'll be down in a minute."

Upstairs, I drew a three-row grid. I wrote *artichokes* across the top and *DZYNVMRL&X* in the center. One by one, I decoded the characters. Six letters in, I paused, certain I knew the answer.

a	r	t	i	c	h	o	k	e	s
d	z	y	n	v	m	r	l	&	x
c	h	e	e	s	e				

I stared at the word. My pulse began to race. I stood up, then sat down, too agitated to stay still. " 'Cheese,' " I said aloud, took a deep breath, telling myself to focus, to

slow down, and then, with a nod, I rushed
to finish.

a	r	t	i	c	h	o	k	e	s
d	z	y	n	v	m	r	l	&	x
c	h	e	e	s	e	c	a	v	e

I hurried back downstairs. Paige hadn't
moved. Her cheeks were wet.

"Paige, do you have a cheese cave?" I
asked.

"Yes," she said, brushing away her tears
with the back of her hand.

Gretchen handed her a tissue.

"Tell me about it," I directed.

"We built it."

"You and Rosalie?"

"Uh-huh."

"Where?"

"In back of the house."

I gawked at her. "The hill in the back
corner?"

"Yeah."

"You made a cheese cave?" I asked, flab-
bergasted.

Paige smiled as she patted away more
tears, then twisted the tissue into a screw.
"It's not much of a cave. It's kind of small."

"Why did you make it?"

"For cheese. Rosalie thought it would be fun to make it ourselves."

"What got her interested in making cheese?" I asked.

"A woman named Michelle Grover, I think her name is. Rosalie heard her speak at some lecture somewhere and got kind of excited. We got a book."

The book on the kitchen counter, I recalled. "What's inside the cave?"

"Nothing. I mean, just the shelves, you know?"

"Tell me about it."

"It's small. It's really just a dome covering a hole in the ground with some shelves and a really low ceiling."

"A ceiling! That sounds pretty impressive."

Paige giggled, her tears, for the moment, dried up. "You wouldn't say that if you saw it. It's just chicken wire, cement, and wood."

I shook my head. "When did you build it?"

"Over Christmas break."

"You did all that in one week?"

"It only took a few days — remember how warm it was over Christmas? It wasn't all that hard."

That's just before Rosalie emptied her storage room at Tim's, I thought. Tingles of

418

anticipation raced up and down my spine.

I picked up the phone. "Officer Brownley?"

"Were you able to decode it?"

"Yup. 'Cheese cave.' "

"What is that?"

"I'll meet you at the Chaffee house and show you."

"No," she said, and hearing the intensity of her response, I paused, fear returning. "I'll come get you. I'll be there in twenty minutes."

I was in appraiser mode, eager to discover Rosalie's — now Paige's — treasure, and in my enthusiasm, I'd lost sight of the larger issue. Rosalie had been murdered and her killer was still at large — and, from what I could tell, as we were circling closer and closer, the police thought there was a chance that the murderer had set his sights on me.

Chapter Thirty

Officer Brownley stepped inside, setting the chimes jingling. "All set?" she asked.

"Give me one sec," I said, and ran up to my office. I dialed her cell phone. "It's me from upstairs. I didn't want to discuss Cooper in front of Paige, but I need to tell you something right away. You know how Rosalie wrote in her diary about catching Cooper with a copy of her journal pages in his hands? We've finished going through her papers — there's no such copy. Apparently it's missing."

She paused, considering the implications. "Thanks."

Downstairs, I grabbed my toolbox in case we needed to open a chest or some mechanism in the cheese cave. Officer Brownley drove.

I'd offered Paige the opportunity to stay at the office and hang out with Gretchen, but she'd chosen to come along. In her shoes, I would have done the same thing.

It was another sunny day, though not as mild as yesterday. Sunlight warmed the New Hampshire winter colors, various shades of brown and gray, lending them resonance and richness. *No wonder Evan Woodricky chose to stay in New Hampshire to paint,* I thought. *Browns and grays aren't only the shades that Whistler preferred, they're also the colors of New Hampshire in winter.*

All at once I realized that I hadn't heard from Wes in response to my question about what happened to Rosalie after she had drinks with Gerry, and then a moment later, it occurred to me that I hadn't checked my voice mail. I patted around inside my tote bag until I found the disposable cell phone Officer Brownley had bestowed on me. It felt odd in my hand.

Sure enough, Wes had called.

"So the answer is that I don't know and I don't think anyone else does either. No one admits driving Rosalie anywhere. According to my police source, both Gerry and the driver say that Gerry got in his limo alone and went straight home. I heard that Gerry's now saying he didn't see Rosalie that night at all, that it was a different night. Even though the bartender says otherwise, try and prove it's a lie. The lounge was packed, so how can the staff be a hundred percent certain it was *that* night she was or wasn't there? Anyway, that's it. . . . Whatcha got for me? Call me."

I closed the phone and slid it back into my tote bag. I shrugged. I was glad when we turned onto Hanover Street and I could stop thinking about where poor Rosalie had been the night she was murdered — and whether someone, most likely Cooper, had lured her to her death.

Pulling up to the house, Officer Brownley hit a huge puddle and cascades of water streamed up on either side of her patrol car. She parked close to the banked snow, and we piled out.

With Officer Brownley and Paige close behind me, I trudged through the yard. I used my arm to sweep away the heavy, wet snow that blocked access to the cheese cave.

The doors were reminiscent of those used in storm cellars, two wooden panels lying at a moderate angle, hinged on the outside, and braced with a crossbar. In the center of the crossbar was a lock.

"Okay," I said, "here goes nothing."

The key I'd found hidden in Rosalie's toiletry box fit, and the doors opened easily. I smiled in eager anticipation, dropped to my knees, and leaned in.

My little flashlight lit up white-washed, dimpled concrete walls and a single row of wooden shelves, maybe ash. *Not bad,* I thought, *for two amateurs and a few days' construction.* Within easy reach, I saw a tan metal box.

"There's a box," I called, my words muffled and echoey in the airless chamber.

"Don't touch it without gloves," Officer Brownley instructed.

Gingerly gripping the handle on the top, I slid it toward me and shone my light around one last time to be certain I hadn't missed anything. I stood up and relocked the doors while clutching the metal box to my chest, as if it were gold.

"Got it," I said.

I sat in the front seat next to Officer Brownley. The box rested on the seat between us. Paige was in the back.

Wearing plastic gloves, Officer Brownley unhitched the latch. Inside was an unsealed, padded envelope, the kind used to mail fragile items. She wiggled it out. Inside the envelope was a see-through plastic baggie, and inside the baggie was a leather-bound book. She reached into her coat pocket for another pair of plastic gloves. Once I had them on, she handed me the baggie.

I extracted the butter-soft volume from its plastic container, and carefully opened it. The title page read, *The Journal of Private Richard Windsor.* It was hand numbered, in an elegant hand, *12 of 20,* and it had been printed by Harrison Brothers of Boston in 1809. I turned a few pages. Even through the gloves I sensed that the paper felt right, heavy and cottony. At first glance, the volume appeared to be in mint condition. I opened to page one and began to read.

"Not one among us knows that I can read and write," it began, *"and I do not intend to tell them. The less the others know, the better it will be for me. When they think you are less educated and knowledgeable than they are, they talk more openly and with less discretion."*

"What is it?" Officer Brownley asked.

"I'm not sure."

This one slim volume was, without question, valuable. But whether it was worth a few hundred dollars, as any leather-bound book in excellent condition from that era would be, or tens or hundreds of thousands — or more — required research.

Officer Brownley watched as I repackaged the book.

"I'll need to take the book in for forensic

examination," Officer Brownley stated.

I chose my words carefully. "I understand that there may be forensic evidence that you need to collect. But you should have an expert there to ensure that you don't damage it."

"Like you?"

"Yes."

Paige asked, "May I see it?"

"Sure." I carefully extracted it from the metal container and padded envelope. I held it up, still inside the plastic bag. "We shouldn't touch it any more until after the police finish with it."

She nodded and stared at the cover.

"It's old, huh?" Officer Brownley said.

"Yeah."

"So why is it rare?" she asked. "Because it's from the early eighteen hundreds?"

"Certainly that's one reason. And it's in pristine condition. And, evidently, only twenty copies were printed, which means it's scarce. Who knows how many of the other copies exist, so it's also probably rare."

"Does it matter what the book is about?"

"Absolutely. We need to research it, but if Richard Windsor did, in fact, write this journal while on the Lewis and Clark expedition, it's priceless. It's of indescribable historical importance."

"Which is why Cooper wanted to steal it," Paige interjected, sounding angry.

"We don't know for sure that he did want to," Officer Brownley cautioned.

"Rosalie said so in her letter."

"I know, and we're investigating it. But we shouldn't jump to any conclusions."

Paige, sitting in the backseat, her arms folded across her chest, seemed utterly unpersuaded by Officer Brownley's reasonable comment. From the look on Paige's face, she was ready to round up a posse and lynch him before nightfall.

"Do you think Ms. Chaffee told anyone about the journal?" Officer Brownley asked me.

"Her book editor," I replied, easing the journal back into the padded envelope and sliding it into the box. "My guess is that's it."

We discussed logistics and Officer Brownley agreed to drop us at Heyer's so I could hang another painting. She glanced at her watch. "I'll call the tech guys while you're there and set something up so you can talk to them before they begin."

"Can I come inside?" Paige asked. "I'd like to see where Rosalie worked if that's all right."

I agreed as Officer Brownley pulled to a

stop at the front door. "Call me before you come out," she instructed, and the hair on the back of my neck bristled.

Inside Heyer's, Paige and I signed in at the reception station.

"Hey, Josie! Aren't you an early bird!" Una said.

"Am I? What time is it?"

"A little after nine — not so early, I guess."

"Well, let's hope I catch a worm regardless," I replied, then realized how stupid that sounded, and laughed. "Well, actually, I don't want a worm. I'm just here to hang a painting. Have you met Paige?"

"I think so. At last summer's company picnic, right?"

"That was a fun time," Paige said, leaving it open as to whether they'd ever met.

"I liked Rosalie a lot and I'm really, *really* sorry for your loss," Una said.

"Thank you," Paige murmured, looking down.

"Why don't you wait over here until I see if it's all right for you to take a look at Rosalie's office, okay? I won't be long."

"Okay," she said, taking a seat in the far corner.

I greeted Tricia, then pointed to the still-crated James Gale Tyler seascape. "Would you let Gerry know I'm here? I'd like to hang it if I can."

She picked up her phone and buzzed through. "Josie's here to hang the painting."

"Josie!" Gerry shouted, sounding as buoyant as ever. Tricia hung up the phone as Gerry poked his head out of his office. "Great to see ya, doll," he told me, winking. "Go to work!"

I pried open the crate, then wrestled the painting out. As I set aside the container, I suddenly had a thought. After Gerry left The Miller House, perhaps Edie followed Rosalie home. Edie could have suggested that they talk about the situation calmly, like adults, and Rosalie, naive and optimistic and deeply in love, agreed, and got in Edie's car.

Edie might have taken her to a quiet place — the Rocky Point jetty, for instance. Maybe she intended only to talk, but Rosalie, euphoric and thus reckless, refused to give up Gerry; probably she even refused to discuss it, instead suggesting that Edie resign herself to the inevitable, and so from Edie's perspective, there were no other options — Rosalie had to die.

Then I thought about Cooper. He had no alibi, which meant that the same time sequence would work for him, too. If he was desperate to get Rosalie to stop her legal actions against him, he might have wanted a private talk. Maybe he followed her, waiting for an opportunity to persuade her to discuss the situation one-on-one, without lawyers. Rosalie, riding high with a book contract and secure in the knowledge that the journal was safe, might have stepped voluntarily into Cooper's car. It wasn't a stretch to imagine Cooper's jealous rage exploding in one disastrous strike.

I shook off the frightening image and breathed in deeply. Finally I turned to Gerry and forced myself to focus on the task at hand.

"So I'm still going to hang the Tyler here, right?" I asked, pointing at an area above two club chairs set off to the side.

"What do you think? Should we hang it in Ned's office?" he asked, squeezing my arm. "He said he likes it."

"Ned?" I repeated, surprised. "Ned likes Western themes, not maritime art. Did Ned say he wanted this piece in particular?"

"Not directly," he replied with a wink. "He admired it, so I said to myself, let him have it. Ned's a helluva trooper, ya know? CFO of a company like this with a CEO like me . . . ," he said, trailing off into a guffaw. "I owe that dude a lot."

"It's up to you, of course, but the Sharp

was a very generous gift."

"Thanks, doll. But with the board meeting coming up, well, let me just say that he's risen to the occasion — really acted above and beyond the call, you know what I'm saying?"

I didn't have any idea what he was saying and paused to give myself time to think. "Whatever you want is fine with me. How about if I offer him the choice — the Tyler or another Western scene?"

He smiled broadly. "That's a killer idea, doll." He rubbed my arm and I drew away.

"If he chooses a Western-themed object, we could sell the Tyler to pay for it."

"Nah, it's only money, right, doll? But I like the idea of asking him. It'll be a sign of respect." He chuckled, amused at I didn't know what. "Whatever you think is best, you go ahead and do. I know you won't rook me."

"Sure. I'll take it over now," I said, glad for an excuse to leave Gerry's presence. He gave me the heebie-jeebies.

"I'll catch ya later, doll," Gerry said, swinging his coat over his shoulder. To Tricia he added, "I'll be at that meeting. Should be back after lunch. Ya need me, ya call."

"Yes, sir," she said.

I selected the tools I'd need to hang the painting from the toolbox I kept near Tricia's desk, then carefully picked it up and headed out of the anteroom. "Tricia, would you ask Una to send Paige back here? Paige is Rosalie's sister, and wants to see where she worked."

"Poor thing."

I stepped into the corridor and waved to Paige as she turned the corner. "I need to show this painting to someone," I told her, pointing toward the seascape. "Would you keep me company? You can see Rosalie's office in a few minutes."

By the time we got to the other side of the building, my arms were feeling it and I was glad to lean the painting against Ned's assistant's desk. I greeted her, introduced Paige, and surveyed the anteroom. There was no obvious place to hang it. The walls were full, overdecorated, in fact. There were three paintings of the Rocky Mountains, one of cowboys sitting by a camp fire, another of a cowboy on a cliff, and several framed artifacts.

"Josie!" Ned said, stepping out of his office. "Paige," he added, "long time no speak."

"Hi, Ned," Paige said.

"Sorry about Rosalie. Quite a shock."

She nodded and looked down.

"Sorry I couldn't make the tag sale on Saturday, Josie."

"You will sometime," I said.

"Gerry said you were going to be working in *his* office this morning. Did our faithful leader chase you away?"

"No," I replied, wishing his sarcasm was less biting. "He wanted to know whether you'd like the Tyler." I picked it up and held it high so he could see it at eye level.

"What do you think of it?" Ned asked.

"I love it," I said. "Tyler's one of the best. He really captures the feel of life at sea. Look at the billowing sail — can't you just hear that wind?"

"You're a good saleswoman."

"I don't mean to be," I said, lowering it. "Gerry asked me to find out if you want it. If not, he said I could buy you a Western art object — more in keeping with your taste."

"Sold," he said, slapping the desk. "We kill two birds with one stone that way. I get an object I actually want and you'll earn another commission. Please thank Gerry for me — and for you."

"That's not why I suggested it!" I protested. He was making me sound like an ambulance-chasing lawyer.

"Of course not," he said as if we were in

league together, grinning.

His cuckoo clock clanged once, marking the quarter hour. *Time to leave,* I thought.

"Okay, then . . . you go ahead of me, Paige," I said, hoisting the painting. "See you later."

"Wait a sec," Ned said.

"What?"

"When will I hear about *my* art?"

I lowered the painting to the ground again and looked through the open door into his office, reviewing the diverse mix of special items — the nicely mounted arrowheads, the knob-handled walking stick, the bear-teeth necklace, the Remington repro. *Maybe he'd like a* real *Remington,* I thought. I'd just read about a sale. One of Frederic Remington's pieces, weighing in at one thousand pounds, called *Heroic Bronco Buster* had sold for $16,000. That was in the ballpark of what Gerry had in mind to spend, comparable to the Tyler.

"Soon," I replied. "Let me put together some ideas for your review. Is later this week all right?"

"Art before business!" Ned said as if that meant something.

With a final "See ya," Paige and I left.

"Are you sure I can't help?" Paige asked as we walked back.

433

"Nah. It's heavy, but it's my responsibility, you know?"

Back in Tricia's office, I leaned the painting against the far wall, then used the key Tricia handed me to open the door to the little storage room that had served as Rosalie's office. Nothing looked disturbed.

"Can I go in?" Paige asked.

"Yes," I said, "and you can look through things, but you can't take anything away yet. And you should try not to disturb anything, okay?"

"Okay," she agreed.

In Gerry's office, I reviewed the location I'd selected. There was ample space for the painting. The mounting moldings and lighting tracks were already installed, so all I had to do was ensure that the painting was level and position the light fixture properly. I dragged the small ladder into place and lugged my toolbox into the room. It took several minutes to adjust the wires, but when the painting was hung and the diffused incandescent light turned on, I was thrilled with the result.

I stretched and glanced at the crystal clock on Gerry's desk. Soup to nuts, it had only taken me twenty minutes to complete the installation. *Not bad,* I thought.

I peeked into Rosalie's office. Paige was

sitting in the desk chair holding the photograph of her and Rosalie eating ice cream, staring as if the image could provide answers.

"Paige?"

She whipped her head around, startled.

"Sorry to disturb you."

"No, it's okay." She slid the photo onto the desk. "I was just thinking."

"What about?"

She stood up. "I was thinking how Rosalie loved ice cream. We always had three or four flavors in the freezer, even in winter."

"What's your favorite?"

She smiled. "Black cherry."

"What do you think? Should we get some for lunch?"

She laughed a little. "Okay."

"The empty crate isn't too heavy. Do you think you can carry it?"

"Sure."

I picked up the toolbox, said good-bye to Tricia, and led the way to the front. Standing by the door, I called Officer Brownley, as instructed, to tell her we were ready to leave.

"Officer Griffin is there. He'll take you to the station house so you can talk to the forensic guys and then he'll bring you back to your place."

"Okay. Where are you?"

There was a long pause and I thought she wasn't going to answer. "I'm en route to Cooper's house to execute a search warrant. I'll let you know if we find anything that relates to your appraisal."

"Wow!" I exclaimed, wishing I was riding shotgun and could help in the search.

Chapter
Thirty-One

At the Rocky Point police station, I showed the forensic examiner how to open the book without breaking its spine, how to turn pages without risking ripping the paper, and how to slide the journal out of the plastic bag without marring the leather.

"We'll treat it with kid gloves," the man assured me as he wrote out a receipt.

Feeling as if I were allowing a stranger to babysit my infant, I watched as the man packed it up. I stood in the entryway buttoning my coat, chatting to Cathy, when Cooper appeared from an inside corridor.

"It's outrageous," Cooper stated, his voice pulsating with impotent wrath.

I watched as he was led into the small alcove where they took fingerprints. I knew where it was located because two years ago, they'd walked me into the same place and taken mine.

Cooper didn't notice me. He was too busy

abusing the police officer, a longtime veteran of the force, for his stupidity and for over-stepping his authority. I noticed that not a hair of Cooper's carefully coiffed mane was out of place.

"Ready?" Griff asked me.

I waved good-bye to Cathy, and with a final glance toward the alcove where Cooper's rant continued, said, "Absolutely."

"Fred's finally gone?" I asked, seeing his empty desk.

Sasha laughed and I turned to her. "Sorry," she said, apologetic as ever, for no reason. "He got interested in the Barkley tallboy and wanted to start researching it, but I made him go home."

"Good — he was half asleep when I left." I turned to Gretchen. "I'm going upstairs to do some work. Do you need any help with the mailing?"

She rolled her eyes. "Always!"

"Paige? Can we draft you again?"

"Sure."

"Great." I headed toward the warehouse. "Oh, one more thing, Gretchen. Get us all ice cream for lunch, okay? Paige, I know, wants black cherry. I want marble fudge."

Her astonished look made me laugh.

■ ■ ■ ■

Ty called as Paige and I were driving to Mr. Bolton's office — the first phone call I'd received on my new phone. I glanced in my rearview mirror. Griff followed close behind.

"I only have a minute," he said. "We're on break. But I wanted to tell you we've picked up the man who ordered your flowers."

"You're kidding!" I exclaimed.

"Nope. The florist did a good job in describing him. He was, in fact, homeless. He received money to take a cab, make the drop, and cab back."

"Who gave him the money?" I asked, my heart racing at the thought that I was about to learn my secret admirer's identity.

"He doesn't know. He never saw the man before and he hasn't seen him since."

"But it *was* a man."

"Right." He paused. "Or a woman wearing a good disguise. He's looking at photos now. But his attention was pretty much focused on the cash the man was holding."

My heart sank. "Another dead end."

"Nope. Another opportunity for diligent police work. We've just begun to show him photos. Give the process a chance to work."

"Okay," I agreed, trying to hide my disappointment.

Brown and white, I thought, *the color of disappointment.*

Everything on either side of the road appeared to be brown or white — brown bark on trees with a few tawny-colored leaves that somehow still clung to branches; white snow edged in brown soot; sunlight filtering through gray-white clouds and stippling the thick woods with specks of white light; brown roofs from distant homes; and the white spire of a small church barely visible through the trees as we drove past. Shades of January, sharply defined, softly etched on the vista. January, a hard month, a month of disappointments.

"Change of subject," he said. "We are staying the week down here."

"All week!" *I hate this,* I thought. *I just hate this.*

"Yeah. They've planned a dinner for all us new guys — and spouses, partners, significant others, you know the drill. So anyway, one guy's wife is flying in from Wisconsin, and another from New Orleans. I was wondering . . . I don't know your schedule and I know it's not really practical, but what do you think? Want to come for dinner on Thursday?"

Thursday, I thought. *Nothing is on the*

schedule that couldn't be changed. Paige will be back with the Reillys. Or maybe she'd be with Rodney, I realized, upset at the thought. I glanced at her again. She was biting her lip, no doubt anxious about the coming meeting with Mr. Bolton.

"I'd love to. Let me see if I can arrange it."

"Great!" he said, and I was gratified by his enthusiasm.

I finished the call as we pulled into the small parking lot at the back of the law office. Griff said he'd wait for us, and Paige and I went inside.

The receptionist said that Mr. Bolton would see us in a few minutes. We sat side by side in Windsor-style chairs, waiting.

I told Paige, "I need to make a phone call."

She nodded and I approached the bay window that overlooked the street. I dialed the office and Gretchen answered with her cheery welcome.

"Is there anything I need to think about if I plan on taking off Thursday and Friday?"

"You? Take two days off? That doesn't sound like you. Are you sure you're feeling all right?"

"I know, I know. . . . I'm living on the wild side," I said.

"Nope, you're all clear! Hey, I just noticed

that your number is showing as private on the phone ID. Did you get an unlisted number?"

"Yeah. It's just for a while."

"Are you all right?"

"Yup. Just being careful," I told her and hoped that it was true.

The invisible danger seemed to be drawing closer. We were keeping me safe, but not addressing the underlying hazard. It was as if I were treating the symptoms of a disease, but not the disease itself.

"Mr. Bolton can see you now," the receptionist called.

I ended my call with Gretchen and turned to Paige. She looked stricken, and I touched her elbow as we walked.

Mr. Bolton was standing as we entered and greeted us both warmly, clasping Paige's hand for a moment as he offered his condolences. He guided us toward a chintz-covered couch by the window and, once we were settled, sat across from us in a club chair.

He cleared his throat and looked at Paige. "I've conducted an extensive background check on your cousin, Rodney Furleigh, and I have good news. He's an upstanding citizen, a sound engineer for one of the

442

movie studios out in California. He's married to a woman named Lucille, who does bookkeeping part time out of their home, and they have one child, a daughter named Mackenzie. She's twelve, by the way, just about your age, and a lovely young lady."

Paige's eyes were huge and frightened.

"Where do they live? What kind of place?" I asked.

"West Los Angeles," Mr. Bolton replied, glancing at his notes. "On the Santa Monica line. A neighborhood called Mar Vista. They have a single-family home with four bedrooms and two bathrooms and a nice yard."

Paige began to cry. Tears streamed down her cheeks, and she closed her eyes. Mr. Bolton slid a box of tissues across the coffee table, and I pulled one out of the box. Touching her shoulder, I said, "Paige? Here's a tissue."

She nodded and took it, but didn't open her eyes or speak or make any sound. Her shoulders shook, then she doubled over, wrapping her arms around her middle and rocking to and fro, just a little.

It was agonizing to watch. I felt helpless and uncertain. I wanted to rescue her, to stop all this talk about Rodney and California, but I couldn't.

"Paige," Mr. Bolton said softly, "nod if you can hear me."

Paige nodded.

"Everyone wants only what's best for you. You are in a difficult situation with limited options. What we're asking you to do is to try living with the Furleigh family. They love kids and are eager to have you as one of the family. If, after you give it a good try, it isn't working, no one — not me, not the courts — *no one* will expect you to stay. Other arrangements will be made. We think you're going to be happy in this environment, but if we're wrong, we'll find another solution."

"Foster care?" Paige whispered.

"Yes," Mr. Bolton replied, "we'd find another family for you."

Rip my heart out, I thought, *and stomp on it right now.* I wanted to offer my house, my home to her — but I didn't. It was too complex a decision from her perspective, and my own, to be spontaneously offered. Objections rattled around in my brain: What would Ty think; I'm never home; she needs a family, not a single woman in a rental house; I'm not capable; and most cutting of all, I couldn't help her overcome the loss since I'm still coping with my own losses.

Paige sat up. "I'm sorry," she managed, wiping away her tears, and swallowing gulps of air. "May I have some water, please?"

Mr. Bolton turned to a phone on a side table and made the request to someone named Angie.

"The Furleighs are here, in the conference room," Mr. Bolton explained. "They are excited to meet you."

Paige nodded. She appeared completely shell-shocked, beyond hope. I reached for her hand and held it.

Water arrived, and after Paige had several sips, Mr. Bolton said, "I know it's hard, but are you able to talk about Rosalie's funeral? The police have told me that it can be scheduled in a few days."

She shook her head and looked at me.

"I think Paige would like Rosalie to be buried in California, near their parents, with a service like the one they had."

"Is that true, Paige?" Mr. Bolton asked gently.

She nodded, then began to cry and covered her face with her hands.

Mr. Bolton cleared his throat again. "Shall we say next Monday?"

"Paige?"

"Okay," she whispered.

I patted her shoulder. "I'll be there, Paige."

She nodded, but didn't reply.

Two tissues later, Paige was able to raise

her head and sip more water. Mr. Bolton escorted her out. I stood up, assuming I'd join them, but Mr. Bolton shook his head, indicating that I should stay behind. Paige's gait was evocative of a death row prisoner en route to the gallows.

"That was pretty awful," I said when he returned.

"She's in for some hard times," he agreed. "And there's no way to ease the transition for her."

I shook my head, shattered at the thought, yet I knew that he was right. "She can stay with me," I said, shocked that I was volunteering for a role I'd proven only minutes earlier was impossible for me to accept. "I'd like to be her guardian."

He stared at me. "That's probably not a good idea."

"Why?"

He shifted in his chair, probably to give himself time to think. "Let me turn that question around. Why do you think you are an appropriate guardian?"

I took a deep breath. This was an audition and I didn't want to screw up. "We've been together all weekend and we like each other. We care. We fit." I fluttered a hand. "My parents died when I was young. I understand her." I took another breath. "She could continue at her regular school, and ballet class, and stay with her friends."

He looked dubious.

"This is a good option. I'm a responsible member of the community. She's had a lot of upheaval in her life. I could represent stability."

Mr. Bolton, whose first name I realized I couldn't recall, didn't comment.

He shifted position again. "If I might change the subject for a moment, could you give me an update on the appraisal?"

I drank some water, and shifted my thoughts from Paige's dire circumstances to her sister's possessions. I closed my eyes, thinking about Paige, trying to listen through the soundproofed walls, and then I switched gears. After a moment, I told him what I knew about the journal.

"That's consistent with what Rodney told me when I asked about the breach. He said that his mother sold an old book to her sister for four thousand dollars. A few months later, after a conversation with a rare book dealer, she realized she'd given away the farm for a penny, and asked her sister either to return the volume or give her a more realistic sum. Her sister said no. Rodney's mother never spoke to her sister again."

"So sad," I said, shaking my head. "Where did his mother get it? Do you know?"

"According to Rodney, she inherited the book from her first husband who was, she told him, a descendant of the author. She was widowed and about a year later married Rodney's father."

"So Rosalie owned the book legally — free and clear?"

"Yes. And Rodney understands that and makes no claim on it."

"Thank goodness for small favors," I remarked.

"So you'll complete the appraisal of the journal?"

"Certainly — and of everything else." I had another drink of water. "So what do you think about Paige living with me?" I asked.

He looked at me for a long time, then said, "I think your offer is kind and a viable next-best option."

I swallowed, abashed. "What about to-night? Will she stay with me? The Reillys? All her stuff is in the trunk of my car."

He stroked his chin. "I think it's best that Paige stay at the hotel with her cousins."

I nodded. "Can I tell her to call me, just in case?"

"Of course."

He pushed a button and told Angie to bring them in.

I met the Furleighs just long enough to say hello. They seemed nice enough, and Paige wasn't crying, which I took to be a good sign. I mentioned Paige's ballet class and Mrs. Furleigh smiled and said that they'd take her if she wanted to go.

We transferred Paige's duffel bag and backpack from my trunk to their rental car and then I turned to Paige to say good-bye. She reached for my hand and held it. And then I hugged her, and she hugged me back.

I leaned into her ear and whispered, "You have my phone numbers, right?"

She nodded against my shoulder. "Uh-huh."

"You need anything, anytime, ever, you call. Don't hesitate. Forever more, kiddo, okay?"

"Thank you, Josie," she whispered, and pulled away.

She gave a tremulous smile, and with a final wave, I left.

I didn't cry until I was in my car and alone.

449

CHAPTER
THIRTY-TWO

Officer Brownley called just as I was about to step inside my office.

"Nothing yet about Cooper. A team is at his office now. And his storage unit." She cleared her throat. "Also, I'm afraid that the man who ordered the flowers didn't recognize any of the photos."

Darn! I thought. *Nothing's easy.* I swallowed, my mouth suddenly dry. "So now what?"

"Now we continue to investigate and you continue to be careful. Any other appointments today?"

Thinking of the trip to take Paige to ballet that I wasn't making, I fought unexpected sadness. "No, none," I said.

"When will you be ready to go home?"

"About six."

"Officer Griffin will escort you."

"Thanks."

I wanted to say more, to thank her more

effusively, to confess how fearful the situation made me and how reassuring it was to have the police nearby, but I couldn't frame my thoughts quickly enough. Instead, I scanned the parking lot and the forest that surrounded it, seeking out, once again, the source of my anxiety, and as before, I saw nothing odd or out of place.

"It's pretty scary," I said finally.

"Yeah."

She paused, maybe waiting for me to speak, but I couldn't think of anything else to say.

"Okay, then," she said.

Inside, Gretchen greeted me with her usual welcoming smile. "How did it go?" she asked, empathy evident in her tone.

"It was tough. The funeral will be in Los Angeles a week from today, next Monday. A couple of people may be calling to ask about it, so you should call Mr. Bolton's office and get the particulars. Also, I'll need them. I'm going."

She nodded. "After we know the when and where, you can tell me how long you want to go for."

"Yeah. I was thinking I might set up some appointments while I was out there, but then I changed my mind." I shrugged. "I

want this to be just about Paige and Rosalie."

Tears sparkled on Gretchen's long lashes.
"You're amazing."

"No. No, I'm not. I'm just doing my best."

Words my father spoke came to me:
*People often say they're doing their best when
what they really mean is that they don't want
to change what they're doing.* I thought
about my statement for a moment. *No, I*
thought, *my father's comment doesn't apply. I
am, in fact, doing my best. I just wish my best
was better.*

Upstairs, I leaned back in my chair and
closed my eyes. I was exhausted. I wondered
how Paige was doing, and what she was doing, and then I realized that I hadn't
checked my voice mail in a long time.

There was one message, from a number I
didn't recognize with a 207 area code. Suddenly, I couldn't breathe. I couldn't swallow. I coughed and finally I opened a bottle
of water from the supply stashed near my
desk; after several sips, I could breathe
again.

Maybe it's a potential client, I told myself
sternly, *a "real" call.* Biting my lip, I took a
deep breath, and pushed the button.

"You didn't listen to me," the husky voice

warned. "You'll be sorry." In the back-ground, I heard clanging, an oraclelike sound of impending doom. "Last warning. Back off."

I slammed the receiver into the cradle and stared at it, hyperventilating. *Calm down,* I instructed myself.

Three deep breaths later, I redialed and listened to the message again. The second time, I heard more than the threatening words — I heard tension in the low-pitched voice and I felt more frightened, not less. My hand was shaking as I replaced the receiver, gently this time. Inchoate thoughts and vague forebodings shrieked in my brain, rattling my aplomb, and I spun my chair half around to stare at my maple tree, try-ing to ground myself and quiet my roiling agitation.

Several moments later, after focusing on my breathing and watching the gently sway-ing snow-covered branches, the noisy terror in my head stilled and I listened to the silence. *Think,* I told myself. No phones rang, no cars or trucks passed by, not even a bird called, and suddenly, I realized who my secret admirer was. I gasped, clutched the chair arms, and said, "Oh, my God!"

I considered the ramifications, and in an instant I realized with petrifying lucidity a question I *hadn't* asked Betty, the hostess at The Miller House.

I called Officer Brownley, and got her voice mail. "I know who did it," I said in a rush, then stopped to gather my thoughts. "I for sure know the secret admirer's identity and I think I know who killed Rosalie. I need to check one thing. What I need is to talk to you — never mind, I'll call the station."

Cathy, the administrative professional, answered the Rocky Point police station main number.

"I'm sorry," she said in response to my inquiry. "Officer Brownley is unavailable."

"When will she be free?" I asked.

"I'm not sure. Do you want to leave a message?"

"This is Josie. Josie Prescott. It's urgent that I speak to her."

"I'm sorry, Josie. She's in a meeting and can't be disturbed. Can someone else help you? Griff is here."

A meeting? I wondered. *Or an interrogation?* I could envision Cooper sitting in one of the interrogation rooms answering unwanted questions about whether he'd appropriated Rosalie's research and sources. He'd be belligerent and argumentative, sarcastic and contemptuous, and he would deny everything with supercilious confidence. I hoped the police found the journal copy soon — they'd need it.

I thought of Griff's stolid demeanor and by-the-book attitude. He'd have endless questions and then I'd be told to back off and let the police do their job. "Thanks, but that's okay. Would you please tell Officer Brownley that I got another phone call from a two-oh-seven area code and I'm going to check out one thing."

I turned to my computer, easily found a usable photo, and reassured myself that I wasn't being stupid. I couldn't not act. Years of frustration, trusting others to take care of problems, had taught me that passivity was harder to endure than fear. *A quick drive to a public place — how dangerous could that be?*

I took the stairs two at a time.

"I'll be back," I told Gretchen as I grabbed my coat and dashed out the door.

I locked myself in my car and surveyed the parking lot. *Nothing.* I headed down the secondary road that led to the interstate. It was only three-thirty, yet dusk was falling. Trees and stone walls cast ghostly shadows along the road.

I looked in my side and rearview mirrors. As I pulled onto the near-empty interstate,

455

all at once, there it was: a boxy, dark-colored car streaked with salt. It was too close, hovering, sliding from one lane to the next, almost passing me, then slowing and skirting to the other side.

I snapped into crisis mode and got ready to cope.

By touch, I found my phone, got my earpiece situated, and pushed the green button twice to redial. I got Cathy.

"Please tell Officer Brownley I'm being followed. She'll want to know."

"Who's following you?"

"The same car. Dark. Salt-covered. No license plate in front. The driver is wearing a hat. Tell her it's the same car and the occupant is wearing the same disguise."

"I'm connecting to emergency response. . . ." After a moment, she asked, "Josie? Are you still with me?"

"Yes."

My heart was in my throat choking me again. The car was tailgating so closely his vehicle appeared to be an extension of mine. If I slowed down, we'd crash. I speeded up, but the other driver paced me.

"Emergency is on the line. Go ahead, emergency."

"Where are you, ma'am?"

"I'm on Route Ninety-five, heading toward the bridge to Maine," I said. "I'm going to The Miller House."

"Police are on the way," the emergency responder said.

The car could hit me, I realized, *little nudges to force me off the road,* and then I wondered why it didn't. I slowed down gradually until I was going only about forty, and at the last moment, with only yards to spare, I spun the steering wheel hard to the right and took the downtown Portsmouth exit.

The boxy car mimicked my maneuver, cutting off a sedan. The sedan's horn blared and kept on sounding, echoing long after I left the highway. I raced along the service road until I came to the next entrance back onto the interstate and swerved on, the dark car close behind.

Think, I told myself. *Damn it. Think. He — or she — isn't trying to kill me. The other car is bigger and faster than mine, so if that was the driver's intention I'd already be dead. Therefore he must want something else. What? To scare me off?* I nodded. *Or,* I realized, more frightened than before, *the driver wants to trap me for some reason.*

I skidded as I sped onto the highway, then, when the car stabilized, remembered the police were still on the line. "Hello? Are you still there?"

"This is emergency response. You okay?"

"Yes."

"What's your current location?"

"I'm on the bridge. I'll get off onto Route One-oh-three."

I heard her relay my location to someone, her mike crackling with static.

The car tailed me the entire way to The Miller House. I snap-turned into the parking lot, parked any which way under a bright light, the boxy car blocking me in.

I grabbed the phone and my bag, tore out of my car leaving the door ajar, and ran up the path toward the restaurant. At a curve in the walkway, I ducked behind a dense growth of rhododendron to catch my breath and watch what would happen next. I clutched the phone to my chest, afraid my voice would carry, revealing my position, if I spoke.

The driver backed out, sending pebbles flying, and turned north, heading deeper into Maine.

"I'm at The Miller House. The car's gone. It's heading north on One-oh-three."

"Copy that," the voice said.

Within seconds, a state police patrol car, its red lights spinning, roared into the lot. I hurried back down the path to meet it, but before I'd taken more than a half a dozen steps, it backed out and went north. The police were in pursuit. The immediate crisis over, I felt suddenly overheated and I began to shake. I thought I might faint. I realized that I'd somehow lost the headset and put the phone to my ear.

"Josie?" Cathy said, sounding concerned, and I understood that she had remained on the line the entire time. "Josie? Josie, can you hear me?"

"Yes. I'm here."

"Officer Brownley is standing by. Hold, please."

A moment later, Officer Brownley said, "Emergency is off the line. Are you okay?"

"Yeah," I said, and I realized that I was trembling. "It was pretty scary."

"What are you doing? I thought you were in for the afternoon."

She sounded confused, not angry, and I appreciated her restraint. I had expected to be reproached.

"It was stupid of me. I thought I'd be fine — a quick drive during the day. I'm sorry."

"You're all right and that's the main thing. What are you doing at The Miller House?"

"I know . . . I mean . . . I'm just really sure —" I broke off, my words tangled in my tongue. I needed to show her, not tell her. "I need to show you something. Can you meet me here?"

"Yeah, okay. Half an hour."

I hung up and paused, trying to still my throbbing pulse. As always when a crisis passed, I felt weak and ill, and anxious.

I reparked the car properly and headed inside. Betty, the hostess, was chatting with a waitress.

"I remember you," she said. "How you doing?"

"Glad to be here. How are you?"

I wondered if my voice was quivering. I was breathing hard, standing with my back to the entryway wall for support.

"Same old, same old." She paused and looked at me. "You okay?"

The waitress smiled at me, picked up an empty tray, and left. "See ya, Betty," she said.

"More or less," I replied, forcing a smile.

"So, what can I do for you today?"

"I forgot to ask you a question." I took a deep breath for focus, dug the photo out of my tote bag, and handed it over. "Did you ever see this person with Rosalie?"

"Oh, sure," she said, nodding. "They had dinner here lots of times."

"When? Do you remember?"

She pursed her lips, thinking, then tapped the photo as she remembered. "Yup. That's right. Last summer."

I knew it! I thought, elated. The final piece of the jigsaw puzzle snapped into place. "When did they stop coming together?"

"Let me think." She paused, still staring at the photograph. "It was an unusually cold day. They had a kind of fight. It was right around Labor Day. Mid-September, maybe."

"Nothing lately?"

"No, not that I know of."

"Thank you," I said sincerely, and extended a hand.

We shook, then Betty tilted her head and grinned. "You're as persistent as a cat tracking a mouse. Bet it makes you one hell of an antiques appraiser — am I right?"

I smiled back. "My dad always called me stubborn. I guess that's the same quality as persistence, just wearing jeans instead of a dress, huh?"

She laughed and told me to come back for dinner sometime. I promised that I would.

I was jump-out-of-my-skin excited. I'd wanted to check with Betty before reporting my conclusion to the police for the same reason that I'd wanted to call Aaron before reporting that Lesha might have committed fraud. Going into any situation ill prepared when you don't have to, when relevant information is available for the asking, is just plain stupid. Except that someone in a dirty car had been waiting for me outside — maybe — so my effort to avoid one stupid event exposed me to another. I walked into the lounge, inordinately relieved that the end was in sight.

I ordered hot tea, and settled in to wait for Officer Brownley. Just after four, the first wave of after-work revelers started arriving, and their presence was reassuring. *There's safety in numbers,* I thought. *If not safety, at least there's comfort.*

When Officer Brownley arrived about twenty minutes later, the first thing I noticed was her expression. She was visibly concerned.

"Did they catch up to the car?" I asked.

She shook her head. "They lost him."

I nodded. "No surprise, I guess."

"No. There are lots of turnoffs." After a pause, she added, "You ready to fill me in?"

"Yeah. The bottom line is that I know who killed Rosalie — and I think I know how you can prove it."

"I'm listening."

"Give me a break, Charlie!" a man said, laughing as he sat at the next table.

"Never!" Charlie replied, joining in with a

low rumbling "ha-ha-ha."

"Not here," I whispered.

"Where?" Officer Brownley asked.

"Heyer's. Let's go."

"What's at Heyer's?"

"Proof."

"You can ride with me," she said, standing up, "and fill me in en route."

I followed her outside, trying to think of how to explain, of what to say to clarify the morass of details and unrelated facts into a cohesive whole. As we approached her vehicle, I hesitated.

"I can drive myself," I said.

"We could use the time to talk."

I shook my head. "It's too complicated. I'll explain later — after we ask Gerry Fine a question."

"What question?"

I shook my head again. "You'll see. His answer will tell you most everything you need to know."

She watched as I got situated behind the wheel, and I could tell from her expression that she was tempted to insist on answers, but had decided to let it ride. I smiled at her and nodded encouragingly. She didn't smile back, but neither did she frown. She was withholding judgment, and I thought, *I won't let you down.*

CHAPTER
THIRTY-THREE

"I'm not walking in that door until you tell what you've got," Officer Brownley said, pausing at Heyer's entrance.

"Chief," I said, lowering my voice as if someone might overhear us. "I've got Chief. And I'm pretty sure that I know where there's evidence that will point to the killer."

"Come on, Josie. Tell me what evidence. *Now.*"

I took a deep breath and started to fill her in. Before I got three sentences out, she stopped me and called for backup.

"You and I will go see Gerry," she said, intense but not mad. "But after that, we wait for the backup. And you will do *exactly* as you're told and *only* what you're told. Got it?"

"Got it," I concurred, grateful she was in charge.

"Josie!" Gerry called as we approached. "Come on in, doll. Officer, you too."

We sat as instructed in chairs on the far side of his desk.

"So, what can I do ya for?" he asked.

"Well, I've got a kind of off-the-wall question."

"My favorite kind. Let her rip."

"Correct me if I'm wrong . . . do I remember you saying that Ned came from aristocracy?"

He roared with laughter, then slapped his desk. "Aristocracy?" he repeated as if the word was the punch line of a hysterically funny joke.

Officer Brownley and I waited for him to speak.

"Oh. God! Don't look at me like that, you'll set me off again. Every time I think of it, I can't stop laughing. That was a joke, Josie. I josh him all the time about it. He's got Injun in him, and he's always bragging that he's descended from an Indian chief. Indian chief, my ass. Ha! More like he's descended from the guy who sold Manhattan for twenty-four bucks and a handful of beads."

I nodded. "Thanks." I stood up. "That's it."

"That's all?" he asked, surprised.

"Yup. You know me. Get it done and I'm outta here."

"You betcha, doll. You're high class all the way."

Officer Brownley and I returned to the front. Una looked at us curiously.

"How's things?" she asked.

"Good, good. Listen, we're waiting for some of Officer Brownley's colleagues. We'll be over there, okay?"

The phone rang, and she nodded as she picked up the receiver.

"What was that about? Aristocracy?" Officer Brownley demanded in a low voice as soon as we sat down in the far corner.

I took a deep breath and turned to her. "Ned is my secret admirer. I *know* it."

"How?"

"It was the bell that got me thinking."

"What bell?"

"That's why I wanted you to come here," I explained. "Ned has a cuckoo clock in his office." I dialed my voice mail and handed her the phone. "Listen."

"And from that you concluded Ned is the secret admirer?" she asked, handing me my phone, her tone indicating that she thought I was batty. "Don't get me wrong. I hear the bell, too. But surely it's not all that unusual. Lots of people have cuckoo clocks."

"Not like this one they don't." I described

the bear and how he strikes an old-fashioned triangle with a tiny metal rod.

"My idea is that you stand near his clock as it clangs and listen to the voice mail. You'll hear what I'm talking about."

"And this Ned guy is going to allow us to come in his office and stand by his clock?"

"I thought you could just do it as part of your investigation."

"You thought wrong. You'd better have something else up your sleeve."

"I do," I said, swallowing dismay. "A couple of things. One is, I think he's the man Rosalie called Chief."

"How so?"

"Once I recognized the background noise as the clock, of course I thought of Ned because I'd just heard it in his office. It got me thinking about him. And I remembered two things — one, that Gerry had made that aristocracy crack, and two, that Ned had a bear tooth necklace hanging in his office suite."

Officer Brownley frowned.

"You don't know what that means, but I do, and I should have realized its significance sooner," I confessed. "Back before guns, it was hard to kill a bear. Only the bravest warriors could do it. Ownership of the teeth proved the accomplishment. Think about it — are you going to put your hand anywhere near a bear's mouth while it's alive? I don't think so."

"So . . . ," she said, her brow furrowed, "I don't get it."

"An Indian hunter who succeeded in killing the bear would typically string the teeth on a leather thong and present it to the leader of his tribe, the chief." I shrugged. "Get it? *Chief!*"

"Maybe he just bought that necklace."

"Absolutely. It doesn't matter whether it's from his family or not, or even if it's genuine or not. Just like it doesn't matter if he *is*, in fact, descended from a chief or not. All that matters is that *he* considers himself connected to a chief. That's why I wanted to ask Gerry that question in your presence, so you could hear the answer. Ned *says* he's descended from a chief. From that fact alone, I think it's reasonable to assume that he'd like to be called Chief as a pet name." I shrugged. "I saw him the other day standing in a diner looking for all the world like Napoleon. He's definitely the kind of man who'd like to be called Chief."

"What else?" she asked, still dubious.

I leaned in toward her and spoke softly. "Last summer Ned and Rosalie were an item."

"Why do you say that?"

"He and Paige knew each other."

"And you know this . . . how?"

"She was with me today. They greeted one another."

"So maybe they met at a Christmas party or something."

"No. It was more than that. I didn't think about it at the time, but it was a greeting of people who *knew* each other."

"What else?"

"I showed Ned's photo to the hostess at The Miller House."

"Just now? You shouldn't be interviewing witnesses!"

"I wouldn't call it interviewing exactly. I'm helping!"

She didn't argue the point, but from the look in her eye, I couldn't delude myself that I'd convinced her.

"You brought me here to listen to Gerry's answer to that question and to stand by Ned's cuckoo clock. Do I have that right?"

I swallowed, aware of how lame it sounded. "Yes."

"Is there anything else?"

"Yes. But I think you're going to get mad at me."

She half smiled. "Heck of a time to start worrying about that."

I met her eyes and was reassured by their twinkle.

"I'm pretty sure that the murder weapon is in his office."

She raised her eyebrows. "Another detail you decided to keep to yourself?"

"I just realized its significance today."

"What is it?"

"Ned's walking stick. It's made of apple wood and it's varnished, just like the splinters in Rosalie's scalp."

"How do you know about apple wood and varnish? That information hasn't been released to the public."

I stared at her, stricken. My foot was in my mouth. I couldn't reveal my source, and I didn't know what to say. Officer Brownley's eyes stayed on my face and I felt myself begin to blush. *She's going to think Ty told me,* I realized in a panic, and I couldn't allow that. "A reporter told me in confidence. I don't know who told him."

"Who?"

"I can't tell you."

She took in a breath that went all the way to her kneecaps. "A leak in the department is serious, Josie."

I didn't reply. Anxiety was pulsating through my body and I felt sick.

"I need to make a call," she said. "Wait here."

She didn't seem angry exactly, just shocked and surprised.

"You okay?" Una called.

"It's been a long day." I leaned back and closed my eyes to avoid having to field further questions. I wondered where Officer Brownley had gone.

Ten minutes later, she reappeared. "I called for an emergency search warrant, and the judge granted it," she announced in an undertone. "It'll be here soon. Until then the backup team is going to stay out of sight and you're going to tell me everything you know. Don't get me wrong, you've been helpful. But if evidence isn't legally obtained . . . ," she said, letting her voice trail off, "well, it's worse than doing nothing at all."

I nodded, dismayed that, unknowingly, I might have ruined the case. She turned to a new page in her notebook.

"What do you know about motive?" she asked.

"There's a couple of things which, taken together, add up to what might be a powerful motive. Ned applied for Gerry's job and didn't get it. Plus, he was involved with Rosalie over the summer and lost her to Paul

Greeley. That was bad — but then *they* broke up. He didn't know that she left Paul *for* Gerry. He thought she was single again, and available. His arrogance isn't an act, it's entrenched." I shrugged. "It wouldn't surprise me to learn that he thought she broke up with Paul because she missed him."

Officer Brownley looked unconvinced.

"I know it sounds a little over the top, but really, Ned might perceive a friendly chat as a come-hither invitation. I swear he's a megalomaniac."

"Have you observed that behavior yourself?"

"Absolutely. He's so full of himself, it's scary."

"So then what did he do? Ask her out?"

"Maybe. My guess, though, is that he started the secret admirer thing as a cute joke, but before he could decide the time was right to come clean, he realized that she was involved with Gerry. Ned was in and out of Gerry's office all the time, and, trust me, their affair was easy to spot. What started as a romantic ploy morphed into stalking."

"Even so . . . ," she said, shrugging. "It's quite a leap from having a pass rebuffed to killing someone."

"Maybe. But from his perspective, he'd

lost both the girl *and* the job to Gerry."

She wrote some notes. "Wouldn't that make him mad at Gerry?"

"Sure, I guess. Judging by his relentless sniping, he is."

Officer Brownley's cell phone vibrated, and she answered it with a crisp "Brownley." She listened for several seconds, then said, "Yeah . . . got it." She turned to me. "The search warrant will be here in about fifteen minutes. When it arrives, you're going to bring up the rear and let us serve the warrant. Okay?"

I nodded dutifully. "Sure."

"The only reason you're going to be there at all is that you know things we don't, like the bear tooth necklace thing. You're to answer questions if asked, identify objects as needed, and otherwise stay out of the way." She looked at me and smiled again. "I don't want you to get hurt and I don't want something you do or say inadvertently to hurt the case."

Before I could reply, her phone rang again. This call was even shorter.

"We got it," she said to me, smiling broadly. "The copy of the journal."

"Hot damn!" I said. "Fabulous! Where was it?"

"In Cooper's storage unit. It was the only

item in there, just the bound copy sitting on the floor. Pathetic, huh?"

How can a human being plot to steal a colleague's work? I wondered. "Completely pathetic," I agreed.

"Back to Ned," she asked softly. "What do you know about opportunity? How could Ned have arranged to get Rosalie out to the jetty?"

"I doubt it was prearranged. Gerry left The Miller House in his limo alone after having a drink with Rosalie. She went home. We know that because her car was there the next day, covered with snow. If anyone knows what happened to Rosalie after then, I haven't heard it, but here's a possibility. Ned could have followed her home and cornered her, begging for an opportunity to talk. I can imagine Rosalie thinking that since ignoring him hadn't worked to get him to leave her alone, maybe talking to him would." I shrugged. "At least it's a possibility."

She nodded and made a couple of notes.

"Here's another thing to consider. Assuming that Edie's lying about having been home all night, she no longer has any reason to keep up the front. Gerry isn't in any danger of prosecution, so maybe she'll come clean. I bet her car wasn't in the driveway because she was, in fact, not home. I'm guessing she started out the night following Gerry, trying to catch him in the act of infidelity. Maybe she saw him escort Rosalie to her car and leave The Miller House in his limo alone and figured this would be a good time to talk to Rosalie, to have it out with her once and for all. I've thought all along that Edie must have known that Gerry's been screwing around for years. My guess is that she's been willing to put up with it because she didn't want to lose her position in life as a CEO's wife." I shook my head and looked at Officer Brownley full on. "Do you see what I mean? It's conceivable that Edie followed Rosalie hoping to have it out with her, but instead of orchestrating a confrontation, she witnessed a murder. If I'm right, I'll bet Edie's secretly glad that Rosalie is dead, and isn't about to help you catch her killer."

A self-important-looking man pushed into the reception area. Seeing us in the corner, he ignored Una and made a beeline in our direction. He was medium-sized and chunky, but nicely dressed. Officer Brownley stood up and greeted him as Harry.

"I'm due back in court," the man said, "but I wanted to be certain you understood that the warrant covers Mr. Anderson's office suite only. Don't go rooting around the entire building."

"Yes, sir," she replied and accepted the blue-covered document he proffered.

He hurried off and Officer Brownley said, "Wait here."

I watched her leave the building, then glanced at Una. Her interest was completely engaged. She looked at me, and asked, "What in the world's going on?"

"I'll fill you in after it's over, okay?"

My phone rang. It was Ty.

"Hey, there," he said. "I just spoke with Officer Brownley. You do what you're told, okay?"

"I promise."

"Call me later."

My ribs hurt from my heart crashing into them and my feet felt leaden. *Later,* I told myself. *You can fall apart later. Once the killer is put away. For now, you need to stay strong.*

Within moments, Officer Brownley returned with four uniformed officers, including Griff.

"Let's go," she told me.

An itchy kind of breathlessness took hold of me, and I felt my energy begin to focus sharply on the events at hand. I was entering crisis mode.

I started down the hallway, and said, "The

second door on the right. That's his assistant's office. His private office is behind it. Same layout as Gerry's suite."

She nodded and pointed that I was to take my place at the end of the line.

"This is a search warrant," Officer Brownley announced to the assistant. "Please stand up and move away from the desk."

She accepted the search warrant, her jaw opening and closing several times. Finally she turned toward the inner office. "Mr. Anderson!" she called. "It's the police."

Ned appeared at the doorway, his eyes skimming over the officers until they reached me. "Josie," he said, his eyes narrowed. To the police, he asked, "What's going on?"

"We're here to search your office. Please stand over there," Officer Brownley informed him. Turning to me, she demanded, "Where's the walking stick?"

"In the far corner on the left," I replied.

"I think I need to request you to stop," Ned said coldly, stepping into the doorway, blocking entry.

"Read the warrant," Officer Brownley told him. "We're coming in."

"No," he stated, and an icy shiver rippled up my spine.

"You gotta move," she told him in a voice

of reason.

"No," he repeated, shaking his head.

"You move or we're going to move you."

"I'm glad I have a disinterested witness in my assistant. I'm sure my lawyer will be glad to know that she observed you threaten me with bodily harm."

"Read the warrant, sir," she suggested again. "Like it says, we're here legally."

He crossed his arms and a sardonic sneer came over his face. He leaned against the doorjamb as if he had all the time and not a concern in the world, and raised his chin in imperial disdain.

One of the officers whose name I'd forgotten was young and big. He stepped forward, put his hands on both of Ned's upper arms, and pushed. Ned hurtled backward. Officer Brownley turned to me and said, "Point it out."

I entered the room and looked into the corner where I'd seen it perch. It wasn't there. "It's not here," I said.

"Where is it, sir?" Officer Brownley asked.

Ned sneered and looked down his nose at her. "I don't know what you're talking about."

To me she asked, "Where's the clock?"

I turned toward his desk and I gaped. The ornately carved clock was missing, too. "It's gone. Look, you can see the bracket," I said, pointing. "It hung right there."

"Mr. Anderson," Officer Brownley said, "I need to ask you some questions. We'd like you to come down to the station."

"No way," he said with a contemptuous huff.

"Sir," she said, her tone reasonable, even kind, "if you don't, I'll arrest you as a material witness. You need to come with us. As a cooperative volunteer or as a noncooperative citizen under arrest. Your choice."

"You're going to have to arrest me. And then I stand mute until my lawyer arrives. Period. End of discussion."

"As you wish, sir," she said, unimpressed, and placed him under arrest.

With his hand on Ned's elbow, Griff walked him out of the suite. Ned turned to his assistant, resisting Griff's directive touch, and said, "Call my lawyer and tell him what's happening. Get a receipt for anything they take."

She nodded and reached for the phone.

"What was his schedule today?" Officer Brownley asked.

"Don't answer that! Don't say a word," he called from the door. "Do you hear me? Not one word!"

Wide-eyed, she looked from Ned to Officer Brownley and back. Ned's angry shouts and instructions faded as he was led down the corridor.

"It's not up to him whether you talk to the police. We could use your assistance and you can absolutely answer that if you want to," Officer Brownley said, her pleasant manner contrasting with his vituperative diatribe.

She smiled. "We got in about the same time. In fact, we met in the parking lot and walked in together. That was just about eight. As far as I know, he hasn't left since."

"Not even for a minute?"

"Not while I've been here." She shrugged. "But I went to lunch around noon for an hour."

"You didn't see him carry anything out?"

"No."

"How about in?" Officer Brownley asked out of the blue. "Do you often arrive at the same time?"

"Yes," she said, nodding. "It happens pretty often."

"On the morning after Rosalie Chaffee's murder, can you recall seeing Mr. Anderson carry anything *in?*"

She thought back. "The leather bag, you mean?"

"Tell me about it."

"Ned was carrying a tote bag. He said it was for Gerry and took it straight to his office. I didn't think anything about it."

Hidden in plain sight, I thought. *Rosalie must have left her bag in his car the night before and he didn't notice it until he got to work. He couldn't leave such damning evidence in his car and he couldn't just drive away without calling attention to himself. As the best of bad options, he carried Rosalie's bag into her office, early, before Tricia and Gerry were in, and left it on Rosalie's desk.*

"Thanks. I'm going to ask that you come with us, too, to give us a statement."

She swallowed. "All right."

To me, Officer Brownley said, "Josie, you can go now. Just in case, I'm going to ask one of the officers to escort you."

I didn't argue or delay. I couldn't wait to get out of there. With the young male officer following, I fled, barely waving to Una. She was standing behind her counter, still openmouthed.

Outside, I paused in the frigid air to take several deep breaths.

"Where are you parked?" the police officer asked.

"Over there." I pointed. "But if it's okay, I'd like to take just a minute and get myself together."

"Sure. No problem. I'll pull up near your car."

I began to pace the parking lot, trying to quiet my thudding heart and quell the sick feeling in my stomach. I came to the executives' assigned parking places and stopped in front of Ned's. I hadn't thought to look before, but here it was — more damning evidence.

I called Officer Brownley on her cell phone. She answered on the first ring.

"What is it?"

"Ned's car. It's dark blue and boxy looking. I don't know what kind of car it is. It's all mucked up, smeared with salt residue and mud. And guess what?"

"What?"

"There's no license plate in front."

"Got ya," she said. "We'll take care of it."

I got in my car and called Gretchen.

"Listen, I'm done for the day."

"Is everything all right?" she asked, concerned at my out-of-character decision to quit work early.

"Terrific!" I said, faking it. "Can you put Sasha on, please?"

"Hello," Sasha said hesitantly.

"You know Lesha's letter and the photos Gretchen took of the palette? Would you please scan in the letter and e-mail it to me,

482

along with a photo of the palette?"

"Sure."

"Okay, thanks. I'll be looking for it."

I laughed as I caught myself checking the side and rearview mirrors. *No more!* I thought, elated. The weight of fear was slowly dissipating. It felt as if I were suddenly free after being trapped in a dark room for days. I raised and lowered my shoulders several times to relax. I couldn't stop grinning. I slipped a McCoy Tyner CD in the player and boogied to the primal beat of a master pianist. After a few minutes, I turned down the volume and called Wes.

"As promised, you're my first call," I told him. "Meet me at the Blue Dolphin at six. In the lounge."

"You got it," he said, and hung up.

When I pulled into my driveway, I saw Frankie shoveling Zoë's walkway to widen the path to the door. He was wearing an unembellished black parka instead of his "bitches" leather jacket. *Good for him,* I thought. I called hello and he waved back. I thanked the police officer for the escort and let myself into my house.

I stripped as I rushed upstairs, and within a minute, I was in the shower. I didn't come out until my skin was pruney. I kept having an urge to laugh. *Relief manifests itself in peculiar ways,* I thought.

Wrapped in my pink robe, I called Officer Brownley.

"I think it's okay for me to dispense with the police escort. What do you think?"

"I think you're right. Evidence is mounting."

"Like what?" I asked, wondering if she'd answer.

"Like the walking stick and the cuckoo clock. They were in his trunk, wrapped in garbage bags."

I thanked her again, and made myself a drink. I smiled as I thought of the largess I was about to bestow on Wes. He would be getting the goods on three separate, interesting stories. Just before I left to drive to the Blue Dolphin, I forwarded him the documents relating to Lesha's attempted grand larceny, the ones Sasha had e-mailed me.

Once we were settled at a corner table overlooking the river, I explained that the police hadn't yet decided whether Lesha would be charged with any crime, but that I doubted that she would be. He was relentless in ferreting out details about Rosalie's priceless journal and begged for photos, a commitment I refused to make. He asked for details about Cooper's motives and his alleged intentions. And he positively lapped up my on-the-scene account of Ned's arrest like a cat with cream.

"You should have taken some photos with your cell phone," he grumped after I'd filled him in.

"You're welcome, Wes."

He shot me a grin. "Yeah, yeah. Thanks." He slipped his notebook into an inside jacket pocket. "Why was Ned stalking you anyway?"

"He was trying to scare me off."

"But you weren't the only person tracking Rosalie's killer. What about the police? What about me?"

"I don't know for sure, but I'll tell you what I think. Ned is arrogant. He wasn't worried about the police, but he knew that I had specialized knowledge that put him at risk. Especially if he thought I had access to inside information because I date the police chief."

"What kind of specialized knowledge?"

"Wood — I can often identify wood just by looking at it." I shrugged. "He'd seen me do it."

"If that's the case, why wouldn't he just threaten you directly? Sending flowers is kind of . . . I don't know . . . not really intimidating."

"He did, but only later when things got

more worrisome for him. Remember the sequence — at first Ned was only a little concerned. He saw how upset Rosalie got when she received flowers from a secret admirer. I bet he decided to see if the same strategy would work to get me to back off. It was only later, after Ned saw us talking at the diner and overheard conversations on my cell phone, that the threats became more explicit."

"What did he hear?"

"You remember . . . one time you mentioned that there were splinters and I confirmed that I could easily identify wood. And another time, when I was talking to Officer Brownley, I described the clanging sound from his cuckoo clock." I shrugged. "So he became more aggressive."

"Are you saying that Ned considered you to be a bigger threat than me?" Wes asked, bristling with wounded pride.

I smiled. "Yes."

He smiled and sat back. "Okay, okay — you're a regular Hootin' Annie."

"Who's Hootin' Annie?" I asked.

"I made it up," Wes said, standing. "Gotta go. Thanks, okay?"

I mock saluted him and sipped my icy-smooth Bombay Sapphire as I watched the beam of a distant lighthouse illuminate the night giving hope to sailors and protecting the coast. I recalled some lines from a Robert Frost poem:

It looked as if a night of dark intent
Was coming, and not only a night, an age
Someone had better be prepared for rage.

No one lit up Ned's dark night and Rosalie was entirely unprepared for his rage. I wanted to be in Ty's arms to chase away the haunting image of Rosalie all alone, hunted, and finally caught.

CHAPTER
THIRTY-FOUR

Three days later, I was in a cab en route to Georgetown when my cell phone rang. I didn't recognize the number.

"Hello."

"It's me. Paige," she said.

"How are you?"

"Okay. That's why I wanted to call. I wanted to let you know that I was okay. So far they seem really nice."

I felt another weight fall from my shoulders. "I'm so glad to hear that, Paige."

"My room faces west and if you squint you can sort of see the ocean."

"That's way cool."

"Yeah, and tonight we're going shopping for sheets and curtains. They said I can pick out whatever I want."

"Fun! Do you know what you'll choose?"

"I think maybe similar to Mackenzie. Her room is lavender and apple green. I love it."

"Sounds like a really good choice. Paige,

thank you for calling. You've made my day!"

"You're welcome. This number is my cell phone. They got it for me."

"Really?"

She giggled. "Yeah. Mackenzie said everyone has one. I don't have all that many minutes, though, on the monthly plan."

"Well, anytime you want to talk, you can call me and I'll call you back."

"Thanks." Her voice cracked a bit as she went on. "Josie?"

"Yes?"

"You're still coming for the funeral, right?"

"Absolutely. I miss her, too, Paige. And I want to see your new room."

"Thank you."

I smiled the rest of the way to the Holiday Inn where Ty was staying.

Ty had left a key for me at the front desk. He'd explained in a voice mail he'd be back by five or a little after, and dinner was at a restaurant within walking distance at six-thirty.

I stepped into the room and was greeted by a Bach concerto emanating from the radio. A bouquet of mixed flowers, still encased in plastic and bound by rubber bands, stood in the hotel room coffeepot. Nearby was a bottle of J sparkling wine chilling in an ice bucket. Next to it was a grocery-store container of grape tomatoes, one of my favorite nibbles. An envelope with my name on it rested against the makeshift vase.

I opened it. On the outside was a cartoon figure of a man, looking downcast, and the words, *When I'm away from you . . .* Inside it read, *all of me misses you.* Ty had added, *I love you, Ty.*

I clutched it to my chest, moved beyond words, heartened and overjoyed.

Showered and wrapped in my favorite pink chenille bathrobe, with my little black dress steam-pressed, hanging on the shower rod, I was sitting on the bed, eating grape tomatoes, reading my Rex Stout, when Ty came into the room.

I leaped out of bed exclaiming, "Ty!" and flew into his arms, nearly toppling him over.

"Whoa!" he said once he got purchase, holding me tight. "I ought to go away more often."

"Thank you *so* much for the flowers and the card and the Champagne and the tomatoes."

"It's sparkling wine, and did you notice it has your initial on it?"

"Only fitting," I said in a queenly tone.

I watched as he turned the bottle to ease

out the cork and poured the wine into plastic cups that he found in the bathroom.

"Yum, this is delicious." I smiled and raised my glass in a silent toast. "Any news about Ned?"

"Yeah. There's confirmation that Ned is the secret admirer."

I took a deep breath. "What is it?"

"The man who ordered the flowers — the homeless guy? He picked Anderson out of a lineup. Without hesitation."

"Wow! I wonder why he didn't pick him out from the photos?"

Ty grinned. "Maybe 'cause we didn't include Ned's photo in the display."

"Yeah, that would do it." I laughed. "Ned sure operated under the radar. What else?"

"Ned's fingerprints match some of the items Rosalie pasted into her scrapbook."

"Wow."

"And Rosalie's fingerprints are on the walking stick — just the way they might be if she fended off a blow."

"And the splinters?" I asked.

"Yup. A definite fit to slivers missing on the walking stick. We've sent out samples for DNA analysis. There's more. We found four disposable cell phones in Ned's office, all purchased in Maine. And, best of all, Edie confirmed that she followed Gerry to the restaurant and then followed Rosalie. She saw Ned and Rosalie stop near the jetty. Rosalie jumped out of the car and ran away, with Ned in pursuit. The moon was bright enough for her to see them tussle. She watched as Ned hit her, and she was there when Rosalie fell. And then she drove away."

"Gotta love a good Samaritan who comes to the aid of a damsel in distress."

"That pretty much sums up Edie."

"I still can't believe she didn't come forward," I said. "She must have known that Ned was the killer."

"She says that she didn't want to admit that she'd been following Gerry."

I shrugged. "Maybe that's true, but I can't help thinking that she stayed quiet for another reason — she was happy Rosalie was dead."

"Maybe," Ty acknowledged, shaking his head.

"But wouldn't Gerry have known she'd been up to something?" I asked. "Edie got home *after* him."

"He says that he went straight to his study, poured himself a cognac, and did some work. Believe it or not, he says he didn't notice that she, or her car, was gone. Really a testimony to their closeness. He just figured she was already asleep. When she got back, she found him in the study. She didn't tell him where she'd been and he didn't ask."

What a ménage, I thought. Self-centered, self-serving, and self-absorbed.

"What do you think? Is Ned's goose cooked?"

"Probably. The splinters from his cane are pretty damning." He shrugged. "But there's no proof he pushed her off of the jetty. She might have fallen."

I nodded, thinking of the complexities of winning a conviction.

"Officer Brownley called this morning. Cooper is insisting that Rosalie gave him the copy of the journal, that they were going to coauthor a paper."

"No way!" I objected.

"The cease-and-desist order she had her lawyer send pretty much takes the air out of that argument."

"Good," I said. "I hope he does jail time."

Ty smiled. "He might, actually. And the Portsmouth police have picked up Lesha Moore for questioning," he told me.

"Really?" I asked.

"Yeah. The ADA doesn't think it'll go to trial, but from what Officer Brownley told me, he was pretty outraged."

"Understandable reaction — it's outrageous."

"They also thought it was pretty outrageous that you discuss the case with the press."

I took a sip of wine and considered how to respond. I knew the police used the media when it was to their advantage by leaking stories, soliciting tips, and alerting them to upcoming events, but I also knew they resented it when private citizens did the same.

"Will I be hearing from them about it?" I asked.

"Probably not," he said, half smiling. "It's pretty hard to argue with the end result."

We finished the sparkling wine and got ready for the evening's festivities.

Later, back in the room, half asleep, after a tasty meal and silly toasts among the new hires who obviously enjoyed one another's company, I asked, "Are you awake?"

"Uh-huh."

"I've been thinking about Rosalie."

"And?"

"She wasn't perfect, you know? But she was a really good sister. It matters so much. I think that Paige will have tons of good memories to sustain her."

Ty reached out and stroked my check.

"You're a good friend to her."

"Thanks," I said, and snuggled close.

When I checked messages the next morning en route to the airport for my flight back to New Hampshire, there was one from Mrs. Woodricky.

"I asked my brother to see if he could find the palette, and he did. I don't want it anymore. Please pick it up from him and sell it."

She left his address and phone number. I was about to call her back when I decided to skip it. I'd need to talk to her about selling it, and the police about whether the real palette would be needed as evidence in Lesha's trial, if there was one, but I didn't need to do it now. Work could wait, I decided, until I was back at work.

Ty called on a break and caught me just before the plane took off.

"What's for dinner?"

I laughed. "When?"

"Tonight. They're letting us out at one, so I should be home by five or so."

"Excellent. What do you want?"

"Let's go out and celebrate."

"Celebrate what?"

"My new job, our being together, and

whatever else occurs to us."

"Date," I said, and smiled the whole flight home.

ACKNOWLEDGMENTS

Many thanks to Amy L., a forensic scientist from a state not far from New York, who researched trace evidence questions for me. While respecting her wish to remain anonymous, I want to express my appreciation for her detailed explanations. Other experts also generously provided information. I'm very appreciative to Kevin Berean, who answered a multitude of legal questions; Steven T. Campbell, who explained technical information about cell phones; and Dr. Douglas P. Lyle, who filled in some forensic blanks for me. Special thanks go to Leslie Hindman, who, with her team at Leslie Hindman Auctioneers, appraised scores of antiques. Thank you all for sharing your expertise; please note that any errors are mine alone.

I would also like to thank my good friend Jo-Ann Maude, who helps me keep everything organized; Katie Longhurst, with whom I share a love of words, for her careful reading; and Carol Novak, my Web queen, for overseeing all things technical.

Also, thanks to Dan and Linda Chessman, Linda Plastina, Rona Foster, Lee and Mike Temares, Sandy Baggelaar, Kathryn Engelhardt, Christine de los Reyes, Karen Roy, Liz Weiner, and Joanne Sieck for their assistance. Thanks also to P. J. Nunn and Ken Wilson, and to my good friends in the Wolfe Pack.

I'm thankful for the support — and the friendship — I've found in the mystery community. Many authors have been especially generous in sharing their knowledge, including Margaret Maron, Donna Andrews, Nora Charles, Karen Harper, Rosemary Harris, Elaine Viets, Nancy Martin, Steve Hamilton, Chris Grabenstein, M. J. Rose, Laura Lippman, and Julia Spencer-Fleming.

Independent mystery booksellers have been invaluable in helping me introduce Josie to their customers — thank you all. I want to acknowledge my special friends at these terrific mystery bookstores: the Poisoned Pen, Mysteries to Die For, BOOK'em Mysteries, Mystery Bookstore, Legends, Book Carnival, Mysterious Galaxy, San Francisco Mystery Bookstore, M Is for Mystery, Murder by the Book stores in

Houston and Portland, Remember the Alibi Mystery Bookstore, Kate's Mystery Books, Mystery Lovers Bookshop, the Mysterious Bookshop, Partners in Crime, Booked for Murder, Aunt Agatha's, Foul Play, Uncle Edgar's Mystery Bookstore, Seattle Mystery Bookstore, Centuries & Sleuths, and Once Upon a Crime.

Manhattan's Black Orchid Bookstore will be sorely missed; Bonnie Claeson and Joe Guglielmelli helped me launch the Josie Prescott Antiques Mysteries at their charming shop. Many, many thanks to them.

Many independent and chain bookstores have been incredibly supportive as well — thank you to those many booksellers who've gone out of their way to become familiar with Josie. Special thanks go to my friend Dianne Defonce at the Borders in Fairfield, Connecticut.

Some of my favorite people are librarians! Sincere thanks to my librarian friends Doris Ann Norris, Mary Callahan Boone, Frances Mendelsohn, and Deborah Hirsch. Also thanks to Mary Russell, who, in her role as director of the New Hampshire Center for the Book at the New Hampshire State Library, chose *Consigned to Death* as its Book of the Week.

I am deeply grateful for the unerring guidance and acumen provided by my literary agent, Denise Marcil, and her entire team. Special thanks go to Michael Congdon, Cristina Concepcion, and Katie Kotchman.

Everyone at St. Martin's Minotaur has been kind and supportive, including those I work with most closely, Hector DeJean, Julie Gutin, Deborah Miller, Christina MacDonald, David Rotstein, and Laura Bourgeois, as well as those behind the scenes. My editor, executive editor Hope Dellon, offered detailed and insightful feedback about the manuscript, helping me add richness and complexity to the story. I'm indebted to her, and to the entire St. Martin's Minotaur team.

ABOUT THE AUTHOR

Jane K. Cleland, who used to own a rare book and antiques store in New Hampshire, now lives in Manhattan. Her first novel, *Consigned to Death,* is an IMBA bestseller and was nominated for the Agatha and Macavity awards. She is president of the New York chapter of Mystery Writers of America and chair of the Wolfe Pack literary awards. Jane keeps in contact with her readers through free, informative newsletters and terrific website promotions, including fun, interactive antiques appraisal challenges.

We hope you have enjoyed this Large Print book. Other Thorndike, Wheeler, and Chivers Press Large Print books are available at your library or directly from the publishers.

For information about current and upcoming titles, please call or write, without obligation, to:

Publisher
Thorndike Press
295 Kennedy Memorial Drive
Waterville, ME 04901
Tel. (800) 223-1244

or visit our Web site at:

http://gale.cengage.com/thorndike

OR

Chivers Large Print
published by BBC Audiobooks Ltd
St James House, The Square
Lower Bristol Road
Bath BA2 3SB
England
Tel. +44(0) 800 136919
email: bbcaudiobooks@bbc.co.uk
www.bbcaudiobooks.co.uk

All our Large Print titles are designed for easy reading, and all our books are made to last.